MELTDOWN

Y0-CCA-467

MARTIN BAKER

MELTDOWN

MACMILLAN

First published 2008 by Macmillan
an imprint of Pan Macmillan Ltd
Pan Macmillan, 20 New Wharf Road, London N1 9RR
Basingstoke and Oxford
Associated companies throughout the world
www.panmacmillan.com

ISBN 978-0-230-53030-0 HB
ISBN 978-0-230-70397-1 TPB

Copyright © Martin Baker 2008

The right of Martin Baker to be identified as the
author of this work has been asserted by him in accordance
with the Copyright, Designs and Patents Act 1988.

All rights reserved. No part of this publication may be
reproduced, stored in or introduced into a retrieval system, or
transmitted, in any form, or by any means (electronic, mechanical,
photocopying, recording or otherwise) without the prior written
permission of the publisher. Any person who does any unauthorized
act in relation to this publication may be liable to criminal
prosecution and civil claims for damages.

1 3 5 7 9 8 6 4 2

A CIP catalogue record for this book is available from
the British Library.

Typeset by SetSystems Ltd, Saffron Walden, Essex
Printed and bound in Great Britain by
Mackays of Chatham plc, Chatham, Kent

This book is sold subject to the condition that it shall not,
by way of trade or otherwise, be lent, re-sold, hired out,
or otherwise circulated without the publisher's prior consent
in any form of binding or cover other than that in which
it is published and without a similar condition including this
condition being imposed on the subsequent purchaser.

Visit **www.panmacmillan.com** to read more about all our books
and to buy them. You will also find features, author interviews and
news of any author events, and you can sign up for e-newsletters
so that you're always first to hear about our new releases.

FOR NICOLA, MY WIFE

ACKNOWLEDGEMENTS

This manuscript has taken over a decade in the research and writing. It has been through thirteen versions, passed through many hands, and been the beneficiary of critical opinions far sharper and more distanced and objective than my own.

Before I get to what is necessarily a long litany of heartfelt gratitude, let me explain the system analysis of *Meltdown*. It is fiction. Absolutely none of the characters is real, other than the occasional historical or political figures who do not drive the plot. So former UK foreign minister Douglas Hurd, the subject of one casual allusion, is real. Samuel Spendlove, Khan, Miller, Kaz, Lauren, Diaz, Nobby, FT, Barton, McMurray et al. are most definitely fictional, and not based on any real person.

The action takes place in the near future, and the financial backdrop is rooted in reality. Samuel is perhaps given his head a little early at Ropner Bank, but the technical data is, so far as I have been able to make it, the real thing. The IT background that allows Samuel semi-secret access to the internet is, I think, just about viable, but is realistic rather than real. And Gallimard, the object of Barton's covetousness, is not of course independently quoted. Nor is there any suggestion that there has ever been any impropriety in any of its financial dealings, so far as I am aware. It is merely an illustrious and rightly admired publishing house which, were it ever to come to the open market, might well inspire the kind of dogfight that is the background to *Meltdown*.

I would like to thank the following for their help and advice. Brad Spurgeon and the library team at the *International Herald Tribune* in Paris provided some fascinating research on bulldozers, which formed part of an early version but, alas, not the final one. Nick Austin, Kerry Lay, Patrick Raggett and Jonathan Lloyd read early versions and made helpful comments. Nick's enthusiasm, in particular, was sustaining.

Sean Chapman, Megan Frost, Damien McCrystal and Martin Fletcher also had one or other of the many versions of *Meltdown* thrust upon them, and I am indebted for their helpful comments.

Two of the cleverest people I know, Gordon Rae and Neil Bennett, read the later versions of the manuscript, independently diagnosed the same structural fault and, miraculously, came up with an identical treatment plan. I truly am indebted to them both.

Mark Griffith, my old schoolfriend, former Oxford pub pool champion and Senior Tutor at New College, booked the Senior Common Room's guest room in that college for me many times. Whatever else Oxford is, it is a magnificent machine designed to promote independent thought. I did a comprehensive job of squandering that opportunity as an undergraduate, but thanks to Mark and the university I may have actually managed to get something done the second time around. Thanks also to Mark's wife, Louise, for allowing me to take her husband away and return him to her smelling of beer and Thai food – all in the name of research, of course.

Much of the early work on the manuscript was done in the Isle of Wight home of Martin and Eleanor Bowen. They opened their house and, in an act of utter recklessness, their fridge door to me. The atmosphere of true happiness and love that pervades their home makes it a wonderful, nourishing environment, and a great place to work. Many, many thanks to them and their children, Charlie and Emily.

Talking of families, my own children, Patrick, Jamie and Madeleine, and their mother, Kate, have had to put up with the flakiness that can – and in my case invariably does – come with being a writer. Thanks and apologies to them – and to Alice, Serena, Rupert, Antonia and Benjie Horlick, who have had to put up with their mother's new husband not just living but also working at home.

My publishers at Macmillan have been excellent. Jeremy Trevathan and Jacqui Graham have been wise, helpful and supportive throughout the extended gestation period. My thanks also to the fact-checking and copy-editing team. I do hope the book justifies all their patience and hard work.

Last and most importantly, my thanks and love to my wife, Nicola Horlick. Without her belief in me and the *Meltdown* manuscript, it would never have been published. It's easy to be impressed by the superficial things about Nicola – for example, having a capacity to organize the Sixth Army's latest move across the Rhine while producing perfect roast potatoes. But her real qualities are an extraordinarily acute intelligence and a drive that cuts through the indecisive and the ineffective like a runaway snowplough. Most impressive of all is the generosity of spirit to deal with the occasional stamping of my own pretty little foot both inside and outside the study. My gratitude to Nicola for this and so much more is truly endless.

The economic system is indeed based on an abstraction, on the mutuality of exchange, the balance between sacrifice and gain; and in the real process of its development it is inseparably merged with its basis and results, desire and need. But this form of existence does not differentiate it from the other spheres into which we divide the totality of phenomena for the sake of our interests.

Georg Simmel, *The Philosophy of Money*

'Result. Monster, monster result.'

Foreign exchange dealer, London, on a colleague's £1 billion coup – made in a single day – in the currency markets

Prologue

'LET'S GO.' He jabbed at a button on the console and waited for the pre-programmed number to dial out.

The New York voice crackled a short greeting from the speaker. They wasted little time on formalities.

'What are you calling the market?'

'Unchanged to five cents down.' He could hear the background noise from the traders on their Manhattan trading floor. His heart was pounding. Time to drop the depth charge.

'OK. Thanks for the temperature gauge. I have an order for you. How close are you to market opening, by the way?'

'We're counting down now. Forty-five seconds.' The trader's voice was relaxed, full of metropolitan complacency.

'Buy five million Brent June on the opening,' he said, his own voice an instrument of authority and command. 'Then let the ripples settle, and buy five more. Then, if we haven't set the place on fire, another two.'

'That's twelve million! It's your business, buddy, but are you sure that you want to take the market on quite so . . . boldly?' There was no urbanity now. This was a year's salary in commission.

'Nice of you to ask, but just go and do it.'

'OK. You got it.'

The background speaker static suddenly turned into a high-volume tank battle. New York had opened. Order placed. The sound clicked off.

Then he put a further eight million into play through Frankfurt. The dealer on the other end of the line swallowed that one whole, no questions asked.

Next up, Geneva.

'Hello?' A heavily accented French-Swiss voice.

'I have something for you.'

Was his tension audible?

'What can I do you for?'

A Swiss joke – it had scarcity value, if little else.

'Three million Brent June.'

'You buying or selling?'

'Buying. A casual interest.'

A whistle. Over $180 million of casual interest.

'Sixty-two dollars seventy a barrel in high activity. Mmm. Do you definitely want to deal?'

'Yes, we fancy oil today.'

'Everything will be taken care of.'

The speaker went quiet, but not for long.

'Whoa! We're at $62.75 and counting! What are you guys up to?'

'We aren't up to anything. Oil seems to be in demand today,' he said, smiling to himself. He shot a sly glance sideways towards his mentor, who was standing close by, nodding slowly.

'Where do you think the demand's coming from?' asked the Swiss.

'Who knows?' said the young man, leaning forward into the desktop speaker. 'Are you going to get that order for us or do I park our business elsewhere?'

'Don't move!'

A frenzy in the oil market was beginning to take hold all around the world. The trader came back in a few seconds, excited but nervous.

'We're filling your order now. I just thought maybe you would be wanting, ah, to come at this a little more cautiously. You know – discretion, valour, that kind of thing . . .'

'Just do it!'

He could feel the surge of excitement, the thrill of power shooting through his veins. Now he was really trading. He was the lightning conductor for all the rich, concentrated vitality of the market, and he could direct it where he liked. He was harnessing all the might of the bank's assets and he was about to muscle a gigantic global market his way. It was as though he could wrap up every floor, every screen, every trader in the world into one huge football and then volley it out into space, booted there by the leverage of his billion-dollar book.

Out in the street, the hurly-burly was just the same – pedestrian bustle, traffic noise, the same tired old urban pantomime. Yet, the world was about to change radically. Billions of people would be affected. Most would become poorer, but he would make some – a few, a very select few – immensely richer.

1

THE PROPRIETOR flicked through the pages of the dossier once more. Pale, piercing eyes fixed fleetingly on grainy photos – individuals, group shots – and small, dense chunks of text. The gaze, baleful and unblinking, lingered for what seemed a long, long time. Occasionally, an exquisitely manicured finger-nail would underscore some passage, or trace the contours of an image for a moment or two. But then the page would be turned, no mark left.

McMurray watched him carefully from the semi-darkness just outside the cheesy yellow pyramid of light issuing from the Anglepoise lamp. Sitting sideways-on to the proprietor was not exactly safe, but sideways was better than opposite. Much better.

McMurray was a newspaper editor, and a respected one at that. At first, he had never really believed the stories about the proprietor. Legend had it that in his own days as an editor, he generated such tension and fear in news meetings that report-ers had been known to faint under his cross-examination – that very same fierce laser focus was now being directed at the document on the desk. McMurray had dismissed these stories as urban myth – tales of marvellous, larger-than-life deeds, the doings of heroes in a Fleet Street of hot-metal presses, outrageous newspaper scoops and twenty-four-hour drinking sessions. A Fleet Street that ceased to exist some time not long after Camelot.

But William Barton was something else. Having worked with the man, McMurray could believe the fainting stories. In the mythology of modern journalism, Barton was Medusa. He could turn you to stone if you glanced the wrong way. Or maybe he was Zeus, all-powerful, king of false gods.

White gold winked and flashed as Barton shot his cuffs and the fingers glided on, soft, tirelessly inquisitive. There was something familiar about the way the proprietor handled the document. McMurray had once seen a blind man in a seaport brothel stroking the face of a girl in just such a way. The money had been paid, the girl's availability established, but the blind man wanted to touch her face before the business began. The eager process of inquiry, the assumption of intimacy, the tenderness of control – this was part of the pleasure. Perhaps it was the pleasure itself.

'I'm not sure. There's nothing not to like, but I'm not sure.' His tone, however, was one of certainty.

The proprietor nudged the dossier an inch. 'What do you think?' he asked softly, eyes forward, averted from the tubby Scotsman.

McMurray twitched as though he'd just been tossed a live hand grenade. Barton was older and more grizzled than McMurray, but slimmer. He was just another man in an expensive suit – just another successful businessman, until he fixed you with that glare. Sitting quite still, he stared straight ahead.

'Well . . .' McMurray cleared his throat.

Barton remained absolutely silent. His silhouette was focused on the bare brick office wall, its bleak designer chic dimly visible in the gloom.

'He's smart. Conventionally and unconventionally,' said McMurray at length.

Barton nodded slowly.

'Agreed. But is he right?'

Barton pushed the file towards McMurray again, this time with the palm of his hand. Still no eye contact.

McMurray swallowed. He wanted a cigarette, hot and cleansing at the back of his throat. How had it come to this? He had edited his first newspaper at his grammar school, a bleak but grindingly effective educational institution in Paisley. His career ascent had been swift and happy: local paper, the big story that took him to the home news desk on a national newspaper in fashionable west London – as locations went, a nice trade. He soon got used to the long hours. There was excitement in finding out how it all worked, how a society fitted together – the power junkies of Westminster, the City boys with their fast cars and faster women. He had experienced the paranoia, low pay and intellectual snobbery of literary London; the dirty, dirty business of professional sport; the decline of Christianity and the rise of Islam. And, yes, the workings of the media. The media held up a mirror to it all, sometimes tilting it slightly, this way or that, according to which supermodel, banker or political groupie had credits in the favour bank.

But this? This was different.

'A precocious scholar,' said McMurray cautiously. 'Went to an obscure independent school in the north of England. Jesuit-run. Took his public exams a couple of years early.'

The proprietor contemplated the tips of his fingers.

'Catholic,' murmured Barton.

'A Taig, yes,' said McMurray, who came from the Protestant side of the west of Scotland divide. 'Shouldn't be a problem. We're not asking him to renounce his faith in the one holy, Roman, Catholic, and pederastic Church.' He grinned slightly at his own wit.

'Yes,' said Barton slowly. 'It could be worse. I suppose.'

McMurray nodded and turned a page. He knew what 'worse' meant. The proprietor had once had a personal assistant – the publishing equivalent of a Parliamentary Private Secretary. The young man was brilliant, dynamic, committed. Could, would and did do the lot: drive, type, play chess, minute a meeting in perfect reported speech, offer a critique of geopolitics from the perspective of anywhere on the planet – you just had to pick a continent, pick a country. But there was a problem when Barton wanted him to work on Passover weekend. The boy couldn't, wouldn't. There would be no more Jews taking religious holidays in William Barton's time.

There were of course plenty of donations to Jewish charities, and many a well-placed, politically astute editorial. And this would continue to be so. It would be inconvenient – no, impossible – for a media baron to be seen to be anti-semitic. But no more Jews on the payroll. Catholics, religious ones at any rate, could also be a risk.

'I don't think Spendlove can afford to be too pious, sir.'

'Why's that?' Barton seemed to be memorizing the tiny differences in shape of each and every brick in the wall.

'He's divorced. Or divorcing. Married an American. A corn-doll blonde.'

Again the nod, as though learning this for the first time.

'Is that a pro or a con?'

'That's a moot point. It could be either.'

'It's not religion that's causing the split?'

McMurray flicked through the file again. It was all there,

but Barton wanted him to restate it, to frame his thoughts out loud.

'I don't think so. She's got a boyfriend. A big bruiser of the red-blooded American sports jock variety.'

Another nod. 'And it's not as though he'd have only just found out that she was – what is she?'

'Episcopalian.'

'Episcopalian.' The proprietor settled on this with the contentment of a dog gnawing a bone.

'He must have known that when he married her,' mused McMurray.

'Have we done the usual tests?'

'Oh yes.'

'And?'

'Passed. Didn't miss a beat.'

A few weeks earlier Samuel Spendlove had attended an interview for the XB Foundation Trust academic exchange programme, named after Barton's grandfather, Xavier, the founder of the family media dynasty. The trust had a series of bursaries for academic research loosely connected to the media. Maybe there would be a chair at Oxford University one day – the Barton Professor of Journalism. As yet, the university was holding out. The name Barton was not liked – but money, enough money, would fix that eventually. It fixed everything, eventually.

'Which restaurant did we use?'

'Camel Toe Heaven in Notting Hill. We hired the whole place.'

McMurray looked down at the file. The interview had gone well. Samuel Spendlove had impressed – sharp mind, great memory, obviously smarter than his interlocutors, but not a bully. Polite, reserved, cool. This was all encouraging.

Interviews, drinks and dinner at Camel Toe Heaven for the candidates, and then the easy transition to a back-room salon. Girls arrived. Cambridge-educated, glossy-haired creatures – beautiful, clever, radiating just the right amount of availability. They were the very best sort of hooker. True predators.

Samuel had been separated from his wife for weeks, but stayed politely aloof. The girls edged a little closer, trying to reel him in, alternating coquettishness with serious conversation, playing the angles. It wasn't often they got the opportunity to enjoy their work quite so much. Samuel was taller than average, dark blond hair, bluey-green eyes, well put together. His pleasure would be theirs.

Fine champagne cognac, bourbon and ice were produced. After the third drink, vials of white powder appeared. A couple of Samuel's fellow interviewees took the easy way. It was just a little toot, after all. It wasn't as though they owned the stuff. It was a bit of fun – like social smoking. You just took someone else's cigarettes, but you weren't a smoker. Someone else's stash? You weren't a user – and pretty girls were offering after all. No harm, surely? Samuel made his excuses, and left.

Barton reached out and took the file back. He flipped a page with a lazy finger. An excellent result. There would be plenty of distractions for the one they chose. An easy social manner was essential to success, but drink, drugs and womanizing were out of the question. Focus, intelligence, an ability to work alone – these were the key qualities.

And yet, and yet. Whoever they chose had to be able to take direction. More than that, he had to be controlled.

'Got any more of that cow cud?'

McMurray produced a stick of nicotine chewing gum.

'Blackcurrant eucalyptus flavour,' snorted Barton. 'Still

tastes execrable.' His new Japanese-American wife, less than half his age and apparently quite comfortable with being Mrs Barton Mark IV, absolutely forbade cigarettes. McMurray, an avid smoker of decades' standing, had taken to carrying ready supplies of gum for the proprietor at all times. It did not do to disappoint.

Barton chewed stolidly. His thin, mildly ravaged face looked sourer with every bite. McMurray watched him in a futile search for clues. He sighed. Maybe their ideal man simply didn't exist. McMurray slipped a stick of the disgusting gum into his own mouth and began masticating in sympathy. He still had a thirty-a-day cigarette habit, but was now also addicted to the nicotine gum.

'Cognitive and memory performance?' asked Barton at last, again as though he didn't know the answer.

'Passed with flying colours. Off the top of the chart in some of it. The eidetic memory helps.'

'Eidetic?'

'I think they refer to it as "photographic" in the file. He did exceptionally well on the anagrams and pattern recognition too. He's not just a photocopying machine.'

'I hope I didn't hear you correctly,' murmured Barton softly. 'You weren't comparing our prime candidate with a piece of office equipment, were you?'

'They might have put more background in the file,' said McMurray, hastily glancing at the document again, which was more than an inch thick. 'Eidetic or photographic memory is not uncommon – about one person in 2,000 has it in some form. It's half natural gift, half technique. You look at a book, a list, a series of symbols, and memorize the shape, rather than the sense of it. Then, when needed, you can call up the image and read it back to yourself. It's a kind of slide show.'

Barton grunted: 'This is too important to entrust to a circus act, McMurray.'

The Scot suppressed a groan. If anything did go wrong, it would be his problem. But Barton had read the file. Barton had hand-picked Samuel Spendlove.

'I absolutely agree, sir. Do you still want me to call him in?'

'If we pick him and he fails, we all fail. Especially you. Do you understand?'

Barton had turned towards McMurray, who now had the full benefit of the proprietor's stare. It was a river of ice. McMurray could feel the leased Bentley, the heavily mort-gaged Docklands flat, and the regular attentions of Karina, his favourite, very attractive, very expensive call girl, all sliding away from him. He swallowed. Or tried to. His mouth was dry, his throat parched.

'Just do it.' Barton poked gently at the file, and gave McMurray a half-smile. His voice never rose above the pitch other people use to ask for a slice of lime with their mineral water. 'But get it right, OK? Or . . . consequences will flow.'

The last words were especially softly spoken. There was no need to raise his voice. The unwavering stare conveyed the message. Then, abruptly, Barton looked away, rose from his chair and walked out.

McMurray remained seated. He ran his tongue thickly over his lips and forced himself to read the file once more. That was what Barton was expecting him to do. McMurray couldn't resist a quick glance at the picture on the wall opposite. It was a detail of a Delacroix painting – a bosomy mademoiselle embodying the nationhood of France and its citizens in heroic struggle against the ruthless control of the aristocracy and the clergy.

Pointless to wonder whether this was an ironic joke or not.

The fact was that Barton was sitting a few feet away, settled at a table on the other side of the painting that was also a one-way viewing screen. The proprietor would be adjusting the volume controls and placing the headset over his ears. Watching, waiting, monitoring everything, and all from behind the large-breasted girl calling the citizenry to fight for liberty, fraternity and equality.

The door opened silently. McMurray pushed his wire-framed glasses up the bridge of his large, greasy nose and squinted into the gloom.

'Hi, Suzi.'

'Hi.'

Suzi Gilbertson slid into the seat next to him, and set a notebook and pencil down on the table. She knew the proprietor was watching them from behind the picture, but seemed totally at ease.

'Show time soon,' muttered McMurray, cursing quietly to himself as he flipped through the file.

'Let's have a look,' said Suzi, a hint of the West Country coming through in the request. She was youngish – no more than mid-thirties – and had the kind of homely charm that went down well with grieving relatives. Suzi was dark-eyed, smooth-skinned, and sexy in a large-shouldered sort of way – she could make the tea or whip up a vodka Martini, depending on the situation and the mood of the contact. Either way, she always got the story. It was known that the proprietor had his eye on her. Some said he planned to send Suzi off to edit one of his American titles, maybe even his New York tabloid. She was a rising star – super-smart, and nearer to Spendlove's age than McMurray. Ideal for their present purpose.

'Pretty thorough, I think you'll find,' said McMurray.

Suzi quickly took in ancient swimming team photos,

photocopied letters from friends of the father, himself an old-time Fleet Street hack, summaries of family background – only child, parents dead, that car crash of a marriage. Pages and pages of information – credit history, political and social interests. Even which way he voted, apparently. So much for the secrecy of the ballot box. The subheadings jumped out at the reader – 'Career history', 'Affiliations', 'Drivers'.

'Bloody hell,' Suzi whistled. 'There's background, and then there's espionage. Who does this stuff?'

'Oh, one of those international intelligence agencies.'

'You mean like Kroll?'

'A bit smaller than Kroll. This one's headed up by failed politicians and retired industrialists. They do reports on the XB Foundation candidates for free as a favour to Barton. They're easy to research.'

'Yeah,' laughed Suzi. 'Open books, and not even particularly dirty ones. I'm surprised they do it for free though.'

'They bill big-time for the real stuff – the captains of industry and the politicians with all the things they pay to hide.'

'I know this is Barton's pet project,' said Suzi, 'but this assignment must be special. I mean – look at this file.'

'I'd love to,' came a new voice.

Suzi jumped slightly in her chair.

'Ah Samuel, welcome,' said McMurray, who had been watching the door carefully.

'Sorry to burst in on you,' said Samuel. 'They told me to come straight in.'

'No problem,' said McMurray. 'Take a seat.'

Samuel Spendlove, young, fit, gifted, and the object of admiration and suspicion in equal measure, did as he was bid.

McMurray reached for the file and quietly closed it, while Suzi crossed to the door and brought the lights up.

'I thought I was the one seeking the research brief,' said Samuel, sitting easily in his chair, legs spread, hands on the tops of his thighs.

'We like to be thorough, but this isn't all about you, Mr Spendlove,' said McMurray, lying directly and smoothly. Compared to dealing with the proprietor, it all seemed easy.

'I've heard a lot about you,' said Suzi, smiling. McMurray looked across. She probably knew at least that Spendlove hadn't gone for the illicit recreation offered by the hookers. Maybe the smile was even genuine.

'Thank you. I don't know whether to be flattered or intimidated.' Samuel flashed a smile back at Suzi.

'You don't look either, as you well know,' cooed Suzi. Her increasingly flirtatious manner was making McMurray feel uneasy. But she was a pro. If this was her style, fine. 'But what I don't really understand is why you're seeking this research brief.'

'Simple. I was invited to apply. And I was at . . .' Samuel looked into Suzi's open, inviting face. '. . . at something of a crossroads.'

'You mean the situation with your wife, Gail?'

'Gail, yes. My wife.'

'You poor thing. Divorce is always so difficult.' A pretty little furrow had developed across her creamy forehead.

Samuel crossed his legs, and folded his arms. His large, wide-set eyes clouded momentarily. Behind the screen, Barton, still chewing on his rancid gum, cracked a slow smile. Vulnerability – an instrument of control. The marriage was long over. The dossier said that the wife had been throwing herself at other men for months before the split. But she still wasn't an ex-wife in Spendlove's mind. He was raw, pained. That was useful; that was good.

'I'm sorry to hear that, Mr Spendlove, I truly am. Or may I call you Samuel?'

'Samuel is fine. But not Sam, please.'

'Of course not, Samuel. I really do feel for your hurt. But I'm still a bit surprised that you'd give up your thesis and the prospect of a brilliant academic career.'

'Well, part of the attraction is money. I am sure you have read about the difficulties Oxford and Cambridge have had in retaining their academic staff. They haven't got the endowments that Harvard and Yale have and it's pretty difficult to live on the salaries they pay.'

'Of course. We know the XB Foundation bursary is a fair sum, especially compared to the pay levels for UK academics. Nevertheless, your record suggests that you would be destined for great things if you stayed on – a professorial chair, the opportunity to publish erudite legal works. I am sure that there are ways that you could supplement your income.'

'You're too kind.'

'Is she?' interjected McMurray. 'How would you rate yourself as an academic?'

Samuel paused for a moment. 'I've been consistently near the top.'

On the other side of the Delacroix, Barton's smile deepened. Near the top, indeed. Spendlove had finished second in his year at Oxford at the degree stage. Then after a spell at Harvard and Cornell he had come back to take the Bachelor of Civil Law degree at Brasenose, his undergraduate college. He had come first in the BCL exams, taking the university's

Vinerian prize, and had accepted an invitation to put himself up for election to All Souls – the ultimate Oxford enclave.

'But would you say you were a completer-finisher personality type?' asked McMurray, dredging up drivel from a recent management training course. He was beginning to feel the proprietor's icy gaze again, even through the screen.

'I'm not a personality type, Mr McMurray, I'm a personality – albeit a flawed one.' Again the smile, this time with a hint of steel.

'We're a team, Samuel,' said Suzi quickly. 'Alan asks the tough questions, I ask the easy ones.'

Barton chuckled quietly. What she meant was that McMurray asked the stupid questions, Suzi the smart ones.

'Easy questions are always the most dangerous,' said Samuel, feeling more at ease now. He uncrossed his legs.

'Could I ask a favour, Samuel?' trilled Suzi. 'I've only had limited experience of people with photographic recall. Allied to your forensic intelligence, it must be an amazing resource. Could we talk about that a little?'

'Happy to, if you really want. But I don't see what this has to do with an academic exchange programme. Surely, what's relevant is my ability to make the most of my work experience and write a paper for the trustees of the XB Foundation?'

'We have to be very careful whom we select for this role, for reasons I'll go into later,' said McMurray. 'It is of course the case that there's a defined remit for the Foundation, but William Barton himself takes a personal interest in these placements – especially this one.'

'How intriguing.' Samuel's jaw muscles flexed involuntarily.

'Would you mind answering my question, Samuel? I'm truly interested,' interjected Suzi.

From their different vantage points Barton and McMurray marvelled at the woman. Suzi had established Spendlove's weak point at the outset, the ring through the nose of the bull, and now she was leading him this way and that. Softening him up.

'Well . . .' Samuel crossed his arms over his chest again.

'We don't have to go through it all here and now, if you don't want to,' said Suzi. 'I could come out and see you in Oxford some time. We could have a drink, maybe.'

Her casual manner made the suggestion seem innocent, giving the impression that she was an eager, amiable seeker after knowledge. But her look said something more.

Samuel held her gaze for a moment, then looked down at his lap. 'What exactly do you want to know? It isn't that difficult a concept to understand is it?' he said at length.

Behind the Delacroix, Barton nodded in appreciation.

To a series of enthusiastic prompts from Suzi, Samuel explained the theory that eidetic memory might be to do with the brain's development during infancy – sometimes little barriers that commonly go up between parts of the brain that deal with sight, sound and what is known as 'recall' might not be created for some reason. So Samuel could 'photograph' whole paragraphs of a book, or a picture, and then 'forget' it.

'But I thought you forgot very little?'

'You sort of put things away. It's like putting pictures in the attic. If you're driving or cooking, you don't need them. But if you want to look at them, you go up there and pull them out of the cupboard.'

'I see.' She was still nodding sympathetically. Once you've warmed up the contact, just let them talk. 'That way, you can get on with real life.'

'Whatever "real" is,' said Samuel, a little wearily.

'It's difficult to believe it's real,' interjected McMurray. 'Is it a normal brain function?'

'I've had lots of tests, and I'm neurologically completely healthy.'

Samuel's back straightened in his chair. Suzi glanced at the Delacroix. She and McMurray would both be in real trouble if Spendlove walked.

'And psychologically?' asked McMurray.

Samuel let a beat pass.

'Psychologically, I'm a total fruitcake, Mr McMurray.'

A shriek of laughter from Suzi. McMurray scratched his head.

'3, 1, 4, 2, 8, 5, 7, 1, 4 . . .' As though to demonstrate his weirdness, Samuel was now staring at a point just over McMurray's forehead as he chanted an apparently random series of numbers.

'What are you doing?' asked the Scot.

'I think he's reciting pi, Alan,' said Suzi, not taking her eyes off Samuel, who was now sixty digits deep into his recital.

The stream of numerals ended: 'Yes, it's not much of a party piece, but reciting pi – that's the ratio between a circle's radius and its circumference, as I'm sure you know – well, it does make it easier for people to understand,' said Samuel.

'It's endless, isn't it?' said Suzi. 'How many figures can you go to, Samuel?'

'I don't really know. I can recite a few thousand, I suppose. I've never really bothered too much about it.'

'There are some people who make a speciality of it, aren't there? They can go on for hours.'

'Yes,' smiled Samuel. 'But they really are fruitcakes.'

'So why didn't you become a maths geek, if your gift is numerical?' asked McMurray.

'I'd have thought collecting degrees in law was quite geeky enough. It could have been worse. Let me demonstrate.'

Samuel settled in his chair and looked at the ceiling. They'd asked for this.

'Education: Plymouth Girls' Grammar School; Downing College, Cambridge. Job history: junior reporter, *Croydon Advertiser*; staff writer and cookery correspondent, *Graziana* magazine; reporter, *Daily Quest*; night editor, *Daily Quest*; managing editor, *Daily Quest*. Interests: wine and water sports.'

Samuel checked quickly on Suzi. Yes, she was staring at him.

'Not sure what that last bit means,' he grinned. 'Maybe it's related to what comes next. "Most inexcusable luxury: Men. Marital status: Single."'

Samuel finished speaking and watched his interlocutors.

McMurray and Gilbertson exchanged glances. Spendlove had just recited Suzi's entry in *Berks' Beerage* – a jokey *Who's Who* of journalism and journalists. But it was taken seriously enough in the profession; the biographical information was accurate. As a feat of memory it was doubly impressive, because Spendlove couldn't have known that Suzi would be there at the interview. He must have looked at the track records of all the senior executives in Barton's empire, and was able to recall Suzi's potted CV in an instant.

'Alan McMurray. Job history . . .'

'No, no need,' said McMurray. 'I get the point. Your combination of skills is unusual, Samuel.'

Samuel considered McMurray carefully. It was a party trick, the memory thing. But it always seemed to work. It was time to move the conversation on.

'This position sounds unusual, Mr McMurray. I need to understand more about it.'

'Well, as you know, it's a research project that involves a challenging and exciting new area of learning,' said McMurray rather shiftily.

'That doesn't tell me too much. It's research and work at the same time – a placement?'

'Yes, it's an office environment,' said Suzi. Samuel turned to her and found himself unconsciously echoing her expression. 'But we thought this might appeal to you after years of being ... well, of being a brain in a box. You'll be with highly intelligent, stimulating people, all engaged in a common purpose.'

Samuel thought of the long, solitary hours stuck away in his law carrel at the top of Oxford's Radcliffe Camera library. The notion of true colleagues and a 'common purpose' was appealing.

'Also, it is located in Paris, and we know you love the city,' added Suzi.

'In short,' interjected McMurray, 'we think this project would be ideal for a fine mind in search of variety and change, a mind such as yours. Very few are considered for a placement such as this. And even fewer are chosen.'

The solemnity – almost pomposity – of this statement was not lost on Samuel.

'But Mr McMurray, what does the Foundation actually want me to do?'

'We want you to work as a top-level analyst-cum-research assistant to one of the most influential financiers in the world, Samuel,' said Suzi. 'It's very well paid, exceptionally well.'

She went on to mention a figure for the three-month placement that was five times Samuel's current annual stipend. He whistled to himself. Three months in an office in Paris. It was very tempting. But it didn't quite make sense.

'I have to ask you,' he said at length. 'Why is the bursary so substantial? It might be a banking environment, but I understood that the Foundation's aims were academic.'

'Partly academic, partly commercial research. The XB Foundation's wealth comes from the media business, don't forget,' said McMurray.

'It still doesn't stack up to me,' said Samuel. 'Who's the financier by the way?'

'His name is Khan,' said Suzi. 'I imagine you've heard of him?'

'Yes ... yes. It sounds very interesting,' said Samuel pensively. Khan was one of a select number of financiers who had made the front pages of the newspapers and the lead item on television and internet news sites. Popular journalism made out that he toyed with currencies and share markets like a wilful child tossing toys against the wall of a playpen.

'I envisaged you'd have some trenchant questions,' said McMurray. 'The answers are contained in these.'

McMurray put two large square envelopes, one red, one yellow, in front of Samuel. 'This isn't a test, merely a form of psychometric profiling. There is no wrong envelope, no wrong or right answer. But I am going to ask you to choose one.'

Samuel sighed.

'This stuff is so dull, you know. If a banana were not yellow, should it be a) blue, b) green, or c) red? It's mildly bonkers. But, all right, I'll have the yellow one.' He held out his hand.

'It's not quite that simple, I'm afraid,' said McMurray. 'You see, there are two combinations of information, brief and money in each envelope. The yellow one has a commission value for a certain amount of money – the figure Suzi mentioned just now was no more than a guideline – and a degree of information as to the nature of what you'll be asked to do in Paris. The red one also has a certain amount of money – perhaps less, more or even the same – but a fuller brief.'

There was a pause while Samuel pondered the options that had been presented to him.

'I'll have the red one, please.'

'Again, not quite so simple,' smiled McMurray. 'The way it works is this: you can open the yellow one at any time. But to open the red one, you must await my return.'

'Your return? How long will you be?'

'That would rather give the game away.'

McMurray and Gilbertson rose from their chairs. The Scot removed his spectacles and looked at Samuel: 'If you open both, each set of instructions is invalidated. If you open the red one before my return, each set of instructions is invalidated.'

'Don't you think this is somewhat childish?' asked Samuel, staring incredulously at the pair.

'It's unorthodox. William Barton's personal instructions.'

'But it's very effective,' said Suzi, patting him on the shoulder as she made for the door. 'Choose well, Samuel.'

TEN MINUTES LATER, Barton, McMurray and Gilbertson were still in the dark room next door, watching through the screen. Samuel was becoming increasingly twitchy. He looked at his watch, paced the room, scratched his nose, put a hand through his long, silky hair. Twice he went to pick up the yellow envelope. Each time, his hand hovered but drew back.

'Is there a set time he has to wait?' asked McMurray at last.

'No,' said Barton softly. 'It's a test in deferred gratification skills. Very revealing of character.'

'How do you mean?' asked Suzi, watching Samuel on his excursions round the room.

'Well, first it's a test to see if he'll take direction,' explained Barton. 'He's playing the game, so that's good.' McMurray blinked. Had Barton actually smiled at Suzi? He must really rate her.

'Second, it's a measure of how much he wants the job. It's fairly clear that the red envelope is the better choice, the one we want him to make. How long he waits is a good indicator of his desire – and his thirst for knowledge. He's been told there's more information in the second envelope, don't forget. And there's a third factor.'

Barton took the gum out of his mouth, and tossed it in an ashtray. Both McMurray and Gilbertson looked at him expectantly.

'Factor number three is deferred gratification skills. If he can discipline himself and wait for a bigger benefit, he will be more likely to operate effectively alone and to do exactly as we wish. People capable of deferring gratification are typically less likely to use drugs, to commit crime, to take the easy short cuts like the vast majority of the great unwashed, the morons that we cater for. In short, they're more likely to be successful.'

'I see,' murmured McMurray.

'If he lasts twenty minutes, go in and put him out of his pain,' said Barton.

'That's really clever,' said Suzi. 'How much extra information and money is there in the red envelope, by the way?'

'None at all. They're both exactly the same.'

'So it doesn't matter which one he chooses, just how he chooses?'

'He has no choice in any meaningful sense. But we'll keep that little secret to ourselves, don't you think, Suzi?' smiled Barton, though his eyes remained deadly cold.

2

SAMUEL STOOD in his Oxford room, lost in thought. It was cold outside and warm within; a gentle veil of condensation covered the window. His gaze focused on the glass itself for a moment and he touched it with his index finger, making a couple of figures of eight before wiping them away with his fist. The lights outside were beckoning. It was time to go. Kempis would be waiting for him, all horn-rimmed glasses and pithy quotes from Ulpian in the original Latin. Samuel put on his gown, opened the door and paused for a minute. This had not been home for very long, but he had grown fond of it; it had been a cocoon for him during a troubled time.

Samuel made the short journey to All Souls as if he was walking to his own execution in a dream. Down the four flights of stairs, out into the New Quad, through the postage stamp-sized Deer Park, into the Old Quad, out of Brasenose lodge, across the cobbles and directly over the Radcliffe Camera's lawn. Had there been any university proctors to challenge him, the men in bowler hats would have immediately withdrawn as Samuel arrived at the Fellows' gate in his gown. Short-cuts, walking on grass. These were Oxford's idea of privilege, devised God knows when, probably in some medieval era when Duns Scotus had ruled and self-abasement was the norm.

The porter looked quizzically at him through the elaborate wrought-iron gate. Samuel adjusted the black, flowing Fellow's gown which enveloped his Ted Lapidus jacket and touched the letter in his breast pocket. He could visualize the Texas postmark, the pre-printed sticky label that said so much. Gail Avoca and Randall Jeffries. An item. Official. Printed stationery didn't lie.

The gate was opened. He returned the porter's grunt with a nod, and strode across the quadrangle towards Kempis's lodgings.

Reluctantly he climbed the chilly, echoing staircase, pulled the outer door back and rapped twice on the oaken inner panelling of the room. The name PBH KEMPIS was painted up, white on enamelled black, in capital letters of impressive fragility.

Samuel ran his fingers through his hair and waited. He knew that the professor would be sitting in his usual chair, that the chilled pale luncheon sherry he favoured would be poured, that the old man would be composing himself, that he would utter the words he always uttered. The command that was really an invitation. He could hear Kempis clearing his throat.

Then, as ever.

'Enter.'

Samuel pushed against the inner door to be flooded in yellowy warmth. The emeritus professor kept a good fire.

Kempis was seated and waved Samuel to a chair. The sherries were poured and waiting. Hedgehog eyebrows, large, ruddy snout, a twinkling behind the thick spectacles. He seemed to be in an unusually jovial humour. Samuel was surprised by how nervous he felt. This was going to be difficult.

'I have come to tell you, Peter, that I have decided to leave

Oxford. It has clearly been a very traumatic time and I need a change. It's for the best.'

Kempis paused for a moment after Samuel had finished.

'Samuel, Samuel. This is ... what is it? Surprising. Disappointing even.'

The warmth disappeared from Kempis's regard. His tawny eyes, tigerish when debating one of the finer points of the jurist Paul or the historical basis of the formal Roman ceremony of manumission, had assumed a distant dullness. Samuel sipped at the pallid lemon tulip of sherry. It was inadequately chilled and tasted sharp. Kempis's glass remained untouched.

'Of course, you're not the first to postpone submission of a thesis. But why, Samuel? Why?'

'I don't know, Peter. It seems I'm looking for something else.'

'But not for the Master of Biblos?'

'Apparently not.'

Samuel stretched his legs and contemplated Kempis, who seemed genuinely agitated. It was bad to disappoint him over a thesis Kempis seemed so keen on – but after the letter from Gail, complete with the hideous little address sticker, none of Samuel's life at Oxford seemed important. The more he thought about it, in fact, the more the work of an eleventh-century master jurist, an unnamed 'glossist' who wrote interpretations of the great Roman Law texts in the margins of huge legal tomes, seemed definitively trivial.

'Come,' said Kempis. He pulled himself out of the ancient brown armchair in which he liked to brood, and walked stiffly towards the door that connected to the bedroom of his three-room set. He beckoned to Samuel, who followed.

The bedroom was cold and clearly little used. Kempis had a huge house off the Woodstock Road in north Oxford and barely managed to fill three rooms there with the basic requirements of his existence. A man of large capacity and little practical use.

'See,' said Kempis pointing to an old freshman's photograph. Brasenose College, Oxford. 1937. Samuel recognized the name of the photographer and outfitter that had retained a monopoly on the printing of these costly mementos for as long as anyone could remember – Sheppard & Woodward on the High.

'Here am I, next to your grandfather. A brilliant man, taken by the war.' Kempis looked at the picture long and hard. But the inspiration or whatever else it was he sought – perhaps some comment from Samuel – failed to materialize. Eventually, Kempis sighed, pushed his pebble-shaped horn-rims back up the considerable slope of his nose and waved Samuel back to the study.

'Your father's picture I don't have. He was taken by other things.'

Samuel felt himself reddening. What did it matter? Drugs, drink. That was what had happened in his father's time, along with the flared trousers. His father hadn't been 'taken', he had simply followed his hedonistic tendencies. But Samuel could see how upset Kempis was. Better to say nothing.

'There should have been three generations of Spendloves teaching at this university. I had been confident of you, at least. The Master of Biblos was a splendid subject.' Kempis stopped and stared at the floor. He could sense that the decision had been made and there was little that he could do to change Samuel's mind.

'It's just that I need something else, Peter.'

Samuel looked at Kempis. He was a world expert in the evolution of the concept of fault in the legal systems of those

societies which used Roman Law as their basic jurispruden-
tial model. Now he was just a watery-eyed old man with
unworldly, donnish clothes and little idea of how or why
anyone should want anything outside his small world.

'At least you aren't pretending that you'll come back and
finish it later. I've supervised too many existential theses, the
hopeful journeymen of academia who never arrive.'

'No. I think the Master of Biblos and I are parting company.'

'You do realize there's an opportunity coming up?' Kempis
picked up his glass. Normally a considerate sipper, he now
gulped half the sherry at once.

'An opportunity?'

'Yes. New College. Mark Stokes has taken the money at
some nameless place in the American Midwest, somewhere
with more funding than sense and an apparently insatiable
appetite for black-letter land lawyers. New College won't
replace him with a full fellowship, but there will undoubtedly
be a well-funded three-year post there.'

'I think it's the material world, the outside world, for want
of a better phrase, which attracts me, Peter.' Samuel kept his
voice level. Whatever else academia had, money was not one
of its attractions. Fellowship of All Souls was charming, a
thing people outside academia thought they understood. But
what did it mean? Apart from a good degree and an essay
that tickled academic sensibilities, it was – how did Gail put it?
– a few dinners a year and the right to walk on a couple more
patches of grass.

'Ah. *Atque cuprina te iacta nunc dimitto.*'

'No, Peter, not money for its own sake.'

Samuel could see Kempis retreating into the synthetic
language of academia, a device the old man used when life
became too irritating. His recitation of an obscure variant of

the phrase for freeing Roman slaves and the simultaneous handing out of a copper coin was typical. Kempis was the master, Samuel the slave. But the slave was conducting his own emancipation ceremony.

'No, of course not,' Kempis reiterated as if to convince himself. 'I would expect nothing so crude from a man who secured his All Souls fellowship with one of the wittiest and most elegant papers ever submitted. Three hours of continuous scribble on . . . what was it now?'

'Vulgarity, Peter. You know full well!'

Kempis flashed him a distracted smile. Night had fallen now. The Victorian lantern lights of one of Hertford's minor quadrangles hung outside below them, baubles on a distant Christmas tree.

'So, what will you actually do?'

Kempis had seated himself before a desktop computer and was booting it up. Some anorak – probably another of Kempis's doctoral candidates – must have introduced him to the technology of a new generation, and the old man now clearly revelled in the pleasures of surfing the net. At the same time, he still took delight in reinforcing the image of the eccentric academic – all tweeds, sweet tobacco and early editions of leading academic texts.

'I'm taking a research job.'

There was no escaping Kempis's gaze. Samuel glanced at a mantelpiece photograph of Kempis as a young man, a gun broken over one arm and a brace of freshly dead pheasant over the other. When he looked back, the don was still appraising him dispassionately, waiting for Samuel to elaborate.

'Yes, well, when I say research, I'm aware that's what I'm doing now. But this will be different. It will have a more practical application.'

'What is it precisely that takes you away?' Kempis was determined to make him account for his decision and was not going to let up.

'It's a very specific research project. I will be able to make a difference, a real difference, in the outside world, Peter.'

He felt an echo of his father, the hand ruffling his boyish hair, the warm, slightly slurred voice telling him that what mattered in life was making a difference.

'It will be interesting work,' he added.

'Will it, Samuel? Think carefully before you use big words like "interesting". You have a considerable, sophisticated intellect. Just as your grandfather and father had. Your father had perhaps a gift even greater than your grandfather's, yet the results were unfortunate.'

Samuel sipped at the sherry and shifted in his chair. The don was the keeper of his father's memory. Kempis had known him as a young man, an advantage denied Samuel. But he was sure that he was doing the right thing, that he could make a difference in a new world away from Gail and academe. Yet by following his instinct and reinventing himself, he was hurting Kempis.

'You have not begun to employ your talents properly. When you do, then and only then will you find work of an interesting nature,' the don pronounced sternly.

'And if I don't?'

'Well, my boy. It was you who displayed a precocious understanding of vulgarity.'

As SAMUEL walked back towards Brasenose College, he felt a real sense of remorse. He had known Peter Kempis all his life and had much to thank him for. He had been grandfather and father to him and he hated to let him down now. But he had to follow his instincts.

When he arrived at the porter's lodge, he saw a red envelope sticking out of his pigeonhole. It had been a week now since he had met McMurray and Suzi Gilbertson, and he had waited patiently for the prize he had been denied on that day. It was so tempting to go for the yellow envelope, but he kept his resolve. McMurray had eventually returned to the room and patted him on the back. The curious, almost biblical, test was over.

The red envelope that they promised him had finally, finally arrived, and he was holding it in his hand. He walked briskly back to his room, opened the door and turned on the lights. It was little warmer inside than out. He turned the two-bar electric fire on – the ancient buildings still did not have the benefit of central heating – and then braced himself before sitting at his desk. He reached for his silver paper knife, one of the few things that he had inherited from his grandfather, and carefully slit the envelope open. Inside was an employment contract and a note from Alan McMurray on XB Foundation paper telling him that he would be employed as a trainee on the proprietary trading desk of Ropner Bank in Paris. He would be reporting to Khan.

Then the language became more opaque. On behalf of the trustees, McMurray invited Samuel to prepare a monograph on the topic of 'risk-management analysis in domestic French security trading, and the matching of risk exposure by setting off different asset classes against each other'. Then there was some fairly technical stuff about bonds versus property versus various types of futures and options contracts. Part of the remit was to prepare a case study, examining share-trading behaviour in the French publishing house Gallimard.

This was puzzling. The rest of the brief was dry investment stuff, but the Gallimard case study seemed to be a departure, an exercise in behavioural psychology. Gallimard published Camus, one of Samuel's favourite authors. He recalled that it had been the subject of a fierce bidding war the previous year. A war that, unless his memory failed him, the Barton empire had lost. Samuel ran down to the computer in the Senior Common Room and checked the website for further detail. It was just a repetition of the text in his letter, and his recollection of the Gallimard transaction seemed to be broadly correct.

The press reports said there was some sort of conflict between Barton and Khan over a media business that the tycoon had been looking to buy. Could that be Gallimard? Talking up tension, creating rivalries – these were media specialities. But Samuel could only assume it was no coincidence that Barton was now sending him to work with Khan. Well, whatever the explanation, he was entering a very different world from the one he currently inhabited. Good.

There was also a business-class open-return air ticket in the red envelope. His start date was the day after tomorrow. Samuel felt strangely elated. He still did not fully understand what his assignment would involve, but he presumed that someone would explain that when he got there. The cloak-and-dagger element to his interview was certainly a departure from the purely academic ones.

Samuel removed his suitcase from under the bed and began to pack.

3

TRADING THE MARKETS could be more than a little alarming for a novice. Samuel came back from the hallway vending machine, punched a command into the keyboard and almost fell off his chair. The screen told him that he had a profit on the day of $200 million. Far from feeling excitement, he had a cold sickness in his stomach that quickly intensified to an icy ball of fear and pain.

He knew something had happened as he pushed through the first pair of soundproof double doors that led to the giant trading floor clutching his Diet Coke. As he walked to his desk, he could sense the huge rush of adrenalin that accompanies a major market move. It was pure animal pheromone: you could smell it for miles, the scent of frenzied trading activity.

Three minutes earlier, Samuel's colleagues had been slumped back in their chairs reading the papers and toying with overpriced chicken salad sandwiches. The sporadic flicking of the Reuters and Bloomberg screens was really quite secondary to the serious business of filling their stomachs.

Now those screens were strobing blue and red, assimilating huge amounts of new information, straining to report the multitude of buy and sell orders which were flooding the market by the second. Most of the dealers were standing up. They were all shouting.

Some screamed into panel speakers, the direct audio links they had with favoured clients. Others held phones to both ears, with third and fourth handsets unhooked and lying abandoned on the desktops. Each individual voice strained louder and louder to rise above the incessant din that it was itself augmenting.

This should have been a moment of newly discovered pleasure for Samuel. The trading floor was no bigger than the St Cross law library in Oxford, but it was packed with professionals, all intent on trying to make as much money as they could for Ropner Bank and themselves. Instead of creaking trolleys loaded with leather-bound law reports, billions of dollars were hurtling around him now, invisibly flowing from Tokyo to Frankfurt to New York, alighting briefly in his rue Auber dealing room in Paris and moving restlessly on again. Billions and billions and billions of dollars.

Samuel had a problem. His trading book had been put together to withstand this sort of mayhem. The carefully constructed portfolio was not supposed to move violently up or down. So where had the gain come from?

He looked at the screen again. His boss, Khan, was away playing the investment superstar he undoubtedly was at an investment banking conference in Singapore. Khan was the principal proprietary trader at Ropner Bank, responsible for the bank's own investments. Samuel had been extremely flattered when Khan had left him in charge of the book, despite his inexperience. Now he could not explain why the book was up $200 million on the day.

A glance at his Bloomberg screen told Samuel that the European Central Bank had done it again, flying in the face of expectations and raising interest rates. That was what had sent the markets into a panic. Investors saw lean times for company profits ahead and even harder times for those who had borrowed to expand. The thinking was to sell now and buy back later at lower prices. Everyone had reacted in the same way, sending the markets into freefall.

Khan had been gone for a couple of days, but Samuel had made only one minor adjustment to the proprietary trading book. He had tried to call Khan before dealing, but without success. So he used his initiative, and switched some tin futures for some copper futures. He had read a very compelling report which predicted that the copper price was going to rise sharply on the back of increased Chinese demand. He was convinced that Khan would be impressed.

A cry went up from the fixed-interest desk, which dominated the Opéra side of the big V-shaped dealing room. The noise was already deafening, but now it had increased to lung-bursting, eardrum-piercing levels. Samuel checked the position again. Slightly down, but still showing a huge profit. He checked his own trade of that morning – yes, a good price hike in the copper price, but not a $200 million bonanza.

Samuel began scrolling through the components of the portfolio, slowly examining each and every asset in search of explanation and understanding. The temptation was to give in to the lunacy all around him – to scream, jabber, and punch buttons with both hands, his fist, his forehead. But he made his movements as slow as possible; he forced the image into his head of a concert pianist cracking his knuckles and flicking his coat tails before settling at the keyboard.

Even in moments of undiluted market panic such as this – especially now, in fact – Samuel was aware that the process of judgement continued on its inexorable, ruthlessly determined way. His new colleagues were watching him. That indefinable entity called the market, the thing of which he himself had recently become a member, was also assessing him.

Who was he? What made him happy, sad, angry, content? Know the man, know the trade. He was being continuously monitored, just as he endlessly monitored everyone else. Life in the dealing room was Stalin's Russia with million-dollar bonuses. If he could simulate a moment's calm amid the panic, he might create a breathing space for himself, bluff a line of credit with the doubters. Yes, there were doubters, those who claimed his presence there was a result of influence, who were jealous of his position close to Khan.

Minutes of measured searching revealed nothing. Not knowing why he had won out so handsomely was almost worse than losing money. In the financial markets, the one thing you definitely could not say was 'I don't understand.' And Samuel still had no idea why his trip to the vending machine had procured him a fortune.

An unexpected profit of $200 million to those in his position should have meant one thing and one thing only: a bonus of at least $1 million. But Samuel, as his colleagues never stopped reminding him, was new to the business. The outside world, which, after having been immersed in this Parisian pressure chamber for a few weeks, he now thought of as the 'real' world, still exercised some influence. To Samuel, $200 million represented something larger than a big cheque; it was a hundred times the life earnings of his father; it was five fully equipped hospitals; it was mansions and cars with several Van Gogh paintings thrown in; it was the gross annual economic output of a city of 300,000 people in one of the poorer parts of Africa.

It was also an anomaly on his screen, one that Anton Miller

would surely ask him to explain any second now. Two hundred million dollars. Up, down or sideways you had to have a pretty neat explanation for that or you were out on your arse before you could programme your wristwatch. It was 14.47. Despite the mayhem, Samuel was surprised that Miller wasn't already there, hovering at his back.

Anton Miller was country head of Ropner Bank, and his dislike of Khan, high-profile king of prop traders, was a simple, well-documented fact of life in their cosy little Paris office. In idle moments, the talk amongst the traders was always of sport. There were three kinds, as identified by Samuel. Conventional sport periodically consumed their collective attention and then there was sex as sport, the brutal classification and interminable discussion as to which women were slappers, sperm trout, dykes or phone queens. And there was office politics as sport, a kind of bare-knuckle boxing, but without the sense of fair play. That was the game played by Miller and Khan.

The senior management of Ropner Bank viewed Khan as a god. He had been responsible for creating 25 per cent of the entire bank's profits the previous year and it looked as though this was going to be an even more successful year, which was why Anton Miller hated him so much. Khan's independent style made it impossible for Miller to exert authority over him. Successful prop traders were hot property in investment banking. They made money in markets few understood except themselves. They were both a necessity as a profit centre and an incomprehensible, impossible management challenge.

Like it or not, Samuel was seen as the creature of Khan, and so implicated in office politics. He sat at Khan's right hand, analysing price charts for companies, commodities and market indices, trying to spot anomalies and assist his boss in making even more money for Ropner Bank and hence himself. His job was to seek out volatility and take advantage of it. Samuel had surprised himself by how quickly he had taken to trading, how intrinsically pleasurable he found it. Up until now, he had been enjoying himself immensely.

Samuel tried Khan's hotel room in Singapore again. Still no reply; the master trader was probably moving in the fiercely protected hinterland of his private life.

Meanwhile, the book was continuing to behave weirdly. According to his screen, the profit on the day was now $197 million, a small retrenchment, which again he couldn't explain. Samuel looked through the opening positions again and did a quick profit reconciliation in his head. He could only account for $2 million of the gain. Where had the other $195 million come from?

Oh God. Samuel checked his current position again. The profit on the day had fallen from $197 million to $162 million. His ignorance had cost the bank more than $35 million in five minutes. Inadvertently making a huge gain was one thing. Allowing it to ebb away was quite another.

Three lights were flashing on his telephone panel. Samuel jabbed at the buttons while flicking through the screens, trying to add and subtract the various price movements in his head.

The first call was from Chuck Stuttaford, a close friend of the chairman of the bank and one of a small number of private investors that Khan deigned to talk to.

'Hello, sir,' said Samuel, cutting through Stuttaford's lengthy introduction.

'Yes, yes, the markets are shifting, sir ...' Samuel stuck a finger in his ear against the background noise. Stuttaford hadn't heard about the rate rise – now the ancient news of ten minutes ago. He asked for Khan's Singapore phone number. Samuel was glad to oblige, and punched the next button.

'Khan?'

'No, Samuel Spendlove.'

At least this would be a quick one. Dee Tungley, a salesman from the bank's Frankfurt office, had been sniffing around Khan for months, in the hope of establishing a regular dialogue and becoming recognized as one of the king's idea generators.

'Hi, Sam. Need some help?'

Tungley was unlucky. Khan was the man who gave the orders and he wasn't there. Samuel quickly passed on the Singapore number, but it was an empty gesture. For some reason, Khan seemed to dislike the American, perhaps because he saw him as being too overtly pushy. There was little chance of Tungley reaching the inner circle.

Button number three.

'Could I speak to Mr Khan please?'

Samuel was distracted as he called up the page on his system that showed the trading profit for the day. It was down again to $119 million now. The profit was evaporating before his eyes.

'Ropner Bank,' he said finally.

'Could I speak to Khan, please? Who's that?'

Samuel felt a sudden pang of anxiety. He knew that voice from somewhere.

'He's in Singapore. Can I help?'

'Hope so. It's José Nissan from the *Mercury Inquirer* in London. Who's that?'

'I'm, erm, I'm his assistant, and I'm afraid I can't talk to the press.' José Nissan. He knew that he had recognized the voice.

'Perhaps off the record? A quick Ropner take on the

mayhem in the markets? Let me know what you make of the situation and we'll run a "sources close to Khan said" attribution?'

'Sorry, no. Really I must go. I can give you Khan's Singapore number though.'

Nissan took the number and hung up. If he recognized Samuel's voice he had disguised the fact well. Samuel hadn't spoken to Nissan for several years – not since they were undergraduates together. And he certainly didn't want Nissan to know he was working at Ropners. That would jeopardize everything.

It was calls like Nissan's and the articles that arose from them which represented the final insult for Anton Miller. Miller was openly envious of Khan's reputation. His trading success alone would have been enough to create bitterness in an office where money was the ultimate lingua franca. But Miller particularly resented Khan's popularity across the investment community and with the financial press. A succession of media interviews had created an ever-spiralling cycle of hype that included such masterpieces of journalism as an article entitled 'King Khan', which featured a collage of the eminent trader's head of steel-grey hair superimposed on a King Kong body atop the Empire State Building: Khan had scaled the heights of the investment banking industry. Unlucky for him that he should be away on such a momentous day in the markets.

Samuel glanced up. Anton Miller, who saw persecuting him as a way of causing pain in the Khan empire, was bearing down on him.

Miller was tall, narrow-framed, and permanently wrapped in well-tailored suits and Hermès silk ties. He was unusually old for an investment banker and had thin, frizzy hair and gimlet eyes that never quite joined in with the rest of his face on the rare occasions when he laughed. Now, however, in the middle of the market crisis there was some kind of a smile playing at the edges of his lips.

'Extraordinary, no?'

Extraordinary, now Samuel came to think of it, was the fact that the head of the bank's Paris office should present himself before the desk of the most junior employee in the flying wedge, as the traders referred to their V-shaped dealing room.

'It's amazing how much noise fifty-seven people can make, that's for sure,' quipped Samuel.

'What's the prop desk's understanding of events?'

'As you know, Khan says the only thing to understand about the Germans is that they're always reliving the aftermath of the First World War, even now. The national psyche is still scarred by memories of hyperinflation.' Samuel flicked through prices on his screen, trying to maintain a cool demeanour.

'I'm aware of Khan's somewhat unoriginal analysis of the market psyche, but what's Ropner's position? Is this good or bad news for us?' Miller had a curious air of stillness about him, the quiet intensity of the predator about to strike and kill its prey with impact alone, the shock of suddenness.

'We are positioned to take advantage of market volatility and to benefit from disorderly markets. As you know, Khan doesn't follow trends. He doesn't make bets on which way things are actually going to move.'

This was a poor response and they both knew it. Miller came closer to Samuel and spoke quietly, just audible above the din.

'Spare me the prepubescent flannel. What is our position?'

Miller continued to stand over him, a dark, threatening presence.

'Hi, Samuel. Insane day, isn't it?'

Kaz Day, by far the most beautiful woman in the office – come to think of it, one of the most beautiful women Samuel had ever seen – was walking over from her seat next to the fat leather chair that Miller normally occupied. He had an office too, of course, but had to have territory on the battlefield, had to be amongst the troops. Miller wheeled round.

'Anton, I think you should look at this. We're down more than $100 million on the fixed-income book. We need the full fire-fighting team on this one.'

Miller was instantly gone, half-running towards the fixed-interest desk. As Kaz followed behind she cast a glance over her shoulder in Samuel's direction.

The trader who had incurred the loss was in tears before Miller got there. For a moment, he stood his ground, staring at Miller defiantly. Then, realizing that his position was hopeless, he trudged off the floor. There was no need for words. The young man knew that for Anton Miller – and therefore for Ropner Bank – he no longer existed.

Kaz was now back by her desk prowling elegantly behind her traders. Women were rare on the trading floor and most of them held relatively junior positions. Special qualities had propelled Kaz to the top of the organization. Ageless in her beauty, she flicked back her tresses of long chestnut hair, offering advice and encouragement as the equities team worked to salvage its positions and generate revenue for the bank. Kaz was cooing to her team now. She wanted them to encourage clients to buy stock after the fall. More sales meant more commissions and a stream of buy orders would help to stabilize the market and preface a recovery.

Samuel was unable to take his eyes off Kaz. Her ability to stay calm in a crisis was impressive.

One of the monitors beeped, and Samuel was brought abruptly back to reality. The book position blinked up at him from the screen, resolutely unfathomable. He dialled François's number for the fifth time. François Morgon was his buddy in the IT department. The bank's trading systems were close to overload and Samuel realized that they must be frantic down there. This time, instead of the engaged tone, the phone answered on the second ring.

'François? Thank God. It's Samuel.'

'This is a bad time, Samuel.'

'I know, I know, everyone's chasing you. But listen, this is desperate. I think there is something wrong with the prop trading system.'

A slight hesitation.

'You know that it's Khan's personal, customized system. We run it on a separate server, so there shouldn't be any problems. You don't trade much. All the computer power is for analysis. Number squashing.'

'Crunching, François. Crunching. Listen, can you just take a quick look and get straight back to me if there's a problem? I'm staring down the barrel of a gun here.'

At least he had been able to confide in someone. François was safe, dependable, and far enough outside the circle of dealers for Samuel to relax in his company.

One of the equity traders was repeatedly banging his head on the desk. The phone rang. Samuel yanked it from the cradle.

'Yes?'

'No problems, my friend.' It was François, back in double-quick time. 'None that I can see. I hope that is good news.'

'I don't know. But thanks anyway.' He replaced the handset.

He checked on his position. The profit on the day had slipped below $100 million and all in the course of a two-minute telephone conversation. There was nothing else for it, he would have to call Miller over again with all the consequences that entailed. Miller would suspend trading on the book, thereby attracting dire publicity for the bank, but especially for Khan. Khan would descend on Samuel like thunder, and he would shortly be sharing the fate of the tearful fixed-interest trader. It was all very well being semi-autonomous within the bank, the Chechnya of the Ropner empire as Khan liked to put it, but Samuel needed someone to give him guidance before the rest of the profit disappeared.

Samuel punched angrily through to the next reporting screen.

'If only the bastard were here in Paris instead of messing around in Singapore . . .' he muttered.

'Well the bastard is here. Where are we today?'

Samuel whirled round. 'Khan! I thought—'

'Yes. I can guess what you were thinking, which is why I came back early.'

Khan always attracted attention when he entered the wedge, but all eyes were definitely on him now. Kaz glanced up for an instant and then continued to prowl behind her team.

Khan took off his jacket, revealing his crisp, white shirt, and gave Samuel a half-second of full-beam smile. His teeth seemed even whiter than usual against his coffee-coloured skin. He had clearly spent some time by the pool in Singapore. The famous bouffant hairstyle was gone; the thick grey thatch had been cropped to within half an inch of his skull. He looked, Samuel thought, disgustingly relaxed.

'Khan, you do realize . . . ?'

'That we're around $100 million up on the day?'

'Less than that. We were $200 million up, but the position slipped. I'm afraid I, er, don't know why.'

This was the moment. If Samuel was going to get the chop, now was the time.

'Dear boy, you weren't *supposed* to know. I was running a little flutter off the book. You'll find, by the way, that we are just over $100 million up on the day. I closed the position on the way into the office.'

'Off the book?'

'I'd just made my presentation on day one and went to the cocktail party afterwards. Plan was to go to bed early. Have you been to Singapore? Asian values, whatever they are, all over the place. Damned boring.'

Khan was slim and short, maybe 5' 6", and sounded like a 1950s BBC newsreader. God knows what his ethnic origin was. Some speculated that he was Indian, others Thai, others that he was an Algerian Jew who had changed his name. It didn't really matter. Khan was clever, with degrees from Cambridge and Princeton and had no interest in Asian values when there was a good time in the West to be had, and another piece of modern art to be collected. He had taken Samuel on board with the nonchalance of a big-budget movie director hiring the latest extra. But now, thinking of the half-hour of hell he had just lived through, all Samuel wanted to do was punch Khan in the face. Not exactly the response of an intellectual – but a rather satisfying notion. Samuel smiled to himself. In his new world, if things worked, that was all that mattered.

Khan was still talking: '. . . and the German Minister of Finance almost choked when I suggested inflation was dead.

That's when I realized that the ECB was probably going to raise interest rates. They're canny chaps these German financiers, but they don't realize what they give away by not saying things. So I set up a little off-the-book bet, and returned early to supervise it. Not early enough it seems.'

'How will "off the book" go down with the compliance team?'

'Everyone does it. Let's say you want to make a speculative play, as I did, once I saw the fear in the eyes of the beast. What you do is you go to another bank – not difficult to find as there are plenty falling over themselves to do business with you – and you borrow against the security of your book. You can usually persuade them to part with about 60 per cent of the value of the assets you put up as security.'

'So you were playing the market with money borrowed from another bank?'

'Exactly. That's why you couldn't work out where the gain had come from.' Khan smiled smugly as Samuel tried to assimilate the new information that he now had.

'You see, Samuel, I hadn't changed anything. There was just an intra-day entry on the suspense account to reflect the loan. If I hadn't closed it out by the end of the day, I would have had to let compliance and the management committee know. But I have closed it out, so the only thing to record will be our gain of . . .'

Khan tapped at the keyboard with a slim finger: '$103.4 million, in fact.'

'But where did the gain actually come from?'

'No rocket science involved whatever. I bought some put options on German government bonds, giant bets that 99 times out of 100 would be worthless, but if the market falls out of bed you make several times your money.' Khan continued to tap away at his keyboard, checking through the book to make sure that he was happy with all the remaining positions.

'But you knew that interest rates would rise, and bonds would fall, so how could you lose?'

'It wasn't a certainty that rates would rise. If it had gone the wrong way, the options could have been worthless and we would have owed the other bank money. But I did make a bet on you, all alone here.' Khan shot him another white-toothed smile which relayed a message of approval. Then the smile faded. 'You didn't say anything to Miller did you?'

'He asked me what our position was and I reminded him of our investment remit.'

'Excellent. That anally retentive buffoon needs to learn a lesson. He doesn't even know what his own people are doing, let alone professional investors like me.'

'But why did you let the profit slide from $200 million to $100 million?'

Khan held up his mobile phone.

'I was stuck in a cab on the way here and couldn't close out the position because my phone had run out of juice and the cab driver didn't have one. $100 million is an irritatingly expensive price to pay for a dead mobile battery, but these things happen. Especially when you have everything so cranked up that every small move is worth $1 million. Anyway, it's probably a little easier on Miller this way. I hear it was our fixed-income team who were on the other side of the trade.' Khan had an even more self-satisfied expression on his face as he contemplated the flak that Miller would get from New York. Samuel did not like Miller one little bit, but he was beginning to feel some sympathy with his plight.

'Don't look at me like that, Samuel. They were playing a

silly game, and they've been taught a lesson. It's just lucky for the bank that I was on the receiving end of the profit. The bank hasn't lost anything. The net result is that I get the credit for saving the day and Miller gets a scintilla of what he deserves for being such an interfering fool. He should find out what's happening in his own backyard before investigating the wide blue yonder.'

Samuel rocked back in his chair. Garnier's Opéra filled the wide bay window. He considered it wildly overdecorated, and didn't much care for it – but perhaps that was because he knew it had been Hitler's favourite building in Paris.

The hubbub had abated considerably now. The activity in the dealing room was no more frantic than, say, the Gare du Nord at rush hour. Samuel raised a hand to his aching brow. It seemed like an effort.

'It's been quite a day,' sighed Samuel.

Khan was tapping busily at a keyboard, working the windows of his Reuters screen. 'Today probably won't even have a name. Not so much a Black Wednesday as a Grey Tuesday Afternoon.' Khan considered his assistant for a moment.

'And you've done well, Samuel. I admit I was worried when my mobile went down on the way in. But you've done well. Kept your head, held your tongue. It sounds like you played the situation very ably. I scanned your trading log and I think the switch from tin to copper was a good decision. That tells me that the risk I took in allowing you to work with me is beginning to pay off. Maybe, just maybe, you have a talent for this job.'

Samuel reddened slightly at the compliment. There were times when he was beguiled by Khan's urbanity and undoubted charm, but he was a world-famous market fixer, and Samuel was briefed to find out the truth.

Khan made hundreds of millions by playing with bonds, currencies, effectively whole economies and the lives of the people who worked in them. And he liked to do it 'off the book' – he played God, but he didn't even play by God's rules. But one man's gain was another man's loss in the turbulent financial markets. The public had a right to know about Khan's unscrupulous methods, driven by an insatiable desire for personal wealth and recognition from his peers. Samuel wanted to lift the lid on this weird game with all its infighting and its ruthlessness. The specific brief in his red envelope was to find out what had really happened to Gallimard, the celebrated publishing house of Saint-Exupéry, Sartre, Camus and Simone de Beauvoir. Khan had made a fortune in the shares, playing bidder off against counter-bidder, playing God again. William Barton had lost out. According to the newspapers, he had been incandescent with rage. But Samuel didn't care about that. He was in a position to make a difference now, and he was going to.

He felt the gentle pressure of Khan's hand on his shoulder and his heart almost stopped. Deceit, even if derived from the best intentions, was a difficult burden to bear.

'Just finish up here. Tidy the daily trading journal and we'll close down for the day. Maybe grab some champagne at Café Marly. What do you say?'

'Sure,' said Samuel without a moment's hesitation. 'Love to.'

'TELL ME A STORY, PAPA.'

'What kind of story? A book story or a telling story?'

'A telling story, a telling story!'

Telling stories were always the best. They were different from the book stories in the way that Mom's pies and cakes were different from the ones that came in a packet. They were more satisfying. If stories could have had a taste, Papa's telling stories tasted better.

'What shall it be now?' reflected Papa.

'The watchtower story! The one about the war, when you were a little boy, like me!'

'Let me see now ... the watchtower story. Let's see if I remember that one.' Papa was smiling, as he always did before he began a telling story.

They both knew the tales, almost by heart. The key details never varied, and nor did the various doings of Oma and Opa, Papa's parents. He noticed that, when Papa finished his telling stories, he had a sad look in his eyes. Maybe it was because the story had come to an end. The little boy didn't like that either. Endings made him sad. But this was the beginning of the story.

'Let me see now. I'd be about your age. Maybe a little older.'

The boy sighed with pleasure and lay back on his bed.

'It was a very cold night. I had to pull the cord of my dressing gown tight round me.'

'Where were Oma and Opa?'

'They were downstairs in our house listening to the wireless. That was how we knew what was going on in those days. There wasn't any television of course. So I put my slippers on, crept out of the house and ran to the watchtower. It was only a few yards away from our house. Then I climbed quickly up the ladder. It was very, very cold.'

'Bitterly cold, Papa. It was bitterly cold,' corrected the boy. Bitter cold was a key detail, a vital ingredient of the story.

'Yes, it was, son. Bitterly cold,' smiled Papa. 'But the cabin was snug, warmed by the paraffin heater, and deserted. There was always a half-hour or so when the eastern watchtower of the camp was empty. It was peacetime; the terrible war that people still talked about was long over.'

'And where were the guards, Papa?'

'The guards felt they deserved a little cocoa and rum on the changeover. For a small boy like me, unable to sleep at night, a trip to the tower was very exciting.'

'It was like being a real soldier,' said the boy.

'Exactly. It was like being a real soldier. Anyway, from the window I could see some of the American soldiers – we called them GIs – returning on a late pass. They laughed and talked loudly. You could hear them far and wide, because the city was very quiet at night. But they quietened down when they got to the razor-barbed wire and the barricades of the checkpoint.'

'And what about the lady, Papa? Where was she?'

'She was there, as she was almost every night, under the street light down below, a couple of hundred metres away. She wasn't American, though. She was German like Oma and Opa. I remember that she was just out of sight of the checkpoint, but clearly visible *from the tower. I used to like to look at her, bathed in the fuzzy glow of the light.*

'Well, this night, the woman cocked her head at the GIs and smiled, and somehow her coat fell open. I remember I saw a flash of cream beneath the coat. It was her skin.'

'So she wasn't properly dressed at all? She really must have been very cold, poor thing.'

'Yes, she must have been cold, son. And the GIs weren't being nice to her as they passed by. They were making fun of her, which made me sad.'

'The Americans were still cross with the Germans, even though the war was over?'

'That's exactly right. Anyway, I remember how one of the soldiers talked quietly and nicely to the woman, and then they went away together for a while.'

'Where did they go in the dark?' The little boy was looking at the ceiling and imagining the couple becoming invisible. He waited for an explanation from Papa as to where they had gone, but he was onto the next part of the story.

'And then I thought that someone must have told a very good joke, because all the remaining GIs were laughing and clapping when the woman and the soldier came back. But the man who had been away wasn't laughing. He was just looking at the floor and fiddling with the buttons of his uniform.

'I remember the GIs were laughing even more loudly and heading towards the camp and the tower where I was when the woman called something out. The soldier she had been talking to turned back and said something.'

'What was it, Papa?'

'I couldn't hear, but I knew it wasn't nice. His voice was harsh. Then the soldier took a few steps towards the woman and threw something on the ground. It looked like money – and something else.'

'What was the something else, Papa?'

'I couldn't see properly at first, but then I saw that it was cigarettes. Cigarettes! The soldier had thrown cigarettes at the woman, and she bent down to pick them up from the ground.'

'You were so brave to climb up to the watchtower, Papa,' said the boy in a small, sleepy whisper.

'It wasn't that brave,' said Papa. 'It was like being on top of the world without anyone knowing that I was there.' The little boy was asleep and so his father kissed him on the forehead, tucked him in and crept out of the room.

4

WHENEVER SAMUEL wanted to speak to Alan McMurray in London, he left his flat and made the call from a public telephone, hard as they were to find in this era of mobile telephony. Apparently, this was what Barton had instructed. Samuel understood his concerns, having experienced the institutionalized suspicion of the French state before.

Years ago as an undergraduate, in what might have been another lifetime, he had been forced to register as a journalist to obtain his *carte de séjour*. He had explained his objective in the rue Cambon offices of the ministry of the interior. His interviewers had been a fifty-year-old bureaucrat, who insisted on being referred to as 'Mademoiselle', and her coiffured poodle.

Yes, Mademoiselle had agreed that he was primarily a student, and that writing about the death of the French brasserie was not controversial, nor was the rise and rise of the École Nationale d'Administration, which produced all France's top politicians and captains of industry, and, indeed, Peter Brook's next French-language production of Shakespeare hardly seemed to merit the attentions of the state security service. But Samuel was an academic, a writer, a journalist – professions which were, in France at least, part of a continuum of the cadre that led to technocratic power. Mademoiselle had smiled; he would surely appreciate the bureaucratic nuance that had brought him there:

'*C'est pas nécessaire, Monsieur Spendlove. Mais c'est obligatoire.*'

During his student stay, Douglas Hurd, then British foreign minister, said he regarded France as a well-governed country. Which, by coincidence, was the very day that Samuel's phone began picking up interference from passing radio cabs. Well, if the domestic intelligence service wanted to listen to Samuel's views on the latest exhibition at the Petit Palais, that was fine.

Revelling in the experience of being in a new city, Samuel had passed a pleasant few weeks exploring the leafy hedonism of the night-time boulevards. He would send reams of understated copy back to the offices of *Stream*, a student newspaper run for the benefit of its careerist staff rather than the readers. Most of his copy even got published, and the official *carte de presse* opened all kinds of doors, including those of nightclubs and the more exclusive bars. Very satisfying, and generally worth the hassle of dealing with Mademoiselle and her mutt.

For all its privileges and attractions, there was something unsatisfactory about being a journalist, something superficial. It was too easy to get away with saying things that were nearly but not quite true. When he read his stories in print, he almost believed them himself. As he sat one evening on the street outside a small café near Notre-Dame, he decided that journalism was not for him. How was he going to explain that to his father?

This time around he wasn't working for a student rag. This was real journalism, but he felt like a secret agent.

There didn't seem to be any obvious radio surveillance of his mobile calls. Nevertheless, public phones were the means of contact with London. Obviously prudent, given the sensitivity of the research. Samuel would sometimes visit a museum or art gallery before he called McMurray. Today he would be making the call from the Musée Antoine Bourdelle, near Montparnasse – just a short Métro ride from his flat in the Marais district.

Samuel glided away from the closing doors, stood on the platform and watched the train withdraw into blackness. The dimmed ruby lights and the flickering tail of silver sparks were eventually swallowed by the tunnel. He walked slowly towards the stairs marked 'Sortie', his footfall in unison with the impartial rhythm of the departing rolling stock.

A tiny black child was playing a skipping game on the exit stairs. Up two, down one. Hop. She played around Samuel's legs. Up four, down two. Jump. Minute black plaits of hair trussed with yellow beads scored the chocolate softness of her scalp. She bumped into his legs, and Samuel stopped for fear of hurting her. The child looked up at him and giggled. But then the wind-rush of a distant train roared softly in their ears, and she tumbled down to the platform and the safety of her mother to watch its arrival.

When trains arrived they carried the urgent promise of destination and delivery, giant worms emerging out of their dark lairs. Samuel had noticed when he was new to the city how he and the other rookies in town leaned forward in anticipation and then stood back fearfully, whilst the seasoned Parisians, perched on the great heights of their urban disdain, never so much as looked up from their *Libérations* and their *Figaros*.

There were other reasons for dawdling on the platform. He could gaze at the advertising billboards, all of which seemed to use semi-naked women to promote their products, and, of course, loitering would make it just a little more difficult for anyone following him to work out what he was up to. The northbound Ligne 4 train sighed to a halt on the opposite platform. A couple of dozen passengers alighted and disappeared. All quiet. Even the little girl had gone. He was being ultra-cautious, maybe even paranoid.

In the street outside, the light was the constant milky grey of a raw spring afternoon, but it seemed steel-bright to eyes grown accustomed to the murk of the Métro. Samuel began to negotiate his way round the vast concrete unpleasantness of Montparnasse – mercifully the only genuine catastrophe the 1960s had inflicted on Paris, apart from the Centre Beaubourg.

The giant electronic notice board on the corner of boulevard Montparnasse and the square proclaimed a message from a publicly amorous buffoon named Michel: 'J'♥ Véronique'. The electronic heart flashed, as though seeking a response; a challenge to the materialism of Samuel's new world.

He turned his back and walked away.

The Musée Bourdelle was a favourite haunt of Samuel's. Sited on the rue Antoine Bourdelle, just behind one of the busiest junctions in the city, it was perennially quiet. Half a kilometre away towards Les Invalides, the Musée Rodin was always overrun by groups of Japanese tourists, aimlessly following a guide with a brightly coloured umbrella held high in the air. Here, the shrine to Rodin's most gifted disciple remained still, a jewel unnoticed amid the urban bustle.

Samuel looked at his watch. Eleven o' clock. Ten o'clock in London. Unlikely that McMurray would be in his office at that time on a Sunday morning, but worth a try. He selected a call box.

'Yes?'

First ring. Alan McMurray, Editor of the *Sunday Inquirer*,

was clearly ready for action. His subordinates no doubt found it horrifying enough that McMurray came in on Sunday, publication day, and supposedly a day of rest. To answer the phone on the first ring at this ludicrously early hour had to be significant cause for wonder. But then from what Samuel had learnt about William Barton over the past few weeks, perhaps it wasn't so surprising. Barton had started his career as a journalist himself and then had been an editor. No wonder then that he read the newspaper from cover to cover on a Saturday night when it left the printing press. If he did not like what he read, the author would be fired. If it particularly offended him, then the editor might go too.

'Mr McMurray? Samuel Spendlove.'

'Spendlove. Good. Any progress?'

Conversations with McMurray tended to be straight to the point. The veneer of respect that had attended their first meeting was long gone. Over the course of their calls it quickly became clear that McMurray had no interest in risk analysis. What mattered was the Gallimard case study. Barton had bid for the publisher the previous year, but lost out at the last minute to a small publisher backed by a Monaco-based trust. Who owned that? No one knew, thanks to the banking secrecy laws in the principality.

But Gallimard was no longer an academic monograph. It was an investigative journalism assignment, and a tough one too.

'Well, no actual progress as such. It's a question of gaining the confidence of the key players.'

'How much bloody confidence do you have to gain? Christ, you've been there for weeks, man. You're not asking them to elect you to the bloody Papacy. I feel as though I'm sitting here waiting for smoke signals.'

'It will take some delicate handling to evince the true story,' retorted Samuel in a hushed voice.

There was a groan on the London end of the line. Samuel conjectured the possibility of a hangover. He imagined McMurray, with his suety face of the palest white, now even more pallid.

'Don't give me delicate sodding evincing, Spendlove. You're buggering around Paris masquerading as a financier and I need some facts to run a story. I don't give a flying fart in a hurricane what you have to do.'

'But it may take time.'

'Listen, Spendlove. As you know, the proprietor is taking a personal interest in this. He has a thing about bloody wonder-boy Khan, whose bags you're carrying. He wants the dirt and he wants it now. He wants to see something in the paper!'

Samuel hesitated. He had a vision of his father stumbling home late at night, grey from the pressures of the noble calling, sad and bleary from the consumption of too much whisky. Samuel on the stairs, his mother wringing her hands. Why so late again? Why the pub again? The first draft of history – a yellow snarl and a pained laugh. Putting something in the paper, filling the empty space.

McMurray seemed to hear the uncertainty, and softened his tone: 'I mean to say, it's an important story that William Barton takes a personal interest in, and he wants us to deliver. I am relying on you, Spendlove.

'So next week I want something, preferably on Gallimard, but we want a result. Soon. Do you want back-up? I can free up Suzi Gilbertson for a week or two. She has reasonable French, and she's bloody good at rooting things out.'

Samuel thought of that direct, challenging gaze, the smiling offer of getting to the bottom of things.

'I'll manage. Suzi's arrival would only complicate the issue.'

'Make sure you do manage, laddie.'

And with that, he hung up.

Samuel listened to the tone for a moment, and gently replaced the receiver. So Alan McMurray was being pushed by William Barton for a 'story'. He clearly thought Khan had prevented him from getting Gallimard and he wanted the hard evidence. And then he would mobilize his media might to discredit Khan using McMurray and Samuel as his instruments of shame. Dirt had to be dug up straight away, which was curious, since he had been told at the outset that this would be a three-month assignment.

Samuel would have to prove that one of the rumours about Khan was true. Gallimard was obviously the key story, but there were plenty of others – Khan's manipulation of share prices of companies big and small was legendary. In the currency markets, his skills were no less. He was credited with having boosted the Thai baht with manic buying of the future and then, minutes later, bringing the Vietnamese dong to the edge of collapse. Khan knew of the stories, of course, and laughed them off. 'How could anyone take a currency called the dong seriously?' he would smile. And even if the rumours were true, Samuel had to prove wrongdoing for there to be a really good story. If he impressed McMurray – or more importantly, Barton – a highly successful career in journalism would be assured, if he wanted it. And he would be able to say that he had made a difference.

SAMUEL SIGHED as he waited for a set of pedestrian lights to change. He needed to be very lucky or very smart to catch Khan and get the big story. To do it all in a week was just about impossible, which was infuriating. Not only was Samuel beginning to enjoy the undercover work, he was finally getting somewhere close to understanding one of the most secretive and exclusive clubs in the world. It was unjust, ridiculous, maddening to be issued with an ultimatum now.

Bourdelle, the little-known sculptor who had been mentored by Rodin, would be his consolation. He paid his three euros to a fat, somnolent attendant, and began his tour. The museum had once been Bourdelle's house and studio, and Samuel liked to begin with the living quarters, where Bourdelle's elegant line drawings, done as preliminary studies for the sculptures, decorated the walls. There was a smell of tallow and clay in the overheated apartment. When he looked at the primitive hand basin by the bed he imagined he could see the great man, stripped to the waist, washing away the sweat of the day's toil.

He climbed the stairs to the upper level of the outside gallery. A huge military sculpture of a mounted general jostled with a gigantic Amazon in what had once been the well-proportioned garden of Bourdelle's courtyard. Now they glared over those who came to pay homage to their master's work. Samuel admired a bust of a laughing Madame de Polignac. Head tilted back, soft, sensuality in the neck, the confident mouth and its full lips. He saw Bourdelle and his model together, he arranging her hair, softly putting that long neck into the desired position – and then, and then. God, it was a long time since he had kissed a woman.

A violent scattering, like gravel against a window, disturbed his reverie. A woman cursed and bent to retrieve the contents of her handbag. She was the only other visitor to the main exhibition hall, a huge, high building stuffed with northern light and gigantic, silently shouting sculpture. A lipstick rolled and rattled down a set of stone stairs, filling the hall with its small metallic sound.

Samuel began to move towards her with an offer of help, but instinctively checked himself. This woman was familiar, very familiar. He realized with a start that it was Kaz. On impulse, he withdrew to the shadow of one of the huge plinths.

He was glad he hadn't called out when the second woman appeared. She was of a similar age and build to Kaz, but different in every other way. This woman had lustrous straight black hair where Kaz's was curly brown; she moved with the raw, confident power of a prizefighter, whereas Kaz had feline grace. And she wore a biker's black leather suit and knee-length boots, which contrasted with Kaz's jeans and sneakers. Her beauty was dark where Kaz's was light. The woman rested her hand gently on Kaz's arm as she bent to help.

Samuel watched from behind a monumental stone carving of what appeared to be an Egyptian alligator-god. The biker woman was speaking to Kaz as if she were a naughty child. Then she picked up an object the size of a small pineapple and pushed it down into Kaz's capacious bag. Samuel was horrified: he recognized the object as a small bronze model of Bourdelle's famous crouching archer, a preliminary miniature casting. Scores of miniatures were kept in unlocked cupboards in the studio next door.

Collecting art was common among people with a lot of money and precious little time to spend it. Art was a fix. But that in itself wasn't enough, apparently. It seemed like Kaz, wealthy though she undoubtedly was, got a buzz from stealing.

The two women were now leaving the museum. The biker woman stopped and was coolly examining exhibits in the sculpture garden, squinting up into the sky where the forty-foot figures were to be lost and found in the wide-fingered foliage of immense chestnut trees. Kaz was waiting, submissively patient. She showed no further interest in the sculpture and evidently wanted to go, but the other woman lingered and looked around and sighed. She seemed to be taking pleasure from delaying their departure.

Samuel withdrew into the darkest part of the shadow. Kaz was becoming somewhat twitchy. If she were stopped that would mean prosecution and inevitably the end of her career at Ropners, and probably anywhere else in the world of finance. Apart from the ethical considerations of putting a convicted thief in a position of fiduciary responsibility to clients and shareholders, banks certainly did not want to employ somebody stupid enough to get caught.

Finally, the women left unchallenged. Samuel made to follow them, but a guard, eagle-eyed for the innocent, stopped him. He was carrying no bags, and a peremptory search revealed that he had stolen nothing.

On Monday, when the inventory was done, the museum would discover the missing miniature and blame Samuel, not the two young women who showed such a polite interest in Bourdelle's masterpieces. He hoped that this would not prevent him going back there. Mere innocence was no defence.

Free of the suspicious glares of the museum guards, he ran to the top of rue Antoine Bourdelle. The women had gone. Now he had a choice. Left would take him towards the Musée Rodin and Napoleon's tomb at Les Invalides. A turn to the right would lead back to Montparnasse. He chose to go right, more in hope than expectation.

He half-ran along the pavement, his mind racing. Kaz clearly had a brilliant future. Some within the bank said she would already have had Anton Miller's job were it not for the inconvenient fact of her being a woman – and a good-looking, especially noticeable one to boot. Whichever way Samuel played it over, Kaz seemed the perfect person to approach for a story on Khan. If anyone could understand how he worked – and whether his methods were truly illegal – she was the one.

And now he had something on her – a thrill-seeking art thief had a certain vulnerability. She would deny it all, make his life hell, and he would be out of the bank in short order, but that would be fine. He would have his story. But where was Kaz?

Samuel's luck held. There they were, waiting for a taxi at the rank just east of La Coupole and the Brasserie Clos des Lilas. The women were at the front of the queue now. Samuel ran to the far corner of the boulevard Montparnasse and hailed a taxi from the traffic.

The cab driver shrugged and switched the meter on as Samuel said he'd tell him where to go. He was used to idiots climbing into his cab without the faintest idea of where they wanted to be.

The women headed south. Samuel's taxi driver became a little impatient at times, particularly when there were hesitations to allow the other cab time to get ahead of them. But eventually the stop–start journey came to an end at the rue d'Alésia in the fourteenth arrondissement. Samuel paid the driver, who took the notes and examined them carefully, as though a half-wit's money might not be valid currency.

Kaz and her friend disappeared through a door in a side street, a minute's walk up the road. Samuel strolled after them and walked by. The door was painted matt black, and was of the heavy-duty, nightclub, drinking-den type. He walked by again. The place wasn't advertised as a club. There were no signs, no stickers in the window, no false welcome in neon.

But then all the clubs with pretensions to smartness prided themselves on their external anonymity. To be cool enough to get into the club you had to know where it was. That was the point of *boîte de nuit chic*.

Eventually, he settled on a compromise. He would knock on the door, apologize profusely if the place turned out to be a private address. If it were a club, he would probably not go in unless he could see there was enough space to lose himself. But even if he didn't go in, he would gain something: he would know where the place was and what it was called.

One firm rap of the knuckles. Nothing. The second attempt was louder and a rat trap opened at eye level. An extraordinary face stared out at him. Intelligent, black-brown eyes set in a smooth oval of flawless, creamy skin, a Joan of Arc earring, in the form of a double-transept cross, dangling from one lobe. Biker woman.

'*Excusez-moi. J'ai la mauvaise adresse, je crois,*' mumbled Samuel.

The eyes searched him. She was beautiful, but slightly scary, and she was looking for something she evidently didn't find. '*J'y crois, moi aussi, mon pote,*' came the laugh eventually. *Sorry, mate, wrong place, wrong time, wrong person.* The rat trap shut just as suddenly as it had opened.

Samuel made for the nearest Métro station. He hoped Kaz hadn't seen him.

What was he to make of all that? It was clearly a club, and clearly not for him. A lesbian club? Kaz would be crucified as a dyke if word got out on the trading floor.

Better to forget all that, and concentrate on the stolen Bourdelle. It would be a horrible business even to have to hint at coercion to get her to talk, but that was the compromise.

You had to accept that sometimes it was necessary to do nasty things as a means of getting at the truth. Especially when you were undercover, struggling for survival in a subterranean world. He wondered what the Master of Biblos would have made of all these fragments, these shards of conflict that constituted his life. Would he have found a pattern, a greater truth?

When he got back to the flat the telephone was ringing. He fumbled with the heavy nineteenth-century door and scrambled for the handset. Maybe it would be Gail, brutally disappointed by the steroid-fed cretin she'd run off with. Or maybe not.

'Hello, Samuel.'

He suppressed a sigh and looked out at the twin towers of Notre-Dame that settled in the gap between the buildings opposite.

'Hello. This is a surprise.'

'I try not to eat into my weekends, nor those of my staff. We all need down time, Samuel.'

'So . . . ?'

'So I've decided to let you have some fun. We're too liquid. I thought I might give you half our cash to play with.'

'How do you mean?'

'Oh, you know, I thought I would let you cast about for some interesting, you might even say speculative, opportunities. I have a few thoughts, of course.'

Samuel took notes now as Khan spoke. His head swam. He was going to get to 'play' with around $50 million of the bank's own money.

After a few minutes he hung up and looked at his notebook. Someone else's money – $50 million of it, in fact. Maybe

Khan really did think of him as a good hire – good enough, at any rate, to embark on a speculative adventure with some of the bank's money. It would be a great chance to see how Khan really operated. Perhaps the truth wasn't going to be quite so difficult to get at after all.

'HERE. SEE THIS? *This is the big secret.*'

The boy climbed up on the stool next to the table and watched carefully. He gazed at his grandmother's shiny old hands. Their purpose and speed seemed mildly bewildering. His Oma was usually so careful, so slow – what she said, where she would go, how she moved. Everything about Oma was old and creaky. But this was a baking session; apple strudel to make, the range hot, long stoked with logs from the Bavarian forest. He loved watching her make strudel: sugar, cinnamon, cloves, fat green apples, flour and wood smoke.

'*See.*'

The boy looked on. Oma took a small pewter pot and shook it into the mixing bowl.

'*Two ingredients. First, we put white pepper to bring out the sweetness of the apples and to make the pastry richer. And the second is love. That's what will make the warm feeling in your tummy, my darling. You'll never be hungry. You'll never be hungry.*'

The fire crackled.

Oma was crying again, quiet streams of silver trickling down her fat pink cheeks. But that was all right. The boy knew what to do. He went to fetch the photograph album and soon felt the comforting clutch of her arm about him.

'Who's this, darling?'

'That's your papa, Oma.'

The boy had never met the sepia-coloured man with walrus moustache, standing so confidently and proudly in front of a big castle that he had not visited. The boy had never met him because the man had been dead long before he was born.

'And do you remember what Oma's papa used to do, my darling?'

'He was in charge of all the money in Germany after the war, Oma. That was the war before the one that Papa fought in.'

'Oh, you are a clever boy! Oma loves you so much.'

And the boy loved his Oma, very, very much. But there were some things that puzzled him. If Oma's daddy had been in charge of all the money in Germany, why wasn't there any money left to buy firewood for Oma? Why did he always have to go and collect sticks for her?

5

SAMUEL STRODE INTO the bank humming a random early-bird tune. He was trying to embrace the life of a young investment banker, exuding arrogance and oblivious to anything except the narrow world of the trading floor. But the process was far from complete. He still noticed the expressions on the faces of the secretaries, the maintenance staff, the janitors and the people who worked in personnel. These people, ordinary Parisians who lived in the real world and who didn't have a job selling shares or bonds with the huge financial rewards that this brought, thought that those who worked in the flying wedge were monsters from Mars. Samuel could see why.

His colleagues worked ridiculous, inhuman hours, for a start, driven by a desire to make more and more money. Most of the team had some kind of business to transact with the East, which meant a very early start. These people were in the office at four o'clock, when even the birds were still asleep.

For every employee of Ropner Bank creeping in before dawn, there was another who did not leave the office until past midnight – until the currency options play on the Philadelphia exchange was squared away or the irate pension fund manager in San Joaquin County, California, had been pacified after being made to swallow another speculative European equity issue. The markets might have become global, but the time zones remained, creating a working day that had become elongated at either end.

Furthermore, the inhabitants of the flying wedge ate and worked like caged animals. Such a shame when the local food was so good. Forget fast food; Paris was the home of the swiftly prepared and consumed meal. In the little cafés on the rue des Mathurins, a glass of red or white wine would be set before you, together with knife, fork and napkin, straight on the zinc counter-top. Before the glass was half-finished, your meal would be there – hot, satisfying, delicious. But the traders in the flying wedge couldn't be away from their desks for the fifteen minutes required to eat a real meal. Instead, they had fat, American-style sandwiches delivered from Lina's, or they ordered in pizzas from Pizza Hut or the Chicago Pizza Pie Factory. A diet of stodge. If the markets were quiet they would throw elastic bands and paperclips and bits of stale bread at one another. But they never strayed far from their screens.

'Hey, big guy, what's up?'

Samuel looked at the flashing button on his screen bank. Dee Tungley from the Frankfurt office came up on the digital read-out.

'I'm fine, Dee. What's happening with the international man of mystery?'

This kind of banality was standard form when the markets were trundling along and no one was screaming. Polite people called it shooting the breeze. In the flying wedge it was shooting the shit.

'The mystery is why I live in this crappy little town.'

'Oh, come on, Frankfurt's not so bad. You can trade anything in Frankfurt.' There had been a time when Frankfurt was a contender to become the European financial centre, but the Americans spoke English, not German, and so London won hands down. 'It could be worse, Dee. You could be in Helsinki with only Nokia and a handful of government bonds to trade.'

Samuel was now worth a bit of banter on a quiet day – an upgrade in status as he made it into Tungley's address book. Tungley had been in Samuel's contact book for weeks. Eventually, the trader came to the point: he was peddling some exotic-looking Italian corporate bond issue.

'Not sure, Dee. Let me talk to Khan.'

'OK. Listen it's a neat story, a pure trade, a clear win. He'll love it. I'll get back to you later.'

The wedge was filling up now. Kaz was sitting at her desk flipping through some research notes. After the Bourdelle escapade it was difficult for Samuel not to stare. She was all poise and elegance; the controlled power of her beauty was mesmerizing. Yet it was the clarity of her thinking that had resulted in her being promoted to run her desk. The fact that she was a figure of authority in this male-dominated world made her physical appearance all the more alluring.

There was a minor negative, though. Kaz was part of a cult of cleanliness that Samuel found faintly alarming. The management of Ropners didn't care if you smoked yourself to death, decorated your Bloomberg screen with half-eaten croque-monsieurs and spent condoms, or burped to the tune of Colonel Bogey every time you made a sale. What counted was the cleanliness and crispness of your shirt, the alpine pungency of your deodorant, and your ability to convey the impression that, no matter how bad your halitosis, you had brushed your teeth that morning. And your hair and fingernails had better be immaculate too. Regulation cuts. No big hair for women, absolutely no facial hair for men.

Samuel's theory was that cleanliness was both an excuse and a justification. You could sell shares in a dodgy company to an unsuspecting investor and then you could look at yourself in the mirror, check the razor edge of the lily-white cuff and tell yourself it wasn't a dirty business. Or if you were feeling a little more realistic, you could say the world was one hell of a dirty place, but at least your little bit was not unduly polluted. Just look at the spotlessness of that tie.

Then there was the dirty game of office politics, a terrible, competitive game played over years and years. The winner was the one left standing after the others were dead. The death could be real – a stress-induced heart attack, a massive brain haemorrhage. Or it could be a protracted, agonizing, office death – death by demotion and humiliation. Or you could die simply by losing it. Death was when you burst into tears because you overheard a couple of secretaries repeating confidences bestowed on them by their bosses which gave you a clue as to your likely fate in the upcoming bonus round. Death was when your voice rose randomly and involuntarily to a falsetto when you were on the phone to a valued client. Death was when you couldn't do the simple, vital arithmetic lightning-quick as a result of exhaustion. If you couldn't do the numbers, you couldn't trade. It was an unpleasant, cut-throat environment, and to an outsider it might have seemed strange that the employees of Ropners were prepared to endure such a place. But trading was like a drug and the ultimate fix was a $1 million bonus. Greed and the pursuit of wealth were the motivators.

Death in one form or another waited for victor and vanquished, for Khan, Miller, Kaz and the rest as they struggled for client accounts and the control of millions of dollars. They all knew that they could only survive if they could prove their commercial value. They knew that they were expendable, irrespective of length of service or the loyalty they had shown to the organization over many years. Each had to fight his own corner and the rewards and penalties were on a scale that most ordinary people could never comprehend.

Khan sauntered into the office looking very pleased with himself.

'Happy?'

'Never happier,' said Samuel.

'Good. Got any new ideas, Sammy boy?'

The markets had been quiet all morning. There was truth in the old aphorism that the financial world doesn't mind bad news, but hates bad surprises. After the initial move downwards following the unexpected rate rise, both bonds and shares had picked up towards the end of the day. The weekend had helped settle nerves as brokers, analysts, bankers and fund managers around the world called each other from their country houses to reassure one another that the sky really wasn't going to fall. Khan's call to Samuel had included a bit of rap about market calm. It was probably just one of many. The informal networking of the financial community seemed to have had some effect. Most of Europe's share markets were up slightly with moderate trading volume – the markets' way of expressing quiet confidence.

Samuel looked at the pile of prospectuses for new companies that were coming to the market. An investment trust which was going to buy shares in small Japanese companies was of no interest. An Albanian government bond issue – another no, even if they were dollar-denominated. A company which specialized in internet security looked more promising.

'What's new?' Khan sat down next to Samuel, who felt a closeness that was discomfiting. It was paternal, an interest that was rapt and personal and somehow flattering. Yet there was something else there, something a long way from two adjacent seats in the flying wedge.

Samuel mentioned Dee Tungley's Italian corporate bond issue, passed Khan a telephone number, and then stood up and walked across the office. He had just seen Kaz glide off the floor.

'Hi.'

He caught her as she was trying to extract a can of drink from the vending machine in the corridor.

'Oh, hello, Samuel.'

She gave him a full-beam smile for no good reason that Samuel could see, a smile that he would be reconstructing inside his head for hours.

'Listen, thanks for saving me from Miller last week. Whew!'

'Everyone needs saving from Anton Miller – especially the man himself.' Kaz laughed in a self-conscious way, betraying a nervousness that surprised Samuel and made him wonder if she realized who had been banging on the door of the club. There was an awkward pause and then Kaz began to walk back towards the trading floor. Samuel followed her exquisitely tailored back into the flying wedge and floated towards his desk.

Khan was on the phone.

'Here's the man himself.' A receiver was thrust into Samuel's hand and Khan gave him a reassuring nod.

'Hey, dude.'

'Hi. Just can't get enough of us, eh, Dee?'

Samuel bought $50 million worth of the Italian corporate bond issue. Tungley believed that it was wrongly priced and that Ropners would be able to make a quick turn. The money would probably only be tied up for a week and he thought Samuel could make 10 per cent. A $5 million profit in a week. In theory.

'That order will have made his day,' Samuel said to Khan.

'His month, at least, I would expect. He's been trying to do business with us for aeons,' chuckled Khan. 'Well done, though. That looks like a good deal.'

As Khan turned back to his screens, Samuel felt a chilling presence, and turned. Anton Miller was standing behind them, watching with open malevolence. Samuel had never seen him quite so suffused with rage; Miller's thin frame was quaking with the pure voltage of his animosity.

Khan too must have been aware of Miller, but chose to ignore him for a full ninety seconds. At last he closed a window on his screen, and swivelled in his chair.

'Ah, Anton. What can I do for you?'

'Isn't it a question of what you have already done for me, or rather *to* the bank?' The question came out as a long, angry hiss. Miller was struggling hard to contain himself.

'I'm sorry, Anton. Not quite with you on all this.' Khan loved to flaunt his British public schoolboy accent. He knew it needled Miller, who spoke in a strangulated mid-Atlantic hybrid.

'I believe you are, but let me acquaint you with the details. Remember Duval, the idiot selling the naked puts on German bonds?'

'You mean the unfortunate fool who had his last scrap of dignity publicly trampled on by you before you sacked him on the dealing room floor just the other day, Anton? Indeed I do.'

'He had just lost this bank more than $100 million through unauthorized trading.'

'Then he was lucky you didn't behead him right here, wasn't he?'

'Please, spare me the adolescent humour. You do know, I take it, that he was selling the puts to Pentangle Trust?'

'And you assume that, as I know the boys at Pentangle, I was on the other side of the trades.'

Miller began to circle the desk like a prosecuting lawyer.

'Do you deny it?'

'No. I was on the other side. I instructed Pentangle to buy the puts in size and your young genius, Duval, was prepared to play.'

Samuel knew that Khan frequently used other firms to disguise his moves in the market. Khan had told him that, once you had a reputation for getting things right, the market makers were wary of trading with you. Dealing through an agent ensured confidentiality.

'You have cost my team over one hundred million dollars.' Miller's voice was quiet, his words carefully enunciated.

'No, Anton. Your little rogue trader was responsible. The fact is that you should have known what he was doing, but you didn't. You should just be grateful that I was on the other side of the trade. The bank's overall position is neutral.'

But from the fixed-income team's point of view, the position was far from neutral. Bonuses were determined on the basis of the profitability of each business unit, and it was going to be difficult for Miller's team to make good a black hole of those proportions over the remainder of the year. Meanwhile, the prop team would clean up again.

Miller turned on his heel and began to walk away. Then he swung back round and walked right up to Samuel. He leaned over Samuel's desk and pointed a finger in his face. Samuel could see he was a tiny step from losing control altogether.

'And you. You're part of this. I haven't forgotten that crap about taking advantage of inefficiencies in the market.'

Abruptly, Miller straightened up and backed off a little. His usual demeanour seemed to be returning. He turned to face them again, and said in a slow, quiet voice that they had to strain to hear:

'You have done wrong.'

'Really, Anton?' drawled Khan. 'Spare us the biblical wrath. What do you have in store for us? A plague of frogs?'

With an intake of breath, Miller swivelled with exaggerated slowness. The drone of the flying wedge indicated no special watchfulness. Then the slim figure stooped forward, bringing his face down to desk level, a matter of inches from Samuel's own. Samuel could smell Miller's deodorant and a minty odour on his breath. The banker's eyes were tiny, viper-dark points of malice.

He looked at Khan, then at Samuel, then at Khan again, and eventually spoke even more softly, even more slowly than before: 'I promise you: I will damage you for this.'

He turned away and retreated to his desk in the far corner of the floor. Khan leaned back easily in his chair and watched him go.

'He's losing it,' said Khan as the far door swung shut. 'I don't give him more than a few weeks – six months at the most.' He smiled at Samuel's grim face. 'Don't worry! Money and success don't always bring you happiness or friends, but you do get a much better class of enemy.'

Samuel gave a watery grin. Part of him fervently hoped that there was nothing to uncover about Khan's startling investment successes. Just because some media mogul disliked the man didn't necessarily make him a crook.

A colleague from the swaps desk came over to talk to Khan, and Samuel's eye was caught by Kaz. How long had she been watching them? They exchanged a tiny flicker of a smile, and looked away. This was dangerous intimacy on the dealing floor.

Khan's mobile warbled. He raised his eyebrows, and began to walk out of the building, the phone clasped to his ear. Chuck Stuttaford was on the line, bleating about the parlous state of the markets. Men as wealthy and as stupid as Stuttaford needed to ventilate their imbecilities on a regular basis. It was part of Khan's job to talk to him.

With Khan gone, Samuel wandered over to Kaz as unobtrusively as he could.

'Hello again.' Her smile was positively radiant. Samuel was struggling to disguise his nervousness.

'Hi. Do you have a moment? It's just that I've got this company that I'd like you to give me your opinion on.' He tossed a document on her desk.

She looked up at him, and tucked an imaginary fold in her silk blouse into the waistband of her skirt.

'What's in it for me?' Her tone was gently mocking, but definitely inviting. He hesitated.

'Not content with subverting the fixed-interest desk are we? Time to sabotage the equities desk,' said Miller, who was suddenly at his shoulder and uncomfortably close.

'Anton, Anton. Nobody sabotages me,' said Kaz with just

the right combination of levity and self-assertion. 'I devise my own bomb plots, thank you.' She continued smoothly, casually picking up the prospectus.

'I told Sam – sorry, Samuel – that I would give him an opinion on a London IPO. If you're really worried that Khan's team is out to blow a hole in the equities team, then don't be. I am perfectly able to look after myself, Anton.'

Miller looked from one to the other, opened his mouth and shut it. Then he retreated to his office and drew the blinds. Before they could exchange another word, three lines burst into life on Kaz's telephone bank. She shrugged and began hitting the buttons.

When Samuel got back to his desk, his mail icon was flashing. He clicked on it.

> Let's discuss the prospectus. Perhaps a post-work ballon de blanc? Is Wednesday good for you? Don't worry about Miller. I have him under control.
>
> K.
>
> PS Is that all you want to discuss, or am I right in thinking that our conversation will lead us on to the fascinating topic of Khan and his trading methods?

He looked up in astonishment. Kaz had been watching him with a half-smile, as though he were a child unwrapping a present. And then she gave him something else, something almost as surprising as the message itself – a slow, knowing, decidedly old-fashioned wink.

HE DOWNED *a glass of schnapps and shuddered slightly. He didn't particularly like the taste, never had done. But it was Oma's drink, her little luxury, and he always kept a bottle with him, wherever he was in the world. The schnapps and the photo album, the constants in an ever-changing, fast-moving world. They were his truths in a universe full of other people's lies.*

Outside the window, London shimmered in the night air. He crossed the floor of the flat and gazed out incuriously before he closed the curtains. London. Apart from the sound of Margaret Thatcher's Tory City boys braying away outside their champagne bars, it could easily have been Boston or Hong Kong, San Francisco or New York. The 1980s. What a horrible decade. What a price to pay for 'sound money'. Whatever that was.

The photo album lay on the arm of a wide, well-upholstered chair. He dropped down into its softness, filled with a familiar sense of exhaustion. His grandmother and another woman looked out at him from the past. A smile began to insinuate itself slowly into his drawn features. There was some joy in all that sadness, after all.

The two women were quite young at the time of the photo. They were smiling and holding a laundry basket above their heads in a gesture of triumph, like it was a sports trophy, one handle each.

He sipped the schnapps again, and could almost feel that soft, inquisitive old hand reaching for his own, much smaller one. He nestled up against the side of the chair, and laid his head against it.

'...and Mariella and Oma decided to take two laundry baskets and get all our money from the bank.'

'You had so much money that it took two of you to carry it in big baskets?' asked the little boy, his eyes wide.

'We had a lot of money, my love, but it wasn't good money. It wouldn't buy very much. Every time we went to the shops, the price of things had doubled from the day before. So the money that we had in the bank was worth less every day.'

The boy looked into his Oma's troubled eyes and nodded, pretending to understand. The exciting bit was coming up.

'So Oma told Mariella that she didn't have to tidy the house that day, because she needed her to come with her into the city. So they went to the bank to take all Oma and Opa's money out and buy as many nice things as they could before all their money melted away.'

'It melted away, Oma? Like ice cream?'

'Yes, darling, a little bit like ice cream, so we had to take it out and spend it before it all melted away. But when we went to the bank there was so much money that it filled both laundry baskets completely, and Mariella and I could only carry one between us. So we carried the first basket out to the entrance of the bank where we could get a cab to take us home, and then went back in to get the second basket.'

'And then?'

'And then we realized we'd left a basket full of money outside on the pavement unattended, and rushed outside. But we were too late. The money was lying on the pavement and the basket had been stolen. Mariella got very angry and ran after the thief, and caught him.'

'And then?'

'And then he gave her the laundry basket back.'

'But what about the money, Oma? Why didn't the thief steal the money?'

'Because he knew it was going to melt away, darling. In a week's time the money in the basket would have been worth less than the basket was. It was much better to take the basket.'

The chair seemed less comfortable now, and the schnapps tasted bitter in the back of his throat. He passed his hand across his brow, and snapped the photo album shut.

Within a couple of minutes he was in bed, trying not to think of the pain that had marked Oma's life. He had an early meeting tomorrow in central London. There was business to do.

6

SAMUEL AWOKE EARLY thinking of Kaz and the evening ahead. He climbed out of bed, pulled on a pair of jeans and went out onto the balcony to watch the new day dawning. It was quiet; still too early for the road-cleaning truck. The odd, somewhat sinister little royalist bar opposite, with its Front National and Maçonnerie Française connections, had only just closed. Samuel suspected that there might have been a fight again; something had frayed the edges of his dreams with a metallic echo of violence.

Light was emerging into the ever-wider sky. To his right Saint Jacques stood atop his tower, guarded by griffins and gargoyles. To his left, the Hôtel de Ville was vast in its morning silence. Beyond them, Notre-Dame squeezed into the angle of two tall, second-empire buildings. The cinereous, crumbling cloudbank was fading to a milky white.

It was 6.25 when he landed in his seat in the flying wedge and the half-dozen people already on the trading floor gave the impression of being well settled into their work. Some of them would have been hard at it for two or three hours, no doubt. They were all, of course, immaculately dressed, uniforms still spotless so early in the day.

Khan was away again. This time he was just a short TGV

ride away, ostensibly attending a conference in Lausanne, but he had made no secret of the fact that this was partly a trip for pleasure. Khan had friends who lived there, who shared his enthusiasm for modern art. Samuel was not sure that it was wise for Khan to be out of the office for spurious reasons whilst Anton Miller was on the warpath, but his boss was so confident of his own position at Ropners that he seemed to care little. The suggestion that Miller might pose a threat was met with a dismissive shrug of the shoulders.

Samuel ran a quick check on their most recent buys. The Italian corporate bond had made little progress – wide spreads made trading expensive, and little business was being done. He might have to wait a little longer than anticipated to make his profit. He looked at the other open positions and whistled softly. There might not have been much movement in the Italian corporate bond market, but the six-month future on the NASDAQ, Khan's pick, was up several per cent.

It was breakfast time. Robert, the short, dark *pied noir* waiter from the Café des Sports in the rue d'Antin, was doing the eight o'clock rounds with his wicker basket of sandwiches and pastries. The traders had fought hard to persuade him to sell sandwiches so early in the morning. It was yet further proof of a barbarism that profoundly shocked Robert. He had once point-blank refused to serve a Canadian trader in his café who had asked for a glass of milk to accompany his steak frites, this being a gastronomic crime against humanity.

With only modest reluctance Robert sold Samuel a non-traditional breakfast baguette, split and buttered, with ham and cheese. Samuel watched the solid little frame retreating. Robert had lived almost all his life in Paris and was proud of it. He was like some rustic peasant, a Rousseau-esque savage in comparison with the levels of deviousness and cunning found in those who worked in the ivory towers of high finance, the city within the city.

It was quiet, and Samuel was bored, already wishing the hours away until his date with Kaz. He picked up the phone. François Morgon in the computer department answered on the second ring.

François was, as always, smoking a cigarette when Samuel found him in the basement which was the IT department's empire. He was tall and black with a skin so dark it seemed sometimes to have an almost bluish tinge. His parents were from Senegal, but François had been born in Levallois in the western suburbs of Paris, and was fiercely, chauvinistically French. The fact that this impeccably dressed black man had been stopped twice to have his papers checked in the street in the few weeks since Samuel's arrival, whereas the Anglo-Saxon dreamboat himself had never so much as received a second glance from a gendarme, did not seem to bother François at all. Or if it did, he was far too cool to let the Englishman know. Samuel suspected that one of the reasons they had got on so well from the very first was an unconscious acknowledgement that they were both outsiders. But this would always remain unspoken.

They shook hands and François poured them both a cup of coffee from the percolator he had personally imported as a gesture of despair over the grimy emissions of the office vending machine. François slowly cleared his desk of what seemed to be a score or more of Escher prints. Typical techie stuff.

'The book must be looking pretty good for you to leave the desk,' joked François.

'It does. And anyway, Khan's away today.'

'So the mice are playing?'

'I just wanted to come and talk to you after that fiasco the other day. Is there any way we can track what we're doing remotely? If Khan's out and decides to trade, is there a way he could update our positions? Dealing is risky and complex enough without doing it in the dark. I'm just concerned that next time, we'll be the ones losing the bank's money.'

François looked carefully at Samuel and, after a moment, gave a minuscule nod of the head.

'As you know, Khan has his own system, and it's relatively simple – a glorified spreadsheet, really. It should be easy to create a screen on-line. I'll write a *petit* programme for you this weekend, my friend.'

'Superb. And if you could explain more fully how the basic system works, I'll be able to deal with any future problems without bugging you.'

'My systems do not have bugs,' smiled François.

'Is that a French technical-department joke?'

'Technology is a serious matter,' laughed François.

'Obviously. But it would really help me with my research, and you know how impatient Khan can be.'

'Anything to help in the pursuit of knowledge,' said François with a mock-serious face. Even in the IT department, the ring-fenced, impregnable fortress of technical nerdishness, they knew that knowledge was power. François was a friend, no doubt of that.

ON SAMUEL'S RETURN, Miller was by his desk, standing silently on his long legs like a marsh bird eyeing a fish.

'Can you come and see me in my office in ten minutes?' Miller paused expectantly. His manner was strained, but civil. 'I would be grateful to you if you could spare the time.'

'Yes, Anton. Of course.' Miller was his ultimate boss, so he could not really say no. 'Ten minutes?'

'Ten minutes.' With a stiff little bow Miller turned and was on his way.

Samuel picked up his mobile to call Khan. It would be as well to alert him to Miller's sudden interest. The small sounds of energy pulses bouncing off satellites scratched distantly in the earpiece as Kaz swept onto the floor. Even amid the minor anarchy of what was turning into a moderately busy day, Kaz was able to create a little time and space for herself. It was the supreme compliment to her poise and beauty. Sales pitches faltered for just a second. A phone was left unanswered for just one extra ring. A chair swivelled. All to pay homage to the 1950s movie-starlet pencil-line grey skirt and jacket, the wide eyes and angelic mouth, the thick hair that hung heavy, precariously banded back, always threatening an exotic overspill. She took her seat and the instant of homage passed.

Samuel saw that she was being softly catcalled by Diaz and his sidekick, a Brit on the derivatives team. No one knew, or at least bothered to remember, what the Brit's real name was. Everyone referred to him as Nobby – mainly because after three drinks he began to think with his penis. He had a perverse taste for humourless Canadian women. Samuel had heard that his first wife had divorced him for infidelity. The second would probably not be far behind. Kaz acknowledged neither the straightforward admiration nor the anachronistic goosing that still survived in financial milieux; she simply readied herself for work. Two French women – Isabelle and Alexandra – looked over at Kaz and sullenly returned to their calls. Isabelle was known as La Petite in the office, and Alexandra was universally nicknamed FT. She only ever read the *Wall Street Journal* and *La Tribune*. But that was the way things were: just about everyone had a nickname on the trading floor, sometimes for reasons no one really knew.

The clicks and jumbled nothing-sounds from the phone suddenly straightened themselves out.

'Russian embassy.'

Khan was clearly in one of his more flippant moods. Perhaps it was the excitement of his imminent visit to see a new art installation, painted tentpegs set into the wall in the foyer of Bergen & Co. Samuel had already been to the lakeside offices of Khan's close friend Jake Bergen in Lausanne. The reception area was crammed full of papier mâché non-representational sculpture, which Khan greatly admired.

'I gather you were expecting my call, tovarisch.'

'Indeed, Samuel, indeed. How are you doing?'

'Fine, but I'm about to step into the lion's den. A cosy chat with Anton is just minutes away.'

'A delicious prospect.'

'What?'

'Referring to the view, Sammy boy. The mountains of Jura. Great food, interesting wines, though I believe the vin jaune is a little overrated, and fossils that Steven Spielberg made famous. *Jurassic Park* and all that.'

'Aren't you concerned?'

'About Miller? No, no. He knows our little adventure was perfectly legitimate. The only one who came out badly was our counterparty, Duval, the fixed-interest dealer he sacked – someone he should have been monitoring in the first place. If Miller wants to see you it'll be because you've wrongly appropriated a box of his department's paperclips, I expect. He knows to back off me and my team.'

'OK, Khan. Just thought you might want to know. The book is doing well, by the way.'

'I know, Samuel. I have been doing more than just looking

at the scenery, you know. If the mountain won't go to the financial world, the financial world must go to the mountain.'

Samuel imagined the great man, looking out over lakes of glacial blue and monitoring the latest profits on his laptop.

'So it must. And now I must head for the world of Anton Miller.'

'Enjoy. Listen carefully to what Miller says though, Samuel. I'm pretty much convinced he's beginning to loop-the-loop mentally. But he used to be a smart operator in his youth. Listen and learn.'

'Will do,' said Samuel. But the phone was already a voided hum in his hand.

He walked across the floor to Miller's office. Only Kaz paid any attention, giving him the briefest of glances.

Miller's executive office had an entirely artificial ambience. No natural light, the air filtered through the giant cooler of Ropner Bank's air-conditioning system. Their faces were powdered with the ghostly reflections bouncing up from the shiny surface of Miller's dark-glass desktop. It was a land without day or night – the land of market forces.

Miller was standing in the corner of the gloom. Wordlessly, he extended a hand towards a chair. They sat on opposite sides of the desk, solemn and quietly confrontational, like steamboat gamblers settling down for the night.

A silence descended, punctuated from the outside by the occasional telephonic warble, a shout, a quick, furious burst of laughter. Samuel let it continue. After all, Miller was the one who had summoned him.

Miller had a miniature Japanese pebble garden in front of him. Apart from the mahogany box that contained the garden, and the Anglepoise lamp clamped to one side, his desk was entirely bare. He began to play with the carefully arranged pebbles, tossing and teasing them, then patting them back into place. Then, finally:

'You, Spendlove, you have potential. I've been watching you. You're good under pressure, or pretend to be, which is pretty much the same thing.'

'Thank you. One can but try.'

'My suggestion, and it is no more than a suggestion, is this.' Miller pursed his lips and pushed a fingertip against them. 'Intelligence. There is no other way to put it. If I am to be responsible for the investment probity of this bank I need to know what is being done in its name.'

A long finger ploughed a furrow through a tiny field of grey-green gravel.

'What happened earlier this week was unfortunate, and, I think you'll agree, quite shocking. I accept that Khan has his own style. It's true that he is ultimately accountable to New York, but the way he trades makes it virtually impossible for me, as the head of the Paris office, to monitor him.'

'Are you saying that you don't know what the proprietary trading team is doing?'

'How can I? First there's the virtual impossibility of seeing how all those options and futures and warrants work together. And then there's the other stuff.' Miller was leaning further forward now, like some giant snake considering the strike. 'Khan spends a lot of time trading the over-the-counter market, which, as I'm sure you know, is basically unregulated. Anyone can deal with anyone else. It's all based on confidence and reputation – the confidence that the players will hold good to their word and pay on losing contracts.'

'But surely all financial markets are regulated nowadays?'

Miller smiled briefly.

'That's the game. The stock markets are regulated, the bond markets are regulated. Even the future and options exchanges are carefully monitored. This bank, for which we all work, is regulated and accounts twice a year to the Banque de France. The entities we deal with are similarly regulated. But a bargain is a bargain, and if Khan calls up a buddy across the world and agrees to swap his bond for the return on a deposit account, a share yield, or a bag of candies, there's no authority on earth that can regulate that. It's like sex. If two entities want to rub the interesting bits of their trading books together, no one and nothing can stop them.'

'It's incredible that Khan bothers to come into the office at all when he can trade his position with anyone he wants over the phone from a train in the Jura, or a helicopter or a car. Or the bath, come to that.'

'No, no. Khan needs the markets. He needs to have the feel of them. That's why he insists on coming in, having a space in the flying wedge.'

Miller had been observing Samuel carefully.

'What I need is someone that I can trust who is close to Khan and understands the risks that the bank is taking. I would like you to be that person, Samuel.' Miller rose from his chair and paced the room. 'So? Will you help? Your cooperation will not go unrewarded.'

'It all seems a little too much like spying. Khan's been good to me, Anton. But I do take your point. I have to tell you that I'm not too sure what Khan's up to myself most of the time.'

'But you sit next to him, Samuel.'

'Can I take a little time to think about this?'

'Sure. I'm certain we can find something that doesn't embarrass you and serves to facilitate better communication between departments. Get back to me soon.'

Silence descended again. The interview was over.

Samuel left congratulating himself on his dexterity. He had mostly kept his mouth shut, and now Miller was under the impression that Samuel was at least considering his proposal to act as an in-house spy. If it came to Miller's knowledge that Samuel had been asking questions, he would think it was on his behalf. Until he got a visit from the French regulatory authorities or saw the story on the front page of the *Sunday Inquirer*, the *Daily Quest*, or another part of the Barton media machine.

Samuel got back to his desk to find a memorandum from Ovid La Brooy, the bank's market strategist. The memo's central proposition was that crop failure and weather patterns, including something called the 180-year retrograde cycle, indicated that times were going to be tough for the markets soon. La Brooy was a brilliant man, but sooner or later he'd end up predicting something really outlandish – maybe a plague of locusts? – and end up out of a job.

The lights were blinking crazily on his phone panel. Samuel cursed the rest of the crew of the flying wedge. Maybe they weren't working for Khan, but they could at least pick up the calls. The callers would imagine that there was no one there or that they were all out on a lunchtime drinking binge. Most of them had rung off, but one blinking light came through with a loud, familiar voice.

'Spendlove? That you?'

Samuel fought the impulse to look round guiltily. It was McMurray, demanding his pound of flesh.

He had to be very careful. Following what had long been standard procedure, all bank calls were taped, which was why Samuel had been careful to follow McMurray's instructions and call from public telephones.

'You're running out of time.' A gruff Scots bark.

'How much have I got?'

Samuel executed a slow 360-degree turn in his chair. No one was watching. Diaz and Nobby were engaged in some simian prank – throwing a ball made of elastic bands at a picture of a movie star on one of the screens. Every time it bounced back accompanied by remarks about balls and rubbers and other sophisticated witticisms. Kaz's chair was empty.

'Very little, or I wouldn't be calling. Call me with something tonight. We're under pressure – you're under pressure. You've got to produce.'

'All right. I'll try and get something. I'm seeing someone who may be able to help tonight. I'll call if anything comes of it.'

'Something must come of it, Spendlove.'

Samuel hung up wondering whether the assertiveness in McMurray's voice was born of desperation, anger or fear.

A twisting column of bright light shafted in through the rue Scribe window. It acted as a kind of spotlight on the folded slip of paper that bore his name. He hadn't noticed it before. Surely it hadn't been there all day? He picked it up from the pile of prospectuses on his desk. A message from the woman herself.

> *Something's come up. Can't do early evening. Sorry. But how about a bite later on at the Café Beaubourg? Say 9.30?*
>
> *In hunger and haste,*
>
> *K*

Hunger and haste. How urgent, how immediate those two concepts were. They seemed to Samuel like a marvellous combination.

7

It was a short walk from Samuel's flat to the Café Beaubourg. He marched up the rue Quincampoix with its ancient, rickety sandstone walls, which provoked contradictory feelings. The close, huddled buildings reminded him of Jesus Lane in Oxford.

As he walked, he thought back to a time when he had been there with Gail, thick flurries of snow robbing the air of sound, their feet tentatively gripping the lightly powdered paving stones. She had been holding his arm, her hair thick and wet against his shoulder. The two of them with big ice-cream cones, purchased from Baskin Robbins, eaten in a snowstorm to the bewilderment of passers-by. They laughed, uncaring, oblivious to the freezing temperatures and totally enwrapt in each other. She had reached up and kissed him, a snowflake eloquent on her eyelash, her lips sweet with almond and toffee. He shuddered as the memory passed.

Samuel was almost running as the clock in the tower of the Église Saint Merri in the rue Saint Martin chimed the half-hour. He was perfectly on time. A waiter in classic black-and-white livery opened the door with a courteous bow and a studied smile of welcome that might have come straight from the court of Louis XIV.

The interior was an advert for the more splendid side of Paris. The place was unashamedly über-cool. The proprietor had spent a considerable sum to secure the services of a smart designer, who had attracted the beautiful people. They had come when the place opened in the late 1980s – and they had stayed. Books, real books, bedecked the shelves, and the waiters swirled over the black and grey modernist floor and the high-tech chairs with the incongruous, old-world elegance of military officers dancing a Viennese waltz. A wide, winding staircase led to a second floor which was really no more than a glorified catwalk – a broad alley running round the walls of the salon. The extra space created an aura of theatre and gave the clientele of poseurs more of an audience.

Kaz was already there, perched up in a first-floor corner. She was looking down at him and smiling. Samuel trotted upstairs and greeted her with a kiss on either cheek – something, he realized with a start, he had never done before.

She had a tall glass with whisky and ice in it. As Samuel called to a waiter she took out a packet of cigarettes.

'I didn't realize you smoked.'

'I don't – except on special occasions,' said Kaz. There was a dancing, teasing look in her eyes. 'And I don't drink either.' She raised her glass in mock toast and sipped.

'Why not?' A glass of ruby-red Vacqueyras, a smoky Rhône wine he loved, was set before him.

'Why don't I drink? Because it makes you lie.'

'No it doesn't,' said Samuel. They both laughed, clinked, drank.

Kaz soon extinguished the cigarette; Samuel was not certain quite what to make of this – a 'special occasion'; it ought to be good, very good in fact. Except that she was a contact, a story lead who didn't even know he was a journalist.

'I see you haven't brought a large pile of documentation.' Kaz beckoned again to the waiter and asked for the menus.

'No. In fact, we've, uh, gone ahead and invested. So . . .'

'So you're here with an ulterior motive. Excellent. I love ulterior motives.' Samuel felt heat in his face.

'Well, your note about Khan's trading style was intriguing.'

'Khan's an intriguing man, no doubt about that.' Kaz leaned closer to him. 'That's what made me put our rendezvous back, as a matter of fact.'

Their food arrived, a simple but excellent quiche lorraine with green salad and a bottle of Pomerol, chosen by Kaz. She led the conversation, and spoke animatedly about many things – anything, it seemed, but Khan. Was Samuel interested in art? Had he seen the excellent Masculin–Féminin exhibition that was so funny and so provocative, but would never go on show in either of their politically correct home countries? Why had he come to France? Why had he chosen finance over academia all of a sudden? But career choices were too close to work, and she was off again, talking cinema and her love for Jean Renoir and Buñuel.

The meal was over and Samuel began to wonder whether their evening was drawing to a close. But Kaz made it clear that she wanted to listen to some jazz in one of the bars on the rue des Lombards.

Out on the street she took his arm and steered him towards a loud bar with tables by an open door. It was a cool night, but they warmed themselves over two Bas Armagnacs and silently took in the sights of the street. The tourists were not out in force, but there were occasional posses of Americans with wide waists, white patent-leather shoes and belts to match. Gangs of barely pubescent boys roamed around, as quick-eyed and light on their feet as underfed dogs. Chic women in their fifties strode by purposefully in mink and beaver and loud gold jewellery. Men and women of the town in the dark colours of the night made for the next drink, the next meal and dance, the latest place on the ever-changing itinerary of the moment's fashion. Looming over it all was the night presence of the Pompidou Centre, a preposterous beached battleship gone belly up, its electric guts exposed to the starry sky.

'So?' Kaz put down her brandy and looked at him.

This was the bit that Samuel found difficult. A beautiful woman was suggesting something. But what? The beginnings of panic descended upon him. Would she place her hand on his, tease him from his cloistered shyness? Into the void stepped the requirement for information, the snarling challenge of McMurray, and his own need to know.

'Erm, about Khan . . .'

Kaz sighed.

'Have you got any coffee at home?'

Samuel nodded.

'Any Armagnac?'

He nodded again, with enthusiasm.

'Here's the deal. You offer me some coffee and I'll do my best to satisfy your curiosity about the great and good Khan. You live near here, right?'

Samuel liked American women, despite his failed marriage to Gail. He admired their directness. The only problem was that he had no idea what Kaz was leading up to. Nevertheless, she knew that he lived five minutes' walk away. That had to mean something. Hadn't it?

Fifteen minutes later they were sitting on Samuel's sofa admiring the illuminated frontage of the Hôtel de Ville. Samuel had just put Bach's *St Matthew Passion* on the CD player. Kaz sipped at her brandy.

'Religious music. You know how to treat a girl.'

Samuel attempted a nonchalant grin.

'I can change it.'

'No, it's fine.' Another sip of brandy and a very direct look. 'I'm going to give you what you want.'

Samuel sat down. Standing up seemed too difficult.

'OK, so here's the first part – the scam on your boss. Khan has been around a long time and has a great track record. He is consistently able to outguess the market. That is, he is better than just about any other prop trader in the marketplace. Sometimes, like everybody else, he gets badly beaten up by making a wrong move.'

She put her glass down and moved a little closer to Samuel.

'Being the best over the long term, year after year, makes Khan virtually impregnable. Which is just as well for him, because he's been getting into more and more exotic shit recently. It used to be he'd come and listen to what we had to say about the market. Sometimes he'd buy a share we liked, sometimes he'd short one of our sell recommendations, but we had to learn to live with the fact that he might just as easily short one of our buy recommendations.'

'That must have been galling, seeing Khan betting against the house view.' Samuel offered her some more brandy and she held out her glass.

'True enough. Hard-hitting stuff, but it happens. That's what Chinese walls are all about, though. We offer investment views to our clients, but we never know whether Khan will agree.'

Kaz took another tiny sip of the Bas Armagnac and murmured her appreciation.

'At least in the old days, I knew where I was with him. I could judge him on each individual trade.'

'There's one that interests me in particular. You remember the Gallimard deal?'

He was off on what old hacks called a fishing trip. None of the newspaper databases he had researched mentioned a Khan connection to the deal.

'The publishing house? Sure I do. That was kindergarten stuff. Khan played two publishers off against each other like fighting dogs. There was only ever going to be one winner.'

'So the Monaco publishers and the other lot fought for Khan's stake?'

'The other lot was William Barton's empire. Thought you'd have known that.' Kaz looked at him quizzically. 'But no, not Khan. The only winner was Khan's backer, the entity that was rigging the market in Gallimard shares, and making sure they were all sold to Khan. Or his favoured champion.'

'Rigging?'

'Well, taking a bigger share than you're supposed to and not declaring it, and then acting together. A few offshore trusts, just the way Khan likes to run his book nowadays.'

'And when they act together, it's called a concert party.'

'Exactly. Simple corporate law stuff – child's play for a top jurisprudent like you, Samuel.'

Bingo. Samuel blinked. Everything he wanted was being placed in his lap by this extraordinary woman.

'So who would that be, exactly? Khan's backer?' he asked as deliberately as he could. His pulse was quickening by the second.

'I have documentation, if you're really interested. Kind of an insurance policy if anyone starts asking questions. Anyone other than you, that is.' She was watching him carefully over the rim of her glass.

'Would you let me see it?'

'I might. It's small potatoes compared with what Khan's getting up to now.'

Samuel reflected for a moment. Kaz was saying that Khan had manipulated the market in a world-famous £300 million publishing company (not a lot of money by Khan's standards, but the company had a priceless reputation). By doing so, the trader had wrested control from one of the world's most powerful media barons.

'How's that small potatoes?'

'It's no big deal compared with what he's up to now. Khan's playing the over-the-counter market all the time. He's trading with his billionaire buddies in Hong Kong and Switzerland and wherever. They deal with each other and have no recourse to anyone, no control from any statutory or regulatory body that I know of. It's big boys making bets behind closed doors.'

'So who knows what's going on?'

'Everyone and no one. The guys in Khan's club, fellow members of the virtual jet set. The trading kings. Because of the secrecy and complexity of the way these things are set up, the only measure the rest of the world really has is how Khan's book performs. As long as he makes money for Ropners, no one here is going to complain.'

'In other words, you can't judge him on an individual trade any more, and no one even wants to – just so long as he's ahead of the game.' Samuel thought he could feel the pressure of her knee against his own.

'You got it. What we all do, that's you, me, Khan, the whole goddam industry, is interpret chaos. We hum tunes in pandemonium; we find seams of gold in bare rock. But here's the difference: when I make a call on a stock or a market everyone can see whether I'm right or wrong. Just call up the price on the screen. With Khan, it's not that way any more. First, you don't really know what the guy's doing till he's done it. Second, even if you see what he's bought and you're sure he hasn't swapped it, you can't say for sure whether there's a profit or a loss. If you try, Khan will tell you that that particular play is part of an overall strategy, and can't be judged on its own. He could be up to anything – and he usually is.'

'It could be he's perfectly straight then. It's just difficult to tell,' said Samuel. Defending Khan was quite fun and surprisingly easy.

'Could be. But there's always the temptation to make a quick buck. People make mistakes. Like that dipstick Duval guy, who basically gave Khan a $100 million profit without even knowing it.'

'But that was legitimate trading, right? Miller knows it was done through an agent to hide our hand in the market. It was better for the bank that Khan was on the other side of the trade than a third party.'

Her whole leg now seemed to be resting against his.

'Shut up, Samuel,' she said softly, and stopped his mouth with a kiss.

She was warm, tender, exotic as jungle air. Her hand rested lightly on his cheek. There was that feeling again, the feeling of delicious weightlessness. He was not sure that he was ready to get involved with another woman. The wounds were still raw. But as Kaz caressed him, kissing him ever more urgently, he began to think that this was different – not Gail, not rupture, not pain. Another misadventure? Maybe.

She was draped across him and he could feel the intensity of her desire, her breath coming in short, stolen gasps. Her fingers began to work at the buttons of his shirt. It was as if she was trying to sate an overwhelming hunger. She had to have him and she had to have him now.

Then, somehow, she lost her balance. Her leg kicked out, caught her handbag, scattered its contents on the floor. Samuel wouldn't have cared if the walls of his flat were being ripped down. All he wanted was to make love to her.

But Kaz was suddenly all consternation. She leapt up and scurried round retrieving toiletries, wallet, phone and a couple of books, mouthing trite apologies as though she were a girlfriend who had spilled a cup of tea at his mother's house. He watched her stuff one of the books into her bag. He recognized the olive and vermilion spine from the café. It was a translation of the hot new American author Jo-Jo Young. Funnily enough, a Gallimard book. Kaz was smoothing her hair down now and walking back towards him.

'You stole that, didn't you?'

'Excuse me?' He could feel the tension rippling through her body.

'That book. The Jo-Jo Young. You took it from the Café Beaubourg, didn't you?'

'What are you talking about, Samuel?' The smile had frozen on her face.

'You stole it. Stealing things is a kick for you, isn't it?'

'Hello. Earth to Samuel. Is anybody there?'

'I was at the Bourdelle museum on Sunday. I saw you with that biker woman. I saw you take the bronze model. And you've taken those books. Why? For the buzz?'

'What are you talking about?' Kaz tried to brush aside his accusations and laughed, but Samuel persisted.

'You know what I'm talking about. The evidence is in your handbag.'

She considered him for a moment.

'Does the idea of taking what you want shock you?'

She moved back towards the sofa and kneeled on the floor, giving him an impish smile. Her slim hand moved to his groin. Instinctively, his erection pushed back against her. With a couple of deft movements the delicate fingers with their glossy pink nails unzipped his fly and found their way inside his boxer shorts.

'I want . . .' said Samuel slowly. It was suddenly difficult to think of just what that might be as she ran her tongue along the length of him. 'I want the crock of gold,' he said at last.

'Oh that.' He could feel her hot breath on him. He looked down at the thick mass of slowly gyrating brown hair. Kaz reached up and pulled back her curls over her shoulder. The exquisite face looked up at him mischievously, inviting him to watch. 'The crock of gold can be yours, but you'll have to get to the end of the rainbow first.' Then she flicked out her tongue and began to bathe him in saliva, watching in delight as he shuddered and groaned, his eyes half-closed.

Suddenly she was standing. Carefully, she removed her skirt, revealing a black suspender belt and stockings, but no knickers. Samuel almost gasped with excitement. Kaz gently pulled him to the ground and then straddled his face, pushing herself towards him. Her thick, glossy pubic hair, abundant where it wasn't shaved, was dripping wet. The animal smell of her desire mingled with the lavender and sandalwood of expensive scents. Samuel began to lap greedily at her with his tongue, savouring the taste of her.

After a few moments she broke free of him and reached for her bag. Very gently, she fitted a sheath over him, then removed her blouse and bra. She let him nuzzle her soft skin and dark nipples for a few seconds, then settled down over him. A soft sigh escaped from her as he entered, then she pushed herself back, arching away from him. Her left hand reached behind her, and he could feel the fingers tracing the delicate contours of where they were conjoined.

'And so?' She looked down at him and smiled wickedly, then tossed her hair back to offer him an uninterrupted view of her perfect breasts.

Samuel looked up at the sensation-seeking thief, the frequenter of mysterious clubs, the star employee, the woman who knew things. He strained to move inside her, but she clamped down on him powerfully.

'I want my crock of gold,' he said at last.

'I'm not sure I'm going to let you have it,' she said. Then moved up and down on him twice, very slowly. Samuel trembled at the depth of the pleasure.

'I'll say this, and I'll say it once only. You're playing a foolish game.' She was beginning to move rhythmically on top of him, pushing down hard, and he could feel the beginnings of an urgent quickening inside her.

'You want your crock of gold, huh? Duval lost his job, Miller's gotta explain the losses, and I'm nanny to a team of airheads.' Her words were coming in short, heavy pants.

She was bouncing up and down, thrusting hard against him. 'Ask too many questions, you'll be in trouble. Just take what you ... can.' With those last words her head tilted back and she let out a groan. The urgency of her orgasm pushed Samuel over the precipice, and he emptied himself as she subsided over him. He felt the heat of her tears on his chest, as she lay forward, spent and shaking.

And then she was climbing off him. A quick glance at the condom to check it was intact, and she was all businesslike attentiveness to the whereabouts of her clothes.

'One other thing, Samuel.' He recognized the confident

stride of the manager, the expert in office politics. 'Khan is one matter, but don't extend your curiosity to me. You'll catch hellfire itself if you so much as even think about challenging my integrity.' She was moving swiftly now, very much in exit mode. She had taken what she wanted. 'So one word more of this kleptomaniac fantasy of yours, one word, and I'll bust your balls – for good.'

She was dressed, and now turned to him and smiled, then blew an icy kiss.

'Thanks for the brandy and the view, both of which were sublime, and goodnight.'

Samuel lay still, listening to the sounds as she let herself out of the flat. Was Kaz running away from intimacy, or had he made her afraid with the confrontation about the Bourdelle museum and talk of the crock of gold? He would soon find out. That hasty exit meant that she would probably come back for more. Once she saw he wasn't going to come running after her like a love-sick puppy she'd be back. He thought of Gail and their early lovemaking. He wouldn't pine for Kaz in the office – he'd done enough of that to last a lifetime.

He was soon recovered and went down to the royalist bar across the street. He ordered a beer and hid himself in a corner, his pocket heavy with 5-euro pieces.

'Yes?' McMurray's voice was drugged with sleep. Samuel pulled the glass doors of the telephone cabin together and loaded in a few more coins.

'Mr McMurray? Samuel Spendlove. I have a take on Khan and on Ropner Bank's trading ethics. One of their teams is led by a kleptomaniac, among other things.'

'Excellent,' said McMurray, now all alertness. 'Just wait till I get my pen!'

'We can't go against the thief, though. She's the one who's

going to give me proof that Khan made sure that Gallimard isn't part of the Barton group.'

'Information is power, Spendlove. Give me what you've got on the brief, and on your source. I want the lot.'

8

'KNOW YOUR ENEMY, Samuel. Know your enemy.'

Khan gave out his most brilliant smile. The enemy he was referring to was sitting a few yards away Ropner Bank's fixed-interest sales team, plus selected recruits from the equities and derivatives desks.

'This is primary market day for a $1 billion issue of nine-year maturity bonds that Ropners is bringing to market on behalf of a big client.'

'Why are they the enemy?' Samuel looked hard at Khan. He did mean that the Ropners team was the enemy, didn't he? Or was there a hint of crocodile in that smile?

'Because they're trying to force-feed everyone in the market something they don't really want. That is irrational, and irrationality is the ultimate enemy. No?'

'Yes, yes, Khan. Reason is God.'

'You make the best jokes. Very good.' Khan swung his feet up onto the desk. 'This is no more than a circus, dedicated to the prestige of the huge chemicals company that wants to borrow money, with a side altar to the vanity of Ropner Bank itself.' Khan smiled with hooded eyes at the nervous fluster about them.

'What I don't understand is how our friend Kaz can miss

the show. This is the kind of spectacle that she enjoys. I wonder how that can be.' Khan gave Samuel a poker player's stare. Samuel tried to return it. Why did Khan notice her absence so quickly? He couldn't know anything. Samuel was just being paranoid. But the question was a good one: where was she?

Miller seemed to have called into service just about anyone on the floor who could spell the word 'bond'. Diaz, Nobby and sundry others had joined the regular fixed-interest team. They were scattered somewhat uncomfortably within shot of a camera at the far end of the trading floor from Khan and Samuel. Miller was speaking earnestly into the cold fisheye of the lens. To his right, the image of Ropner Bank's Singapore bond team was projected onto a five-foot-square screen. The video conference image switched to a grizzled man in his sixties. Khan identified him as Jeremiah Westcott, the head of Ropner's gigantic US fixed-interest team.

'They are serious about this one,' said Khan.

This was impact day for the bond issue, the day that investors gave their orders to the Ropner Bank's sales team. Or not. Once a bond had been launched, it would find its own level in the market. The objective was for Ropner Bank and its worldwide team of bond salesmen to get the issue into the market at the asking price. Failure was unthinkable.

How they made their clients buy was down to personal and professional idiosyncrasy. For the women who 'gave good phone' it was a question of finding a good connection and making their voices nice and husky. For jocks like Diaz it was a sporting bet. He took his clients to games. The barest anatomical details of what was on offer, plus plenty of reminders that life was a game and you had to take a risk constituted his best line on bonds. Nobby used a similar pitch, although he implied that life was not so much a soccer match but an orgy, just waiting to happen.

Khan and Samuel sat at their desks and watched the tribal ritual of the bond sales team psyching itself up for action. The video conference was over. Everyone dispersed to their desks and began calling their clients.

'You know Metternich, the diplomat who kept the Austro-Hungarian empire alive for half the nineteenth century?'

Samuel nodded, and bit into a breakfast sandwich.

'One of his many *bons mots* was a splendidly accurate, if non-substantive, definition of the truth.'

'I believe I know it,' said Samuel through a mouthful of cheese and bread. 'Truth is that which is confidently asserted and plausibly maintained.'

'Exactly. He would have made a wonderful bond salesman.'

And a passable journalist, thought Samuel.

Miller was pacing the floor, rounding the desk of the bond sales team. They watched his retreating back.

'How was your chat with the delightful Anton, by the way?' asked Khan. If there was even the slightest trace of concern in his voice Samuel hadn't noticed it.

'Oh, you know. Took me to the top of the mountain and told me all this could be mine.'

'Did you believe him?' Khan was still casual.

'Would you have?' They laughed. It was good for Khan to know that Miller was courting him. It could only mean more status for Samuel, which would give him greater access.

Something was happening in the far corner of the trading floor. People were pointing at screens. The Chinese had agreed an Asian trade protocol and Taiwan, while not a signatory to the agreement, was mentioned as a participating country in the schedules. This gesture of political reconciliation meant that the value of the bank's Taiwanese clients' factories and its huge Asian division would be much greater.

A flood of euphoria now burst over them – a tidal wave of optimism that had travelled seven thousand miles in five seconds. Miller was patrolling the aisles, patting backs, cajoling and encouraging. The sales team picked up their phones and screamed that this news made the bond an unmissable buy. The bonds began to sell and the rich smell of victory hung in the air. The Paris bond team had needed to sell as much of the issue as they could to make up for the Duval losses, and they had done it.

Then, suddenly, the excitement began to ebb. FT and La Petite were chatting quietly. Diaz and Nobby draped their jackets over their chairs and left the office, arms round each other's shoulders. Miller had looked almost relaxed at one stage before retreating to his darkened lair.

'Genius.' Khan nodded in the direction of Diaz and Nobby, who appeared to be leaving for a long, late and decidedly liquid lunch.

'How so?' High intelligence was the last attribute Samuel would have ascribed to either of them.

'It's the jacket-on-the-chair genius of the bull market,' said Khan. 'Those two have done their allotted duty of ramming these securities down the throats of anyone who's had the misfortune to stray into their contact books over the past five years. When they come back from the trough they will find that the bull market has made those sales look even better than they already are. In a bull market, people get complacent; open a position, leave your jacket on the chair, and one six-hour lunch later you're a genius. Close it out, and go home.'

Samuel nodded and looked around. Whatever the reasons, there was certainly an air of high contentment about the place.

'These people are cheats and thieves on one level,' sighed Khan. 'It can be difficult to have to play their game.' For a second the façade seemed to have dropped. Was this some sort of admission?

The moment was punctured by what looked like a fight. A female figure, clad in black leather, was struggling with Miller. A security guard bellowed something incoherent from the stairwell and Miller had come out of his office to try to head the woman off at the entrance. There was more shouting, and then the glass doors burst open. The occupants of the flying wedge were used to commotion, but actual riots tended to grab their attention.

The whirling limbs and Gallic oaths got wilder and louder, until they were right by the proprietary trading desk. The woman was being frogmarched out by the security guard, who was smaller than she was, and Miller, who was taller but would probably have lost to her in an arm-wrestling contest. She was shouting something and trying to break away from her captors when Samuel realized who it was. The woman from the Bourdelle! The beautiful biker!

'Enough!' she shrieked. 'I will go now! Enough!'

Calm descended as Miller gave the order to release her. He and the woman stared at each other, chests heaving, and then she averted her glance and caught sight of Samuel. There was a flicker of recognition.

'It's you I have come to see. I want to know what you have done with Kaz.' She spoke in accented English now, and pointed a long finger at Samuel. 'You. She went out with you last night to talk about your crappy boss. But she hasn't come back. She's not in work. What have you done with her?'

The entire flying wedge was craning to get sight of Samuel now. The woman was flushed and furiously angry.

Samuel reddened under the pressure, and turned to Khan to protest his innocence.

But the chair next to him was empty. Samuel swivelled back, nonplussed.

'Well?' The woman sensed the moment was hers. 'I'm waiting.'

THERE WAS no such thing as a free pass into Harvard, that much he knew. True, it helped if your father was an alumnus who had donated a couple of million to the university endowment fund. Having a father or grandfather who had been President of the United States didn't hurt either. But to get into the Harvard Business School you had to be both outstandingly smart and ferociously hard-working. So how come so many on the class list behaved like grade-A morons?

Maybe the intensity of the work had effectively lobotomized his co-students. They were mostly younger than he was, that might have been part of it. And maybe he saw the worst in them. He had already experienced what it was like to earn a living. Most of them had been in full-time education for years, spending the summers in the Hamptons with their families or going to Nantucket. Although he had been born in the US, he had inherited the immigrant mentality that had been engrained in his parents.

But it wasn't the idiotic social behaviour that bothered him. No, what annoyed him was the sheer stupidity of the herd mentality. As these talented individuals walked through Harvard Yard towards the Co-op and Cambridge town centre, the talk was of real estate investing. That was the career they all seemed to want for themselves. Even the pretty, red-haired Yvonne, one of the few to ask *him questions about himself, said that real estate was attractive. Sure, it was a sector that had done well. Fortunes had been made there. But couldn't they see it was an asset as old as time itself? Land was one of the most ancient and primitive measures of wealth.*

He had told Yvonne that graduates of Harvard Business School were supposed to be innovators. He wanted to engineer new forms of capitalism, to wipe out the enemies of stability. Financial insecurity had ruined his father's health, had made his Oma so sad and generally blighted his family for generations. It must never come again – but it would if the supposedly smartest people on the planet behaved like a herd of cattle.

They shared a chocolate malt at the Co-op's chequered Formica bar, and he told Yvonne she was too smart to be part of the madness of crowds. It was a well-known fact that the career choices of Harvard MBAs were a good indicator of which part of the world economy was going to fall apart next. It was possible for lots of clever people with individually high IQs to have the collective intelligence of a baby trout. They hadn't come to one of the hottest schools in the world so they could obsess about real estate and chant 'location, location, location' in unison. Had they?

The Bugle, a free student newspaper, mocked the collective idiocy and the trendiness of its readers – in clothes, haircuts, career choices – in a sneeringly clever way. The editorial that went with the career analysis was a masterpiece of low-key vitriol. It was authored by another postgraduate, listed in the school of journalism. Well, whoever he was, William Barton was on to something.

Yvonne laughed, told him to turn on to a milder vibe, and held his hand for the first time.

9

SAMUEL LOOKED INTO the woman's eyes. The last time they had been mocking and derisory behind that little peephole. This time a dark fire of accusation burned within.

He stood up slowly. Phones hung in mid-air; squawk boxes remained unanswered. Everyone in the flying wedge was watching him.

'I don't know who the hell you are. And I don't care.'

'Liar! You were following us on Sunday. You came to the museum, you came to the club. What have you done with her?'

Miller stood ramrod-straight, considering her words, trying to make sense of what she was saying. He rotated his head slowly in Samuel's direction, then spoke very quietly.

'What is she talking about, Samuel? Tell me this is all a fantasy.'

The woman took a step towards Samuel: 'He was with her last night to spy on his boss. But she didn't come back. Where is she?' She whirled towards Samuel. 'Lying drugged in your flat? What have you done with her?'

The security guard laid a hand on her arm; she shook it off angrily. From the corner of his eye, Samuel could see sly grins on the faces of Nobby and Diaz. They were clearly thrilled that

Khan's minion seemed to be in some kind of trouble. Miller's eyes narrowed and he hissed from the side of his mouth:

'Samuel, give me something here.'

Samuel walked right up to the woman. She was still flushed with anger, and stared him defiantly in the eye. There was almost an electric feel to her beauty. What a pair – if they were a pair – she and Kaz would make. He stepped right up to her and put his face an inch away from hers. She did not flinch.

'What gives you the right to come in here asking questions? And who are you anyway?'

She almost spat in his face: 'I am Lauren de la Geneste, of Labastide Beauvoir. I doubt you will have heard of me or my family. And I have the right to ask about Kaz because she is important to me.'

A long moment of silence passed, before Samuel said, slowly and clearly, for everyone to hear.

'Well, listen to me, Mademoiselle de la Geneste! I . . . do . . . not . . . know . . . where . . . she . . . is.'

He turned abruptly away and gave Miller the coolest look he could muster.

'I'm going for a break. This is ridiculous.'

Miller watched him go, pondered a moment, then nodded to the guards.

'Throw her out.'

The wrestling match began again. Samuel marched across the floor, as the woman was noisily jostled away. He retained his composure until he was safely locked in a lavatory cubicle, then sat down and held his head in his hands. Playing the public school boy – self-assurance without substance – did not come easily. He tried hard not to hyperventilate. Where indeed was Kaz? What would Khan and Miller make of her accusations? And where the hell had Khan disappeared to?

Samuel washed his face and examined himself in the mirror as he dabbed himself dry with a paper towel. He felt strangely tired. He ran down the back stairs and slipped out of a side exit onto the rue Auber. Home seemed like a more appealing place than an office full of questions he couldn't answer.

He slammed the flat door shut, poured himself a beer from the fridge, and disconnected the phone. Then he lay on his bed and pondered what to do next. Soon he was in an uneasy, fitful sleep, his mind still going over the events of the last twenty-four hours. Kaz had been in his flat and now she had disappeared. What had happened to her?

When he awoke it was dark, and he still had no answers. He could see the girl in the flat opposite. She was pretty, so far as he could tell, with short, auburn hair and a lithe, youthful figure. She was perhaps twenty, no more. Her bedroom light cut a hole in the evening sky.

He had watched her a couple of times before. It was the motion that had attracted his attention that first time, the upward arc of the arms as the sweater came over her head. He had been transfixed, a rabbit caught in the powerful glare of her unabashed sexuality. He had been frozen where he stood, unable to move or take his eyes from her. She had slowly removed all her clothes and then pottered about her room a little, examining magazines and tossing them aside. At last she had pressed herself up against the window and fixed him with a sullen, urban stare as she drew the curtains. Five floors up, thirty yards apart, they were separated by an entire city.

The following night, Samuel had been better prepared. Once the clothes had begun to come off he had snaked out a hand and switched off his living room light so as to observe her from the comfort of darkness. As soon as he did this, however, she too switched off her bedroom light. When he switched his light on again, light flooded back into the girl's bedroom – and the undressing continued. Samuel had understood. She would undress, but only if she could watch him watching her. So who was the voyeur, Samuel or the girl?

Samuel shook the sleep from his eyes. She was moving about her room fully clothed. He flicked the light on, so that she could see him. There was no immediate reaction, but after a few moments the girl turned to face him across the street. Her hands moved slowly up to her neck and began to work the buttons of her blouse.

His mobile rang, giving Samuel a fright. The girl was still there, slight and intense, bathed in the golden yellow light of her bedroom. Her blouse was gone and she turned to face him as her fingers moved to the buttons on the fly of her jeans. In the next-door room, her television was on and he could see the ghostly silvered flickerings of a screen in the darkened salon. The phone continued to ring. The number was withheld, but he answered it anyway.

'Je vous écoute.'

'What the hell are you doing, Spendlove?'

Samuel was in no mood to talk to McMurray.

'What do you mean?'

'Don't you know that your phone line's down? We agreed to talk this evening, Spendlove.'

'It's not down. I disconnected it. Didn't want any interruptions. And anyway, I thought we agreed that I would only talk to you on public telephones.'

'To hell with that. I want the story you've been promising me, Spendlove.'

'Kaz Day's friend, possibly her lover, came into the office and confronted me today. I felt compromised.'

'What did he do, this guy? What do you mean, "compromised"?'

'It was a woman.' An obscenity came down the line. Samuel continued: 'She came in and marched up to my desk and asked me what I'd done with Kaz.'

'It'd be nice to think you'd got some bloody information out of her. Has she produced, this Kaz woman?'

'She didn't give me what she promised. She didn't show up at the bank. Her girlfriend did. Kaz must have told her what we were talking about, and then she just went ahead and shouted out in front of everyone that I'd been "spying" on Khan. See what I mean about compromised?'

The girl opposite seemed put out by the sight of Samuel with a phone in his hand. She flounced out of view.

'Mmmm. How did Khan react to that?'

'Good question. He just seemed to disappear. When I looked round for him he was gone.'

'Well, laddie, I think you'd better find this Kaz girlie and get what you can, as fast as you can.'

McMurray rang off. The window opposite was dark, offering a silent, lifeless rebuke.

SAMUEL RANG Kaz's number. Her evenly modulated voice announced in French and then English both her absence and her eagerness to receive messages. He did not leave one.

Samuel grabbed a jacket and headed out. He had no clear idea of what he would do. The office directory of addresses was just that – a list of where people lived. It did not include door security codes, so Samuel would not be able to get into the building and knock on her door. Perhaps he would find a bar or a convenient place to wait and catch her as she came in

– always assuming that she was in or screening her calls, and not really drugged up in some stranger's bed.

Maybe he should have left a message after all? No. Too sensitive. He would go to her place first and telephone as a last resort.

Kaz lived in a large, modern apartment block on the boulevard Lannes, on the very edge of the sixteenth arrondissement. Further down the boulevard was the modernist concrete unpleasantness occupied by the Russian embassy. Across the road was the furtive night market of the Bois de Boulogne. Truck drivers parked up there and slept in their cabs. Samuel had never been there after dark, but knew from the dealers' talk that this was a favourite spot for transvestite hookers. Beautiful creatures with full breasts, soft faces, and an abundance of erectile tissue between their legs.

Samuel got out of the cab and looked around. He could see no hookers. This was inconvenient in a way, since there were few people about and no obvious place to await Kaz's return. The street was brightly lit, and the nearest café was back the way he had come at Porte Dauphine. That would be a five-minute walk and would take him too far away to be able to monitor the building. This part of the city was notorious for its lack of street life. The sixteenth was the home of the itinerant rich, the international diplomatic corps, the elderly and the executive classes. Unlike other parts of the city it was not well served by the brasseries and the all-night groceries run by Vietnamese and Arabs. *Faut pas oublier le sel*, said Parisians of the sixteenth. If you ran out of salt, you wouldn't be able to pick some up on the corner of the street.

He glanced down at the scrap of paper on which he had written her address. Fourth floor, right. Right and left were usually determined by the way you were facing as you ascended in the lift. But all the flats on the fourth floor had their lights on. So Kaz was either screening calls or coming home soon. She would almost certainly not be in bed.

He looked up and down the empty, wind-scoured street. Traffic was backing up at some distant red lights. Soon the cars would be upon him. As a pedestrian he felt something of an oddity.

The darkness in the trees of the Bois de Boulogne beckoned. The reputation of the Bois, and the intensity of the blackness next to the fuzzy orange neon of the road lights, made him uneasy. If he wished to avoid being seen, there was no other option. He walked quickly across the road and stood under a tree some five yards back from the edge of the wood. This was the perfect spot. He could not be seen from Kaz's building and yet he could watch anonymously in the silent, dark solitude.

After a few moments his eyes became accustomed to the murk, and he began to realize that he was not quite as alone as he imagined. The wood was teeming with a special kind of nightlife. Most of the figures Samuel could make out were men. Some were young, some besuited and decidedly middle-aged. He could discern the occasional woman, dressed in short skirts of flamboyant colours. Many sported huge beehive wigs. He supposed that these were the transvestite prostitutes. What Samuel found strangest of all was the silence. The whole sexual meat market, the ritual of cruise and counter-cruise, was conducted with no more than an occasional murmur of consent or a tiny, choked giggle. Beyond that, he discerned the sound of bodies crashing onto soft grass, the vigorous shaking of shrubbery and the snapping of small twigs and branches. It was like watching a set of badgers at play – only these badgers had crew cuts and a taste for amyl nitrate.

'*C'est combien la passe?*'

'*Comment?*'

A large, florid-faced man in a dark suit appeared out of the darkness. He seemed to have mistaken Samuel for a prostitute. The man asked again what the price of a trick was. Samuel explained, somewhat weakly, that he was just there to take a rest. The man backed off warily. Perhaps he had noticed Samuel's English accent; perhaps he thought he was a policeman. Whatever the man surmised, it was clear that Samuel could not spend much longer in the wood. He wondered how surveillance experts managed to blend into the background. It would have been easier if he had come in a car.

Samuel edged a little further along the tree line until he had a perfect view of all the fourth-floor flats. Then he took his mobile from his jacket pocket and dialled Kaz's number.

Her phone began to ring – and, yes, a dark shape occluded one of the windows on the fourth floor. The glass was bevelled, and there were thick net curtains, so he couldn't be certain it was Kaz. The answering machine kicked in again, and Samuel hung up. Once could have been a coincidence. He waited for two more minutes amid increasingly feverish activity behind him. He redialled. Again the figure on the fourth floor rose, and again the machine kicked in. Twice was too much of a coincidence. Kaz was in her flat monitoring answering-machine messages. It was time to go and pay a visit.

Getting into the building proved surprisingly easy. Just as Samuel was crossing the road a taxi drew up outside the front entrance and disgorged an amorous couple. A lingering embrace outside the doors gave Samuel enough time to walk up behind them as the woman disengaged herself from the man's clutches and punched in an entry code on the alphanumeric keypad. They opened the doors and headed for the lift. Samuel slipped in behind them and took the stairs.

When he reached the fourth floor, he bumped into the couple again. The woman was fumbling to get a key in the lock. They must have been tampering with each other's clothes in the lift for at least a couple of minutes. The man murmured an embarrassed good evening to Samuel, who nodded non-committally and tried not to loiter too obviously outside Kaz's door as the couple stumbled into the flat opposite.

Once they had disappeared he inspected the name tag by the doorbell. DAY was spelled out in bold capitals. This was the place, no doubt. Kaz would be surprised, certainly. Furious, probably. But he had to do it.

He rang the bell and stepped back.

'*Oui?*'

The door had been hurled back, and filling its frame was a large black man, around 6′ 3″ tall. He gazed impassively at Samuel.

'Ah. *Excusez-moi de vous déranger si tard dans le soir, monsieur.*' Samuel was in a state of utter confusion. 'I'm a colleague of Kaz. Is she at home by any chance?'

The man was wearing blue jeans and a white T-shirt that revealed an athletic build.

'Do you speak English?' Samuel presumed this was Kaz's flatmate, and began to ask if Kaz could possibly spare him a minute since something urgent had come up. But he found himself pinned against the wall. The man held his neck by one very powerful hand. Samuel could feel the pulse of anger in his aggressor. The man threw him to the ground and stood over him.

Samuel was half-sitting half-slouched against the door of

the flat opposite. The couple from the lift were well into their rhythm by now; the man was shouting and the woman was making noises that sounded as though she was being sawn in half. They would never hear any cries for help.

The man stood over Samuel and produced a wicked-looking Stanley knife. He was breathing hard. With a sudden movement he kicked Samuel's legs apart, and he found himself sitting squarely against the door. The man bent down and waved the knife in Samuel's face.

'Here's a good one for you. You can tell this one to your office buddies. What's white and ten inches long?' He spoke in French-accented American English.

Samuel could not take his eyes from the blade that glittered in front of his nose.

'Well?' He kicked Samuel roughly.

'I, er, I don't know.'

The man bent towards him and pushed the knife to his cheek. Samuel could feel the cool razor-edge of its point.

'I'll tell you what's white and ten inches long, Mr Samuel Spendlove. Nothing.' There was the unmistakable sweet smell of pastis on his breath. He tweaked the knife slowly beneath Samuel's nose.

'What's the matter? Lost your sense of humour? Worried you might be losing something else?'

The colour drained from Samuel's face. Had he just been called by his name? How did this man know who he was? The woman in the flat opposite was discovering new universes of orgasm, whilst he found himself the victim of a violent attack.

'But don't worry. You can keep your little pecker. For now.' He dived for Samuel's leg, locked him in a wrestling grip that pushed him face-down to the floor and began tearing at Samuel's shoe. Samuel bucked and reared and hammered with

126

his fists against the door, but the man was a solid weight holding him fast. A hand grabbed his flailing foot, pulled at his laces.

'No!'

Samuel gave a frenzied kick, but only succeeded in loosening the shoe further. The man chuckled as he pulled it off.

'Thanks.'

Then cold clamminess as he ripped Samuel's sock off, the glinting steel of the blade against Samuel's little toe. Samuel went wild, bucking and struggling. He didn't feel the blade go in; only sudden, sticky warmth enveloping his foot.

'*Qu'est-ce qui se passe?*'

The neighbour's flat door opened. The man was wearing his lover's pink dressing gown and looked down on them with fear and astonishment. The disruption was enough to break the concentration of Samuel's assailant. Desperately, Samuel flipped onto his side, broke his grasp and grabbed at the hand holding the knife. They began to roll around on the landing. The man in the dressing gown watched for a few seconds, then retreated into the flat and slammed the door.

It was an unequal struggle. Samuel was smaller and much lighter than his foe. They wrestled for control of the knife, but Samuel knew he would not be able to resist much longer.

Upstairs, the sound of the ancient lift cranking into motion issued down the central well. Samuel tried to conserve his strength by rocking backwards and forwards on the ground, hoping to use the weight of the bigger man against him. He could see the lift heading towards them through the gaps in the ornate brass trelliswork. It was nearly at the fourth floor.

His attacker was almost on top of him now. Samuel knew the man was preparing to lunge for him with the knife. The thrust came at the perfect time. Samuel suddenly released his grip and ducked to the side. The knife and his assailant's hand slid through the trelliswork just as the lift came down. The man tried to get his hand back in time, but it was too late. Samuel jammed his arm against the grid. The lift dashed the knife to the bottom of the well. There was a sickening snap and a scream.

Samuel rolled away and jumped up. His adversary had blood all over his shirt and was nursing a right hand that was minus a little finger.

'I'll kill you for this, you bastard. I'll kill you,' he cried. Samuel could see that he was in shock. As was the elderly lady in the lift. She sank beneath them, staring out through the diamond-frames of the safety guard, her face crumpled in horror and disbelief.

The man was sitting on the landing floor cradling his hand and crying softly to himself. Time to go. Samuel's shoe and sock had been lost in the scuffle, but his little toe was still there. He half-ran, half-hopped down the stairs to the foyer. The old lady was just climbing out of the lift as he arrived. She hurled herself into a corner. She too was now crying.

Samuel let himself out and hobbled across the road. He could hear the wail of sirens, and decided to take refuge again in the darkness of the Bois while he considered what he would say and do when the police came for him. Even if his attacker escaped, phone records and the testimony of the neighbours or the old lady put him at the scene of the fight. He stood in the cover of the trees and counted the wailing blue sirens. Four, five altogether. The residents of the building were looking out of their windows, wondering what this latest urban atrocity might be.

Samuel, his naked right foot bleeding and hurting badly, realized that if he wanted some rest away from the police he could not go home that night. He would have to check into a hotel, or maybe stay at François's place. Neither of which would be easy to do discreetly with just one shoe. His chances of re-establishing contact with Kaz had almost certainly been destroyed. The repercussions of the fight would be incalculable. So getting any sort of story – let alone a crock of gold – seemed highly unlikely. His cover was about to be blown sky-high, and his new career was aborting before his eyes. Maybe Kempis had been right. He should have stuck with academia.

He cursed quietly to himself in the shadows as police car number six arrived. A man with a military haircut, leather jacket and a studded dog collar emerged from the darkness and asked as to the price of Samuel's body. He told him politely that it wasn't for sale as another wailing siren drew nearer. Christ, thought Samuel, as he flitted from tree to tree in the direction of Port Dauphine, things are really and truly beginning to unravel here.

10

THE SUN ROSE on a beautiful spring morning, ruined by the fact that Samuel had a foot that felt like twenty pounds of hamburger.

He had spent a relatively comfortable night on the sofa in François's roomy avenue de Friedland flat. François had been amused by the naked and bleeding foot. Samuel avoided his questions and his host immediately imagined exotic causes involving bondage and foot fetishism. The Englishman indulged his friend's tendency to believe that the world was one giant sexual conspiracy taking place just outside his door.

The taxi journey to the office took far longer than it should have. Monsieur le Président was entertaining a visiting head of state from a small African country, a former French colony, and several streets had been closed. This kind of inconvenience was routinely greeted with resigned indifference by Parisians. But try changing someone's parking space at work and you had a war on your hands, complete with quotations from the Declaration of the Rights of Man.

It was a risk to go in, but if the worst came to the worst he would walk out. Everything in the office seemed normal. The security guards were as sullenly indifferent as ever, the team in the flying wedge as routinely raucous. There were a couple of lengthy glances in his direction, but nothing more. People had minor nervous breakdowns all the time in the flying wedge. Neurosis, violent rows, individuals bursting into tears and storming off the dealing floor were common enough. The events were noticed, but then they were forgotten. Perhaps no one was surprised by what had happened the day before.

Samuel limped to his desk and sat down amid minor flurries of gossip, sniggers and stolen glances. It was after nine o'clock now, and everybody should have been in. But Khan was nowhere to be seen. Nor was Kaz.

Miller was gliding around the floor. He sauntered by Samuel's desk and spoke quietly into the middle distance without breaking his stride.

'Let's take a coffee break, shall we? I think we should talk.'

Samuel began to get up.

'Not now. L' Entr'Acte. Five minutes.'

Miller rolled on and almost bumped into Khan as he strode through the main doors. They exchanged bows of mock politeness.

'What did he want?' Khan appeared and draped his jacket over a hanger and glanced at the screen Samuel had on display. If he had heard the biker woman's accusations he was too cool to let on.

'The usual, I expect. A weapon he can use to club your brains out,' said Samuel with a rather feeble attempt at humour.

Khan flicked to a screen showing his positions at the previous night's close.

'And you, as spy-in-chief, will be providing him with that, I take it?'

Samuel felt himself beginning to blush. His mobile rang and he hurried off to a corner of the flying wedge.

'That you, Spendlove?' It was McMurray. 'Good. Listen. Arses are on the line now. Ours. You've got to find someone who will give us hard evidence for next week, or else.'

'But this is a three-month placement,' hissed Samuel. 'I'm supposed to have six more weeks.'

'Deadlines change. Especially when William Barton's setting them.'

The days of Samuel only communicating with McMurray via public telephones were definitely gone. They could both sense that the opportunity to get a big story on Khan was now a matter of urgency. Caution was being thrown to the winds. But why?

'Hi. Good to hear from you. What can I do for you?' said Samuel loudly.

Samuel looked about him. He was still attracting more than his fair share of attention because of yesterday's scene, but nothing else. Khan was half-turned away.

'Listen, you've still got the option of getting some dirt, even without this girlie's evidence. Don't care how you do it. Just do it. This man has to be nailed.' McMurray's manner never changed.

'Thanks. A bunch.'

'I don't expect gratitude, Spendlove. Just deliver!' The line went dead. Samuel shook his head, and trotted back to his screen and began to log off the office network. He was late for Miller.

'So, would that be your editor?' enquired Khan. He was humming lightly to himself as he flipped through a customized investment program.

'Excuse me?'

'That would be your editor, I expect. Demanding something

juicy on whatever it is you're writing about. I am the topic, unless I'm horribly mistaken.'

Samuel felt his eyes widen. He opened his mouth, blinked, then snapped his jaws shut again. He rubbed his chin and smiled ruefully.

'How did you know?'

Khan laughed. 'Dear boy, you came recommended by an Oxford man, a friend of your friend Dr Kempis. There are some people who regret only having ten fingers when there are so many pies in the world. One of the pies this fellow is sticking a finger in is the media magnate William Barton. Or it may be the other way round. You had to be a journalist. Or a researcher with a special mission, whatever you want to call it.'

'You knew all the time?' Samuel's hand was jammed in his jacket pocket; he fingered his handkerchief like a nervous schoolboy.

'No one ever knows anything for certain. I suspected. I did what the market calls due diligence on you before you ever set foot in the country. Dr Kempis is well known in his field, so you came with an impressive background, even if your mission was possibly to be a spy.'

Samuel nodded, his mind racing. Was this good or bad? Was he sacked forthwith? He assumed not, if Khan had sort of known all along.

'Now why do you think I didn't mind?'

'I really have no idea,' Samuel said, truthfully.

'Two reasons. First, I've nothing to hide. Second, I think something smells about this bank's operation too. That was off the record, by the way.' A sardonic smile.

Khan reached over and patted Samuel on the back. 'Cheer up. Nothing to worry about. I shan't tell Miller, satisfying as watching his nervous breakdown would be. You look as though you're on your way out. See you later.'

'And, Samuel.' He stopped and turned back to face Khan. 'Apart from anything else, I think you could actually have a future as a prop trader.'

Miller was sitting on the upper floor of the Entr'Acte café at a rich mahogany table in the corner. The thick belt that drove the two fans on the ceiling was turning busily. The fan's blades, set amid heavy brass bunches of grapes, shifted just enough air to create a pleasant breeze.

Miller gestured with a palm, and Samuel sat.

'So. Where did you disappear to last night?'

'Went home to do some thinking.'

'And ended up falling on the dance floor?' Miller nodded at Samuel's foot. 'I don't suppose that mad woman who invaded us knew what she was talking about, do you? You weren't trying to seduce one of my senior colleagues, were you, Samuel? It would have been doubly profitable if you really were spying on Khan.'

'As I said, I've no idea where Kaz is. None whatsoever.'

'But you were with her the other night? We're beginning to get seriously worried.'

'Is that real concern, or just bank policy?'

'Samuel, come, come. She's a senior employee, a very hard-headed and responsible woman who's suddenly just not there any more. Of course we're worried.'

Samuel sighed and picked up his cup. 'She strikes me as a very capable woman. What is it you want, anyway, Anton? Khan's waiting for me.'

'You're employed by the bank, not by Khan.'

Samuel gloomily surveyed the bustling street. He had been a fool to think he could step into the role of undercover journalist. Of course Khan, with his perception and his contacts, would see him coming before he even decided to make the journey. He had been stupid and vain even to imagine he might deceive the king of opaque behaviour. Now he was embarrassed – humiliated even – and beholden to Khan for his dignity and restraint.

All of which left him in a mess. Just about everyone in his life had a call of some sort on him – Khan, Miller, the bank, McMurray, Kempis and the Master of Biblos and the idea of truth. And then there was The Story That Would Make a Difference. Would he, could he make a difference?

The waiter brought them two more *cafés allongés*. Samuel sipped. He was beginning to get a caffeine headache, especially now his cover had been blown.

'I can understand why you want to monitor Khan, but I don't see how I really can be of much use to you, Anton.'

'Let me be the judge of that. Just watch and listen and keep notes. Sooner or later you will have something useful for me – an unbooked investment, an off-the-book catastrophe where one of his sudden speculative thrusts goes badly wrong. I feel confident that you will produce something that will be mutually rewarding.'

Samuel looked at him. Who had more to hide? Khan the clever manipulator or Miller the man whose team member booked a $100 million loss?

'He did say something the other day, something I thought was strange.'

He had Miller's undiluted attention now. He fixed the older man's gaze and waited to see how he would react when the revelation came.

'Khan said the other day that it was difficult having to play the same dirty game as the others in the market.'

'Did he indeed?'

'Yes, Anton. But I shouldn't be too delighted by that. I'm pretty sure he thinks the bank is one of those playing dirty games. I should look out. Khan might be watching you too.'

'THESE PEOPLE are here to see you,' said Khan, clearly put out by the very presence of two individuals whom he would have termed 'civilians'. Khan turned away from Samuel to the bank of phones and screens. New York was falling out of bed, losing two per cent – more than $30 billion – in half an hour, as it sometimes did just before the close of the European markets on Fridays.

The man before Samuel was short, tubby, balding, and wearing a woollen cardigan over a creased shirt and frayed tie. Brown corduroy trousers and a tweed jacket completed a look that told Samuel he was not a banker. Nor was his female companion, who was also in her mid-forties and shared her friend's miserable dress sense.

The man produced an identity card that proclaimed him a police inspector. Samuel examined it carefully. It looked real enough, and the Cinquième Bureau would probably not impersonate domestic police officers.

'What can I do for you, Inspector Blondeau?' asked Samuel. His companion had also waved a card at him that identified her as Sergeant Bouchinet.

'It concerns events at the home of your friend and colleague, Mademoiselle Katherine Day,' said Blondeau.

'I would hardly call Kaz Day a friend. We had a few drinks together once. Look, Inspector, do we have to do this here?' Once again Samuel was the universal object of attention. For the flying wedge, this was more exciting than a whole panto-mime season of bin-liner redundancies.

'Well, we could always have this conversation at the station.'

'Inspector Blondeau, may I have a word?' Khan's manner was all calm and reassurance. 'I believe I recognize your name. We certainly have friends in common.'

Within seconds Khan had taken the policeman by the arm and was leading him away from the desk. After a brief, uneasy interlude during which Samuel and Bouchinet tried not to look at one another, the two men returned. Khan still had his hand on Blondeau's arm.

'Good, good. That's settled then. Next week, your offices. Very good, officer.'

Miller arrived at a stooping near-run. 'What's this? What's this?'

'Something you weren't here to take care of, Miller. May I introduce you . . .'

Moments later the police officers left.

Samuel's stomach was still churning when Khan reappeared, his diplomatic duties done.

'Khan, I have to say thanks very much. What did you say to them?'

'Mmm. I've been wondering about this,' said Khan avoiding the question. 'Would you like to come to lunch on Sunday?'

Samuel was nonplussed.

'Lunch? Why, yes, very kind. But what happened with the police?'

'Oh, we have friends in common, as you'll see. Inspector Blondeau fielded a call from a frightened old lady about a couple of men rolling around outside Kaz's flat the other night.' A pointed look. 'He knows one of them was you. I managed to convince him it was just a routine fracas. It can be sorted out in the presence of the bank's lawyers next week. There shouldn't be any problems.'

'Well, thanks. I really don't deserve this.'

'Maybe you don't.' Khan's voice had a hard edge to it. 'You owe me. You should stay away from Kaz, by the way. Spying in this country tends to have painful consequences, and she's not worth troubling over. The woman is . . . expendable.'

The last words were spoken softly to a screen, as though Samuel, or anyone else for that matter, wasn't even there.

SAMUEL ARRIVED punctually, but when he rang the bell of Khan's avenue Matignon apartment, the great man was not ready. A muffled apology came down the intercom and then he buzzed Samuel in. He took the lift to the seventh floor and found the flat door open. Except it wasn't so much a flat as a gigantic penthouse with the kind of view of the city that estate agents liked to call panoramic. It was truly breathtaking.

The Eiffel Tower loomed in the near ground, to its left the Alexander III Bridge, the old train station now transformed into the Musée d'Orsay, and he could also see the Tour Montparnasse and Les Invalides. If he turned the other way the Arc de Triomphe dominated, with the Grande Arche de la Défense, a large modernist echo, some kilometres away. The west-facing wall was entirely glass, and the place was flooded with late morning light.

Khan descended a spiral staircase. He was dressed in jeans and an olive linen shirt. His hair, Samuel noted with some amusement, was wet. That would never have done at the office.

'What do you think?'

'It's stunning.' Samuel had seen a similar view, at the

Maison Blanche restaurant on the same street. But this was far, far better. He told Khan so.

'Yes, I bought it for the view. Not one of my better investment decisions. But then if everything were an investment, life would be so dull, don't you think?'

On the street they took a taxi east, towards the Marais. Khan talked about the fall in New York share prices that had happened on Friday after the European markets had closed. He told Samuel that it was nothing too serious. There had been a sharp, sudden fall just before the close, which smacked of computer-generated profit-taking. Khan was sure that the market would bounce back on Monday.

Samuel was finding it hard to concentrate on what Khan was saying to him. They passed near his flat, and he looked out anxiously. Samuel had not ventured back there since Friday night. He would go soon and get some clothes for the office. But he felt deeply uneasy there now. Better to stay in François's flat for the moment.

The taxi disgorged them on the rue des Archives, by a large sandstone building with an armed guard. Khan turned in to the main entrance. Samuel had understood they were going to a private lunch given by one of Khan's friends. Now it seemed they were about to visit a museum.

The guard on the interior door that led into a large cobbled courtyard checked their names against a list. A walkie-talkie crackled in his hand. Yes, they were expected.

They stepped inside. The courtyard was rectangular, with a large statue of Henri IV. Its dimensions and elaborate architraves gave it the look of the Bodleian back in Oxford. A tower dominated the north-western corner of the quadrangle.

'You are about to witness something that should tell you any number of things,' said Khan. 'The conclusions you will draw are of interest to me. But I suggest that you save them for later.'

One of the first conclusions Samuel drew was that Khan was better connected than he had dared to imagine. The long, straggly hair and frameless glasses by which he now found himself confronted were known all over France. Lunch was being provided by Patrice Gourdon, the French minister of culture.

'*Patrice, je te présente Samuel, un collègue à moi. Un jeune homme brillant.*'

This was kind of Khan, but Samuel hardly felt he merited the epithet of brilliance, given his recent track record. Particularly as Gourdon was renowned for his intellectual abilities and linguistic prowess. They exchanged formalities in French. Samuel, who had seen Gourdon dispensing his knowledge for the television-watching masses in flawless English several times, was expecting him to speak to them in English, but he did not. Samuel's French had long been past the stage of fluency; Khan's mastery of the language was excellent, but heavily accented.

Khan and Gourdon were discussing the refurbishment of a printing museum in the fourteenth arrondissement as they entered the salon through wide double doors. A long dining table was set for sixteen people. A huge display of tulips was set in a large white bowl in the middle of the table.

Samuel realized that, despite the guards, this was actually Gourdon's private house. On the gilded Louis XIV walls were pictures of the politician as a young man. He had been famously fixated on Saint-Exupéry and had followed his flying adventures around Africa. Gourdon's subsequent book had been well received. Combined with his top position in the *classement* at one of the Grandes Écoles, he had been well set in French public life from the age of thirty. Ardent horticulturalist, art historian, master of wine with an interest in one of the best vineyards in the Saint-Julien area of Bordeaux, and a mightily respected polymath, Gourdon had been an ebullient minister for three years.

As the lunch progressed, Samuel saw that Gourdon's renowned passion for things French had perhaps coloured his private life. Gourdon was reputed to have considerable mastery of English, Greek, German, Italian, Spanish and Mandarin, plus a smattering of many other languages, including one from Papua New Guinea spoken by fewer than five hundred people. But from this base of dazzling eclecticism the great multiculturalist had become a doughty defender of French values.

Seated round the beautiful walnut table were an American writer, a Pakistani academic, a Hungarian poet and a Russian choreographer, whose work with the Royal Ballet had received excellent notices. The French contingent – a party colleague of Gourdon, a film director and a gaggle of television folk – were barely in the majority. There should have been an easy co-existence of languages; the American, the Russian and the Hungarian were talking mostly in Russian, with some English. The Pakistani clearly preferred English as a lingua franca, as did Khan. But Gourdon continued to speak French.

White-liveried servants brought a cress and nutmeg vichyssoise, a confit of duck on caramelized spring cabbage, cheeses, and a clafoutis of kiwi fruit. Gourdon then invited them on a tour of the house, as he put it. The guests left the table and began to stroll through the immense, high-ceilinged rooms of the minister's palatial mansion. The man had the most incredible collection of artefacts that Samuel had ever seen. He was walking next to Khan toward the rear of the crocodile, and said as much.

'No, no, dear boy. This is state-owned.'

'So this is a museum after all?'

'No. This is Patrice's ministerial residence. These things all belong to the state. There isn't the room to show them all. There are cellars under the building packed full with more gems, and it's the same with all the state-owned buildings. There simply aren't enough walls to display France's cultural wealth.'

'That's a Leonardo da Vinci cartoon.'

'It's only a cartoon, Samuel. Nowhere near the merit of a proper painting.'

'So when Patrice is out of office, he'll have to return everything?'

'Probably. The loaning of objects by the state has become something of an established practice. People are relaxed about it as part of the system. Gourdon's three immediate pre-decessors have not handed back all of the things that were on loan, as far as I'm aware. It's a question of having uncommon taste, of offering to house objects that will not be sought after by the larger public.'

'You mean objects that won't be missed?'

'Objects that will not be required urgently for exhibit. Their whereabouts are known.'

Gourdon was at the head of the group, offering his views on the Tang dynasty to the film director and the academic. With a theatrical clap of the hands coffee was summoned. It appeared on silver trays, accompanied by petits fours. As the guests began to form themselves into little groups around the trays Gourdon nodded at Khan, and headed through a rosewood-panelled double door. Khan followed, motioning to Samuel to do likewise.

They tracked the minister along a wide corridor and up a

spiral staircase. The light that had suffused the display rooms soon seemed far away. The winding stairs became increasingly narrow and dark. Eventually, Samuel's shoulders were brushing the walls as he peered into the gloom. Then Gourdon opened a door set into the stone of the wall and the liquid grey light of the afternoon flooded over them. They were in the turret of a tower, presumably the tower he had noticed on entering Gourdon's palatial home. Inside, the turret had a bench seat that ran around the walls; cushions were strewn on the floor. The only furniture was a tiny trestle table, on which rested a black 1950s-style telephone.

'Well, my friend,' said Gourdon, speaking in English for the first time. 'To business.'

Khan picked up the phone and began to call numbers in New York, Singapore and Hong Kong. The introductory patter was different each time – customized was the word you would have used in the markets. Wives' names were uttered, enquiries as to children's health and education were solicitously made. Then came the crunch: there was nothing to worry about in the markets following the nosedive in New York just before the close on Friday. Technical reasons: it had happened before, it would happen again. All that was needed was a few loud, confident noises when the markets opened. Plus some buy orders and things would be fine. Khan was with his close personal friend Patrice Gourdon, who sent his regards.

Sometimes Gourdon himself had a cordial word, but this was not usually necessary. Within an hour they had made calls to twelve expatriate managers of leading French institutions not wholly owned or directly controlled by the state. Insurance management in New York, chemicals executives in Sydney – all got the same message. They were to make bullish noises with their brokers in Tokyo when the sun rose on the new financial week. If they stood fast, their cooperation would be rewarded. Maybe not now, but well before they went to heaven. Samuel, as he had been bid, listened, watched, and said little.

They rejoined the party. The guests were playing chess and backgammon and hardly noticed their arrival. Flutes of tawny Barsac and an array of fruits were being served. Some guests had fat-bellied glasses of port or cognac in their hands.

Samuel stayed and watched Khan play and win against all-comers at backgammon. Eventually the clock moved towards supper time; a good half of Gourdon's guests remained. A six-hour luncheon was clearly nothing out of the ordinary.

Samuel was just beginning to wonder when the acrobats in the white suits would magic dinner in their direction when Khan rose. The promise of imminent departure in his posture drew Gourdon over from a game of mah-jong. They bade farewell with quietly spoken words and small bows. The food, the walk, the games and the slow, continuous drip of drinks had mesmerized the minister's guests. Their departure was acknowledged by the others, but as no more than a ripple on the surface of their concentration on the trivial pursuits in hand.

'*Au revoir, Samuel. À la prochaine,*' said Gourdon as they were leaving.

They stepped out into the cool night air.

'He liked you, Samuel.'

'Really? But I hardly said anything.'

'Precisely.'

They headed west a little and then turned up the rue du Temple. In its southerly marches the street was ancient, narrow and crumbling. There was little traffic, but cars were parked recklessly on the pavements, adding to the claustrophobic atmosphere. Khan walked swiftly, looking straight ahead.

'So. What are your conclusions?'

'That if there are a dozen people to know in the world, you are probably one of them.'

'Ha. I doubt that. Don't let the view from the flat or Patrice's Cézanne blind you. Go on.'

'That the markets probably won't fall out of bed on Monday.'

'Yes. The qualification was important, of course. We can never know for sure. What else?'

'That maybe the conspiracy theorists have a point. Maybe we are all being manipulated – even you, Khan.'

'There's something in that. But don't get carried away by conspiracy theories. No one's ever organized enough to be in charge. Just as no one's ever disciplined enough to take orders, even if one were foolish enough to try to give them.'

'You mean all those calls for support in the markets may have been in vain?'

'Naturally. Most of those captains of industry and finance will be looking at early losses tomorrow. They know that, and the temptation to make a personal profit should never be underestimated. But most will do as we asked. No, I'll rephrase that: most will behave in a manner we indicated would be looked on with favour from Paris.'

'So there is a kind of benign conspiracy then.'

'Not a conspiracy, cohesion. France is still a product of dirigisme. People expect direction from the centre; all their upbringing, their cultural instincts tell them to accept that direction, and they choose to do so in most cases. That's far from being a conspiracy.'

They were heading towards the Place de la République now. Marianne, the spirit of the fourth republic, fat arms holding a comically delicate olive twig, came into view.

'When one is really well connected the conversation may not have a high level of intellectual density,' continued Khan. 'But the factual background can be fascinating. My move on German rates, remember, came about because of something a German minister didn't say at a cocktail party. That's not insider trading. That's having access to important people and using your brain. Lateral thinking. Occasionally, there comes a time to repay the favour of inclusion.'

'Witness today's round of calls?' Samuel interjected.

Khan nodded.

'My name is known in the markets and, by adding what weight I carry in the financial world to the authority of the state, one can pretty much guarantee a good response from the francophone world. There will have been conversations like that going on all over the developed world this weekend. The golf-club lines will have been melting with the volume of mutual reassurance. Which may or may not work. It's a question of time and confidence.'

'I see, I think. It's not a question of bucking the markets, but making people understand that they are the market, collectively speaking.'

'Put it this way. Do you really imagine a cohesive society like France would allow its industry to be sold off to faceless people on the other side of a bargain? To foreign capitalist adventurers, men like William Barton? It would be like the Brits selling the Crown Jewels.'

Samuel privately expected that the Brits might well sell the Crown Jewels one day. If not outright, a sale and lease-back arrangement seemed entirely possible.

Khan was looking round the gigantic square for cabs. He raised his arm, and a taxi dived out from the throng and extinguished its light. 'You must remember, Samuel,' said Khan as he climbed into the back of the cab, 'that this is a well-run country.'

Samuel watched the taxi hurtle off, breaking a red light. A well-run country? He had heard that opinion somewhere before.

HE LOOKED AT *his wristwatch. The programmer was late again. Why was it that those who could design a clean structure for a computer system were uniformly unable to catch a plane or meet any deadline? He hated lateness as much as he hated scruffiness. Yet he had to tolerate the beards and the jeans and the dubious personal hygiene of the contractors he employed. They were the best – they knew it and he knew it.*

He sighed and picked up the paper. The business section was full of the crisis in the real estate market. He smiled. Not going into that market had been the correct call. It had overheated, and suddenly everyone wanted to sell at the same time. Residential real estate had dropped precipitously too, even in the smartest areas and especially in Manhattan. Now, it couldn't be given away, and thousands of bankers, many with good MBAs from top universities, were looking for jobs.

He glanced up again at the clock on the wall. It was uncertain whether setting up a consultancy to design computer systems for banks had been quite as clever as avoiding the real estate market. Maybe he should have stayed in the business of manufacturing hardware. But his instincts told him that software was the forward. Even if you had to deal with air-headed techies, who didn't understand that the world needed order and precision.

He put down the paper and wandered off to the bathroom to wash his hands again. They were clean already. But they could never be too clean, could they?

11

You are on the right track. The Day woman has what you
need. Keep going.

Samuel looked again at the message blinking up at him from
the screen of the new titanium Mac that Khan had given him
a couple of days earlier. An anonymous message from some
Yahoo! address, probably created while he was still having
lunch with Khan. Kaz – the right track? Or to be avoided,
expendable as Khan had said? But where was she?

He needed a favour. François picked up his mobile on the
first ring, and, of course, agreed to Samuel's request with
the minimum of fuss. So instead of lounging in front of a
movie on his friend's sofa bed Samuel hunted around for car
keys. Soon he was sitting in the leathern comfort of François's
1966 Citroën Safari within sight of Kaz's boulevard Lannes
flat. In one hand a flask of coffee, in the other a copy of Ovid
La Brooy's latest memo from hell, something to do with a
correlation between the number of mentions of 'bull market'
in newspaper headlines and the imminence of financial doom.
Journalists almost always got it wrong – but not quite so
consistently that you could make money by doing the opposite
of their analysis.

The clock set in the walnut dashboard glowed a faintly phosphorescent 1.45 a.m. at him. Ovid's memo had sent him to sleep again. Kaz could have come, gone, and left naked on top of a tank, and he would have missed her. He would never get his story now. This was his last chance.

The lights were still out in the flat. He picked up his mobile and dialled. The ringing, the message. He was sure somehow that he had missed nothing, that nothing had happened there while he slept. No one was in the flat, and he was in the wrong place. He just knew it. He dialled again. The answerphone message reprised.

It was time to go home. Tonight he would spend a final, fretful night on François's sofa. Tomorrow and thereafter he would go back to his still unburgled, unsullied flat.

Then he saw her. But the creature moving in the shadows of the apartment block on boulevard Lannes was definitely not Kaz. He had noticed her a few minutes earlier, and had taken her for an upper-class hooker cruising the street. But now that she moved and walked in the dull orange glow of the street light he knew instantly who it was and why she had seemed familiar. It was Lauren de la Geneste.

He looked up. Still no light in Kaz's flat. So she had been waiting for her too. And now she was walking away, giving up and going home.

Samuel reasoned that whether Lauren had, like him, been staking the place out, or whether she had been there for an appointment that Kaz had failed to keep, she was definitely worth following. She might even be about to look for her elsewhere, a favoured haunt perhaps. All the more reason to stick close.

She stepped into a small van, an ancient, light-coloured Renault Quatrelle, and moved off briskly. Samuel turned the key and brought the heavy old Citroën stumbling to its knees. He followed her with considerable difficulty as she zipped around – it was like stalking a deer from atop a camel. But the lights and the luck of the traffic were with him. Soon she dumped the car and Samuel slipped out onto the pavement behind her, leaving the Citroën illegally parked. He trailed her down the rue de Rivoli. Incredibly, they were about to pass his flat. He could have stayed at home and done as much effective surveillance. Lauren walked on, glancing neither left nor right.

The royalist bar was noisy tonight. He was glad of the distraction it provided. Lauren turned up Samuel's little street, the rue St Bon, and he quickened his pace. He had the unnerving feeling that he was about to witness her breaking into his own flat. He ran to the corner to see where she went.

But he was wrong. He was just in time to see her disappear into a door a few metres along the street from his own building. Lauren had gone into Chez Simone!

Samuel had been regularly teased in the office about living close to Chez Simone ever since *Sept Jours à Paris*, a city listings magazine, had published its survey of Parisian *clubs échangistes*. Samuel had somewhat naively expressed surprise on the trading floor that he should be living so close to a sexual exchange club. Diaz had pounced. No doubt it was convenient for Sam, eh? Saved on the cabfare home after a – ho, ho, ho – hard night?

Samuel shivered quietly in the cool of the evening. Lauren had already shaken him off once by vanishing into Paris's clubland. Not this time.

Or so he thought. The woman at the counter behind the door was polite but adamant. There could be no question of Samuel going in alone. This was a club for couples – men and women only. Unaccompanied adults of either sex simply did not gain admission. But what about the client who had just come in? She had been on her own; Samuel had seen her.

The woman smiled. She reminded Samuel slightly of his mother; all dyed hair and matronly authority.

'*Non. Vous vous trompez, monsieur. Elle est partie par la contre-allée.*'

With the knowledge that she had left via the side entrance, Samuel retreated. Lauren and Kaz were quite a pair: they got their kicks from stealing art objects, going to women's clubs – and, it seemed, hanging round places for straight twosomes. Well, Kaz certainly had an interest in men, whether or not she was intimate with this woman. It was getting to the stage that nothing surprised him about her.

He went back to the crowded royalist bar and ordered himself a cold, golden beer. He nursed it at a corner table and sipped ruminatively. They knew all about sex clubs in the flying wedge. It was probably a function of the jobs that they did. The men threw their life force into their jobs, and married women who thought they had solid, respectable citizens for partners. But at the end of a long day of eating and being eaten alive, a quiet supper with a kindly woman while the kids were tucked up in bed was the last thing most of them wanted. They lived dangerously; often they gambled with their own money as well. Consequently, they needed a powerful sedative to come down from the emotional high of combat. Strong drink, recreational drugs, the company of fellow market warriors, the sexual favours of a stranger. These were the principal avenues through which they could vent their animal pain.

As for their female colleagues, they lived with the same pressures, accentuated by the unabashed ethic of female-baiting. If Kaz – variously described by Diaz and Nobby as a clued-up doxy, a major piece of ass, a significant hard body and a flash piece of mutton – wanted to hang out with the groovy girl in the leather gear and occasionally take a man for a lover, who could criticize? Certainly not Samuel, who had very much enjoyed being taken.

'*Qu'est-ce que vous faites ici?*'

Dark and beautiful and dangerous, Lauren took the chair opposite.

'*Moi?*' Samuel was shocked. His thoughts had materialized. He tried to improvise something witty. '*Je bois pour me souvenir.*' I'm drinking to remember. Not great, but marginally better than nothing.

'You are looking for Kaz,' she said. Statement, not question. There was something else in her eyes this time. Not anger. Anxiety? Fear?

He nodded towards a drink. She accepted the silent offer with another nod. After some difficulty Samuel attracted the attention of a boy in a soiled white coat. Lauren ordered a demi Leffe, and lit a cigarette.

Samuel didn't know what he found harder to believe: her composure or the marked change in her manner. Instead of hostility there was something approaching acceptance or resignation. Having taken the drink she made no attempt at conversation, but sat there wreathed in cigarette smoke.

She wasn't wearing leather today, but a black jacket and skirt. Samuel guessed it was a Kenzo or a Cerruti. It was smart enough to wear to work, except that the skirt was just a little too tiny. He looked at her exquisite legs, veiled in dark stockings. They were crossed, and the skirt had ridden up. It had the substance of a large belt, and no more. About her neck she wore a long black feather boa. On a less beautiful woman the effect would have been idiotic. But she carried it off with perfect poise: the contrast between the frilliness of the boa and the sexy plainness of the suit worked, somehow.

Lauren leaned forward and stubbed out her cigarette. She seemed quite happy with silence, but her dark eyes burned into Samuel. He sipped his beer and waited.

'Tell me,' she said at last. 'Do you believe Marx has any relevance to the new millennium?'

'I saw where you went earlier,' said Samuel, gesturing over his shoulder towards Chez Simone. 'What's the relevance of Marxism to sexual exchange clubs?'

It was a game of dare. Dare to ask, dare to hear the answer.

'You know his theory on sex,' he added after another long pause. 'That in the utopian society appearance would be almost irrelevant. For logic would dictate that if sexual favours were granted mostly by the beautiful they would quickly become undesirable. Who would want to soil his lip drinking from the well-greased rim of the communal cup?'

'So?' she asked with a slight frown. She looked him full in the face. 'All that matters is desire. Need. The satisfaction of physical appetites. Practical matters.'

'So you're a practical person?' he asked.

'As a lawyer, I have to be.'

Samuel let this sink in. This biker woman came from a smart family with a 'de la' in the name. Now she had presented another little surprise.

'A Marxist lawyer?'

'One can respect the analysis of the capitalist system without struggling to destroy it. Better sometimes to do so from within.'

Another silence. This probably made her a Trotskyist in Samuel's reckoning. Her gaze was unnervingly steady.

'So why did you go to Chez Simone?' said Samuel at last.

She looked away, then fixed upon him again.

'I accept that you don't know where Kaz has gone. Why else stake out her flat? What I don't understand is why you want to find her.'

Samuel shrugged slightly and tried to parry her poker player's stare.

At last, she nodded slightly, and rose from the table. 'Come with me,' she said and took his hand.

The woman at reception in Chez Simone showed no surprise when Samuel reappeared with Lauren. Another two punters getting together to get round the couples-only rule. Lauren paid with a 100-euro note, and went into the bar. The room was small and quiet. Music from one of the local radio stations issued from speakers set in the ceiling.

There were two couples in the room. They were nursing drinks at separate tables and talking quietly. Samuel had expected to see the equivalent of sexual minesweeping: all parties on full 360-degree radar scan every thirty seconds. But the atmosphere was more evocative of one of the quieter nights at a suburban golf club.

He and Lauren sat in a corner and sipped at their beers. Marx and Kaz had slipped out of their lives now, as had all conversation.

After a few minutes Samuel decided that the sexual exchange club scene was really quite sedate. They finished their drinks and Lauren touched his hand gently. She nodded in the direction of a door that Samuel had assumed led to a lavatory. He looked at her, nonplussed. She got up; Samuel followed.

'Kaz comes here often,' murmured Lauren. 'She could be behind this door. At least there may be someone who knows where she is.'

She turned the handle and pushed on to enter a land of shadows. Samuel could hear rustling and soft moaning, but there was no substance or detail to what he saw. Shapes flitted by and settled in obscurity. Lauren's hand was cool in his as she led him to an indistinct mass that translated itself into a sofa.

'This is your first time here, no?'

Samuel nodded.

'So we should act the part.'

She handed him a papier mâché, faintly feline mask, which he slipped on. They were in what looked like a corridor, though in the dark and dreamlike world they had entered it was difficult to tell. Then she held him close to her, as a lover would. Her body was taut and firm, and he detected a subtle, rich scent mingled with tiny traces of smoke. Her glossy hair was pressed against his cheek, her hands flat against the small of his back. Someone stumbled by them in the semi-dark. Samuel felt himself responding to Lauren's embrace.

She pulled away, gently but firmly.

'We should act the part, no more.'

Samuel nodded and followed her as she took his hand once more. After a few moments he began to think that someone had turned up the lights, but it was just that his eyes had become accustomed to the gloom. He realized that there were many passages and niches leading off the corridors, and the sounds of quiet revelry were somehow more distinct when he could distinguish the outlines of the moving shapes.

'She may be here,' whispered Lauren. 'Let's split up. I'll go this way.' Samuel watched after her, and within seconds she was gone. Most of the inhabitants of the series of interconnected rooms seemed to be in various states of undress; Samuel took off his shirt in sympathy and began to wander.

As he roamed the rooms and tunnels he was filled with an increasing sense of wonderment. Had Kaz really frequented such a place? It was like a scene from Hades, the very celebration of unabashed carnal pleasures that once upon a time had constituted his personal vision of hell. This, surely, was what the Jesuitical fulminations from the pulpits of his youth had been all about. This was the world of sexual comfort that the priests said was Satanic, that Gail said was impure. It was a world in which he had never travelled because every important person and idea in his life told him it was wrong. Yet now it was neither threatening nor erotic, just faintly absurd.

There were men and women of all ages, shapes and sizes. Some, like Samuel, were partially dressed in street clothes. Others wore costumes of rubber and leather with zips and buckles that deliberately exposed a nipple or a testicle. Some – a few, mostly young women – wore nothing at all. Some had masks. One man wore a Viking helmet. Some were lying on sofas and cushions kissing and touching one another. Others watched with drinks in their hands.

But where was Lauren? Had she found someone? Had she found Kaz?

There was a bed on a raised dais in the biggest room. A tall thin man was blindfolded and handcuffed to it; he was whimpering with fear and pleasure every time he heard a footfall near him. A woman in green leather trousers, naked from the waist up, knelt over him, rubbed herself against him and began to bite his nipples. The bound man bucked and groaned; a fat man in his fifties wearing a gorilla mask, a pinstripe jacket and no trousers or pants that Samuel could see was walking around rubbing a fat, lazy-looking penis in his hand. He stopped briefly before the bed, rubbed a little more vigorously, and moved on.

Then he saw her. At least he thought it was Kaz, moving away from him, towards the door at the far side of the crowded room. She flicked her thick, curly hair back over her shoulders in that distinctive way. He gave a small shout and tried to push through the throng. But the crowd was too dense, and people instinctively moved to block him. Shouting and pushing were frowned upon in Chez Simone. By the time he got to the door, she was gone, disappeared into the maze of anterooms and chambers.

He spent another half-hour wandering the corridors, stopping passers-by and asking if they had seen the woman he was looking for. But before he could even begin to describe Kaz, there was a shrug of indifference and they moved on. This, after all, was a place where people came to lose their partners, at least for a time.

He drifted into another room, slightly darker than the rest. Samuel noticed a line of men, patiently queuing up, as though to collect a pension. On a sofa in front of them, legs spread wide, was a young woman. Her body was arched so that her face was almost completely hidden. Samuel would have had an excellent view of her genitalia, had they not been obscured by the furiously bobbing head of the man at the front of the line. The woman's cries were becoming louder and louder, creating a noise that seemed to breach the etiquette of quiet depravity.

The bobbing head stopped, distracted by a tap on the shoulder. There was a brief hiatus, faintly reminiscent of Confederate Army balls that Samuel had seen in old movies. One quick tap and a new gentleman cut in to dance with the Southern belle.

Except that the new head did not belong to a gentleman. The woman was positively wailing now, as a head of corn-yellow hair moved up and down. For a dreadful moment, Samuel thought it was Gail. But, of course, it was a woman with only a passing resemblance, save for her hair. She was naked from the waist up, except for a feather boa similar to the one Lauren had been wearing. Then he saw Lauren looking on, cool, but nodding in quiet approval. He kept silent and observed her watching the women.

The woman on the bed reached down and lifted the black feather boa from the blonde, who now gave way to a youngish man wearing a wolf's-head mask. The mask was pulled back over the man's head as he knelt to his task. The man behind, shorter and decidedly podgy, began to murmur words of encouragement. The woman on the bed was now losing all semblance of control. Soon the plump man was speaking quite loudly:

'Go, Nobby. Go for it! Do that thing mightily!'

It was indeed Nobby. He was being encouraged by Diaz, dressed in frilly pink suspenders and a Brooks Brothers button-down. Soon Diaz pulled Nobby aside and began churning his head in a circular motion around the woman's groin. She was now thrashing about, arms flailing, legs jacked apart and trembling.

Suddenly Diaz stood up. He wiped his chin and turned to Samuel.

'Your turn, buddy.'

Samuel hadn't been aware of how close he had crept to them. Thank God he still had his mask and had kept silent. His colleagues surely wouldn't recognize him with his cat mask. As he dithered the woman looped the feather boa over him, and pulled him abruptly down to her. At first he was hesitant, but soon found a rhythm, thinking of oysters and salt and the faint taste of earth in his mouth. Above the screams of the woman he could hear the happy laughter of the two men.

'That's my baby! You got it, Five Tongues!'

'Go for it, FT!'

Soon she could take no more. Samuel rose and quickly turned into the darker shadows of the corridor. From the gloom he looked back to check. Yes, it was FT! Alexandra from the bank was slumped on the sofa now; she was soaked in sweat. Diaz was smiling and tossed her a towel. Well, this certainly was an evening when he was getting to know his colleagues a lot better.

'Would you like your jacket back?'

Lauren held it out to him. He suddenly felt cold. What on earth was he doing?

'Have you seen Kaz? I'm sure I saw her. But I can't find her any more.'

'Your research methods are original.'

'You told me to act the part.'

'Kaz loved it here. For me, it remains a diversion. But as for you, Monsieur Spendlove, your dedication to journalism and the cause of truth is heart-warming. Almost as if the last person to see her alive was you.'

Samuel said nothing.

Lauren motioned to him, and he followed her to the bar. Samuel could understand now why it was so quiet and relaxed. Everybody was exhausted, not to say sated; the last thing anyone wanted to do was to play a courtship game in a well-lit room.

'So,' she said as a beer was placed before her. 'She's not

here. I am certain of it. I looked everywhere, but there was no point. I felt it before I went through the place. Every room.' She exhaled loudly.

Samuel responded with a sigh. 'But I'm sure I saw her here.'

'So you say. Tell me. Did you enjoy? Is your appetite satisfied?'

'Is that why you came here with Kaz, to satisfy your hunger?'

She blew smoke away from him.

'Appetite is all there is. Appetite and gratification.' She had a vacant look.

'What about affection and love?'

'These are bourgeois myths. They do not exist,' she replied sharply. She looked away. Samuel placed a hand on her shoulder. The gentleness of his touch seemed more intimate, more personal than all the lewd acts in the dark.

'We all have our myths, our sacred beliefs. You believed in those myths once, no?'

She half-turned towards him, hesitated, inhaled hard; he could have scooped her sadness out of the air. She shook her head.

'If love and affection are sacred today it is because they are scarce. Today, here, sex comes before affection and before love.'

'Satisfaction and appetite, buy and sell?'

'Exactly.'

Her eyes were troubled but full of defiance.

'So you didn't love her then?' he asked.

Lauren looked down for a second. 'Shall we go?'

For some reason he wanted to walk out with her. Was it just because they had gone in together? As they picked up their coats their eyes met and she put a cool hand over his, a first gesture of intimacy.

'Tell me, where is she, do you think?' The question was delivered with quiet concern.

Samuel returned her stare, and they both realized that Kaz was no longer around Ropners, nor the wild night scenes of Chez Simone, nor anywhere that Lauren frequented. She inhabited neither of the worlds they knew. So where was she?

12

'LADIES AND GENTLEMEN, may we request a moment of your attention while our cabin staff inform you of the important safety procedures that will be used in case of emergency? Safety doors are sited at the front, mid- and rear sections of the aircraft . . .'

A ripple of laughter spread across the flying wedge. Diaz, tethered to his chair by a long string, was walking up and down the aisle in between the securities desk and the derivatives traders. He was 'in character'. Diaz had just the two personae in his repertoire: an air hostess and the Pope.

As the air hostess he minced around imitating engine noise, passing round sweets, performing the elaborate pantomime of safety drills, pushing a cumbersome, non-existent, drinks trolley. At other times, he would climb onto his chair, wave to the multitude in St Peter's Square and begin to offer blessings to the assembled company in many execrably pronounced languages. On the whole, the traders preferred the air hostess character. It was more upbeat, had punchier dialogue, better special effects (the vacuum jet door sealing itself was more fun than *Adeste, fideles*), and was generally more in tune with an upward-moving, bullish market.

Diaz meandered over to the floppy-haired television

reporter, who was practising a twenty-second stand-up to camera. The journalist looked gloomily at the fat little trader. He had the joyless task of reporting a non-story. The markets hadn't crashed, as the Sunday newspapers had been screaming they would after Friday's mini-dive in New York. The most interesting thing on the dealing room floor was the corpulent little weirdo – and even he was a bore after a couple of minutes.

Samuel watched and smiled at the air hostess act. Khan, sitting at his side, was as unamused as the reporter, but for his own reasons.

'It's harmless, isn't it?' asked Samuel, peering at Khan's frown.

'Harmless self-abuse,' said Khan shortly. 'It's perfectly comprehensible that Diaz should behave like that. It's a conflict between the rational and the irrational. He is debasing a mind not without resource to guess what will happen next in a volatile, fundamentally irrational market.'

Samuel looked at the fifty or so highly intelligent, utterly dedicated people in the flying wedge. Miller, trying to ignore the space next to him where Kaz should have been, flicking through screen after screen; La Brooy, intent on more research, a cowboy tie setting off the gleaming dome of his head; the contented climbers and the frustrated plodders of the various desks; FT, whom he hadn't quite been able to look in the eye since their nocturnal encounter, and Isabelle, speaking softly into her phone. Nobby was inviting people to the house party that was his version of the market.

Could it really be that they were all involved in no more than a fool's enterprise? A kind of futuristic parlour game with lots of electronic gadgetry where the only object was to guess what Simple Simon would do next, a billionaire's version of blind man's buff?

He wiped his brow, and picked up an internal memorandum envelope. At first he thought it was a mistake, that someone had sent him a memo but forgotten to put the paper in. He put his hand down deep to the bottom of the ochre folder and felt again. Yes, there was something after all, but it wasn't paper. He chased it around, pulled the object out and found himself holding it in front of his nose, blinking at it rather stupidly. Between his forefinger and thumb he twirled a long, black, furry object. It was a plume from a feather boa, possibly Sunday night's feather boa.

Diaz gave him a long, slow wink, and advised the wedge to buckle their seat belts, as they were entering a zone where turbulence was anticipated. Samuel looked down at his desk. These were smart people. They didn't miss a thing – and he was close to becoming one of them. They accepted him already. They didn't care about last night. Or if they did, they approved – it was a rite of passage in their eyes. Perhaps he should forget the whole thing, abandon the whole idealistic nonsense of seeking the truth, of succeeding where his father had failed, making a difference. He would make a good trader, after all. Khan had said so. Maybe he should substitute power for truth.

'Here. Take this.'

A paper floated out of Khan's immaculately manicured hand onto Samuel's desk. It was a buy order for 50 million barrels of Brent Crude oil futures. With the price of spot oil at around $60 dollars, this represented an investment of $3 billion.

'I want you to handle this one for me,' said Khan. 'But remember, we have to pay only a tiny percentage of the contract's notional price. If things go our way the clearing houses will not require us to pay any more than our initial deposit – there'll be no margin calls. Now, tell me how you propose to execute such a transaction.'

Samuel reflected. There was little in the market to beat a modicum of common sense and plenty of low, animal cunning.

'The oil futures market is highly liquid, but I suspect an order of this magnitude will move the price significantly if it isn't handled properly.'

Khan nodded.

'So the thing to do would be to spread the order around as much as possible. Put it out to, say, half a dozen firms.'

Khan raised an eyebrow.

'OK, maybe a dozen firms, in smaller parcels. That way you keep the price reasonably low. Like laying a big bet at the racecourse. You get lots of people to make largish bets, and that way the bookies don't notice the amount of money going on one horse until it's too late. Whereas if you make one huge bet they shorten the odds straight away.'

'OK, but what's the downside of your strategy?'

Samuel considered. He had never been asked to improvise a plan involving a few billion dollars' worth of anything before.

'Erm, confidentiality, I suppose. On the basis that nothing's a secret if more than one person knows, this kind of move is going to get out.'

'Right. It's trading in a goldfish bowl. The best that you can hope for is that most of your parcels of five and ten million can be purchased before the market notices the move and ratchets the price up.'

Samuel scratched his head. What made Khan so certain that the oil price was going to shoot up?

'There isn't going to be a war in the Middle East, if that's what you're thinking,' Khan said in that uncanny way he had of answering unvoiced questions. 'It's just that I have it on rather good authority that there have been some particularly nasty private beheadings in Joqar this past week.'

'How many kinds of beheadings are there?'

'Well, one doesn't normally expect the prisoner's family to be obliged to watch, Samuel. Just not the done thing.'

'And the crimes?'

'The crime. Singular. The crime is that of knowing too much about one of the biggest cover-ups in the history of the financial markets.'

Samuel looked out of the window at Garnier's master-piece of a marshmallow wedding cake. The Opéra was still there. The world was still turning. Everything appeared just as before.

'Falsified geology reports. Mass manipulation of the market. Three billion barrels of oil supposed to be lying under the earth in Joqar. The biggest reserves in the world. Ninety per cent of it does not exist.'

'Who would lie about that?'

Khan sighed slightly. 'Just about everyone. The Americans, in particular, don't want and can't afford expensive oil. The rise that they have had to bear over the last few years is as much as they can take. The political and racial tension there is already twice as bad as a decade ago. Toss the spark of a severe, oil inflation-induced recession into the powder keg and you get a pretty explosion of the race-war variety. Nine/eleven dented confidence around the world. This will make a more fundamental difference; the world will become a much, much more expensive place.'

'And the Joqars? Wouldn't they object? They've got something that's really more precious than the market's now pricing it, and it's being sold off at a discount? Why would they want to do the Americans and the West a favour?'

'Domestic power struggle is the short answer. Joqar is sophisticated in part, but is fundamentally tribal. It has its competing dynasties. Better for the powerful tribe to remain so with the help of the Americans. That way the ruling house, rather than its rivals, gets to spend the wealth of the nation. If it has to be done at a brutal discount to keep the West happy, so be it.'

'It's an incredible story.'

'But probably true. The vicious slaughter of all those in any way connected with the cover-up tends to lend credibility. And I had the information from an impeccable source. Someone I met at one of Patrice Gourdon's backgammon parties, you know.'

Diaz strolled by, offering a choice of mignons of ostrich steak or golden-breaded goujons of sole, followed by an in-flight movie.

'But anyway, Samuel.' Khan shot his cuffs and smiled a buccaneer's smile. 'To business. The call I've been waiting for for two days came through just now, and we are going to set Ropners athwart the high seas of finance. Three billion dollars of her own capital at notional risk. Where's Brent Crude trading?'

'But if all this is happening in Joqar, why aren't we playing the Joqari sweet light contract?'

'Too obvious, dear boy. And not practical. We can't place big orders in Joqari sweet light. The market's too small, and the price would rocket after the first buy was satisfied. We'll have to go into Brent Crude, which is much, much bigger. If the news is too big for the market, trade in Joqari sweet may even be suspended. Oil is oil is oil. If the Joqari reserves are mainly fictional, oil everywhere becomes far more precious.'

Samuel looked at him with new respect. If Khan knew this kind of thing and still remained calm, what did he do for excitement?

'OK, Samuel. Right or wrong, let's get to work. Name your counterparties.'

Samuel had already moved into overdrive. How sharply would the oil price rise on the news that a major oil reserve was no more than a figleaf for American political stability? Fifteen per cent? Fifty? It would be the Six Day War all over again, and after it would come falls in the world stock markets, credit squeezes, and a long, horrible recession. But Khan and Ropners would come out of it with a huge win. A result, as the traders liked to say.

Samuel named a few banks and names he trusted.

'Let's go,' said Khan softly. He jabbed at a button and waited for the pre-programmed number to dial out.

The New York voice crackled a short greeting from the speaker. They wasted little time on formalities.

'What are you calling the market?' asked Samuel.

'Unchanged to five cents down.'

He could hear the background noise from the traders on their Broadway trading floor. His heart was pounding. Time to drop the depth charge.

'OK. Thanks for the temperature gauge. I have an order for you. How close are you to market opening, by the way?'

'Oh, we're counting down now. Forty-five seconds.' The speaker-phone voice was relaxed, full of metropolitan complacency.

'Buy five million Brent June on the opening,' he said, his

own voice an instrument of authority and command. 'Then let the ripples settle, and buy five more. Then, if we haven't set the place on fire, another two.'

'That's twelve million! It's your business, buddy, but are you sure that you want to take the market on quite so ... boldly?' There was no urbanity now. This was a year's salary in commission.

'Nice of you to ask. Just go and do it.'

'OK. You got it.'

The background speaker static suddenly turned into a high-volume tank battle. New York had opened. Order placed. The sound clicked off.

Then he put a further eight million into play through Frankfurt. The dealer on the other end of the line swallowed that one whole, no questions asked.

Next up, Geneva.

'Hello?' A heavily accented French-Swiss voice.

'I have something for you.'

Was his tension audible?

'What can I do you for?'

A Swiss joke – it had scarcity value, if little else.

'Three million Brent June.'

'You buying or selling?'

'Buying. A casual interest.'

A whistle. Over $180 million worth of casual interest.

'Sixty-two dollars seventy a barrel in high activity. Mmm. Do you definitely want to deal?'

'Yes, we fancy oil today.'

'Everything will be taken care of.'

The speaker went quiet. But not for long.

'Whoa! We're at $62.75 and counting! What are you guys up to?'

'We aren't up to anything. Oil seems to be in demand today,' he said, smiling to himself. He shot a sly glance sideways towards Khan, who was standing close by, nodding gently, the corners of his mouth turned up slightly.

'Why's oil climbing?' asked the Swiss.

'Who knows?' said Samuel, leaning forward into the desktop speaker. 'Are you going to get that order for us, or do I park our business elsewhere?'

'Don't move.'

A few seconds of frantic noise from the speaker filled the air. The fire was beginning to take hold around the world. The Geneva trader came back, excited but nervous.

'We're filling it now. I just thought maybe you would be wanting, ah, to come at this sideways. You know – discretion, valour, that kind of thing?'

'Just do it.'

He could feel the surge of excitement, the thrill of power, shooting through his veins. Now he was really trading. He was the lightning conductor for all the rich, concentrated energy of the market, and he could direct it where he liked. He was harnessing all the might of the bank's assets at their disposal, and he was about to muscle a gigantic global market his way. It was as though he could wrap up every floor, every screen, every trader in the world into one huge football and then volley it out into space, booted there by the leverage of his billion-dollar book.

Out in the street, the hurly-burly was just the same – pedestrian bustle, traffic noise, the tired old urban pantomime. The world was about to change radically. Billions of people would be affected. Most would become poorer, but he would make some – a few, a very select few – immensely richer.

Two minutes later, Geneva was back to him.

'Hi, Samuel, we've news for you. The . . .'

'Yes, yes. What?' Samuel was crouched forward, shouting into the desktop speaker, just like everyone else in the flying wedge, just like everyone else in this vast, global market. But the speaker was silent. The display was wiped.

'What's this?' He turned to Khan.

'Looks like circuit failure, localized to us.'

Samuel saw that the rest of the floor was still moving at the same frenetic pace, the traders gabbling volubly, transfixed by their screens.

'Damn. We're almost there. I'll get that Geneva number, in a second. It's downstairs in my document store, in my address book old fashioned paper, would you believe?'

'I would, Khan, I would,' Samuel grinned at him. 'But we may not need it. I have it, I think . . .'

Samuel focused on the blank screen in front of him and dredged up the image that had disappeared. He hadn't paid much attention to it, maybe, maybe he could bring it to the front of his mind – the colours, the number, the caller ID, the full number just below it. He picked up a handset and quickly jabbed in the eighteen-digit specialized dealer number for the Geneva bank – 00 41 22 3472 . . .

'There you are,' said the French-Swiss voice. 'What happened?'

'Just a glitch,' said Samuel. He could feel Khan's approval, but did not look at him. The victory had to be claimed first. 'So what's the news?'

'Good, basically. It's done, but the market's up near the limit. We had to fill the last batch at $62.90.'

'What's the average?'

'About $62.83. Are you guys about to drop a nuke on Baghdad or Riyadh or something?'

Samuel laughed, intoxicated by the feeling of power and control: 'You saw what the Gulf War did to the oil price? The market was flat as a pancake for weeks. And nobody's ever going to be fencing nuclear weapons while the words "September 11th" mean anything to the CIA. We're just in there for a quick turn.'

'Whatever. Rumour is that Ropners is behind this buying wave. I bet this isn't the only order you've placed today.'

Samuel said nothing. A massive roar came from the Geneva end of the line. The day was not so quiet after all. The trader screamed that he had to go and hung up.

Khan turned away from his desk and locked into Samuel's gaze. There was a similar light in their eyes, a mutual acknowledgement of the feeling of excitement and power they shared: And On The Eighth Day He Created The Market.

'What's the limit on the Brent June?' The moment had passed. Khan was all business now.

'$63.10, I believe.'

Trying to restrain his excitement, Samuel resolved to adopt the pose of the Whitehall Mandarin. Because of the volatility of the oil futures contract, the regulatory authorities insisted that it only be allowed to rise or fall by a specified amount – usually one dollar – per day. So speculative losses and gains, and above all the frenzy that went with speculation, were stopped. Once Brent June reached $63.10, trading would be over for the day – unless someone was prepared to do a deal below the limit.

'Bought four million at $63.05. Repeat four at $63.05,' screamed an almost unintelligible Euro-trader voice out of one of the speakers at Khan's desk. The Eurotrader's accent and grammar had crumbled under the gargantuan pressure. 'Working four more. It will be a scramble to fill it below your limit.'

'That's my boy,' called back Khan. He turned again to

Samuel. 'That's also my last order. We're loaded up once this one's done.' Khan began to reach for his jacket, which he filled with an assortment of phones and beepers. 'At which point I believe I shall be able to make my engagement for tea after all. You know how to reach me, Samuel. In case of emergency, send a taxi to Angelina's on the rue de Rivoli.'

Samuel nodded. Khan had just put the vast majority of the bank's proprietary capital in play, and was now heading off to a fashionable teashop. But then Khan had taken his stance and already seen that the market was with him. The cracked voice of the Eurotrader announced that the order was executed, just under the Brent June limit. And – amid a deafening shout from the Eurotraders' pit – the limit had been reached. Ropners was sitting on a position that could treble the size of its proprietary trading book if this move continued.

The rise in oil futures had at first hardly been noticed in the other markets. But inevitably, the price of 'spot' oil, which wasn't subject to a limit, had risen sharply in response to the price that the market was making for the commodity in three months' time. The higher oil price and the rumour of a significant open futures position had created concerns among share traders. There were losses across the board, with the exception of oil refiners and explorers, who were expected to benefit from the move. At $63 per barrel, oil-shale fields on the west coast of Wales would become profitable, Khan had murmured with a small grin. Samuel had wondered if his boss had already bought some property there.

An animal wail from the far corner of the room.

'Bloomberg! Oh God, look at Bloomberg!'

Somebody punched up the wire service onto the presentation screen at the back of the trading floor. There was a moment's silence.

16.50 GMT. URGENT. ATTENTION FOREIGN AND
ECONOMICS EDITORS. EX: BBN/BLOOMBERG
BUSINESS NEWS. URGENT NEWSFLASH.
URGENT.

JOQARI OIL MINISTER QADIF ANWAR
BEHEADED YESTERDAY. JOQARI GOVERNMENT
SPOKESMAN CITES CRIMES AGAINST STATE.

ENDS

A moment of pure, stunned disbelief and fear in the flying wedge. The fear of not knowing. What did it mean? And then everyone began shouting at the same time. The Reuters screen was showing spot oil activity. Prices were heading upwards. Fast.

'Keep in touch. I'll be back in an hour,' said Khan. Samuel watched him leave the floor. A slow, deliberate walk. The swing of the immaculately tailored suit somehow made him seem taller, more powerful. Almost like a – yes, that was it! – like a gunslinger. The slight, milk-chocolate-coloured man had the power to stun a universe hanging loosely, invisibly, from his impeccably manicured fingertips.

Now, with their position at least momentarily secure, Samuel could watch developments. From a quiet morning with Diaz as trolley-pusher, there had been a seamless transition, via sporadic barking and shouting, through small, intense bursts of mania, to the scene he now beheld: a group of adults doing an impromptu rendition of full-blown tactical nuclear warfare, with telephones and screens for weapons, and no fall-out bunkers. It seemed that everyone in the flying wedge was screaming and shaking. Phones were slammed, direct-link buttons punched in a spirit of fury and vengeance. It was gospel-house hysteria, and the god was Mammon.

The equity markets were moving down sharply now. With them went bonds, as investors sold, fearing higher inflation on the back of the move in the oil price which could lead to an upward move in interest rates. The derivatives desks were going mad. Positions with stop-losses were being redefined by the second. There was no doubt which market was in the driving seat. The mainstream markets in shares and bonds plummeted as oil, the lubricant of the world economy, shot up. Samuel watched Nobby on the derivatives desk. He was standing up, a phone in each ear, bellowing something inaudible at a patch-radio link. Samuel doubted that the person on the other end could hear much either. Then, with no warning, Nobby slammed down the black phone in his right hand and shrieked into the radio link.

'Sell two million at 146. I mean buy two million at 146!' A minute later, he picked up the phone again and shouted, 'I meant buy two million at 146!'

'Sorry, Nobby! You've already dealt.'

Nobby crumpled onto his desk, with his head in his hands. The dealer on the other end of the phone managed to buy back two million of whatever contract Nobby had been trading at the same price. The result was that Nobby's position was unchanged, except for the deduction of the commission on the transaction that the counterparty would make. 'Heart of stone, mind of steel. On the phone, do the deal' – the dealers' mantra. Seeing Nobby's despair made Samuel feel guilty. He was finding it hard not to show his delight at the chaos that he and Khan had caused in the markets, but now he realized the distress that others were feeling as a result was real.

A light flashed at his desk.

'Khan?'

He felt faintly amused that his boss wasn't so relaxed as to enjoy his tea with perfect equanimity.

'Everything's fine, Khan. Brent June's never going to pop out of limit with the spot market going up a yard a second. We have made a ten per cent profit on our position already and counting.'

'And everything else?'

'The equity markets are rolling around in the gutter, as you predicted. Have you been selling short? Not that a few million would make much difference to Ropners given the kind of leverage we've got in Brent June.'

'And how much is that again?'

'Why, you know . . .' A cold, spiky ball of fear expanded inside his stomach and then shot out through his limbs. By the time it reached his fingers and toes it had transformed itself to the unwelcome, jittery heat of pure panic. That voice. So perfect an imitation. It wasn't Khan.

'Who is this? Who is this?'

'This is José Nissan from the *Mercury Inquirer*. Thank you for confirmation that Khan is behind today's rape of the oil market. Did he know about the execution in Joqar, or did he just arrange it?'

'I have nothing to say to you,' replied Samuel in his most professional voice.

'You've already said plenty. Tell me, do Khan's analytical staff have names, or can anyone pick up his phone?'

'You have no right to call up impersonating a member of this bank.'

Samuel had to get off the phone before Nissan recognized his voice. He could see the screaming headlines: 'OXFORD DON DOES DIRTY IN OIL MARKET'.

'Says who? I called looking for Khan and ended up with a

data dump. For which thank you, by the way. The one thing I don't have is your name, but I think I know who you are, anyway.'

Samuel was furious with himself. They both knew that Nissan had tried to sound like Khan. But Samuel had been overconfident, proud, drunk on the power of it all. The price of hubris was instant.

The scene about him now was almost unendurable. Human beings were not supposed to sustain this kind of intensity for so long. The phone princesses were screaming and chewing gum, a senior trader was running up and down the equities and derivatives desks, urging people to 'close it out, close it out!' Nobby was back on the phones; Diaz was talking manically into his console and biting at his nails in between times. Miller had emerged from his lair and was on the phone at Kaz's desk. The eyes staring out of his thin face seemed to see a vision of Gethsemane hanging somewhere just outside the window. Ovid was steadfastly backfielding calls others were unable to take. He was repeating the house line that this was a sharp correction. But he must have been suppressing a tremendous urge to claim vindication of his views.

Now Samuel envied them.

He knew what was coming, and monitored the news wires. There was little information from Joqar itself. Samuel guessed that this would not be for lack of reporting, so much as the cleverness of the news editors. They had their correspondents in place, and they had to strike a fine balance between reporting what went on and keeping their people out of jail. It was easy to go to jail in Joqar. The Joqaris were not renowned for their respect for Western concepts of justice, let alone freedom of speech.

The email icon flashed on Samuel's laptop screen. Khan had been monitoring the markets from whatever teashop or art gallery he was in, and was pleased with the day's developments. He would be in tomorrow. Samuel had been gathering the nerve to call him, but, until the news of Khan's involvement actually hit the marketplace, maybe it was better to keep quiet. It wouldn't affect Khan's market position – if anything, the oil price would move up further.

Khan would know soon enough, as the wires flitted across his own laptop screen. But Samuel felt an acute sense of paralysis. He would have to tell Khan that Nissan had duped him as his phone was recorded. How swiftly he was paying for his few moments of glory. He was now ignoring incoming calls, leaving the voicemail to deal with them as he watched the oil market continue to go Khan's way.

It happened just before nine. The team in the flying wedge were exhausted, just about ready to wind up for the day, when it came through on the wires. The London newspapers habitually 'flashed' early electronic copies of their front pages to the news agencies, in the hope of attaining extra publicity for their best stories, and of course a few extra sales.

Agence France-Presse was first with the story. Samuel saw the bullet identifiers in the list of newly posted items, and clicked it up on his screen.

19.41 GMT. MARKET SLIDE-KHAN-GURU.
EURO/FIN NEWS BUDGET. ATTENTION
FINANCIAL EDITORS

By Nat Kumble

London – Today's calamitous 12 per cent fall in stock
prices, wiping more than £180 billion ($350 billion) off
share values, was partly the result of proprietary trading

activity, according to a report in the *Mercury Inquirer*, a London newspaper.

The *Mercury Inquirer* alleges that the proprietary trading desk at Ropner Bank in Paris was instrumental in driving oil to five-year highs. Traders in London said that shares and bonds sank on twin fears of recession and inflation occasioned by the spike in oil.

The principal proprietary trader at Ropners, which is understood to have made a $3 billion-plus bet on a higher oil price, is the enigmatically named Khan. The trader was unavailable for comment Thursday, but an unnamed source within Khan's Ropner Bank offices in Paris confirmed his involvement in the oil futures market.

Investment industry observers see Khan's oil play – perfectly timed ahead of news of internal troubles in the oil-rich state of Joqar – as the latest move in a series of spectacular market coups that have catapulted the trader to international prominence.

The rest of the story was a reworking of cuttings about Khan. Typical news-wire copy. The journalist had rehashed Nissan's story and tacked on a few clichés from library clips. Not much chance of picking up a phone and doing some research himself, given the time pressure those guys worked under.

'Unnamed source within Khan's Ropner Bank offices in Paris.' That was pretty specific. The journalist must have lifted that directly from Nissan's copy in the *Inquirer*. He began to gather his things together in preparation for the journey home.

'You messed up.'

Miller had ghosted to his desk. Samuel looked up. The thin mouth was toying with the idea of a grin.

'Excuse me?' Samuel looked calmly into Miller's emotion-less eyes.

'You messed up, Mr Unnamed Source.'

Samuel blinked and remained silent.

'I'll be listening to the tapes of the day's trading tonight. It seems that by staying loyal – sorry, by trying to stay loyal – to your rock-star boss you've done him a bigger disservice than anyone could have hoped.' There was a definite smirk on Miller's face now.

And then he was gone, padding silently down the corridor. Samuel wondered how much money the man had lost for the bank and for his clients that day. Probably tens, maybe hundreds of millions. But Miller was happy, because the Khan desk had screwed up.

Samuel ruminated for a few moments, then picked up the phone to call Khan. May as well get it over with.

'Excuse me, sir.'

Samuel looked round. Miller was standing there again, eyes glinting. With him were the two police agents, Blondeau and Bouchinet.

'Yes? I thought we were going to sort this out in your offices later in the week.'

Blondeau looked at Bouchinet, smiled, then turned back to Samuel. 'Yes, sir. But that was before. We have found your former colleague, Mademoiselle Day.'

'Thank God!' The relief was palpable. At least something good was happening that day. 'She'll confirm what I told you then.'

'I doubt it, Monsieur. Mademoiselle Day is dead. Her body was discovered this afternoon in the canal by Parc des Villettes. Not only were you the last person seen with her, but her mobile telephone shows that yours was the last number she called.'

'What! This is ridiculous. You're joking!'

'I'm afraid not, sir.'

'Let me call Khan. This is incredible.'

'There's no time for that, sir. I must ask you to come with me now.' Blondeau laid a hand on Samuel's shoulder – the ancient gesture of arrest. 'Immediately, please.'

'I HEAR you speak good German.'

'That's correct. My family came from Germany.'

He wondered how much else the older man knew about him. The call had come to his office, a casual invitation to lunch from a total stranger. One who wanted to discuss 'government business'.

'Would you say that you were good at languages?'

'Well, I'm developing some good skills in computing and finance – languages all of their own.'

The older man didn't smile at the pleasantry. The awkwardness was ended by the arrival of a matronly waitress at their booth who took their sandwich order and served them a refill of coffee.

'What do you think of strikes?'

'Pardon me?'

'Strikes. People withdrawing their labour. What do you make of it?'

'Well, I guess I would say I approve of what President Reagan did with the air traffic controllers back in the 1980s. He broke the union. The country can't be held to ransom like that.'

'That was years ago. What about now?'

'I guess we're facing different problems. We've beaten Communism...'

'You can never be complacent about that,' said his host.

'Absolutely, sir, absolutely.'

He instinctively put his hand to his head and felt the bald patch on the crown. He understood what was happening all right. But while the guy quizzing him was hardly subtle and might not beat him in a problem-solving contest, he was obviously very shrewd. The older man's eyes had a searing, penetrative quality about them. They were the kind of eyes that would spot a phoney word in an instant.

'If you're wary of Communists, how come your father used to go on business to East Germany?'

'It's where my family came from, where he was born.'

'Is your family important to you?'

'Family is important, yes. I hope to have kids of my own one day.'

'Good, good.'

Their food arrived. The older man asked for catsup, and talked about sports and the crazy liberal bias of the media for the rest of the meal. There were a few honourable exceptions – that bright young newspaper guy William Barton, he was a good guy. Pro-business.

The older man picked up the tab and made the waitress sign the back of the receipt. Just in case it wasn't quite clear that they were spending taxpayers' money.

13

'So ...' Inspector Blondeau's heels clicked on the tiled floor of the windowless room. He stopped, reached out a hand, and twitched at a plain white sheet covering an object on the table. It fell away at once, like a conjuror's device, to reveal a cold, white, naked body. Samuel gasped. He saw flowery blue blotches beneath a skin rendered translucent in death. The hair was matted and dank, and when he forced himself to look again, he noticed scores of small cuts, abrasions and puckerings. There was also a large gash near the hip that looked very deep, with what might have been bite marks of some sort at the edges of the aperture. He shuddered.

'Three days in the canal, we think. Maybe four.' Blondeau paused and lit a cigarette with elaborate care. He exhaled: a blue-grey smoke that rolled out of his nostrils and drifted over the body's slender abdomen – a minor act of desecration. At last he looked up and caught Samuel's eye. 'The eels and parasites had only just begun to enjoy their feast. Even beauty such as that possessed by Mademoiselle Day does not survive three days in the water.'

Samuel averted his eyes from Kaz's ravaged, water-wrinkled face. Blondeau was looking directly at him.

'A tragedy, no?'

Samuel did not respond.

'Here. Relax.' Blondeau stepped lightly next to Samuel, and took his hand. The next second the policeman pressed Samuel's palm to the dead woman's thigh. 'Here, Monsieur Spendlove. This is how the dead feel. The texture of waxy bacon. And so cold. The coldness of death.'

Samuel could smell the tobacco on Blondeau's chesty breath. He looked away, into the corner of the strip-lit room, trying not to think of Kaz's chilled skin against the puffy warmth of his fingers. He was aware that Bouchinet and the two uniformed men by the steel door were watching him intently.

'Stop this. Stop this,' he managed to breathe. He could feel acid pumping in his stomach. 'What do you want?'

'It has an unforgettable texture, no? The dead flesh. Some who handle corpses claim that the smell stays with them for days. Personally, I find washing-up liquid and a little lemon juice quite remove the odour.'

Samuel still did not look down. Blondeau maintained a steady pressure on his hand. He could feel the cold, slightly greasy hairs of Kaz's pubic mound against the side of his fingers. Blondeau looked up into his eyes. The two men were inches apart, a parody of lovers united in grief.

'You will tell me the truth, Monsieur Spendlove, before our esteemed colleagues and friends from America come poking their noses into a crime committed on French soil. Why did you kill her?'

'I didn't kill her.' How to make this man desist? 'I ... did ... not ... kill ... her.'

'Of course not. You didn't smash her head with whatever it was. A car jack? You didn't stab her in the side. And when we rip her womb apart, it won't be your semen we find, will it?'

'How dare you!'

The blow landed almost as the words left Samuel's mouth. Blondeau struck him a short, hard jab to the point of the chin. The power of the punch lifted him backwards, and he fell to the floor. Bouchinet retreated to the corner of the room

'No, no, Monsieur. The question is, how do you dare? How do you dare to come to this country and set yourself up as a king? You and your friends and your international bank and your international ways of living. You can eat, drink and fornicate like pigs. You can treat the people who made this country what it is like peasants. "Love France, shame about the French" – that is the way of these barbarian imbeciles, no? You can do all these things. But you cannot violate our laws. You cannot take life at your pleasure. This is one piece of shit that you and your clever banking friends will have to pay to clean up.'

Samuel got up slowly and rubbed a hand across his lip. As he took the punch he had bitten his cheek, and blood trickled from his mouth. He smeared it away, scenting briefly the smell of dead flesh on his fingers. He looked around. The two guards gazed back at him impassively. Bouchinet was smiling slightly at his discomfort.

'Look, Inspector. Have you considered the man who attacked me? The big, black man who hit me outside Kaz Day's flat on Sunday night? The neighbours opposite will back me up. And there was an old lady night-walking her dog.'

'We have talked to one of the neighbours, yes. But she is old and her memory is, well, unreliable. And we have you. You, at least, are not a fantasy.' Blondeau walked across to Bouchinet. Without a word she produced a handkerchief. Blondeau's anger seemed softened by his outburst. He gave it to Samuel.

'We are looking at a number of things, Monsieur. But we are looking very closely at you. Why were you so interested in her? It was more than sex, certainly.'

'Why do you think I was so interested in her?'

Samuel was standing next to the trolley where Kaz lay. Blondeau and Bouchinet occupied two fold-up seats, side-by-side, like a pair of auditioning directors. Bouchinet withdrew a packet from her inside jacket pocket. One of the guards walked across to Samuel with it.

'I see.'

Samuel flipped through the sharp-focus black-and-white pictures – outside the Bourdelle Museum, loitering by the club in the fourteenth, the dinner in the Café Beaubourg, the night walk back to Samuel's flat.

'Well, if you've had me under such close surveillance, you'll know that I didn't do this.'

'That's just what we don't know. You disappeared after your fight with . . . after your fight.'

'So you do know about the fight, then?'

'We know that you were the last person to see her alive. We know that yours was the last number she dialled from her mobile. What we don't know is why you killed her.'

There was a sharp knock at the door before Samuel could respond. A guard moved.

'If that's Pathology, tell them to wait. I'm not finished here,' said Blondeau, staring directly at Samuel.

A quiet conference followed across six inches of space. The door eventually closed.

'It's not Pathology, boss . . .' began the guard, but he was interrupted.

'No, it's not. I am here to represent my client, and I demand to know by what right you detain and question him.' Lauren walked slowly across the room, all dark-suited business poise, and looked into Samuel's face. She touched the side of his blood-smeared mouth lightly, and turned to Blondeau.

'What's this, Inspector? A fall, I suppose.'

'This man is a suspect in a murder case. I have every right to interrogate him . . .' Blondeau looked down at the business card that Lauren had deposited in his hand. 'Maître-Avocat de la Geneste.'

'And this? You have the right to do this?' Lauren wiped a handkerchief over Samuel's mouth and held up the blood smear. 'And this?' She gestured at Kaz's body without looking at it. 'What kind of interrogation procedure is this, Monsieur l'Inspecteur? You know that my client is entitled to legal representation and yet you have embarked upon an extremely unorthodox course without affording him that right.'

'I was confronting this man with his crime, no more.' There was an edge in Blondeau's voice that belied the confidence of his statement.

'This is irregular, and you know it.'

Lauren placed a hand on Samuel's shoulder. 'Come. It's time we left here.'

'You will do no such thing. I have more questions to ask.'

'Until Monsieur Spendlove has no more teeth in his head? We shall of course entertain questions and assist in every possible way with your inquiries, Monsieur. But given the gross breach of my client's civil rights and the serious denial of human rights, plus flagrant abuse of the procedures that natural justice requires under the European convention, I propose that any further interrogation should take place at my offices at a time to be agreed, and in my presence.'

Blondeau's eyes hardened, but Lauren did not shrink from the challenge.

'Unless, that is, you have the evidence to charge him now.'
Blondeau half-turned from her, then flapped a hand.

'Very well, Mademoiselle de la Geneste. But I shall require
surety from you, an undertaking as to his good conduct, and
the surrender of Monsieur Spendlove's passport. He is an
important part of our investigation, a very important part.'

'Done, Inspector. Shall I attend to the formalities with your
colleague?' Lauren shot a look at Bouchinet, who stood up
even before Blondeau nodded agreement. Lauren sidestepped
the mortuary table without so much as a downward glance,
and stalked out of the room with Samuel at her heels.

'I shall see you again, Monsieur Spendlove. Very soon, I
believe,' called out Blondeau. Samuel closed the door behind
him, somewhat bemused by Lauren's unexpected intervention.

The formalities were conducted by a deliberately unco-
operative desk sergeant, and took the best part of an hour.
Eventually, Lauren and Samuel settled in the back of a taxi and
began to head west, finally free to talk.

'Lauren, you were brilliant. How did you find me?'

Lauren stared at the back of the taxi driver's neck and said
nothing.

'Are you OK? Thanks a thousand times for retrieving me
from that mess. I don't know what I'd have done without
you . . .' Then he noticed a large tear running down Lauren's
cheek.

'What's wrong? Can I help?'

He took her hand. She did not resist, but shook her head
slowly.

'Lauren, please speak to me. What's wrong?' He spoke in
English now, as a way of keeping the driver at a distance. He
squeezed her hand gently, but got no response. The wheels
thrummed on the cobblestone boulevard. At last she spoke.

'You don't understand, Samuel. It's not your fault. You don't understand.' The last words were spoken as a choked sob. Samuel stroked her hand gently, and waited.

'I . . . I didn't come to see you, Samuel. I came to see her.'

Samuel drew her to him, and clasped an arm over her shoulder as she began a long, shuddering series of silent sobs. The taxi thundered on towards Trinité and Saint Lazare. Twilight was falling, and Samuel didn't really know where they were going.

14

THE DOORBELL RANG.

'*J'arrive, j'arrive,*' grumbled Samuel, and reached for his dressing gown. For a moment he couldn't remember where he was, then it flooded back – the cab ride to Lauren's flat; her tearful refusal to be comforted or to let him stay; the fear-filled and lonely journey home; the glugged bottle of wine, the troubled dreams – brutal assailants in the shadows, the dead, naked Kaz walking towards him, demanding his passport.

The bell went again, and Samuel cast around despairingly for something to wear. His clothes were fetid and pushed into a crumpled pile, like leftover salad. He kept up a continuous, audible mumbling as he searched vainly for something to lend him an air of respectability. Eventually, he settled on a bath towel.

'You?'

Samuel wasn't sure what he'd been expecting. Certainly not the large, red-haired man who filled the doorframe.

'You look like shit,' said McMurray. 'You do realize your phone's out of order?'

He glanced down to his right. Yes, the phone jack had been pulled out of its socket – one way of ensuring a good night's sleep. McMurray pushed brusquely past him. Samuel gestured with a hand.

'Do come in. Please.'

'Well, I will, but this is not a social call. Here!'

The editor thrust a newspaper and a heavy black refuse bag at him. Samuel put the bag down and stared at the paper dumbly, as though it were a tablet of hieroglyphs.

Eventually it made sense to his fuddled brain. His old acquaintance José Nissan had eaten him up and spat him out. Nissan got a good, solid start on Khan's coup in the markets, and had quoted Samuel as the source in Khan's office. There was an ancient picture of Samuel as an undergraduate, wearing an academic gown and a foolish grin.

'You've buggered up, Spendlove. A few weeks in Paris, in the sodding sweetheart centre of it all, and you've not just been scooped – you're the prime source for the opposition's story!'

But Samuel was a side-show – the main side-show, admittedly – but still minor compared to the major attraction. The paper was dominated by one word in 56-point bold type:

MELTDOWN

The *Mercury Inquirer* had marshalled its forces well. Writers in New York, Frankfurt, Tokyo, Hong Kong and London had a joint byline on a piece that chronicled a day of mounting panic across the world's markets. The rampant oil price, the failure of the international regulatory authorities to take joint responsibility and coordinate their action, the lack of sustained, publicly announced government intervention – all these had helped panic turn into financial freefall.

The splash was a masterpiece of popular journalism, entitled 'How They've Betrayed Us All'. The article was a collage of discontent, fear and anger across the wide spectrum of those directly affected by the crisis. There were interviews with pensioners, whose nest eggs had suddenly dropped 20 per cent in value, with car dealers who said that Jaguars and Porsches would lose most value as investors' wealth was eroded.

Financial dealers predicted a massive recession and thousands of job losses. Some estate agents claimed that there would be a flurry of interest in property as money fled from shares into 'something solid'. But the older agents knew that when wealth evaporated in shares, it inevitably had a catastrophic effect on residential property. A senior partner at a national estate agency predicted huge price retrenchment, and 'a downward spiral of perhaps ten years, unless the authorities can produce a miracle'.

Some of the more extreme international reactions had been included: the proprietor of a New York bar, The Raging Bull, just off Wall Street, told how his windows had been smashed by a mob seeking vengeance on the money types who they felt had stolen their savings. The bar owner, pictured next to the shattered shop front, was a model of equanimity as he stated that, even though thousands of dollars of damage had been done to his business, he 'understood how the perpetrators felt'. In Hong Kong, the government had moved in to quell the protest marches in the financial district. There was a big picture of a soldier with red stars on his tunic sitting outside a tank in front of the Hong Kong stock exchange. Finally, there was a brief quote from a stress helpline spokesman. There had been an 'unprecedented' number of calls the previous day. He expressed concern that worry and depression could lead to stress-related illness, and ultimately a significant increase in the number of suicides.

The financial overview piece was a detailed market commentary by each correspondent. The New York story told how the Dow-Jones industrial average of leading shares had started the week near the 10,500 mark. The last price for the index before the authorities called for an early close to trade on Friday was below 8,000 – the lowest price since 1996. The whole US market had been valued at almost $6.9 trillion. Now shares were priced at something less than $5 trillion. In other words, twice the annual economic output of France had been lost in the space of two trading sessions. The other market stories told tales of similar losses.

The paper's editor had written a leader, boxed in the centre of the second page of meltdown coverage. In it, he questioned the fundamental efficacy of market correctness. Should society be more concerned with ecology and morality than profit? asked the sage. Samuel smiled to himself. Funny how commentators discovered a conscience when things went belly-up.

The 'basement' piece at the foot of one of the pages was traditionally devoted to something light, witty and irreverent. Not this time. The mood at large was clearly one of undiluted anger; this piece did not ask why the collapse had occurred, but who had made it happen. The answer was swift and stinging – the jackals of capitalism, basically anyone involved in financial markets, but especially proprietary traders and hedge-fund managers. Khan was cited as a major culprit, although the lawyers must have insisted that his absolute denial of personal responsibility be inserted after this allegation. Proprietary traders and hedge-fund managers, readers were told, made billions when markets moved either up or down. They needed to be reined in, or banned from practising legalized criminality. The piece made the people running investment banks sound like pimps – they perverted decent people, seducing them into the markets when they could have been doing something useful in society, like being a physician, an engineer – or an academic.

Samuel swallowed hard at this pointed reference. He looked at the old picture of himself. The word 'gleeful' was printed beneath it, a reference to his triumphalism when Nissan had called.

It was little consolation, but the other obvious targets got vicious treatment. The regulators, who often met for a jolly at their International Organization of Security Controllers conferences, were roundly castigated. 'Why didn't they stick to their elaborate plans for safety nets and shared responsibility?' asked the journalist, more or less reasonably. Instead, the bureaucrats had reverted to recriminations and finger-pointing. So much for the strong relationships forged over many late-night drinks in expensive hotel bars around the world.

Samuel sat down at the little table he worked and ate from, pushed aside an empty bottle of Châteauneuf-du-Pape, and shook his head slowly. He opened the refuse sack; the contents of his desk in the flying wedge were inside. He looked up at the big Scot.

'The concierge here gave it to me when I asked for you,' said McMurray. 'Seems like you've been a bit careless – lost two jobs in one day. The XB Foundation trustees will be writing to you in due course.'

'I was on to something.' Samuel fought a desire to be violently sick. 'But Kaz promised me red meat and then went mad at me, then . . .'

'Then she disappeared, and came to a sticky end,' volunteered McMurray. 'A bit like you, in fact, Spendlove. Where were you when we needed you? The biggest bloody financial story since 1929, and you're nowhere. Well, I'm afraid it's the end of our little arrangement. You're history.'

McMurray reached the door, and turned.

'To be a good researcher requires dedication, talent and a genuine thirst for knowledge.'

'And I just have a genuine thirst – but not for knowledge, right?'

'Yeah, I've already done the hangover check – eyes like M&Ms, little piss-holes in the snow? Empties on your desk? You want to watch out you don't turn into a pisspot like your old man, Spendlove.'

'Good. I'm sacked. No more journalism, no more bank. That's that established. Now do me a favour and go.'

'You, Spendlove, you're a fucking liability.'

McMurray slammed the door, leaving a silence to unfold round Samuel's gentle but persistent headache. He ran to the bathroom where he retched excruciatingly and emptily into the lavatory three times. Then he poured himself a glass of water and went to stand on his balcony. He saw McMurray climb into a waiting taxi.

He watched the taxi negotiate its tortuous way through the teeming traffic, and sipped his water. This was the price of pluralism. You tried to do several jobs, and ended up with none. You tried to please several masters, and everyone was unhappy. He had forsaken academia, Kempis and the Master of Biblos for the thrill of power and the markets. For a moment, a brief moment, he had thrown his lot in with Khan, and had been the master of all he surveyed at the centre of the financial world. But he had discovered that power was the most difficult master of all. He looked down at the jumbled office bric-à-brac in the bin bag, the remnants of his career in finance, the broken shards of academic hopes.

Samuel wondered where Khan was. He could hardly be happy with the media coverage and the blame that was being heaped on his head.

But something told him that he would have to wait to find the answer to these questions. Two police cars had weaved through the traffic and drawn to a stop outside his building. The policemen had got out; some were looking up. It was clear that they had come for him.

'BUT WHY ARE we interested in this company, Frank? It isn't making money.'

The man watched the keen new member of the mergers and acquisitions team ask their senior colleague what ought to have been a perfectly valid question. He himself had been like that once. He used to have that charming naivety. After leaving Harvard, all he wanted to do was to make his millions by building software's version of a better mousetrap. Millions of cleanly earned dollars. It had been so simple then.

'Well, it's about synergy, about how the assets fit with our client's business portfolio and the geographic fit,' responded Frank, who was known as the silver fox of the M&A world and with good reason.

'Their assets? This company makes house bricks for virtually no profit in Portland, Oregon. Our client is a Californian software company that makes good money from a totally different business.' The new recruit turned his attention from Frank. 'Didn't you once run your own company in this sector? I'm sorry to be so dumb, but I just don't see where the fit is here.'

The man smiled, and pulled at a thin wisp of hair – a nervous tic nowadays.

'It's as Frank says. It's the assets we're targeting. Not the operating business.'

'The assets?' A look of understanding was beginning to spread across the new recruit's face.

'The target company has a pile of cash and a site which is worth a fortune to a real estate developer. The market is valuing it on the basis that it's a brick maker. For our client, it is a source of cash, which it needs to continue to grow its business. We could go to the market and do a secondary offering, but this is a much cheaper way to raise the cash.'

'So we're buying the company to strip it of its assets?' asked the trainee.

'I didn't say that,' said Frank. 'But once we've assumed operational control of the company, let's say we will be looking at how to deploy the assets more effectively.'

The novice looked down, said nothing, and the team meeting ended a few minutes later.

After Frank and the trainee had left, the other man stayed behind and doodled briefly on his notepad. He remembered all too well the impulse to talk during such meetings. When he had first joined the bank and been involved in similar deals he wanted to talk about injustice, the unfairness of making an aggressive move on another company and potentially taking away people's livelihoods. But that hadn't stopped takeovers occurring for simple reasons: that someone wanted to get their hands on a company's assets and take the extra cash. The bank wanted the transaction to proceed because it wanted its fee. To a young trainee, it seemed wrong somehow, but one got used to the moral dilemmas that investment banking presented.

That was then, and this was now. He still hated deals like this one, but he had long ago realized that it wasn't his role to shape the strategy of the people who ran the bank. He had another mission next week. That was what he considered his real job. That was his consolation.

15

SAMUEL MOVED QUICKLY round the flat. His eyes flitted back and forth. Suitcase? No. Keys? Yes. Duffel bag? Yes. Laptop? Yes. Wallet? Where? Mobile? Yes. Wallet? Where was the wretched thing? No time. He slipped out of the door, pulled it quietly shut behind him, and trotted down the stairs. The lift was in use – perhaps the police on their way up? Samuel didn't wait to find out.

On the second floor he took the corridor that his building shared with the next-door tenement, slipped down to the sous-sol of that building and was walking out of the back alley into the roar of the rue de Rivoli traffic within two minutes. He cast a swift glance back over his shoulder. The two police cars had aggressively half-mounted the pavement; their lights had been left flashing. Had they come for Samuel? They certainly weren't collecting somebody's parking fine. He fished the mobile out of his duffel bag and dialled.

After fifteen minutes' walk along the river quais, he entered a secluded courtyard in Saint Germain des Prés. The office was on the fourth floor of the old building, and the lift grudgingly hoisted him up with the action of a 1920s sewing machine treadle. At last he pulled the doors aside and rang on the door marked 'Cabinet Mercer'.

A buzz, and he was shown into a tiny waiting room that seemed to have come straight out of the life of Proust. The walls were tiled with cork; the leather furniture had been there for decades. The only modern touch was a large pile of glossy magazines strewn on an ancient coffee table. At last the receptionist beckoned him. He followed her down a narrow corridor to a mahogany door. She knocked and retreated to her desk.

After a few moments, when Samuel had heard nothing, he knocked again.

'*Entrez*,' was the immediate response.

He pushed open the door and found himself looking at a room of subtly ordered, opulent clutter. The space was small and gloomily lit by a tiny window set to the east. Hundreds of leather-bound volumes of decisions of the Cour de Cassation and the Conseil d'État lined the walls. Three tables stood heavily burdened with files and practitioners' textbooks. The atmosphere, designed to impress clients into parting with exorbitant sums, as all such lawyers' parlours were, was one of oppressive erudition.

Lauren looked pale, almost washed out, but her manner was calm, her gestures deliberate. She waved a graceful hand, and he took a seat. He thought of the cab ride, and her terrible distress. His instinct was to step forward and offer a comforting arm. But this would clearly be a mistake. Lauren was all professionalism and had taken out a large Mont Blanc pen and was making notes on a sheet of paper. Samuel waited for her to finish.

She looked up at last.

'You're early. Several hours early.'

'I know. I'm just a bit jumpy staying in the flat at the moment. I feel like a sitting duck. So when I saw the police arrive . . .'

'The police?'

'Yes. I can't be certain that they were coming for me, but I wasn't going to wait to find out.'

He smiled at her. She managed a twitch of the lips in response.

'Lauren, are you all right?' he blurted. 'I . . .'

'Wait, Samuel.' She stood up briskly. 'You can stay here. I have much to do. You will have to amuse yourself. Is that possible?'

'Yes, yes, Lauren. Um, could I just check my emails on the laptop?'

'Of course.'

He half-rose in acknowledgement of her departure, but she didn't look at him. The door clicked shut.

He rummaged impatiently in his bag. It was less than forty-eight hours since Kaz had been found, and, true, Lauren had saved him from God knew what kind of torture by the police. Kaz had clearly been very special to her, but her refusal to be comforted or to acknowledge her pain was difficult to deal with. He was beginning to realize that he too was feeling Kaz's loss. There had only been a few brief minutes of intimacy between them, but if she had survived, their relationship might have developed into something more substantial. He might have been able to save her from the moral decline – the thrill-seeking, the petty thieving – that had taken hold of her. He would have relished the challenge.

His computer was small and light, the newest Super-iMac, a top-of-the-range model. Trainees were not normally allowed to have such swanky kit, but his friendship with François and his status as Khan's boy had allowed him to jump the queue.

He switched the machine on, heard the deep, melodious

power chord as the computer sprang to life. Using the infrared port on his mobile, he logged on for messages. Amid the offers to reduce his debt and enlarge his penis was a file marked 'Samuel – Need To Know'.

'Greetings.'

Samuel did a double take. The computer was speaking to him. The voice was deadened and flattened by the computer read-text programme, but it was recognizable – definitely Khan's. Read-text programmes had advanced significantly over the past few years, but the intonation was still faulty: Khan as robot.

'Just trying out a new wheeze with the speech program. You speak twenty-eight words into the microphone, and the computer has all the vowels sounds, diphthongs, plosives and consonants it needs. It adapts them and adopts your voice. Quite something. If you prefer, Samuel, you can disengage the sound by pressing the control and period commands at the same time.'

Samuel got rid of the sound. Apart from being no fan of primitive cybernetic voice technology, he could read more quickly than the voice speaking the text in the machine.

The note was brief and generous. Khan thanked him for his efforts, his resilience in a crisis and his general helpfulness. He regretted the manner of Samuel's departure and asked him to keep in touch via email. Because of Khan's constant movement this was far more reliable than telephoning – and more intellectually satisfying, 'since one takes the trouble to distil one's thoughts into words rather than just babble down a telephone line'.

Samuel wondered what particular thought-game Khan was distilling with the markets – and with Miller – at that moment.

It was mildly surprising that Miller hadn't repossessed his fantastic laptop. This meant he probably didn't know Samuel had it. There were some consolations in life.

François had also sent an email expressing regret that he'd left Ropners. He thought that Samuel would like to know that Duval, the trader who'd fallen for Khan's fixed income play, had left the country. No one knew where he was, or when he'd be back. As for the mystery emails Samuel had asked about, the best François could come up with was a sender location somewhere in Switzerland. They should have dinner soon, he said, after the unpleasantness was over, and signed off. Samuel sighed and looked at the leather-bound legal volumes in a vain search for inspiration.

He almost deleted the next message. He wanted to see what the internet newswires made of Kaz's death. American, glamorous, a high-powered banker found in a Parisian canal. She had to be a big story. But there was something about the title of the message that told him it wasn't quite the junk it first seemed.

Further And Better Particulars had legal resonance – it was part of the pre-trial pleading in English and Welsh common law cases. The message was from a Yahoo address.

Keep going. Solve Kaz's mystery and you will find what you want. Don't give up, my friend.

Samuel forwarded the latest message to François, more in hope than expectation that he would trace something useful. Then he reread it. *Don't give up, my friend.* Someone was claiming to be on Samuel's side. But who?

He had little time to ruminate on this before Lauren was back. Whereas she had been taciturn before, now she seemed determined to talk. Or should that be lecture? The evils of capitalism were a favoured topic.

'. . . and so we have the final, crushing irony.'

'Excuse me?'

Samuel had endured nearly ten minutes of diatribe, and was beginning to wonder about this woman's mood swings. But he needed her right now. She was his lawyer, his place of sanctuary.

'Institutional Marxism is dead. China is a business anyway, and Cuba has been bankrupt for years. But now they are looking like havens of quiet and peace compared with the failure of the capitalist enterprise.'

A slight sigh, a shifting of her dark suit. Her eyes seemed to be fixed on a point just above his forehead.

'Lauren, I have no urgent need to talk about the forces of history. Tell me about Kaz. What did the police tell you?'

Lauren lit a cigarette and exhaled through her nostrils. 'The police are hopeless. It really does seem that a talent for brutality is all that is required of them. But it's a useful quality in some respects. Reminds one of the truth of one's beliefs.'

Samuel sensed more propaganda on its way. A strange manner of dealing with Kaz's loss. Sure enough, the monologue arrived: 'The instrument of law and the actions of those who enforce it are simply mechanisms for maintaining the control of the establishment and reinforcing the bourgeois sham of equality before the law. If they keep accusing you, soon you will even feel guilty yourself. Guilty of a crime you have not committed.'

She looked at him, suddenly engaged, alert, back in the real world.

'Have you?' She looked at him quizzically.

'Why would you accept my word now, when you yourself thought I'd . . . that I'd . . .'

'Abducted her? Killed her?'

She crushed the barely smoked cigarette.

'No, I don't believe you did those things. When I came to your offices to confront you, I was ... I was distraught. However, it is, as the English say, irritating that you have no alibi – you say you were walking through Paris barefoot at the approximate time of the crime.'

'I told you I was attacked by this huge guy outside Kaz's apartment who tried to dismember me.'

'I know. I know. I have been doing my own research.' She continued, her voice slightly halting now. 'When I discovered the police interest in you, when I heard of the orders to interrogate, their wilful ignorance of this man you fought at Kaz's flat, I knew the machinery of imbecility was grinding into gear again.'

'How did you know they had me, anyway?'

'I am a lawyer, a good one. And I have friends in the police. Perhaps I should rather say contacts.'

'Do some of them frequent that club with you?'

'When and if I choose, yes. I choose what I do with my life, Samuel.' Her tone was that of someone explaining something to a child. 'I choose what kind of company I keep. I choose who shares my bed, what man ... what woman. Whatever I want, in fact. Kaz reserved the same right to choose.' She looked at him intently. Was she waiting for a reaction?

'I'm sorry. I had no right,' said Samuel at last.

'Correct. But it will not surprise you to know that I cared for Kaz. Very much. And I will not let you be the victim of some trumped-up charge. My sources tell me every effort is being made to bring a murder charge against you. You seem to have made a powerful enemy.'

Samuel rubbed instinctively at the knot in his stomach.

'Who? Do you know?'

'It's difficult to tell. The police are such whores. All I know is that someone with a lot of influence doesn't like you. This guy you fought could turn himself in tomorrow and they'd still be looking to pin Kaz's death on you.'

'What a mess.'

'And that's not the least of it. Have you read the French press, maybe watched television here recently?'

Samuel shook his head.

'It's full of the wickedness of the markets. But they miss the point. The wickedness is not the manipulation of the system, but the system itself. Your friend Khan is highly unpopular, as are you.'

Samuel handed her the paper that McMurray had brought by.

'Not just in France. The British press too.'

As Lauren began to read, one of the phones on her desk uttered an urgent digital warble. Samuel dabbed at his laptop and began to scan the newswires as she spoke. By half-focusing on the screen he could gaze over the top at her with relative anonymity. She was just about the most enigmatic woman he had ever met.

He tapped idly at the keyboard. The news from the markets, which already seemed so far away, was no better. A subsidiary of one of the big French banks had ceased to trade. It looked like the French authorities were trying to get ahead of the game – liquidate their assets, cut credit lines, let the weak go to the wall. Shares were down again across Europe, with America expected to open lower yet again. The falls were already far steeper than 1987, 1998, or even those sparked by the Enron and Worldcom scandals or the 9/11 attack.

Lauren was dealing with what sounded like the finance director of a multinational. She was assuring him that if he really had been badly advised by his bankers of course he could sue. Samuel made a motion to leave, to allow her a moment's privacy. She gestured for him to stay.

With highly volatile derivative products, she continued, the risks had to be properly explained and the advice had to be continual. Otherwise it would be like selling guns and live ammunition to children. She looked at Samuel and smiled properly for the first time. He could see she relished the power she had over whoever it was on the other end of the line. With a few gentle words of reassurance she managed to finish the call.

'Banks,' she said. 'Corporations. Eating each other alive. Sometimes it is a pleasure to help them do so.'

The smile melted away and she became businesslike again.

'Now ... Why didn't you tell me you were a journalist? There is automatic low-level surveillance of foreign journalists in this country. And considerable attention is paid if they do anything suspicious.'

'I have never been a proper journalist. Hard as it may be to believe, my placement was part of an academic research programme. It was fun being a banker for a while, though. Being a proprietary trader at a major investment bank gives you immense power in the markets. Look at how we managed to affect the oil price.'

'Power corrupts, Samuel. Not having power can be a delicious experience.'

'I'm not sure I'd agree.'

'You and I both want the same thing for different reasons, Samuel. We both need to know what happened to Kaz and why. To find out we're going to have to trust each other.'

'And my reasons? Why do I want to know?'

Lauren looked at him and smoothed her hands down the torso of her suit. It was as though discourse and conflict had sexually stimulated her. He could see how she must relish the cut and thrust of legal practice.

'Beyond the obvious issue of personal liberty, there is some deeper force. I think that your initial interest was on behalf of a newspaper, but I think you are seeking a higher truth now, a truth about the world outside that can only be discovered by learning what is within you.'

Samuel looked at her. Her chest was beginning to heave.

'Lauren, is this some sort of game?'

'Is seeking the truth a game?'

'OK. I have got two questions for you. First, how do we discover the truth, and second why do you think we have this common purpose?'

'It's about trust, Samuel.' Lauren clicked on the intercom.

'Marie? I am in conference and do not wish to be disturbed under any circumstances.'

She was prowling round him now like some wolverine. Samuel noted again the extreme smallness of the window, the sound-deadening banks of leather books, the sense of isolation. This would do as an interrogation cell.

'Put your hands behind your back,' she said evenly.

'Excuse me?'

Samuel began to jerk his head round, but was stopped by a soft, restraining hand.

'Please,' she said, and kissed him softly in the ear.

He hesitated, then did as she wished.

There was a faint swishing sound, and he felt his wrists being tightly bound to the back of his chair by what he guessed was a silk scarf.

'Don't look round,' she commanded.

He heard her cross the room. There was a gentle click from the lock of the door. Then she was standing next to him again.

'Now. What comes next?' She whispered softly in his ear. He could feel her breasts nuzzle against the back of his head. Suddenly he was in darkness. She had placed a silk scarf over his eyes and was tying it – tightly, but not too tightly – to his head. Within seconds he was blindfolded. She kissed his ear again. This time she put her tongue deep inside. He groaned. It was as though some wild, voluptuous animal were scrabbling to climb into his head.

'You tell me,' he said at last.

'No. You misunderstand. It is for you to tell me.'

He felt something cold and metallic against his cheek. He turned his head, only to find the coolness had transferred to the other side. Then, swiftly, she bound both his ankles to the chair. He struggled and fought to check the bindings, at first in play, then in earnest. She remained silent as he did so.

For a while only the sound of the captive's short, hard breaths were to be heard.

'Do you trust me?' she asked.

'I don't know.' Samuel was trying to remain calm.

He breathed in. Presumably this woman did not tie all her clients up. Sanity surely must prevail. All the same, as he had seen when she stormed onto the trading floor, she was dangerous; she gave off an aura that might have panicked many men.

'You have to trust me enough to tell me exactly what happened that last night you saw Kaz. This is not just need-to-know, Samuel. This is a truth we are pursuing, even if it makes the client–lawyer relationship a little difficult. This is a truth I need to know, because ... because it was Kaz.'

Then he felt the coldness of the steel again. This time by

his ankles. There was a tearing, rending sound and he realized that she had a knife. She was cutting his jeans apart with it, upwards from the floor. He could feel the air of the room fresh on the newly exposed skin. She cut all the way up one leg to the waist. Samuel was beginning to quiver with fear.

'I don't think you killed her. But you may have slept with her, if you were lucky enough to be chosen. Did she fuck you? Did she?'

'I, why . . .' he laughed, trying unsuccessfully to make a joke of it.

'Do you trust me, Samuel?'

'I don't think you are going to hurt me and I believe that, like me, you want to find the truth.' His mind was racing now. Lauren had been doing her own research. A denial could be fatal, truly fatal. 'Look, if we did have sex, what difference does it make? If Kaz did choose me, what was the meaning of that single act? From what I can see, she had sex with plenty of people and that didn't affect your relationship with her, did it?'

'Ha. "What is the meaning of a single act?" That's something men say when they have sex with a woman, and then they regret it. "Why did I do that? It doesn't mean I care for you. It may not even mean I'm straight." Although I do think you're straight, by the way.'

Lauren was cutting the second leg of his jeans away, and there was a rising tide of animal fear and visceral excitement within him.

'Do you trust me?'

'Lauren, I have to. I am powerless.' A few minutes earlier, he had been bragging about the thrill he had got from flexing his muscles as a proprietary trader and now he was tied to a chair, totally at the mercy of a woman with a sharp knife in her hand.

'You have to want to,' said Lauren emphatically. 'Almost every time a woman has sex with a man she has to want to submit. She has to want to trust that it will be the bourgeois activity of making love – at the very least that the subjugation of her person will not be too brutal.' There was a pause. Samuel could hear the regular rhythm of Lauren's breathing. She was standing very close to him.

'You've seen where we are. Down the corridor in the old servants' quarters. You could scream all day and no one would hear you. So, tell me again. Do you trust me? You will only get the delicious feeling of powerlessness if you admit the power of the other. Do I have your trust?'

One hand was massaging his groin now. The other was cutting away at what remained of his jeans. Within a matter of moments she had finished and discarded almost all the flaps of fabric.

'So, Samuel, do you trust me?'

She laid the steel of the knife blade against his cheek. He could feel the cruel sharpness of its serration. Now its coldness moved to the last remnants of his boxer shorts. She could either caress him or castrate him at will. Suddenly Samuel let go. He leapt into the abyss of powerlessness. He was hers to command, her familiar, her thing.

'Yes, yes, yes. Oh God, yes, I trust you.'

'Good, Samuel, good.'

He felt the soft enclosure of her mouth over the tip of his penis. But the moment was brief, ended by the harsh buzz of the intercom, and the worried voice of the receptionist.

'Madame, I'm so sorry to interrupt, but the police are here to see Monsieur Spendlove. I've explained they're early, but they say it's urgent, that they have a warrant for his arrest.'

HE ATE ALONE, *occasionally glancing distractedly at the book he had brought with him. It was a medium-sized restaurant on the fringes of the fashion district, just off the rue Marbeuf, between Matignon and George V. The place was expensive, not quite good enough to be crowded on a weekday, but not so quiet that he stood out. He toyed with his steak and waited until the appointed time. Not before 21.45, the voice on the phone had said.*

Sure enough, when he went to the restroom in the sous-sol, it was there. Halfway down the pile of lavender-scented tissue paper a small white tab of paper with an address and a name. The address would be real, the name fictitious. Hide-and-seek, silly names, party games – the timeless essentials of spy craft. Was he really a spy? He felt like a civil servant, a secret servant of the state, more like.

Within half an hour he was back in his hotel room with the television, as always, tuned to CNN. Tomorrow he would take the flight to Frankfurt, his suitcase stuffed with notes. He had memorized the name and address and would deposit the case in the usual manner. There had never been any problems going through customs on any of the earlier missions, and he didn't expect there would be any tomorrow. Pinstriped bankers in business class did not get stopped. The United States had a big empire to run, one that consumed vast quantities of cash.

He flipped CNN over to WBC7, a Barton Corporation channel. Yes, plenty of cash and the right sort of coverage. In combination, money and good publicity kept the masses happy.

Tomorrow would be fine, of course. It had been before, and would be again. What worried him occasionally was the simple thing, the piece of idealism that he hadn't lost, of whether he was really doing anyone any good.

16

'QUICKLY!'

Lauren pulled off the blindfold and slashed through the bindings on Samuel's wrists and ankles. She sprang to the door and checked it was locked, just as the handle began to turn. Samuel rummaged frantically in his duffel bag for his spare chinos as the commotion began outside.

'Police! Open up! Open in the name of the law!'

'One moment! I'm in conference. This is an outrage!' shouted Lauren. Samuel buttoned up his trousers and stuffed the remains of his jeans in a waste bin under the desk. There was another thunderous knock at the door, then Lauren looked at Samuel, nodded, and opened it.

'Good afternoon, Mademoiselle de la Geneste,' said Blondeau. He walked into the room followed by Bouchinet and a couple of strapping men in plain clothes. 'And Monsieur Spendlove. How pleasant to see you. How fortunate, indeed, that you are here.'

'We surrendered my client's passport and arranged for a further discussion of the Day case as you requested. So why are you now seeking to arrest Monsieur Spendlove?'

'Because circumstances change, Maître-Avocat. Circumstances change.'

'Sufficiently to justify brutalizing my receptionist and barging in during a conference between me and my client?'

Blondeau looked at Bouchinet and smirked.

'Such a shame about your friend, Monsieur Spendlove, don't you think?'

'As I have already explained, Inspector, Kaz Day was a colleague. I hardly knew her.'

'Oh no, I'm not speaking of the tragic death of Mademoiselle Day. No, it's your other friend I'm referring to. Your friend and trading partner – Mr Tungley.'

'What? Dee Tungley? What are you talking about?'

'Who is Dee Tungley?' asked Lauren.

'He's someone I do business with at the bank. He works in the Frankfurt office.'

'Worked in the Frankfurt office, Monsieur Spendlove. He's dead.'

'I don't believe it. Tungley was . . .'

'Don't say anything further, Samuel,' interjected Lauren. 'In any event,' she turned to Blondeau, 'a death in Frankfurt is nothing to do with you.'

'Oh but it is. A suspicious death of a second American citizen, with whom Monsieur Spendlove had close business contact, is too much of a coincidence, Mademoiselle de la Geneste. Our German colleagues are sending a detective to interview your client about their relationship. All their conversations are on tape, of course.'

Lauren was scrolling through the newswires on her computer. The news suddenly leapt out of the screen at her. It was a short, flash story.

15.33 GMT REU-WIR GEN. FRANKFURT KILLING
US NATIONAL.

FRANKFURT – Frankfurt police this morning confirmed
the identity of a body found hanging under Amspel Bridge
as that of American citizen Dee Tungley, 28. Tungley was
an employee of Ropner Bank.

ENDS

'It's true. Tungley's dead,' she said.

'Two American nationals dead, both of whom you had
recent contact with, both of whom were your colleagues,'
Blondeau continued. 'I repeat, too much of a coincidence I feel.'

'I'm not the only one with connections to both of them.
Have you interviewed Khan?'

Blondeau smiled thinly. 'We shall of course talk to Monsieur Khan, amongst others. But he is not so central to the
case as you, Monsieur Spendlove.' He lit a cigarette and
inhaled. 'No other person that we are aware of was the
recipient of a telephone call from Mademoiselle Day on
the night she died; no one else had an intimate dinner with
her that night; no one else's fingerprints were found on her
thigh.'

'You put them there! You forced me to touch her.' Samuel sprang up, and the two heavies took a step forward.
Samuel looked at Lauren. 'She'd been dead for days when
I touched her. That will show in the forensics, won't it?'

'It ought to,' said Lauren slowly. 'I'm not sure what prolonged exposure to water does to human skin.' A look of
misery flashed briefly across her face.

'One is entitled to conjecture, however, whether Monsieur
Spendlove's dinner companion was not touched by him on
the night of her death,' continued Blondeau smoothly. 'The
forensic examination reveals traces of spermicide and sexual
lubricant in the vaginal canal and at the base of the womb.'

Samuel could feel Lauren staring at him. He needed her help now more than ever.

'It is clear that she had sexual intercourse on the night of her death,' said Blondeau, hammering home the nails. 'Moreover, fingerprints matching those on your *carte de séjour* were found on the person of Mademoiselle Day, who our investigations lead us to believe was a close friend of yours, Mademoiselle de la Geneste.' Blondeau offered a poison-toad smile. 'You must have been very upset at the morgue the other day. Quite a performance.'

Lauren shot him a look of pure hatred. 'A professional performance, naturally,' said Blondeau, lingering over the words as though each syllable brought with it a minor sexual frisson.

'I don't see that you have a case, Monsieur,' said Lauren. She was controlled and correct, but Samuel could feel the heat of her anger.

'Enough of a case for the examining judge to issue this.' Blondeau waved a piece of paper.

'May I look at that?' asked Lauren.

'Certainly.'

Lauren's dark head bent over the elaborately franked document.

'And now I must ask you to come with me to Nanterre, Monsieur Spendlove.'

'Don't be absurd, Inspector Blondeau,' said Lauren, now openly angry. 'We agreed that my client would be questioned here, in my office. I am not coming to your offices in Nanterre.'

'No, Mademoiselle, you are not. Your client is to be taken for examination by the presiding judge. In camera. Neither prosecutor nor defendant is to be represented. Questions of national security are involved.'

'But that's ridiculous! How can my client be a threat to national security? In any event, it's an abuse of natural justice. I'll fight you.'

'In the courts, perhaps, Maître-Avocat. But after Monsieur Spendlove has been examined in accordance with the exceptional and urgent needs that national security require. Now, good day to you.'

And amid Lauren's furious but futile protests, Samuel was marched away.

THEY HAD TOLD HIM *nothing could go wrong, but something did, of course. And it was a warning, no doubt of that. Maybe he had committed some error, some careless breach of security. Maybe his paymasters had changed. There was a new man in the White House. You just never knew.*

He had left Charles de Gaulle in the usual fashion. The man in the business suit and his briefcase were waved through Fast Track with scarcely a glance. When the short flight to Frankfurt was done, he and his fellow Business Class travellers were among the first passengers to alight. He had no baggage to claim, and was striding confidently though customs control, part of him feeling like he was coming home, when he was drawn to one side by an official.

'Good morning, sir. What's in the case, please?'

'Papers. Business papers.' The business traveller didn't know what was in the case. He had merely picked it up, as bidden.

'I see, sir. Please open it.'

'Pardon me?'

'Please open the case, sir.'

'I'm on business here,' he said, trying to convey with a stare that they were all on the same side. His business was the business of saving the Germans' fat arses, amongst other things. That was why he was risking his own.

'Open the case, please.'

'I've lost the key, I believe.'

'Very well. Let me help you.'

The customs official took some small metal implement from his pocket, and flipped the locks in a matter of seconds. The business traveller couldn't resist a peek himself. He had never seen the contents of one of the cases. For a moment, he was engulfed by the hideous possibility that he had been duped all along, that really he was a drugs courier. But there they were, bundles and bundles of Deutschmarks

'Come with me please, sir.'

He was led away and seated in a comfortable waiting room. He asked for, and was given, a receipt for the case. After an hour or so, he was served coffee and sweet biscuits, and an hour after that a man from the US embassy arrived.

'C'mon, Mister,' said the attaché, when they were alone. 'Let's get out of here.' He didn't address the businessman as 'sir', even though he was considerably younger. The death of manners was apparent, even in the diplomatic corps.

'Just like that?'

'Not quite just like that. We've got some talking to do.'

17

SAMUEL SAT AND pondered the few items he could call
certainties. First, he was in an interrogation cell – a real one,
not a venue for a lawyer's role-play. He was buried deep in the
guts of a giant concrete block a few hundred metres from
the western autoroute sign welcoming visitors to Nanterre.
Nanterre was twinned with Watford, which did not necessarily
make Samuel any more cheerful. The other certainty was that,
save the dual companions of powerlessness and fear, he was
on his own.

They left him for almost half an hour before they came. It
was an effective tactic. By that time Samuel was sick of staring
at what there was to observe – tiled walls, a table, two chairs,
a single-filament, low-voltage light and a thick prism of gluey
Perspex which passed as a window. After a few moments, the
gravity of his situation dawned on him. But then France was a
'well-governed' country.

He heard them well before he saw them. The corridor
outside was long and echoic, and the dull thump of feet on
linoleum sounded like an execution squad approaching his cell.
Blondeau and Bouchinet entered, followed by a third man. He
was thinnish and in his forties, and repaired to the furthest
corner of the cell. He did not look directly at Samuel. He was

hiding behind the thick, black-framed spectacles that dominated his face.

'So, Monsieur Spendlove, you continue to find life entertaining in our country,' purred Blondeau. A statement. Samuel did not qualify it.

'Cigarette?'

'No thank you, Inspector Blondeau. Tobacco is not my vice.'

'So it would seem. At least you enjoy the others. Drink . . . sex . . . even philosophy.'

Blondeau briefly pasted a smile on his face, then lit a tipped Gauloise and sat opposite Samuel. Bouchinet stood behind Blondeau's right shoulder, partially obscuring the thin man.

'But don't worry. In France, we like a man who enjoys his pleasures.'

'I don't suppose there's any hope of being told what I'm supposed to have done, why you're holding me, and whether the British embassy knows I'm being detained. Is there?'

Blondeau exhaled and brushed ash from his sleeve. Samuel noted again how badly dressed he and Bouchinet were. If, as he now supposed, they were intelligence officers of some sort with a brief to blend into the background of the city, Paris was a very poor choice of place to dress down.

'Oh, Monsieur Spendlove, we have much time. Just as long as it takes. But if we had till the end of eternity, there would still be no opportunity for you to ask questions.'

Blondeau walked to the table and tossed a metallic object onto it. A pair of handcuffs. He rummaged theatrically in his pockets and looked sideways at Samuel to check he was enjoying the performance. Then Blondeau pulled a long wire out of his pocket and held it aloft to ensure that Samuel could see what it was.

'Are you planning to start a car?' asked Samuel. The sight of the jump leads and thought of electric current made him feel sick, but he could not show Blondeau his fear. The policeman smiled and shook his head, then carefully withdrew a long, thin hammer from his jacket and placed it softly on the tabletop. The face of the hammer head tapered into a conical grey tip that looked cruel and sharp.

'Now, where shall we begin? We have so much to talk about.'

Blondeau walked over and stood next to Samuel again. He was empty-handed, but there was something about the over-casual way he swung his arms that suggested an easy transition to violence.

'What was your relationship with Katherine Day?'

'I've told you. It was a superficial, professional relationship.'

'And nothing more? You never touched her?'

Blondeau walked slowly over to the table with its horrid implements, turned and looked at Samuel, then walked back, still empty-handed.

'Well, I kissed her once. But you seem to know about that. The only time I did anything more than shake her hand was when you planted my fingerprints on her in the morgue.'

'We can do this the easy way or the hard way, Monsieur Spendlove. You do not want to sample the hard way.'

Samuel looked over at the table. Blondeau had undoubtedly used those things before.

'All right, all right. We had sex, if you need me to tell you. But it was consensual. We used a condom, for heaven's sake.'

'Good. We are making a little ground at last. It's true, though, isn't it, that a rapist and murderer seeking to hide his identity would do well to use a sheath?'

'What, putting it on with one hand while subduing his

victim with the other? Inspector, Kaz had the condoms in her handbag. Check. The contraceptive was hers – she put it on. Having consensual sex with a colleague is not a crime. You must have a better reason than that for detaining me.'

Blondeau drifted by Samuel's chair again, and swung the back of his hand into Samuel's face. Something sharp caught Samuel's cheek, which began to bleed profusely. There was no discernible movement from Bouchinet or the man in the corner.

Samuel felt a surge of anger within him. If he went for Blondeau now he would probably get in a couple of good blows before the others tried to restrain him. They were waiting for him to react, but if he fought back, it would not do his case any good. He had to exert some self-control. He forced himself to relax, and put a hand to his cheek, dabbing at the wound.

Blondeau laughed briefly, and tossed Samuel a soiled cotton handkerchief.

'Good, good. A wise reaction after a rather foolish answer. Please remember that I am conducting this conversation, and you will respond to my questions, not comment on them.' Blondeau paused, looked at Bouchinet, then the thin man. 'All right, we'll leave that subject for the moment. What about Dee Tungley?'

'Tungley?'

'Your relationship with Tungley. Do not make me lose patience with you again, Mr Spendlove.'

'Tungley. Well, you said that you had done your research, so you'll know that I had a superficial professional relationship with him.'

'You have a lot of superficial relationships.'

'Well, that's business. We used him very sparingly.'

'When was the last time you spoke to him?'

'Oh, a few days ago.' It seemed like years. 'It's all in the trading logs.'

'And in the newspapers. You're quite a darling of the media.'

It occurred to Samuel that no one was attempting to note or record his comments. The cell was probably bugged anyway, but the fact that there was no pretence of observing due procedure for the recording of evidence was alarming. It simply underlined the point that they felt they could do whatever they wanted with him.

'And you always booked all your deals under your own bank identity?'

'Correct.'

The cut on his cheek was beginning to sting.

'I see.' Blondeau tossed his cigarette to the floor and stepped on it.

'Then how do you explain the fact that Katherine Day is supposed to have executed several trades with Tungley on days when she was not in the office – but you were?'

'I don't. I'm not a bean counter or a computer boffin. Ask Ropners. They'll have the explanations.'

'Their explanations are unacceptable. She seems to have conducted several trades whilst sitting at your computer terminal. One of them occurred when she was most certainly dead. You will concede that this is an impressive feat.'

Samuel blinked. Another logical cul-de-sac; whoever it was, whatever it was, was tightening its grip on him. 'I have no explanation for that. How can you expect me to? This is the first I have heard of trades being executed by Kaz through Tungley. Can't you see this is nothing to do with me?'

Samuel was standing up now, voice raised, indignant. The

man at the back of the room took a step forward. Samuel sat once more.

Blondeau waited a moment, then began again. 'You are aware of the term rogue trader?'

'It's a phrase incompetent managers use to explain away their own negligence and inadequacy. If something goes wrong, it's not because of slipshod management control, it's just that one of the workforce has gone mad. Funny that a billion-dollar hole in the accounts should escape the vigilance of the management.'

'A billion dollars?'

'I was speaking hypothetically.' Or was he? He could think of more than one instance where the management of a major institution had tried to excuse gigantic ineptitude by pinning the blame on a single man.

Blondeau's back was turned.

'You know, you are lucky to be here,' he said quietly.

'Really?' Samuel put his hand to his cheek.

'Yes, really.'

Blondeau tossed a copy of that evening's *France-Soir* newspaper into Samuel's lap. It carried a screaming headline.

PARASITE!

There was a picture of Samuel. He wasn't just a financial jackal, but a lurid journalistic version of one. The paper fulminated in condemnation of the threat to national security that Samuel had allegedly posed through his trading activities. He was apparently solely responsible for trying to manipulate the oil market and there was no mention of Khan. The newspaper condemned him and the evil festival of speculation that was the global market. A short article squeezed into the left-hand column reported that jewellers in Toulouse had been looted for their gold; an old-age pensioner in Béziers had committed suicide, believing herself ruined – all the fault of evil speculators like Samuel.

'If I turned you out on the street, the mob might just rip you apart. Whatever happens to you here will at least occur for a rational purpose.'

'So my choice is between the madman and the paid executioner?'

'Possibly neither. You must tell us what you have done. If you confess all, there is hope for you. Perhaps.'

Samuel could feel himself falling into an abyss. He would never be able to satisfy them on any of the things they wanted to question him about – his dealings with Kaz, with Tungley, the mystery trades.

Then Blondeau turned to Bouchinet and nodded. She left the room, but was back within seconds carrying Samuel's laptop. She placed the computer on the table and switched it on.

'We allowed ourselves the liberty of collecting your mail for you,' she said. Bouchinet clicked on the mail icon and stood back. The computer version of Khan's voice issued from tiny stereo speakers. There were two messages waiting, dated and timed for that afternoon. Khan's voice droned on, into message number one:

'Greetings. Times are diverting enough without extra entertainment. But I fear there may be more fun and games ahead if the entry of the police into our little world is any indication. Perhaps you should call me. Warmly, Khan.'

The second message was timed a few minutes later. The voice was still a tinny echo of Khan, but the substance was altogether different.

'Remember what you came for. Keep going.'

The mechanical voice stopped abruptly. There was no sign-off.

'Who sent the second message?'

This from the thin man. He spoke from the corner, but did not look at Samuel.

'I don't know.'

'Are you sure?'

'Certain.'

'Then who sent you these?'

Blondeau had printouts of the earlier anonymous messages.

'I see you've been working closely with the computer department at the bank ... You know the answer; I told you, I don't know. I asked the computer people to find out, and they came up with the log-on of someone who's convalescing in a Swiss rest home, to the best of my knowledge.'

There was a silence as this was digested by all parties.

'You know,' said Blondeau at last. 'Your knowledge is not very impressive. You could find yourself here for a very long, very painful time.' He got up and walked out of the room, followed by Bouchinet.

The thin man stayed and stared at Samuel for some moments, squinting from behind his glasses. The lenses were extremely thick, as opaque and dense as miniature television screens. Samuel returned his stare, hoping he would say something and explain who he was and why he was there.

But, of course, he didn't.

The thin man simply walked forward and picked up the computer, putting it under one arm. With his other hand he struck Samuel a vicious blow to the side of the head, using some kind of concealed soft cosh. By the time Samuel had fallen to the floor unconscious, the thin man had already left the room.

WHEN HE CAME ROUND, the room was spinning. At first Samuel thought it was just a side-effect of his headache, until he realized that the room really was rotating. Or rather that the extraordinarily comfortable bed in which he found himself was turning itself slowly round. The room wasn't moving at all, it was the easy mistake of relative displacement – the moment when you can't be sure if it's your train or the one next to you that has begun to move.

He lifted his head – there was a little pain, but not too much – and looked about him. He was indeed in a slowly gyrating waterbed. Paris sprawled beneath him, gaping and gorgeous through vast, lighthouse-style windows. The dizziness he felt now was cognitive rather than physical: he didn't have a bad head, just no clue as to where he was – or why.

And then he thought he knew where he was. But this was impossible, surely? Yet he recognized the view. It had to be.

'Orange juice?'

Climbing up the spiral staircase, wrapped in a silk bathrobe, came the owner of the view. In his hand he carried a lacquer tray laden with tall glasses and a jug of freshly squeezed orange juice. Samuel flopped back on the pillow in disbelief.

'Khan,' he said, mainly to test that he really wasn't still dreaming.

'Rest, Samuel. Agitation is not good for you. Enjoy the view. Take refreshment when it suits you. These are Moroccan oranges. Small, and with quite a low juice yield. But there is a hint of caramel in the after-taste that makes the extra labour worthwhile.'

Samuel accepted a glass, beaded with cold. The dark ochre liquid was indeed delicious.

'I don't wish to seem ungrateful, Khan, but could you stop the bed turning? It's disorientating.'

'Of course, how thoughtless of me.'

Khan had been sitting at the foot of the bed. He jumped up and flicked a switch on the wall. In his silk robe he looked slight, like some minor servant in a Sheik's harem. Then he skipped back to the foot of the bed. For the first time, Samuel wondered whether Khan might have some kind of sexual interest in him.

Samuel sipped at his drink again.

'I had been expecting to wake up in a dungeon. This is a pleasant surprise.'

Khan smiled and reached for the jug.

'I must say, you do seem to have made one or two people rather unhappy. Their minions have certainly been heavy-handed.'

'Who were they? Surely not regular policemen?' asked Samuel, looking up at the ceiling. There were no mirrors or other signs of interesting sexual gadgetry that Samuel could see. But then, with Khan you could never tell. Everything could change at the flick of a switch.

'Far from it. I didn't realize the severity of your problem until I discovered you were in the hands of – well, what are they? – civil servants, I suppose.'

'Civil servants?'

'Those people may describe themselves as police, but if you look at their identity cards you will see they belong to a division that was formed in Algeria when it was still a French colony. The colony is no longer a colony, but, technically, the domestic police force and civil service still exist. That is a wonderful convenience for the bureaucratic mind, Samuel. An empty box to fill with whatever you wish – a container in which to hide the inconvenient.'

'And that's me, of course. Inconvenient.'

Samuel fingered the monogrammed K at the breast of his silk pyjamas, and propped himself up again. He was beginning to feel less delicate now. Presumably he had been fed some drug that was wearing off.

'Correct. You seem to have a talent for annoying people at the moment – the journalist jackal who's stealing the people's savings, the fraudster, the abductor, the killer. That badly dressed gorilla Blondeau hates you – if you went out on the street, he'd create a mob and feed you to it.'

'Oh God.' Samuel's headache was getting worse again.

'But you do have friends. Patrice Gourdon likes you, and I haven't given up on you – yet.'

The last word was accompanied by a careful sideways look.

'What have I done to you, Khan?'

'Would you like the list in order of importance or alphabetically?' There was a sharper tone to his former boss's voice now. 'You've played havoc with the way I run my business, brought massive publicity to the whole operation that's got the bank running scared. They're a very secretive lot, you know.'

'God. Sorry. This is appalling.' He looked up after a while. 'Did Gourdon get me out of there?'

'He discovered where you were. I was the one who actually got you out. It took every ounce of influence we had. You have made a very dangerous enemy somewhere, Samuel. If Blondeau and his cronies had been able to prove that you were masquerading as Kaz, and dealing with Tungley, I wouldn't have been able to do a thing. I told you he was trouble, didn't I?'

Samuel nodded. An image flashed into his mind of the way Khan would wince whenever the American called.

'But the Algerian police forgot one crucial point.'

'Which is?'

'They adduced proof of your misdemeanours that was a little too convincing.'

Samuel waited for the plum.

'They had apparent proof of your impersonation of Kaz Day that went back a considerable time. Your persistent underhandedness was really quite compelling. Except for one key factor.'

Khan walked over to the window and admired the view once more.

'They alleged that you were trading as Kaz Day on the fraudulent Tungley trades – there was a lot of money that was never booked in Frankfurt, and was siphoned off into some account or other. It looks like a real mess. One can only presume that Tungley paid for his riches with his life. But suggesting that you were involved in market rigging when you weren't even working at Ropners blew their case apart. They had to release you, fancy warrants notwithstanding.'

Samuel's head ached. He was still thirsty, and Khan's suaveness tired him.

'So am I off the hook, no longer a part of the inquiry?'

'I'm afraid not. They're still very interested in you. They say that the fingerprints on Kaz's body incriminate you.'

'But that's bullshit!'

'I know, I know. But it may have to be proved in court. And then there's the sexual activity.'

Samuel reddened.

'Sex is not violence, Khan. It's not a crime. She chose me.'

'That's true. At the moment they have a financial case that is too clumsy to be believable, and a poorly manufactured piece of forensic evidence. Your admission of having sex with her weighs heavily against you, though. So often the lover turns murderer. Snatching you away from your lawyer worked against them. Patrice made much of that. But it's understandable that they still want to keep very close to you.'

'They have my passport, so I can't leave France.'

'But that's not how the bureaucratic mind works over here. Testimony and practicality are not evidence. Documents and money orders are what count. Which is why I've had to put up half a million euros and make a solemn promise to the courts that you will not attempt to leave the country and will generally be a good boy.'

'Well, I'm immensely grateful to you, of course. But what do I have to do? Wait for the next Buddy Holly look-alike to come and bash me over the head?'

'No, Samuel. Stay close to me until things have been cleared up. Interesting things are set to happen, and your help may be useful. Perhaps even more so now you no longer work at Ropners. Just stay around, my boy. I haven't finished with the markets yet.'

THE VOICE OF the television reporter pierced his dream. He recognized the nasal, self-important whine that poured out of the surround-sound speakers Khan had set in the corners of his bedroom. The world's financial markets were, it seemed, in meltdown. Samuel blinked and looked about him.

Afternoon had crumbled into night, and the evening was

just beginning to pull its cover over the city. The neon signs of the street cafés reached up to lay light fingers on the unlit ceiling. He felt clean-limbed, springy, as though he had slept for a very long time. The television reporter was droning on about the losses at Ropner Bank's Frankfurt branch. They could not be explained, he said. Investigations were under way into whether the calamitous holes in the bank's balance sheet were connected with the death of American trader Dee Tungley. This was another non-story. The reporter was long on supposition and very short on fact.

Samuel then watched a brief item on the latest round of panic buying around Europe – sugar was suddenly scarce again; people were queuing for everything. The former Communist states in Eastern Europe were being rallied by a ragged coalition of anti-globalists and a few diehards who hadn't thrown their Communist Party membership cards away. There were bread riots in Prague and Bratislava, and there had even been looting in relatively affluent Budapest. The Balkan states were on the brink of war yet again, and far away in Finland the government had imposed an emergency curfew.

Samuel yawned, pointed the remote and switched off. Yes, it was terrible and life in Paris seemed pretty cosy by comparison. But it was all far away, somehow unconnected with a man in silk pyjamas, safe in Khan's perch at the top of the city.

He got up. The flat was empty; he could feel it. Samuel smiled grimly. He could feel emptiness all right.

After a shower he donned some clean clothes that had been left out in a neat pile for him. Then he made an omelette with unsalted Normandy butter and fresh chives, poured himself a glass of red wine, and devoured the view.

He finished his meal and looked out on the bustle and

noise below: Khan was out somewhere in the night. The neon fineries on the ceiling were bright and bold now. Samuel washed up his plate and began to wander about the flat. Khan had asked him to stick close, which seemed eminently sensible advice. But where was Khan?

Samuel slowly walked the perimeters of the apartment, tracing his finger lightly over random surfaces – a Bauhaus table, the white-pebbled fireplace, the mini-cupolas on a low skylight, the exquisite, animal-dark of a Chinese lacquer cabinet.

One of the cabinet doors was slightly open. Inside were hints of treasure, obscure outlines of objects precious to Khan.

Samuel walked away and sat down. This was the man who had saved him from the Algerian thugs. This was his host, and the laws of hospitality demanded extreme circumspection from a guest. And yet, and yet.

He walked up to the cabinet, and away again. It would doubtless have several internal surveillance cameras trained on it. But did that matter? It was hardly as though he were riffling through Khan's private papers. This was no more than an opportunity for the discreet inspection of the admirable taste in *objets d'art* of one of the wealthiest and most sophisticated individuals in the world. Would opening the cabinet door be treachery? No – more like flattery. And besides, there was Samuel's duty to himself. Khan had been generous in every way except the most important one – offering the truth. Anything that might help him discover the truth had to be done.

Samuel marched up again and opened the door wide. He pulled out an object the size of a small grapefruit, and smiled. It was a Fabergé egg, extravagant enough to please the most sybaritic Romanoff. He set it down on the coffee table. It was somehow typical of Khan to make great display of hideous modern art, of papier mâché tent pegs, but to hide a fantastic artefact of exquisite craftsmanship in a cabinet.

A series of much smaller objects was ranged on the left-hand side. Samuel reached in and pulled out something that felt cold and smooth. He gave a soft whistle. Celtic chessmen – either from the priceless Isle of Lewis set or one just like it. He looked into the tallowy brown face of the piece he held in his hand. It was a pawn, a foot soldier with a walrus moustache and a comically mournful expression. He felt an odd sense of kinship with it. Did Khan ever play? Or just keep this treasure up here, a joy to none but himself? There was a switch at the side of the cabinet; he flicked it on, and gasped out loud. At the back was a drawing in a glass case. It glowed dully in the unlit room. There could be no mistaking the hand – it was a Cézanne. Stunning, a treasure, a piece of pure genius.

And then he noticed something that set his head reeling, his mind whirling. Samuel reached in, but did not dare to bring it out. He peered in to make absolutely certain that he had made no mistake. He had to be sure that there could be no ambiguity about what he was seeing. No, no, there was no mistake. It was definitely what he thought it was.

Suddenly the Cézanne seemed less impressive, less important. Samuel switched off the light, replaced the Fabergé egg, and sat down on the sofa. Were there cameras on him? Was this a test? Did Khan want to send him this signal? Samuel's heart beat wildly in his chest amid the gathering darkness. The last object in the cabinet was one he had seen once before, quite close up. It was undoubtedly a miniature sculpture of a crouching archer. And the last time he had seen it was in the Bourdelle Museum – in the hand of Kaz Day.

THE BIG BLACK MERCEDES *sped through the bustle of a Frank-furt city centre made greasy by relentless rain. The gates of the embassy, just outside the financial district, swung open to receive them, then clanged shut the instant they were through. The young attaché, having promised lots of talking, kept silent throughout the trip. So all there was to look at was the stiff, razored neck of the driver and his companion in front. Both were Marines. He tapped the thick bulletproof glass of the windowpane. The car would undoubtedly be strengthened to deal with bomb blasts – he was travelling in a luxury tank.*

He was shown into a room similar to the one in the airport, except that there were windows giving onto the street. The coffee served was American, and there was a big bowl of candies, including Reece's Peanut Butter Cups, his personal favourite.

The man who came to see him introduced himself as Tony Burrows. He had a face that was difficult not to like – kindly lines, full of experience and wisdom, a warm smile, a twinkle in the eyes. Of course, Burrows knew all the background, and they chatted about Vietnam, the 1987 crash, the property market, the incredible things that could be done with computers nowadays. Burrows felt very sympathetic about Yvonne. To lose your fiancée to a skiing accident was a terrible thing and he could understand why a man would be reluctant to commit again. You could only give your heart once, couldn't you?

It was only after three hours of answering similar, but not quite identical, questions over and over again, that the businessman began to get angry. They hadn't even discussed the incident at the airport, where he had risked liberty and possibly his life for the sake of his country. It was as though they thought he had somehow arranged to have himself arrested and his package impounded. The idea of being treated as a criminal made him furious, and he told Burrows so.

Burrows said he was sorry, and that he shouldn't take it like that. But he did take it exactly like that. He caught a flight back to the US the next day. But he didn't use the ticket that the embassy had offered. He paid for his passage with his own, purely acquired, money. No burden to his employer, nor the taxpayer.

18

SAMUEL LAY BACK on the sofa seeking calmness, a moment of reflection, but his heart was beating wildly. Random thoughts raced around his head. The night seemed to have thickened further. Its darkness was suffocating now. He dared not even turn on the light.

Images of Khan fizzed back and forth across his mind's eye – the disdain for Tungley, the constant warnings about Kaz, that she was not worth the bother, that Samuel should drop his interest in her. He thought of Khan's benign smiles as Samuel tried and failed to spy on him – so knowing, so certain that he was in control of the game. Now the Bourdelle miniature had appeared in Khan's apartment. It must have come directly from Kaz, who was dead. Samuel had known of no connection between Kaz and Dee Tungley and yet the bank's dealing records linked them. Khan had to be the spider at the centre of the web, but what had been his purpose and why had he needed Kaz and Tungley?

A jazz bar in the street switched on its sign. Blue light bathed the front of the room with a flickering, ghostliness. On-off, on-off, on-off, cool fingers reached up to stroke his cheek. What was he to do?

Perhaps he should take the archer miniature as proof –

inconclusive but damaging – that Khan had something to do with Kaz's death. Lauren would swear to having been there when Kaz took it, even if that made her an accomplice to theft. But ... Lauren. His heart pumped even harder. Maybe ... Maybe Lauren had given the archer to Khan. In which case she was implicated in Kaz's death, and Samuel was the victim of a giant conspiracy.

He could feel the sweat run cold down the small of his back. His mind was turning over like a car engine in neutral with the accelerator jammed down. He was thrashing around, making no progress – and the fear, the fear within, was rising all the time.

He must have spent several minutes sitting in the semi-dark, shivering. Until, at last, a semblance of calm came over him. It was as though he was kneeling at the feet of the Master of Biblos himself, conducting the forensic exploration of the external world in harmony with the rational models that described internal and external reality. He was discovering the external probabilities by extending the inner certainties.

He was breathing evenly now. He moved quietly across the flat and got a glass of water. There was another set of clothes, which he slipped into a sailing bag. He looked about him in a darkness punctuated by slow, strobing blue. Then he crossed to the cabinet, reached in, took the archer figure, and stuffed it into the bag.

He opened the windows, walked onto the terrace and swung a leg over to the balcony of the *chambre de bonne* next door. Khan apparently used this as a box room, and though he had never been there, Samuel's instincts told him to go next door, not to leave by the main door of the apartment. The frames pushed apart easily enough – fifth-floor windows were not designed to prevent forced entry.

The room was tiny, featureless, and empty of anything but a camp bed and a couple of cardboard boxes. Samuel had his hand on the door to let himself out, and was just beginning to turn the handle, when he froze. There was the distinct sound of a footfall outside, and a low curse at the creak of the ancient parquet flooring. Then silence. Samuel pressed his ear to the door, straining to hear any noise, however tiny. Finally, the minute metallic click of a key in the big safety lock next door made itself heard. Someone was trying to work the door of Khan's flat. Silence fell again. Samuel waited a minute, then slipped out of the *chambre de bonne*. All was quiet, apart from the shallowness of his own breathing as his body fought to control the adrenal urge to flight. After a moment of agonizing stillness, he crept away from the flat, towards the tiny iron staircase that led to the fire escape.

After a few minutes of stealthy climbing down the stairs, he found himself in the comforting anonymity of the street. In his bag he had a spare set of clothes, a phone, computer kit, and an art sculpture. Apart from that, his only asset was his judgement.

SHE ARRIVED slightly early. Despite the tiredness that showed darkly under her eyes, heads still turned when she walked through the bar and down to the *sous-sol* snug where they had agreed to meet. Samuel watched the ripple that Lauren caused from a far corner. As promised, she had come alone. And if she hadn't, it mattered little – he had made his call, and now he had to act on it. He glanced at his watch. It was near midnight, but the Café aux Sources by the place de la République was one of a host of bars that stayed open twenty-four hours a day. They had plenty of time – or perhaps he had run out of it already, without knowing.

He approached her table from behind and slipped into the seat opposite.

'Samuel! Thank God!'

She reached across the table and kissed him. Samuel did not pull back, but did not respond either. Lauren frowned slightly.

'What's wrong? Where have you been? I've been losing my mind. First Kaz, then you . . .'

'I said I would explain, didn't I?'

She began fumbling for a cigarette. 'Well explain, then. God, I thought you were dead. You probably would be if Khan hadn't intervened.'

'So you're a friend of Khan's?'

'What is this, Samuel? Don't be ridiculous!' She exhaled angrily. 'He's your friend, your mentor. I simply phoned to inform him you'd been legally abducted from my office. Whatever one may think of him as a jackal of capitalism, he's an influential jackal.' She pulled a face – angry, tired, a little scared too, he thought. 'Come on. What is this? You wouldn't explain on the phone. Tell me where you've been for the past forty-eight hours. Tell me now.'

Samuel looked at Lauren and held her eyes. He thought of the exquisite sadness he had seen arise within her when she saw Kaz's body. Was it sadness at the loss of a loved friend, maybe a lover? Or was it just a reaction, relief from giving a performance, as the odious Blondeau had described it?

Samuel was still peering intently into Lauren's face, desperately seeking answers. She even looked as though she might care for him beneath the battering life was handing out to them both. He tried to smile. Of course Lauren's grief was genuine. Maybe other things were too.

He watched her light a cigarette with an unsteady hand. He

reached down into his bag, and silently placed the archer sculpture on the table in front of her.

'What's that?' Lauren stared in stupefaction at the tiny crouching figure with its broad, bent bow. 'Is it? It can't be, can it?' She looked at him, eyes bright with inquiry.

'That confirms what I was almost certain of, anyway. It is the same sculpture, isn't it? The one that you encouraged Kaz to steal from the Bourdelle?'

Lauren nodded. Tears began to fill her eyes.

'But, Samuel, where did you get it?'

'You mean you didn't give it to the person I got it from?'

'You're speaking in riddles. How did you get this? Where have you been? I've been frantic.'

'Are you sure you don't know?'

'I really have no idea what you're talking about.' She was staring at the figure as though it had a magical quality, as though it would bring Kaz back, transport them all to an earlier, happier time. Samuel watched her intently.

'I believe you,' he said at last. 'I don't think you know how I got it. The answer is I got it from Khan's place on avenue Matignon, where I've been recovering these past few days. Probably drugged up, for all I know. Time certainly seems to have flown by.'

'Khan had this?'

'Yes.'

'But that means . . .'

'I'm not sure what it means. If you didn't give it to him, which I have to believe, then it proves that there was some connection we don't know about between Khan and Kaz.'

'Oh my God. Do you think . . . do you think he killed her? That he had her killed?'

'I don't know. But I think we need to find out. Unless we do, I'll be jailed for at least one murder and the biggest financial scam in the history of the world. That much is clear.'

'And neither of us would ever know the truth.' She choked on a smile and angrily brushed aside a dewy tear, struggling to make sense of what Samuel had told her.

'Ah yes. Finding the truth. Was that one of the games you played with Kaz?'

'Samuel, you're the one who likes games. What is this ridiculous test?' she spat back. 'Truth, taking risks, daring to play the game of love – knowing all the while it can be a game that becomes real. Yes, we played those games, Kaz and I. We tested each other that way. And to think I was considering playing some of those games with you.' She gave him a hard, angry look, and reached for her drink.

'Look, Lauren.' He reached for her hand. She kept her gaze averted, but did not withdraw. 'This isn't a game. Not a truth game, not a love game. It's deadly serious. Two people are already dead.'

He breathed deeply, and squeezed her hand. She looked at him now. 'Lauren, I trust you. I decided that before I left Khan's flat. And now he'll find me gone, and he'll notice that I've taken something that connects him with Kaz. It's war. Will you help me, please? It'll be dangerous, but then I know you like taking risks.'

She smiled at him weakly. 'And I like doing what is right, don't forget. OK, Samuel, I'll help you. We'll do this for Kaz.'

They finished their drinks. Lauren listened to the story of the mystery intruder at Khan's flat and agreed that it was too much of a risk for him to go home with her. They found a cheap hotel on the rue Vieille du Temple. Lauren, who seemed to know how these things were done, paid for their room in cash.

EARLY LUNCH in a little café off the rue Montmartre. The smell of soap on zinc slowly eroded by kinder aromas of butter, onion, garlic, seared red meat – then sharpened at the top of the register with a little tobacco.

They were alone in the *sous-sol*, definitely not being watched by the Algerian police. At least while they ate. Samuel had rabbit in mustard sauce. Lauren devoured a pavé of rump-steak.

Robert, short and busy, bustled about them. He dumped down a small pichet of Côtes du Rhône and headed back to the basket of sandwiches he was preparing for the lunchtime run. Business was quiet, as it had been for a few days now. Any sort of quiet was reassuring when Samuel considered what else had been going on in the world lately. In France, there had been none of the runs on the banks that Russia had seen, with vast, hysterical queues seeking to withdraw all their money.

Nor had there been the panic buying, the desperate stock-piling of commodities, that Asia had experienced after the financial crisis had virtually destroyed public order. Shop-keepers and restaurateurs had been brutalized by angry crowds who would not accept the merchants' sudden reluctance to be paid with paper money for goods. Some Moscow cafés had multiplied the rouble price of a meal by ten during the course of a lunchtime. That was the kind of inflation that occurred when there was a crisis of confidence.

They ate in silence, with an air of concentration. It had been a long night. Once she had begun to talk it had been difficult to stop her – a necessary unburdening for the woman whose childhood had been crippled by the brutal Marxist zealot who had been her father. A self-hating aristocrat, he had tried to revolutionize his life, but could not give up the posh 'de' in his name, nor the privileges of the family estate.

Different from the other children in her class, Lauren's childhood stories were paternal tales of heroes of the class struggle, inflated somewhat by brandy and revolutionary fervour. The little girl knew none of the commonplace flopsy-bunny fictions of the nursery, but of the events of 1968, and the inevitable triumph of Communism, she had a precocious knowledge. Then there was her father's violent death – Samuel had been chilled at the pallid, emotionless way she recounted finding him, his skull split open after falling downstairs drunk. After that, Lauren had stopped resenting the ideology that separated her from the rest of the world and had embraced it. Suddenly dialectical materialism had seemed comforting – it was her father's final legacy.

Samuel watched her as she drank the dark, sun-drenched wine and sawed through her steak. She had talked for hours in the night, and yet she remained somehow opaque and impenetrable. She wanted something different, more than sex, certainly. Samuel kept thinking of their blindfold trust game – sex was part of it, perhaps, but only a small element of a bigger picture. Part of him wanted to hold her and comfort her, but he knew that the moment was wrong.

They had lain in separate beds and talked, sometimes a little edgily, of the things they cherished. They had discussed truth and love in abstract terms. Had she found those with Kaz? Would Samuel ever be able to really trust a woman again after Gail? Was this adventure with Samuel just a means of rediscovering excitement for Lauren, a way of holding on to what she had once had with someone else? She seemed to treat relationships as a game and saw the possibility of falling in love as a necessary risk.

'So. Are you ready?' she asked finally.

Samuel nodded. They pushed back their chairs, picked up the scissors from the table, and disappeared with Robert into the small, cramped staff lavatories.

Twenty minutes later Robert emerged with a new sandwich assistant. Short, spiky hair dyed black, brown contact lenses, and the white jacket of the junior waiter – Samuel had become a sallow Mediterranean sandwich vendor. He was unrecognizable, or so he hoped.

SAMUEL NEED NOT have worried. The new bank security guards waved them through with minimal scrutiny. The stiff, unnatural jab of the forearm, horizontal and pivoted about the waist, emphasized the fact that these were armed men, newly hired for times of crisis. He doubted if even the old security crew would have recognized him as a former employee, but the new men merely knew Robert and his sandwiches from the previous few days, and waved them both through with little more than a glance.

Samuel could understand the precaution. People were looking for scapegoats. And Ropners, as an American institution, simply could not be too careful. Nevertheless, seeing the short-nosed Uzi barrels in the marble grandeur of Ropner Bank's atrium was an almost visceral shock.

He stepped out of the lift to be met by two more security guards. Only one was toting a gun this time. The other stepped forward, uttered a brief apology, and frisked them. Samuel smiled to himself: paranoia in the financial markets.

Maybe it wasn't paranoia though. After the 1987 crash, which wasn't nearly so bad as the present crisis, a Merrill

Lynch client had walked into the firm's Miami offices after losing his $11 million portfolio, shot the office manager dead, seriously wounded an account executive and then put a bullet in his own brain. Perhaps those Uzis were a prudent measure.

Samuel shook his head as Robert was ushered onto the trading floor. As planned, he headed upstairs to the security guards' main control room. He would not test his simple disguise by selling sandwiches to his former colleagues. The guards, especially the new guards, were much safer. He looked about him as he climbed the stairs. Everything seemed as normal. This was an insane risk to take for almost no prospective gain. What had he expected to find? A signed confession of guilt to some unspecified crime lying on Khan's desk? Or Miller's?

The security control room was state-of-the-art 1990s, a combination of the sophisticated and the primitive. The bank's senior management had probably decided to avoid the computer-controlled-environment buildings that had experienced so many teething problems. They had eschewed the self-adjusting sunblinds and self-varying air-conditioning systems in favour of things that worked: diligent human beings and banks of video surveillance screens. Just about every room in the building, including lavatories and lifts, had CCTV.

Samuel played dumb, not wanting the two guards in the room to know that an Englishman was selling them their lunch. Much better that they thought a half-idiot cousin of Robert's from Marseille was hawking food.

Both men were well into middle age. Ex-police, Samuel judged, probably retired a little too early, perhaps after an injudicious piece of graft. They had little pistols tucked into the belt holsters that trussed their ample stomachs. The radio played Cherie FM – the Parisian housewives' station of choice.

The mixture of bland American rock music and the tinselly drivel that the French called 'le rock' drowned out the low-volume ambient noise that accompanied some of the screens. Of course, to the monolingual guards, any English conversation they might hear was just that – ambient noise and no more.

Samuel had stalled for as long as he could, and was fumbling in his pockets for change, when the moment came. He heard the oath.

'*Regarde-moi ça.*'

Samuel's customer turned to the bank of screens at which the other guard was staring. The entrance hall was a scene of considerable confusion as a young woman in high heels and a tiny micro-skirted dress started screaming about the crimes committed in the name of capitalism. It was Proudhon's foul-mouthed half-sister down there. What was property? Property was evil, capitalist, fuck-pig theft.

The combination of Lauren's looks and the mayhem she was causing had the two men scuttling from the room. In a second, Samuel was alone with the bank of security screens. He quietly shut the door and then turned to look at the choice before him. There were sixty-plus screens, and he had just three microphones – high-frequency bugs with a transmitting distance of a couple of kilometres. The kind of thing that legal research agents keep under their pillows for the next contested matrimonial case – the kind of kit that lay in abundant, disorderly piles round François's flat.

He looked about quickly. The first choice was easy. Once he had identified Miller's office, he slipped the bug onto the head of the co-axial cable. It would pick up the sound from the room's microphone irrespective of the volume level in the control room.

Now – Khan. But Khan didn't have an office. So Samuel

opted for the main dealing room receiver. That would be like listening to the construction site for the tower of Babel, but no matter.

He had one bug left. Where to put it? The boardroom, of course. But he couldn't see it on any of the screens.

Then, as he scanned the monitors, he saw Anton Miller. Miller was headed along one of the upper-level corridors. He flitted off one screen, and appeared a second later on another. Samuel couldn't be sure but he sensed that Miller was coming his way. Any second now he would be trapped. He jammed the last bug under a cable for the nearest screen. With a flash of irritation he realized that this last one, marked 'cave', was dark. He had had three chances to monitor activity at Kopners and had completely blown one of them by bugging the cellar.

But there was no time for regret now. The footsteps were approaching. Discovery was certain. One of the screens showed Miller outside the closed door of the control room. Now his hand was on the door handle, Samuel looked over his shoulder and saw the door opening. Miller was certain to see straight through his disguise. He was finished.

'Monsieur Miller! Monsieur Miller!'

The door remained half-open. The screen showed a guard in the corridor running to Miller. Further down, Samuel could see Lauren bucking and rearing in the middle of a melee of uniform, doing a magnificent job. The guard and Miller hurried off to deal with the emergency, and Samuel, as quickly as he dared after their departure, slipped out of the room and headed back to reception.

19

ONE OF THE LEGS of a horse mounted by Henri IV needed repairing. Samuel watched the green-uniformed men work away in a tiny place tucked off the main street, just visible from his hotel room window. After an hour or so, the statue was bound in bright orange tape and trussed up, nice and tight, by the machinery of government.

Samuel crossed the room and poured himself another glass of water, avoiding eye contact with the faintly ridiculous, black-haired punk figure in the mirror. Lauren was sitting up, rubbing sleep from her eyes. He envied her ability to relax.

She yawned, stretched, considered him: 'Shall we go?'

'We have to go somewhere, that's clear. But where?'

'Your flat. Let's get those credit cards.'

Samuel reflected. He had broken Khan's surety, and if Khan had told the police or whoever the Algerian thugs were, they would be watching his flat. But something told him that disclosing information to other people was not Khan's way. The security at Ropners was slow-witted. That probably wasn't a major concern. Once he had retrieved his wallet, he would be a citizen of the world again, with perhaps half a chance of sustaining his freedom.

'OK. Let's do it.'

Within half an hour they were inside Samuel's flat, and two minutes later he had a bag of clothes and his wallet in hand. The place seemed untouched. It was time to go. No need to ride their luck.

As they let themselves out of the flat, the downstairs front door, five floors below, opened and shut.

Samuel and Lauren looked at one another and instinctively held their breath. Down there somewhere the sound of soft footfalls on the parquet entrance floor was just discernible. There was a brief silence and then they heard someone cautiously mounting the ancient, creaking staircase. Samuel's mind raced through the possibilities. Why was this person not taking the newly installed lift? Was it for the pleasure of exercise, or was it to check on the status of the flats on the way up? Whoever had clambered up the first flight was now beginning the ascent to the second floor.

Samuel motioned to Lauren to stay silent, called the lift, and crept back inside the flat. Seconds later he returned with a radio in his hand. Whoever it was had now reached the third floor and was still stealthily climbing. The silent visitor would reach the fifth floor in less than a minute.

The lift arrived. Samuel opened the doors, and placed the radio inside. He tuned it to a station that broadcast religious monologues non-stop, pressed the ground-floor button on the lift, and stepped out. Seconds later the wire-frame lift cage was earthbound, as a sonorous clerical voice recited a string of trite pieties.

Whoever it was stopped on the staircase. The lift descended slowly, and the priest's voice continued its spiel. Lauren and Samuel crept up one flight of stairs and waited.

There was no sound in the stairwell for many seconds.

Then came the unmistakable creak of a footfall – a heavy foot-fall – on the stair. The mystery man was still coming up.

Hardly daring to breathe, Samuel watched through the wire grille panel of the upper stairs as the man came into view. The shock of recognition hit him like a cold wave. It was the big black guy; the man who had fought him at Kaz's flat.

The man stopped when he saw that the door of Samuel's flat was ajar. Then he began to creep back downstairs. Samuel imagined at first that they would be stuck there until his assailant called for some henchmen. But then there was thunder on the stairs. The man was running back up, this time with some kind of heavy metal implement, perhaps a monkey wrench, in his hand. There was murder in his eyes as he burst into the flat.

Samuel fought the impulse to instant flight. He ran down-stairs and pulled the door of his flat shut. There was a cry from inside, followed by a hammering sound. Too late. Samuel had turned the heavy key of the door three quarters of the way then kicked it, jamming the lock. His burglar was effectively a prisoner.

As the cursing and the raging continued, Samuel and Lauren ran downstairs and hurried out onto the street by the main exit. If the authorities were watching, they would pick them up now. But all was quiet.

Lauren led them up the tiny side street of rue Saint Bon to a large green and pink candy-striped motorbike. Samuel was no connoisseur of two-wheeled transport. He merely recog-nized that the name Triumph carried a certain kudos among those who were bothered about these things.

Lauren opened a pannier on the back of the bike and drew out a set of black leather dungarees. Samuel averted his gaze as Lauren removed her shoes and whipped off her skirt. Within seconds she had stepped into the bottom half of the dungarees and was unbuttoning her suit jacket. This was duly discarded and seconds later she was zipped into the biker's suit and had donned a pair of boots. She folded her business suit and placed it in the box, from which she had already withdrawn a pair of helmets.

'Here.'

Samuel quickly put his helmet on. He looked about him. No crazed assassin running down the street. Other than the dog owner, there were no surprised onlookers to witness Lauren's striptease-cum-pit stop. Within a minute of leaving the apartment block they were edging their way onto rue de Rivoli.

The traffic was particularly bad that day, and Lauren stopped and started as she tried to find a way through the metal chain of bumper-to-bumper vehicles. Samuel looked up at the Tour Saint Jacques. To his surprise, he saw that work was being done on the statuary here too. There was a man up on the second parapet, just behind one of the saints. He was wearing dark glasses and looking down at the street. A few hundred metres back Samuel could see his assailant out on the balcony of the flat; he was gesticulating and waving at the man in the tower. The man appeared to be some kind of surveyor or engineer as he was using a theodolite, training its focus on the crowds below.

Except that it wasn't a theodolite.

Samuel lurched forward hard against Lauren, almost pulling them over. She turned angrily to protest, and then bent forward over the handlebars, opening the throttle and urging a meaty roar from the bike's engine.

The first bolt missed Lauren by a matter of inches. It shattered the ribcage of a tartan-coated poodle as it crouched to make its own contribution to the daily mountain of Parisian dog shit.

Samuel looked up to his left. The figure in the tower was reloading what was some kind of crossbow. He was going to fire at them again. This was lunacy. Behind them a crowd had begun to form round the distressed dog owner.

'Get off the street! He's going to shoot again!' screamed Samuel.

'I can't! The traffic!'

They dodged the wheels of a bus, and several cars screeched to a halt and blared their protests at them in the few seconds it took to reach the junction of boulevard Sébastopol and the rue de Rivoli. But a gendarme had been watching their progress. A white-gloved palm was held up and a whistle blew furiously. The pale blue-shirted traffic policeman stepped into the street, but Lauren swerved and accelerated past him. Samuel's knee caught him as they were racing by; the gendarme twirled around, his arms flailing, his face stupid with surprise. A bolt had pierced his abdomen.

Out of the corner of his eye Samuel saw the next bolt hit home. A girl dropped to the ground clutching her chest. As they sped by Samuel realized that he knew her. It was the girl from the apartment block across the street; the girl who used to undress in the window. He felt tears of fear and anguish pricking in the corners of his eyes. He wanted to leap off the bike and attend to the girl, fresh-faced and in the prime of youth, now felled to the ground because of him.

But Lauren did not look back. Within minutes they were speeding out of Paris.

'Where are we going?' shouted Samuel above the rushing wind.

'To a place where you will be safe,' Lauren yelled back in response. 'It looks like you're definitely a wanted man now.'

20

THE MOON WAS almost full. Strong enough to cast a silvery half-light on the quiet sibilance of the garden fountain. Samuel watched the flicker and splash of the water from the impenetrable safety of a bank of yew hedge. The darkness and the mild summer night eventually offered some comfort. Whatever else happened, he had a moment's solitude. The trip from Paris had been urgent and wordless. They were expecting a hand on the shoulder at any moment – from the gendarmerie, the Algerian police, the black assailant, or some agent of Khan's.

Lauren had promised to return soon, after giving Samuel a quick tour of the house, which belonged to a cousin of hers. It had been some time before he had ventured outside. But now here he was, breathing in the sweet night air, listening to the chuckling of the ancient fountain, the gentle, mechanical whirr of nightjars and cicadas, and beneath it all, the soft reassurance of his own breathing. They had not caught up with him yet and they could not destroy this moment.

The bushes parted and a gloved hand touched his back. He shouted aloud and another hand immediately applied itself to his mouth. But the instinct to struggle was quelled when he saw who it was.

'What the hell?' he hissed.

'Sorry. Sorry.'

Lauren backed away, holding up her hands.

'You looked almost like a statue. I wanted to touch you to make sure you hadn't turned to stone.' She gave him a friendly pat on the back.

'Marvellous. Convinced?' He was breathing heavily, trying to overcome his fear and surprise.

'Sorry,' she said again.

Was that a flicker of a smile that he could see through the veil of darkness?

'Here!' She handed him a mobile phone.

'Where did you get it?' Samuel asked in surprise.

'Believe me, these things are difficult to come by out here where people don't know the meaning of the word technology. There's only a weak signal, but it just about works.' She gave a very Parisian shrug. Small wonder Paris and its inhabitants were hated in the countryside. 'We should have at least a couple of hours before it's missed. There will be no tap.'

'Not on this phone line, at least,' breathed Samuel. The other end of the line he was about to call might well have an attentive listener or two.

'Allô?'

'François?' Samuel's spirits were lifted by the sound of a familiar voice.

'You are famous, my friend.'

'So long as it's just for fifteen minutes.'

'It will be longer than that. You are the rogue trader, an Englishman who revels in letting blood. Kaz dead, Tungley dead. Your neighbour from across the street, dead. A traffic cop in hospital, sadly not dead.'

'So you've been reading the newspapers, François?'

'And it's been on the television, of course.'

Samuel groaned.

'Don't worry, they're using an old identity photo that looks nothing like you.'

Samuel hesitated and then asked if François had anything else to tell him. He knew that if the French police were listening, then François would suffer, but this was his only hope of saving himself. He silently made notes. When he was sure that he had an accurate record of what François had told him, he whistled softly to himself.

'OK, thanks. Take care.'

'No problem. I'll be here in case you need me again.'

'You're a good friend, François.'

'Well?' Lauren was waiting for him by a van at the top of the garden. She was wearing an ancient black leather jacket and tightly belted jeans, and had the general look of teenage jail bait.

'Seems like there may be a way out for me after all.'

Lauren exhaled a rich plume of smoke into the evening sky, threw her cigarette down and began to walk away.

'Where are you going?' called Samuel softly. He had to run to catch up with her as she climbed into the battered old Renault Quatrelle.

'Where do you think I am going?'

She bounced into the seat, and the van's ancient suspension trembled beneath her. Samuel levered himself in next to her and looked across. Since reading that morning's papers and seeing the half-page photos of the stricken gendarme and the dog, he didn't quite know what to think any more. The shops in the little village that Lauren knew from her childhood didn't sell English newspapers; Samuel dreaded to think of the full-scale crucifixion he would be getting from the UK press, complete with chicken sacrifices and burning in effigy. He could imagine the dramatic headlines that would be screaming from the front pages of the tabloids.

Lauren had teased the motor to life and was scudding through the manual gears on the steering column. They careered round a corner following a sign marked *Toutes Directions*.

Samuel gazed out into the darkness and mused. What would Kempis do? What would the Master of Biblos have done?

Here he was, with butchered, dyed hair, sitting in an ancient Renault in the middle of nowhere on a dark night, with no idea of where he was going other than *'Toutes Directions'*. He had to keep moving, physically and mentally, until a long-term solution presented itself. There was craziness and fear and panic abroad, and the hunt was on for someone to blame. Bankers, journalists and foreigners were the perfect targets and Samuel qualified on all three counts. It was a witch hunt, and he was everyone's favourite witch. He was on the run, and no matter how swiftly he moved or how cleverly he hid, eventually the French authorities, or another mystery assailant, or maybe just a mob would find him. And he would be beaten to death.

François had offered some hope. He tapped the dashboard.

'Are you all right?' Lauren shot him a worried look.

'Yes, I'm fine. Keep driving. Where are we headed, by the way?' he asked. Lauren was gunning the little engine for all it was worth as they followed the blue motorway signs for Paris.

'We're going to get you a passport. You need time and space, and you'll never get that as an Englishman on the run in France.'

'So you'll get me a passport. Just like that?'

She veered onto the motorway; the van creaked and tilted precariously.

'Just like that, Samuel. It'll be easy.'

THE CLUB 2000 in Fontenay-sous-Bois on the eastern fringes of Paris seemed quite a remarkable place to Samuel. He had used business centres before, but that had usually been in airport lounges and hotels catering for a business clientele. The fax machines, the laser printers, the array of newspapers and the desktop computer, labelled with its email address for the club members, seemed perfectly proper and eminently usable. It was just that Samuel didn't associate such machinery with a sex club. Gadgets of other sorts, yes, but not the mundane tools of the office environment.

He made himself sit down and read the *Inquirer* article again. The piece had been run under a single-word 42-point headline: 'KILLER'. Without saying that Samuel was definitely a murderer, it pointed out that he was wanted for questioning in connection with the death of Kaz Day, that he had traded extensively with 'rogue trader' Dee Tungley, and that he had been present at the 'William Tell-style slaying' of the girl. There was no mention of the homicidal maniac who had been pursuing him. The thrust of the rest of the piece was a rehearsal of Samuel's involvement in the markets at the time of the crash. It was a masterpiece of smear and innuendo. Undeniably true facts were juxtaposed in such a way that even the dimmest reader would be able to draw scurrilous conclusions. And of course the British newspapers knew their market – the picture of the dead dog dwarfed that of the girl and the injured gendarme. The only mitigating factor was that it had all happened in Paris, and foreign death wasn't as interesting as domestic death – so the paper had run it big, but on page three.

He looked at his watch. Lauren had disappeared behind the green door that led to the bar at least fifteen minutes ago. He felt oddly protective of her, worried even. What was she doing back there to buy him a little more anonymity? If she failed to appear in – he looked at his watch – ten minutes – he would go and find her.

A fax machine whirred into life and produced a short message in Spanish for someone called 'El Grosso'. Samuel wondered who El Grosso might be. Whoever he was, El Grosso certainly wasn't in the business centre. In fact, Samuel had had the place entirely to himself for some time.

He picked up the *Inquirer* again and threw it down. Samuel knew the unmistakable touch of the man, and was furious. How could McMurray betray him? And who had steered the blame in his direction within Ropner Bank? Miller? Khan had to be a possible candidate. He must have discovered the disappearance of the archer miniature by now. The meaning of its absence would be very clear.

There were lots of hard questions, no clear solutions. For the moment, he needed a passport and plenty of luck before he could even think about the next stage of his plan.

He wandered back to the bar, where he was relieved to find Lauren waiting for him. He noted with satisfaction that she looked relaxed and in control.

'Are you OK?' he asked. The look was one of incredulity more than straight inquiry.

'Of course.' She tapped the pocket of her leather jacket and lowered her voice. 'There is something about fat British businessmen. They're quite happy to wander round with no trousers on in a club like this, but they're embarrassed to be seen without a jacket and tie. Why is that I wonder?'

'Probably something to do with the divisive private education system that we have. Most things are,' said Samuel smiling.

'Anyway, that's good for us. There is much for them to surrender. Once they are distracted.'

Samuel gave her a sideways glance. Distracted? Well, it was none of his business what Lauren chose to do. At least in theory.

They walked out onto the street and breathed in the cool night air. It felt fresh and good. Lauren rummaged in her pocket and gave the passport to Samuel. The owner was a rubicund, red-haired man of thirty-eight or so.

'I can never pass for this guy.'

Lauren smiled. 'That can be taken care of. Where to now?'

'Aha,' said Samuel, with a slightly forced levity. 'That would be telling, wouldn't it?'

21

DUSK WAS SETTLING into night, and they had little time. At this time of day, the network of tiny streets at the back of the Gare d'Austerlitz teemed with illicit life. Most of the drugs sold in the shop doorways were straightforward stuff – hash, poppers, various mutant combinations of speed and LSD masquerading as ecstasy, cheap brown heroin from the poppy fields of Afghanistan, a little coke cut with lactose, or nasal decongestant, or, if you were unlucky, something worse.

But the good thing was that the police left the area alone. They had no interest in it, for reasons Samuel well understood. He had noted the sublime insouciance often to be found inside a blue uniform. The semi-official line was that these were dangerous times, dangerous people. Let the *Beurs* kill themselves if they wished, the police had families and pensions to think of. Just ring-fence the place with a few cars at night and let them do their worst. Only if crack cocaine came onto the market, and the fantastic, crazed violence that followed then produced unfavourable newspaper headlines, would a clean-up operation be ordered. Then there would be a huge, sudden swoop – massive force, a few arrests, a trial – followed by another couple of years of glacial indifference.

By day, the shops around Gare d'Austerlitz sold cheap

clothing and cheaper jewellery. And electronic equipment – lots of it. Polaroid cameras that printed scannable pictures, digital recorders, videocams, personal computers, laptops, and every conceivable gadget needed for the transporting, importing and synthesizing of information, with or without cables.

Samuel gazed impassively at the dense bank of matt-black casing and infrared phone ports piled up in one window display. Out of the corner of his eye he followed Lauren's progress. The streets were beginning to fill with the animals of the night. They were scurrying about their own business, and hardly a head turned in the direction of the young woman in biker gear.

Several of the technology shops were open, their windows warm, saffron oases of light in the rapidly deepening blue of early evening. Lauren stopped briefly before the shop they had selected, and went in. Samuel had trawled through the area during the day and identified one that had a reasonable range of goods, and whose proprietor had a shifty look that indicated he might be receptive to the delicate transaction they had in mind.

Samuel waited in the doorway of a pharmacy, its windows shuttered and bolted. Large notices saying no drugs inside, no point in breaking in, had been pasted to steel window sheets. Apart from a couple of paranoid side glances from junkies, no one paid Samuel any attention.

After fifteen minutes he could stand it no longer. The bureau and the police would be looking for a couple. The last thing that Samuel wanted to do was to enter the shop and identify himself as Lauren's partner. But fifteen minutes was too long.

The door opened with a saccharine chime.

The owner, a small, sallow man who Samuel guessed was

Tunisian or Algerian, was on to him in a second. Sorry, terribly sorry, but they were closing. Were closed already in fact. All hand waves and regretful smiles.

Samuel looked about him. Lauren was nowhere. The shop was quite small. It was the work of a second to see that there was no one else there. Lauren had not come out of the door. So she had to be in there somewhere.

Samuel found himself feeling very calm. There were two possible courses of action here. He could play along, perhaps try to offer a large amount of cash for a gadget he didn't want, and work on from there. Or he could play it heavy.

The owner was still jabbering and backing him slowly towards the door. Samuel nodded, and looked briefly around once more. He half-turned to go, and then turned back, as though he had just remembered something important to say.

He brought his elbow round sharply into the side of the little man's head. His momentum and the total surprise of his move had a devastating effect. There were two soft thuds – the first, the sound of the hard ball of his elbow making its impact on the shop owner's skull; the second, a larger, scuffled sound as the man dropped to the floor. Instinctively, Samuel looked over his shoulder. The world outside continued to transact its business.

Samuel stepped over the prone figure, locked the door and switched on the 'Closed' sign. It was surprisingly difficult to shift the small man to one side, but he tidied him out of sight with a little effort. Samuel noted with relief that the shop-keeper was still breathing.

He slipped round the back of the counter. There was a nightstick propped against it. Samuel picked it up and tested its solid weight, the comforting smoothness of the wood in his hand. He pushed gently against the door that led into the interior of the shop. His breathing became heavy and loud. His body was flooding his system with oxygen, preparing him for fight or flight. With a conscious effort he controlled his heaving chest. He had to. There was no going back now.

The door gave way to his push, and he found himself in a dark corridor illuminated dimly by a small red light bulb. He flattened himself against the wall as his eyes grew accustomed to the gloom. At the end of the corridor was a set of stairs. Samuel crept along the narrow alley; the sound of his own breathing now seemed deafening. Eventually, he took a tentative step down towards the lower level.

He was in a basement, with three doors. To his left, he could see a door fortified with bolts and mortise locks. This had a small square window with thick glass and a protective wire screen. Night had fallen completely now, and no light issued from what would be the yard. The other two doors were interior.

He stepped gingerly towards the first, closed his grip on the handle and turned. It was a store room. A confused array of boxes of various sorts, with import ticketing, mostly from Asia, stamped all over them. He closed it quietly, and moved along to the second.

Very softly, he pushed the door open. The pungent smell of hashish, as smoked pure in a bong, assailed his nostrils. He could hear music, modern Arab rap music in French. He had entered a sort of anteroom, and whoever was smoking the dope and playing the music was on the other side of the small door set in the wall in front of him.

Against the muffled throb of the music he could hear voices and a small gust of cruel laughter. The door was marginally ajar and he circled round to peer inside. A fat white man's rear blocked out his view; the man was holding a video camera to his shoulder and chuckling at whatever it was he was filming beneath him. Then he moved away in a small arc, his camera still focused downwards.

Samuel stifled a gasp. He could see Lauren now. She was turned three quarters away from him, bent forward over a high leather bench, her wrists tied. Lauren was naked from the waist down, and her mouth had been gagged. The second man, an athletic-looking Arab, was standing over her, his jeans round his knees. He said something in a guttural voice to the other man. It was in *verlan*, the back-slang of the cities, and Samuel couldn't make it out. Whatever it was, the fat man, who was out of sight now, found it very funny.

The Arab produced something from his pocket and bent over Lauren. Samuel heard the buzzing noise before he saw what it was. A big green vibrator, with bumps and crenellations. It was gyrating slightly in the Arab's hand, and looked almost alive in its cruelty – like a cross between a carving knife and a crocodile leg. The Arab had some kind of cream that he was smearing on the sharp tip of the instrument. Laughing, he rubbed it against Lauren's cheek. She struggled to turn her head away, but could not.

That was when she saw Samuel. She shook her head almost imperceptibly, and Samuel instinctively knew what she meant. The time was not quite right. Not yet.

The Arab man was fully in front of him now, with the fat man somewhere out of sight. Samuel calculated that he was to his right. He would need to take two steps into the room before reaching the Arab and Lauren. He had to wait a little longer until they were both really engrossed. He listened to another few seconds of the brutal amusement of the men. They were taunting Lauren with the sound of the vibrator.

Finally, he kicked open the door. The Arab was pushing

her buttocks up with the intention of inserting the vibrator in her anus. He was so intent on what he was doing that he scarcely noticed that the door had pushed the fat man to the ground. The Arab would have had no time to react in any case. A short, brutal arc from the stick felled him instantly. The fat man was now in the process of getting up from the floor. The videocam had smashed against the wall. Samuel saw with disgust that the fat man's flies were undone.

It took two swings of the nightstick to dispose of him. The first was partially parried, and only succeeded in breaking a cheekbone. The second was a backhand that caught somewhere at the back of the head. The fat man lay motionless as a walrus on a sunny rock.

Samuel rushed to untie Lauren and cradled her in his arms for a second. Fleetingly, she hugged him back.

'Come on,' she said. 'Let's get out of here.'

She pulled her jeans up, dusted herself down, and was ready to go. Samuel marvelled at her composure. Then he looked at the two men. The fat man was still breathing, but the other looked ominously still.

'Have I killed him?' he asked, suddenly appalled.

Lauren rolled him onto his side and smashed her foot into his testicles. Once, twice. The second, sickening impact elicted a small groan.

'Unfortunately not,' she said. 'Come on!'

'This way,' said Samuel. 'We can't leave by the front door.'

He took a ring of keys from the fat man's belt, and left Lauren to work on the bolts of the door. The second room contained what he wanted. There, with a Korean label, was a 'For export only' tone box. Able to replicate the tonality of any phone system in the world, this was the hot property for any computer hacker who wanted a near-guarantee of not being traced. Most transactions involving these boxes were tightly controlled. Export was illegal and involved large amounts of cash. Samuel could only guess what had happened when Lauren mentioned her interest in these boxes, but one thing was certain: the shopkeeper should simply have taken the money.

Lauren had undone the locks, and they stepped out into the night air. It was warm, but Lauren was shivering. Samuel took her hand. Now they had to negotiate the wall of the dank yard.

'Come on, let me help.'

He made a bridge with his hands for her to step on, and soon she was over the wall. Samuel scrambled up after her and dropped down into a narrow, cobbled alleyway, the only light the dull yellow of studio windows.

'What exactly happened in there?' whispered Samuel, pulling Lauren towards him.

'I'll tell you later,' came the brusque response as she pushed him away. 'We need to move.'

They had parked the Renault in one of the small streets near the place d'Italie, and picked their way towards it in silence. Then Lauren stopped suddenly and laid a hand on Samuel's arm.

One look at her stricken face told him what to do.

'Here.'

He folded her into his arms, and rocked her gently. She wept. Big shuddering jolts racked her body. He could feel her tears against his neck, could smell lingering hints of hashish in her thick lustrous hair. She was crying freely now, repeating 'Why? Why? Why?' over and over.

After a few moments she stood back from him, and began dabbing at her smudged mascara. She was brushing back her hair now and pushing him further away from her, adopting a determined and businesslike posture.

'Look.'

She pointed behind him.

The sky in the street where their car was parked was flickering with an electric pulse, like a cinema screen with a faulty projector. They both knew what it was. Police lights.

'Perhaps it's nothing to do with us,' said Samuel. Lauren looked at him and did not speak.

They reached the corner of the street to find, as they both had really known, that the street was blocked off. The little Quatrelle was surrounded by meat wagons and the heavy artillery of the Paris police.

'What a show,' murmured Samuel. 'What are they trying to say here?'

The idiocy of it, the heavy-handed arrogance of the authorities, suddenly provoked him. He began to push forward. He wanted to confront these fools, to remonstrate with them for their indolence, their corruption, their blindness.

But Lauren put her hand to his arm.

'Stop,' she hissed. 'Don't be such an imbecile. Come with me. We need to go. Do you have everything?'

Samuel checked. He had his bag, the tone box and plenty of cash which they had withdrawn before their cards were cancelled. He also had the stolen passport and a data stick of information copied from the laptop, which unfortunately was in the Renault. And, of course, he had Lauren.

He nodded. 'Everything I need.'

22

THEY SLIPPED AWAY quietly into the night, through the scaly maroon entrance arches of the Métro. Soon they were engulfed by the welcoming darkness beneath the place d'Italie. Within half an hour, the acrid smell of stale cigarette smoke and warm engine oil greeted them on the grand concourse of the Gare St Lazare. And twenty minutes after that, a long carriage of overlit shiny orange seats populated only by an old lady with a tiny dog in a voluminous handbag promised to be their sole companions between Paris and St Malo. Safety and a slow train were heavenly; the early morning and the stiff backache awaiting them were trifling in comparison.

Samuel waited until they were far out in the suburbs and the light from the urban sprawl of the city was dissipating. Such dwellings as there now were emitted light like glowing coals scattered on a night beach.

'So?'

Lauren had been largely silent during the trip across Paris – she had hardly spoken since her ordeal. She lifted her head.

'Please don't ask me to relive it, Samuel. I know you are concerned, but I don't want to think about it.'

'No. Obviously not.'

He took her hand. She allowed him to hold it for a moment.

'We need to eat,' he said, gently running his fingers through her hair.

She passed him one of the slightly middle-aged sandwiches they had bought at a kiosk on the station. Samuel bit into it. It was tuna, which he hated, but he was so hungry that any-thing would have tasted good. He encouraged her to eat and she eventually took a tentative bite of the second sandwich.

They chewed solidly for a while. France passed them by. Slowly, reassuringly. When they had consumed every last crumb of the sandwiches, Samuel took Lauren's hand again. She stared at his hand and gently caressed his fingers with hers, lost in thought. After a while, she spoke, almost in a whisper.

'I couldn't move, you know. I couldn't move.' She began to cry, slamming her fists on her knees. He put his arm around her shoulders.

'You're OK now. You're safe.' He pulled her to him more tightly and gently kissed her temple. 'I should have come sooner.'

'You came in time. I'm fine, I promise. That's not why I'm upset, Samuel.' Her voice faltered again and she let out a sob. 'Kaz is dead and nothing can bring her back.'

Samuel gave her his handkerchief. Better to be practical and useful than offer banal niceties. She was right. Nothing could bring Kaz back.

They looked out of the window for a while and Lauren gradually became calmer, helped by the regular sound of the train's motion and Samuel's warm embrace. It was he who broke the silence.

'You need to sleep,' he said. Lauren nodded, and eventually

they found a row of seats where one of the chair partitions was broken. Here Lauren was able to lie down with her knees drawn up and sleep in relative comfort. Samuel sat opposite and drifted in and out of a tentative slumber.

An hour or two later he was woken as the train came to a sudden halt for no apparent reason in the middle of the bitumen-black countryside. He looked out of the window, his heart hammering in his chest. He could not detect any sounds of police boarding. Just the routine banging and clanking of a slow night train.

At last they began to move again, and he tried to settle. But sleep would not come this time. He touched his inside pocket and resisted the impulse to withdraw the document. The passport had in the end been surprisingly easy to fake.

Lauren had told him that all he had to do with the burgundy-coloured pan-European version, which she had so effortlessly stolen, was to leave it in the freezer for an hour, then take it out and zap it with maximum force in the microwave for fifteen minutes. At which point the heat-sealed plastic inside cover simply uncurled, and a new photo could be inserted. Only if the document was held under ultraviolet light to test the seal would it be possible to tell that it had been tampered with.

Samuel had to trust Lauren's expertise. She seemed confident enough. But would the passport control on the Jersey ferry use ultraviolet? It was hard to know. He had been lucky until now, managing to evade his various pursuers. It could only be a matter of time before one of them caught up with him.

The sky was a torn grey, and his neck hurt by the time they got to St Malo. He must have slept for three hours in the hideous discomfort of the train. At least Lauren had managed to sleep a little. She was now busying herself with greeting the new day. This involved vigorous washing, the miraculous production of a bottle of mineral water, and a cigarette. They were in a non-smoking carriage, but the wrath of a train guard hardly seemed to matter much any more.

No one was lurking on the station platform. The place seemed as sleepy as anyone could expect on an early summer's morning. A middle-aged woman with dyed, aubergine-coloured hair walked towards them, stopped, fumbled in her bag in front of them long enough for them to imagine she might be rummaging for a warrant card or a gun. But all she produced was her ticket. Small morning sounds of wind on shutters and warbled birdsong filled the air. To judge from the wide, well-used roads, it would not be long before the low hum of the traffic drowned the early morning sounds of nature. They made their way to a rank, Samuel carrying their bags, and took a taxi ride with a sullen, taciturn driver.

Deposited at the ferry terminal, they were soon walking again, a cool breeze chilling their faces. The first boat was due to leave in thirty minutes. Samuel advanced to the ticket counter, but Lauren pulled him back.

'Just one ticket.'

'What?'

A lone seagull wheeled over them, cried out and then flew away.

'Just one. I can't come with you, Samuel.'

He looked into Lauren's face and saw how pale and drawn she looked. The loss of Kaz, the terror of being pursued and the near-rape had taken their toll.

'If you stay, I stay. I can't leave you like this,' said Samuel, devastated at the thought of being without her.

'No. I have made my voyage of discovery.'

'How do you mean?'

'You and Kaz.'

'But . . .'

She raised a hand gently to his lips.

'Let me speak. I have seen her in places like those clubs. I have seen her in many places, in many situations. And I know now for certain that you were one of the people she chose. I didn't want to believe what those police cretins said, but now I feel it. Please.'

Samuel stopped himself. It would have been useless to protest anyway.

'I want to come with you, Samuel, but you stand a better chance on your own. I need to be on my own too. Just go. I thought I was doing this for Kaz, because it was the right thing, because it was a way to uncover the truth about her death. But when I was on my knees in that room, about to be raped, I couldn't be as brave as I wanted to be. I realized I was just doing this for myself, for the adventure, the game.'

'Is that all we've been doing, then, playing a game?'

'Who knows?' She shrugged, and looked out to sea. 'I do know that I am sick of games. I know I am the only one who can help myself right now. And to do that, I need to be alone.'

She sighed.

'You must go, Samuel. Go to England. It is your country. You'll be safer there.'

'Please.' He tried one last time. 'Come with me. I want you to come with me. I want you to help me. I . . . I want to help you if I can.'

She smiled, shook her head and kissed his fingertips. They sat on a bench in a small cobbled square, and held hands for a while, like lovers at ease with each other. Eventually, Lauren pressed a wad of euros into his lap, and stood up.

'Is this goodbye?'

'Maybe au revoir, and not adieu. Good luck, Samuel.'

She gave him a long, lingering kiss on the lips, took her bag and then she was gone, leaving Samuel to board the ferry alone.

23

SAMUEL STARED AT himself in the mirror. So far, so good, but the strain was beginning to tell. Far from using ultraviolet light, the border guards had waved him straight through, but soon he really would look like the thirty-eight-year-old his passport claimed him to be. He put out a hand to steady himself. If no police were waiting for him on the station platform, this would be the end of the easy part, the end of the physical journey. What would follow promised to be more difficult.

In the confines of the train toilet, he applied a little more foam to his scalp and continued the delicate business of shaving his head. A simple move, but a bald head might just get him past a casual eye. Moreover, the black hair dye was ludicrous; it had a faintly tarry tint in the sun, and generally looked like boot polish. He nicked himself slightly on the top of the head, and grimaced.

He finished, wiped his scalp and looked at himself. Then he returned to a different carriage and gazed out at the soft green dimples of the southern Oxfordshire countryside, staring occasionally at the dome-head he caught looking back at him from the reflection in the train window.

They would be there in a matter of minutes now.

He had sent the statement from an internet café yesterday, just after disembarking. He imagined it winging its way across the ether to José Nissan's electronic mailbox. From the detail, Nissan would know it was authentic, despite the anonymity of the hotmail ID. Would he use it? Maybe. More likely the police would have traced the message back to the café in Jersey. Well, he was long gone now. And – he felt the cool top of his newly shaven head – they were welcome to the security camera pictures of him coming through immigration.

The train was moving like an earthworm with no clue of where it really wanted to go. Samuel sighed. This was typical of the British rail system. Whether private or state-run, it had never recovered from decades of governmental apathy. The one thing you could rely on was plenty of random delay.

He looked around him. The old lady who had been giving him sympathetic looks, perhaps imagining that he was a cancer sufferer, must have got off at Reading. He was all alone in the carriage, whose arthritic wheels were grinding to a halt with a long, excruciating shriek.

He looked out of the window. A few cows gazed back at him. It was too late by the time he saw the dark figure in the reflection of the windowpane. He turned and tried to stand up, but a swift, brutal blow to the side of the head sent him sprawling back on his seat.

Then, before he could cry out a very strong hand clamped itself over his mouth. The stench was disgusting – like hospitals and hayseed, but oh so sharp, like hot knives stabbing his nostrils, then filling his head with a whirring, blurring pain. Just as he was losing consciousness he realized it had to be chloroform, which was why his flailing limbs suddenly felt so heavy, then became impossible to move. The last thing he noticed before the darkness descended was that the hand placed so tightly over his mouth was quite badly damaged. There was a bloodied bandage where the little finger should have been.

He had the sensation of coming up from beneath a great weight of water, struggling to get to the light and air. Then, at last, he broke the surface, and found himself gasping.

So he wasn't dead after all. That was something. Then the pain hit him. He had a brutal headache that made him want to weep for the intensity of it. He gasped, and felt the air rattle in and out of his lungs. His body was drenched in sweat. He moved to wipe his forehead, but he was bound hand and foot. A leather restraint bit into his wrist. He forced himself to relax his arm, and slowly worked the muscles to loosen the tourniquet slightly and improve his circulation.

His head still felt like it was going to explode. The pain boiled in his brain every time he looked towards the sun filtering in through the skylight. He was in some sort of attic, tied to a big, musty bed. The place stank. He realized with a stab of schoolboy shame that it wasn't just sweat that covered his body. He had soiled himself.

The door opened with a creaking noise that was like a rifle shot inside his head. The frame was filled with the outline of a big man. He squinted to make out who it was, but he already knew. His assailant walked towards him slowly, holding up his damaged hand, a cold smile on his face.

'You don't smell too good, son.'

Samuel tried to respond, but his throat was too dry. He coughed miserably. The rattle and heave of it pained him, as did any movement of the head.

'Well, I'm not cleaning up your shit,' he said and disappeared. Samuel could hear him stamping heavily down several sets of stairs. Within moments the door opened again as his captor returned, walking towards him and breathing hard. He didn't notice the buckets until the first one was being poured over him. He almost shouted. It was full of cold, soapy water.

'Now for the rinse.'

His captor was smiling, clearly taking pleasure in the ritual of humiliation. Another bucket of cold water. Samuel was bucking on the bed from the shock of it, but glad nevertheless to be a little cleaner.

'And now.'

His captor held up a knife, the one Samuel recognized from their fight on the stairwell in Paris. For a second he thought that the man was going to cut his fingers off, one by one. Or perhaps just slit his throat and have done with it. But instead he slashed through the restraints. Then as a shivering Samuel began to rub at his arms and legs, the man pointed at a pair of jeans and a T-shirt.

'Those are for you. There's some food and a couple of newspapers you might find interesting next door. Here. Dry off.'

He threw a rough towel at Samuel's head.

'Someone likes you,' he said, as Samuel removed his shirt and began rubbing as vigorously as he could. His accent somehow lent his words extra menace. 'For me, I'd kill you now. Maybe I will kill you one day.' He caught Samuel's eye. 'I'd like that.' He left the room again and Samuel heard a key turning in the lock of the door.

Someone liked him? He had been beaten about the head, drugged and tied to a bed. Did that constitute liking him? Samuel dried himself off and then used the towel to clean himself up as best he could. He changed into the jeans and T-shirt. The clothes were too big – probably the black guy's own gear. He stood on a rickety chair and tried to work out where he was by peering through the skylight, but the opening was small and set near the top of the roof. All he could see was the sky. He looked around the room for clues as to where he was, but there were none. He could be in England, France, or New York State for all he knew.

Suddenly he was very hungry. In the next room, which was even smaller, there was a camp table with a plate of sand- wiches, a bottle of water, and some newspapers on it. He sat down and began to eat. Corned beef sandwiches. Bizarre. He hadn't had those since he was a little boy, when he had only eaten them under duress, but now they tasted delicious. Best of all, the water felt like nectar from heaven as it ran down his gullet.

Eventually, he reached for the newspapers. Whoever it was who had taken him prisoner wanted him alive and informed. More in hope than expectation, he reached for the *Mercury Inquirer*.

Yes. Incredibly, yes. There it was, the lead story on the front page. 'Meltdown Fugitive's Denial'. With José Nissan's byline. The paper had run more or less the full content of Samuel's statement. After the usual flourishes and chest- beating about the exclusivity of the story, the piece carried his communiqué with only the tiny stylistic alterations that sub- editors made when they felt like justifying their existence. Nissan's copy was naturally couched in legalese, with plenty of words such as 'alleged' to satisfy the lawyers. It seemed that Nissan had been able to convince his editor that it really was Samuel who had sent the message – a couple of details of their last conversation would have been good enough for that. An ancient picture of a young man with curly blond hair, whom Samuel scarcely recognized as himself, adorned the article.

MELTDOWN FUGITIVE'S DENIAL
ROGUE TRADER PROTESTS INNOCENCE
Inquirer Exclusive by José Nissan

Fugitive trader Samuel Spendlove, wanted by French police in connection with a series of alleged crimes ranging from murder to market rigging, has sensationally pointed the finger of blame at former colleagues, the *Mercury Inquirer* can exclusively reveal.

In a secret electronic message to this newspaper, Spendlove has denied any responsibility for the murder of former colleague Katherine Day, the head of European equity sales at Ropner Bank in Paris. Spendlove has also claimed that at least one other of his former colleagues was involved in the manipulation of share and currency markets on a regular basis. Those responsible for the alleged market rigging used proxy accounts and temporary 'suspense' accounts to conceal their actions, according to Spendlove.

Spendlove, who reported directly to Ropner Bank's renowned proprietary trader, Khan, has also alleged a connection between the death of Ms Day and the death of one of the bank's Frankfurt-based traders, Dee Tungley, another US national.

The British and French police are cooperating closely on the case, with the Americans taking a detailed interest too. The *Mercury Inquirer* has opened up its computer records to technical experts so that they can try and trace where Spendlove's message was sent from. Police believe that he may be in southern France, and have warned that the public should not approach him, as he could be dangerous.

Samuel put the paper down and scratched his head. It was strangely, weirdly funny to read about himself as though he were a criminal – a dangerous criminal! Well, he was a prisoner now, so no one need fear him.

His head still ached, which made thinking difficult. He tried to work out why he'd been captured, but not killed. The answer certainly wasn't that someone liked him. That someone – if it happened to be the same someone who'd had him picked up in France – certainly didn't like him. The only answer he could think of was information. Either he already knew something without understanding its value, or the 'someone' thought he knew something he didn't know at all. Whatever the answer, he was alive – with a brain that ached terribly.

He wandered back to the main room and examined the door. It would give if he tried hard enough to force it. If he could find his shoes there would be no difficulty kicking it down. But why would he do that? He felt awful, and his captor at the base of the attic stairs would need no encouragement to inflict damage on him. And then he would just be running away again, offering himself as prey to one of the other parties that were so eager to take him.

He went back to the small room to reread the newspaper article. The first part of the strategy had worked well, maybe too well. Was that why he was here? It was the afternoon and the sun had come out. Rays of light were forcing their way through the boards behind him. He tested them. It was a window that had been boarded up years ago. Again, the slats would be relatively easy to force, but secure bars were not the issue. His captors did not seem to wish to impose serious physical constraints. Which meant, he realized with a flash of anger, he'd been tied up just for the sadistic fun of it.

Samuel heard heavy footsteps on the stairs again. The key turned and the door creaked open. His captor walked across the bedroom and then had to stoop to enter the small room.

'Did you enjoy reading about yourself, Mr Spendlove? Do you think that trying to shift the blame onto other people is going to make the slightest bit of difference to your fate?' The black man shot him a look of pure hatred and fingered his wounded hand again, a constant reminder of their first encounter. 'If you are thinking of making a run for it, be my guest. You will never escape from me. Once my friends have finished with you, don't think that will be the end of my interest in you, Mr Spendlove.' He held his hand up. 'We have a score to settle.'

Samuel did not respond, sensing that it was better to say nothing.

'How's your luck today?' asked his captor. 'Feel like a race down the stairs?' Still no response from Samuel. 'Give me trouble and I'll give you trouble.' There was a leer painted on his captor's face now. Samuel considered. He was being given a head start. He looked towards the door of the main room. He might just make it to the stairs, but then he had no idea what was out there, what sort of booby traps might have been set. Nor who else might be waiting for him. He sensed that this man had waited long enough to exact revenge on him and was determined to have his fun. Filaments of sunbeam framed the captor's shoulders.

Samuel finally spoke.

'No thanks. I'm happy to stay here and read the paper.' The man relaxed and looked to leave the room.

Without warning, Samuel swept the things off the top of the table, picked it up and ran at the man, ramming the table into his midriff. He pushed hard. A burst of adrenalin gave him real impetus, and the shock of the move worked surprisingly well. The man bent double, lost his footing, staggered back, and crashed through the boarded window.

Samuel hurled himself to the floor to avoid falling through

the window too. Springing back up, he heard his captor's screams and saw that his feet were hooked over the edge of the old window frame. His body was supported by a small bit of slated roof. Samuel edged up to him. He could see now that they were high up. The huge man was almost vertically inclined with his head downwards, like a naval coffin about to be tipped into the sea. Samuel could see that the slightest movement would send the Frenchman crashing to earth.

'Help me! Help me, please!' The big disfigured hand extended towards him. It would be the work of a second to send his tormentor to an ugly death.

But that would be murder, and if he saved the man's life there was the chance at least that he might give him useful information. He must follow his instincts, as the Master taught, not fight them. He wasn't a killer. Samuel held his hand out and the man reached up to take it.

But just as he felt the warmth of his skin, the window casing finally gave way, and the man slid down over the roof and plunged to the yard below. Samuel gasped with horror.

He dared not look down. His captor must be dead. He could not have survived such a precipitous fall. Samuel was finding it difficult to breathe, hardly able to believe what had just happened. Eventually he leaned out of the hole in the side of the building that had once encased a window frame. The man lay spreadeagled on a car roof below. He was very still.

Samuel looked, listened, tried to get his bearings. It was a bright, sunny day. On the horizon, he could see the spires of Oxford. No one ran out of the house to see what had happened. They must have been alone.

Undoubtedly there were people who knew their whereabouts, and if his jailer did not contact them, they would want to know why. There could be others in the house who had not heard the commotion, although this was unlikely. He would only know for sure if he ventured outside.

Samuel walked tentatively down the stairs. The house was sparsely furnished – a holiday rental, he guessed. He had to move quickly now. He found his shoes and bag, which had been dumped in a spare room, doubtless waiting for the arrival of whoever it was. He quickly checked the contents of the bag – the miniature sculpture of the archer was still there, and his electronic equipment. There was a stash of euros, pound notes, skunk and cigarettes in the kitchen cabinet. He stuffed the whole cache in his pocket and wandered out into the farmyard. He could use the drugs and cigarettes to barter with.

Samuel stood looking at his former captor for a moment. After a while, he moved slowly towards the car. He extended his hand and touched the body. It was still warm, but there was no discernible pulse. He shuddered.

He walked briskly towards the barns. They were all empty, except for one, which had a couple of motorized scooters in the corner. One had a key in the ignition and a helmet on the seat. Well, it was better than nothing. He placed the helmet on his head and quickly ripped the cabling from the other scooter. Then, pulling his bag over his shoulder, he hopped onto the first one. From his vantage at the top of the house he'd seen the criss-cross of bridle paths that would take him to Oxford, his destination. It wouldn't be a quick trip, but it was faster than walking, and the helmet afforded some anonymity.

He headed off in a northerly direction on a wide, flat path. He guessed he had no more than seven miles to travel. He'd be there, with a bit of luck, in half an hour. He breasted the first hill of the valley and fancied he saw a dark blue car take the turning for the farm. He didn't wait to see whether he was right. Oxford beckoned.

SAMUEL DISCARDED the scooter in the forecourt of the Kite pub, just off the Botley Road. He would do the last section of the trip on foot. As he passed Oxford railway station, he thought that it looked surprisingly quiet. The mass of push-bikes in the forecourt made it look like a vast box of hairpins. He was relieved to see that no crazed assassins, no bad suits from the French police or sturdy members of the Oxfordshire constabulary were discernible.

He wandered along Park End Street towards the centre of the city. Before long he was swinging his bag and whistl-ing. The summer was beginning to evaporate in Oxford, and the Michaelmas term was approaching. Some of the keener students had come up early to study for the exams that each college set at the beginning of term.

Times had changed. Samuel was no longer studying here. The university and Gail were his old life. The grid references of his new existence were written in fire: murder investigations, secret service agents, mega-deals and the billionaires' casino of world finance. Kaz, Khan, Lauren were his new companions – but he was separated, estranged or divided by death from all of them. Which just left him with his plan, the one plan that made sense.

Samuel came to a coffee house just off Carfax. It was a quiet spot out of term, and was as yet uncluttered by tech-nology and the ever-growing tentacles of the internet. He settled at a table, and ordered a jug of water, plus a large espresso and four slices of toasted soda bread with thick-cut marmalade.

He gave an impulsive shudder. Maybe they – whoever they were – were watching him now, waiting. He looked around him. The only other customer was a middle-aged woman with shopping bags. She looked almost too tired to draw on her cigarette. He could relax for a minute at least.

He ordered another coffee and sat, reflecting a little more. It was certain he would be found in the long run. All he could realistically hope for was to engineer a little space and time to make sure that he found what he needed before they caught up with him. Nevertheless, he could not go to ground yet. He dared not make a call, and would just have to wait until the hour when he knew he could meet his man.

He leafed idly through the sports section and let the world pass him by for a moment. Then a headline jumped out at him from the large pile of old, discarded newspapers by the window. That name again – Khan – he was everywhere. The piece, a minor story on the front page of last week's *Financial Times*, was certainly interesting.

The poacher had turned gamekeeper and had seemingly been forgiven for bringing havoc to the world markets through his manipulation of the oil price. Khan, king of volatility and counter-intuitive plays, was calling for stability in the markets. The latest crisis was in Poland, which had just about managed to organize its economy and dedicate it to the market ethic in perfect time to have everything swept away by the financial tempests raging around the world. Khan was calling for IMF support, aid from the European Investment Bank, the European Bank for Reconstruction and Development, and coordinated soft loans from a number of agencies, including the World Bank. He also wanted to establish a currency board – a committee of 'wise men' – to dictate monetary policy, and implored the G8 group of rich Western nations to offer a rescue bond of several billion dollars to inject liquidity and confidence into the ailing Polish financial system.

Samuel was now all set to complete the final and shortest leg of his journey. But having read the *FT* piece he sat there for a few moments more and pondered. Khan had been cast in the role of financial guru. The Chaos Kid was suddenly on the side of order and regulation. Maybe he was about to take some very large positions in the Polish zloty. If Khan had expressed the view that the international community should do all it could to support Poland, then taking such a position could be interpreted as being part of that effort. And then he could not be criticized for trying to make profit out of the distress of others. His time at Ropner Bank had changed Samuel from a naive, fresh-faced youth into a cynical man.

24

SAMUEL PULLED UP the collar of his leather jacket, jammed back his sunglasses, and checked his baseball cap. He walked towards All Souls, but this time there was no easy assumption of privilege, no confident stride, no scholar's gown – just the feeling that he was being hunted by an enemy that could emerge from any shadow.

He skirted by the paved forecourt of St Mary's church and presented himself at the porter's gate.

'Yes?'

The same sullenness of tone, the same understated belligerence. The porter hadn't recognized him, but even if he had and there'd been a reward of millions on his head, the custodian of the All Souls gate would not have admitted to knowing Samuel. The porter had one asset – an arrogant ignorance of the rest of the world. This he would not relinquish at any price.

'Dr Kempis. I'm expected.'

'Name?'

'Jeffries. Randall Jeffries.'

A list was checked with feigned studiousness.

'I'm afraid you're not down on the list, sir.'

'But Dr Kempis is in at the moment. He's invited me for sherry. Perhaps you could telephone him?'

'Oh, no. That'll be all right, sir.' The sherry seemed to have convinced him, even if Dr Kempis's visitor did look a little odd. Samuel wondered whether the porter was covering up an inability to keep a simple appointment diary. Or maybe picking up the phone was just too much trouble.

Samuel listened patiently as directions were given to a place he had visited scores of times. Moments later the echo of his footfall sounded as it always had on the stair; the outer door above the shakily inscribed 'PBH KEMPIS' was open and he knocked twice, as usual, on the stout inner door.

Suddenly Kempis was standing in front of him.

'Yes? This is not my usual hour for visitors . . .' He started. 'Is that you, Samuel?'

'Yes, Peter, it's me. Can we go in?' Samuel was suddenly very conscious of their voices booming through the stairwell.

The old man was plainly delighted to see him.

'Come in, do,' he said, pumping Samuel's hand. Kempis gestured towards a chair. He put his bag down and sat.

The sherry bottle was instantly uncorked, and Kempis was pouring.

'My boy, you have been going through interesting times. Let me look at you.'

Samuel removed his cap, feeling somewhat like a circus freak.

'I suppose a shaved head acts as some sort of disguise. You look tired,' said Kempis in a concerned voice. 'You have much to be tired about, no doubt. Tell me, is what one reads in the newspapers true in any fashion? You are, of course, a celebrity in the university now. Infamy is at least as good as fame, if not better.'

Samuel sipped at the sherry. The instant hit of the alcohol, the sight of a familiar face and the unchanging nature of their sherry ritual comforted him. Kempis was naturally sympathetic; he was an old family friend, a cohort of his grandfather, a mentor to his father and then to Samuel himself. And like all genuinely intelligent men, Kempis knew how to listen. It took over an hour, and a couple of refills, but at the end of it Samuel had unburdened himself of his few certainties, his several confusions, and the structure of the only potentially workable plan he could think of. When he had finished, Kempis sat and considered, his fingertips forming a cage, a matrix of possibilities and strategies.

'And how long do you need?'

'I don't know. I may never find what I'm looking for. But they're certain to find me sooner or later.'

'You have everything you require in that little bag?'

Samuel nodded.

'May I?' He gestured towards Kempis's computer. It was an Apple, perhaps a couple of years old. Samuel quickly checked the applications. Kempis only used the net browser and the email functions, but the Super Java and the high-function algorithmic code language that Samuel might need were all in place. That was technology for you: a few hundred dollars' worth of kit was all you needed to hack into the Pentagon or win the Nobel Prize for economics. But that had always been the story of Oxford – pen, paper, or nowadays a small computer, plus a little wit. These were the university's instruments of world domination.

'Yes, this is fine,' said Samuel after a couple of minutes of putting the machine through its paces. 'I have everything that I need.'

He looked at the don for a moment. 'Peter, may I ask you a question?'

'Of course.'

'Have you been sending me emails?'

'My dear boy, you know I have. Despite your hasty departure, I feel a sense of obligation . . .'

'No. Not those emails. Anonymous emails offering help and guidance with all this mayhem surrounding Kaz and Tungley? Using a false user identity?'

'The anonymous emails you referred to earlier? Do you think it likely, Samuel?'

'That's not what I asked. Did you?'

Kempis removed his spectacles and rubbed them thoughtfully. 'The answer, of course, is no. I have been conducting my research. The paths of my investigations led me to Byzantium, not your exotic doings in Paris.'

'Ah. I see. I'm sorry.'

Samuel looked down, suddenly aware of his uncouth appearance, his incursion into Kempis's civilized world.

At length, Kempis spoke: 'Given the delicacy of your relations with the forces of law and order, I take it you would appreciate a little hospitality from an old friend?'

'You mean I can stay here?'

A nod.

Samuel beamed. 'Thanks, Peter. But . . . what about the scouts?'

Kempis waved a hand.

'The servants? Bill and Martha? They will think nothing of it. Simply a question of leaving the "Do Not Disturb" sign up, and they will leave you alone. I often withdraw completely here for days on end if I am writing a monograph. I believe I spent nearly a week here last year, writing a paper for the *Cambridge Law Journal* on – what was it now? – ah yes, comparative evidentiary values for expressed will in contract formation for selected civil and common law jurisdictions. They didn't set foot in the place for the whole week.'

'Actually, Peter, I was hoping that I might draw a little on your intellectual resources too. As this thing progresses – if I can make it work at all, that is – I will need someone to subject my analysis to scrutiny. And I can think of no one better than you.'

'But, my boy, finance is not my field.'

'No, but thought is. You are the perfect man to help. I have been imagining what the Master of Biblos would have done in this situation, and his brand of practical reasoning has worked out extremely well. I think you're the closest living being to him.' Samuel sighed. 'In any event, you're in the best position to help since you're the only person I can trust.'

'Well, put like that, I can only offer my humble best. Though humble it may be.'

'Good.'

'So when do we start?'

'Well, now. Unless that's inconvenient.'

'THIS IS MOST ENTERTAINING, my boy. Most entertaining,' said Kempis, picking up one of the cables and suddenly replacing it as though in fear of somehow contaminating it. 'All I ever use this computer for is to gain access to research papers, pictures of exhibits and that sort of thing.'

Samuel flipped through some of the browser screens. Kempis had bookmarked a number of websites that Samuel himself knew – the University of Texas, the University of Fribourg, an academic publisher in Heidelberg.

'And now we're going to use it as a vehicle on what people

used to refer to as the information superhighway. This is the dangerous part.'

'How so?'

'Because we can be traced. The so-called superhighway is really no more than a conflation of little bits and bobs of information conveyed down tiny phone wires or big fat fibre optic and co-axial cables. Two billion people use GSM – that's the Global System for Mobile Communications – and they and their computers all travel on the highway using a digital vehicle that has its own distinctive engine tone. They can have the latest Kray supercomputer, a BlackBerry, or a prehistoric Apple laptop with an external modem. The trick, though, isn't really about computing power, but knowing where to go, and how to get there secretly.'

Kempis picked up the tone box, an anonymous brick of matt black plastic with a row of small red lights, and began to examine it, as though looking for a set of instructions.

'We use that to get on the highway by invading the phone system,' said Samuel. 'If you like, we scramble down the banks of the motorway and start trucking, so that anyone watching the entry roads will never find us.'

'Entry roads?'

'Yes. Here in Oxford there is a straightforward automatic electronic exchange. When you want to look at a document in Fribourg, for example, you enter the Oxford University mainframe, and gain access to the internet that way. You are charged only for a local call, and the access to the internet, your slip road, is via the Oxford local system. The tones of the call to the local computer tell the exchange where to place the call, but they also leave a very clear trail for anyone who wants to trace you. It would be the work of minutes to determine how often you had logged on, and where you were when you did so.'

'Now this thing' – Samuel pointed at the box, which was now plugged into Kempis's phone socket and into his computer – 'offers us a different way.'

'Was it expensive?' asked Kempis with a look of fascination.

'Obtained at a very high price,' said Samuel sombrely.

He pulled out his diary and dialled the number of a free-phone service in the US, explaining what he was doing to Kempis all the while. It was an international software exchange forum that made its money from carrying advertising to the vast amount of traffic it processed.

Samuel then switched to the tone box's options function. The phone was ringing, using high-frequency, near-digital quality sound – close to wireless and Bluetooth technology in terms of speed, but far harder to trace once the user was logged on. The ringing phone sent an instruction to clear the line for communication at 3,200 hertz. This signal effectively told the international call control centre to end the call. But the tone box then sent a slightly higher 3,600 hertz signal that jammed the request to end the call. This seize tone had the effect of opening another line – a free call that was logged between the two exchanges in New York and the UK. Best of all, the source of the call would be untraceable. The original call had in effect never connected, and the free call would be registered only as coming from New York.

'You lost me a long time ago, Samuel. Are you telling me it's perfectly untraceable and safe?' asked Kempis.

'Nothing's foolproof, Peter. But so far, so good,' said Samuel, as the reassuring burr of the open line issued through the PC speakers. 'Now . . .'

He looked in his wallet and pulled out the single sheet of

paper he had scribbled on during his last call to François. Hurriedly written, but quite legible, was an anonymous grouping of pencil figures; he tapped in the site identity that François had given him. And there it was, on the undernet, a simple subgrouping that enabled those with the right access code to survey the information. Someone with an ID Samuel didn't recognize had set up the website. Perhaps François too had invented himself a new ID. It was easy enough, after all.

The information he needed was now sitting in front of him. Samuel had gained access to the digitized versions of the recordings registered by the bugs he had planted in the security control room at Ropner Bank.

He clicked on the first icon and whistled. François had not just posted the unedited recordings, as promised, but had used a voice-activated transcription program to create text versions of whatever the microphones had captured. It would obviously have taken too long for Samuel to listen to the tapes in their entirety – it might have been days before the bugs had been discovered, as they surely must have been. There were potentially three or four days of tapes for each microphone he had planted. Scanning through the text would give him a better chance of spotting something quickly. Quite what he was looking for he still wasn't certain, but knowledge was power, and he needed all the power he could get.

He began the long, arduous task of sifting the information, all the while aware that, in addition to all the other parties who were anxious to find him, the UK police would now be looking for the killer of the man in the farmyard. Time was running out.

SAMUEL AWOKE to a crinkling sound. He had fallen asleep reading the transcript, the text versions of the audio files. They were mostly jumbled words, snatches of conversation. Confusing and desperately dull, but he had to pan through it all in the hope of finding a flake of gold.

There was a knock at the door. Samuel sat up abruptly. Had he remembered to put the 'Do Not Disturb' sign up? Would Bill and Martha walk in on him? He heard shuffling sounds outside. Perhaps this was it. Maybe there was a squad of police officers at the door, come to take him into custody and explode his theories and his proofs and his hope of liberty. Well, there was only one way to find out. He sprang up and flung the door wide open.

'THERE IT IS. *Don't ask how I got it. Not that you would.'* He tossed a mini-disk onto the café table.

'We'd never ask you to do anything that we felt was morally unjustifiable I tell you that as one operative to another.'

The man opposite slid his copy of the International Herald Tribune over the disk, to be picked up unobtrusively on departure.

He sighed. They might both be 'operatives' engaging in schoolboy field craft, but somehow he could never feel that this man was a colleague. They just happened to have a common enemy, that was all.

'Hey, hey,' said the other man, as if reading his mind. 'We're the guys in the white hats, remember?'

'Oh yeah. Gott mit uns, and all that. Except, of course, you don't like Germans, do you?'

'Myself? I have no problem with the Germans. The French, mind. They're different.'

'Not you. I mean the Agency.'

'Keep your voice down.'

'You're the one saying you've got problems with the French. We're right in the heart of Paris in case you've forgotten.'

He blanked the stare coming back at him across the small table. These guys – a combination of paranoia and arrogance – not unlike some market players he knew.

They watched the buskers and the skateboarders do their stuff by the entrance of the Forum des Halles. The waiter came with a coffee and a small beer, together with a printed bill asking them for euros in the name of the Bon Pêcheur.

'So. Did he do it?'

The operative nodded at a long feature article in the financial newspaper Les Échos. The writer was excitedly describing how the American hedge-fund icon Yuri Pildorossian had stacked a currency play that made him €5 million for every cent that the British pound weakened against the euro.

'What? Crush the pound? Sure he did it.'

'How?'

'You care. I like that.'

'Not really, but I'm interested. How did he do it?'

'Simple. These hedge funds are like a ball of unfocused energy. They can be stretched out like safety nets, or turned into diamond-tipped torpedoes. With all these short-term market coups, it's the torpedo function. What matters then is secrecy – placing your bets in the marketplace through lots of sources so you get maximum surprise and the best price and all that.'

'So did he really make all that they say he made?'

'And more. And more. He moved the market – or rather the market moved, who knows? You release the right story to the media, and it gets eaten up. Those guys – power without responsibility.'

'Who, the hedge fund managers or the media?'

'Both. Anyway, it was 26 cents in our man's favour before the UK government raised interest rates two per cent.'

'Whew!' A low whistle. 'That's €1.3 billion.'

'Someone sure found a crock of gold.'

He sipped his beer and gestured towards the paper and the disk hidden beneath. 'Well, there you have it. Different fund, different position. Not €1.3 billion on that play, but it's a fun few hours on the laptop – trading records from a very private accounting system. There's nothing illegal there, as far as I'm aware. Speculation is just an amusing game – even if it can bring a whole country to the edge of the precipice.'

'No. Not illegal,' said the other man, sweeping up his newspaper and the disk beneath it. 'Just very, very interesting.'

The Agency man sipped his coffee and tapped his paper, now neatly folded, against the edge of the table.

'Thanks. You've done well. Just one more question.'

'What now?'

'How'd you get it?'

25

'OH. IT'S YOU.'

Samuel was almost disappointed to see Kempis, all sprightly and excited. The don had left late the night before, for the long, slow cycle ride up to north Oxford. He was now clutching a bag that was gradually turning transparent. A rich odour began to fill the room.

'Sorry. Did I wake you? I see I did. Breakfast?'

'What time is it?'

The fatigue hangover would not go away.

'Eight.'

'Eight?'

'Yes. I've been up for hours. One needs little sleep as one gets older. A banality, but a truism nonetheless.'

'What's in the bag?'

Samuel realized that he hadn't eaten for hours.

'Provisions. Fogarty's in the covered market had just finished baking as I was walking past. I couldn't resist.'

Samuel opened the bag, and groaned.

'Pork pies?'

'The best in Oxford. Hot water crust at its finest. I also have some rolls. And there is orange juice in the fridge.'

'Nutrition more fitting for the human constitution. Not all of us have the dietary habits of the mountain bear, Peter.'

'We'll see what you say about that at lunchtime,' laughed Kempis, positively boyish in his enthusiasm. 'Now, I'll make some tea and you can tell me about the result of your labours.'

'Little to relate, really. The dealing room is what you would expect – lowest common denominator stuff. A few exclamations, the occasional piece of bawdy nonsense shouted across the room. Nothing. A public exercise in chatter, and no more. Painful to read. Talking of reading, is there anything in the newspapers?'

Kempis shook his head. 'Nothing about your terrifying experience with the chap on the farm, if that's what you mean. Reams and reams of stuff about how the roof of the world is falling in.'

Samuel nodded thoughtfully, and turned to the other bits of paper on his desk. The transcript of Miller's conversations had been more interesting, but hardly beneficial. A discussion about feng-shui, a brutally short conversation arranging to meet someone in a café. Samuel found this mildly surprising, and guessed it was a lover. Whether male or female it was impossible to tell from the text.

Kempis arrived with tea, orange juice, and toast made in the traditional Oxford way: risking death by electrocution, or at least badly burned fingers over the bars of an electric fire.

'Thanks. I need this.'

'Have you unearthed anything?'

'Nothing remotely interesting, unless you count Miller's latest fad as stimulating.'

Samuel shrugged slightly. It was incredibly frustrating to have put both himself and Robert at risk planting the bugs, and then to have allowed François to jeopardize himself in monitoring the tapes and downloading them onto the net. And for what? Two electronic treasure chests full of sound but no fury, and a third that wasn't even worth opening.

As it transpired, the bugs had gone undetected for nearly three days. They all finished at almost exactly the same time, months before their batteries would have expired. There must have been a routine security sweep. The annoying thing was that whoever had something to hide within the bank – and someone had, Samuel was sure – might then have been panicked into making an indiscreet call. But they would only have done this after the discovery of the bugs, so Samuel would never know about it.

The computer had flicked into life.

'Right. Let's join a pornography network, shall we?'

Kempis looked at him uncertainly.

'Peter, whatever else happens, this will not turn into a news story. "Oxford don in porn ring", or whatever.'

'I should hope not. But why your sudden interest in pornography?'

'Well, I don't want to go back to New York. We got away with nearly four minutes on a protected website that I thought wasn't being monitored. The call was untraceable, a routine call between two international exchanges. After I got the information I logged off straight away. Hence – despite the intense interest in Samuel Spendlove, arch-criminal – the absence of pursuers.'

'None of this explains the imminent arrival of buttocks and breasts.'

'Well, I'm not going to use New York, so I'll repeat the trick using different frequencies on a different exchange. Preferably a heavily used site, such as the porn site we're about to go and see in Copenhagen.'

'Samuel, this is most discomfiting.'

'The essay on vulgarity, remember? Sometimes it is exquisite to be vulgar. In any event, you have nothing to worry about.'

Kempis sighed and shook his head as Samuel repeated the process with the tone box.

'Now,' said Samuel, as he dialled the mainframe number of Ropner Bank in Paris. 'The game begins.'

'I'm intrigued by your daring, Samuel.' Kempis was watching intently now. 'Won't it take a long time to penetrate the defences of a sophisticated investment bank?'

'In theory, yes,' breathed Samuel. He could imagine the flickering and whirring of red and green monitor lights somewhere in an air-conditioned sub-basement in Paris – a tiny electronic ripple below the surface of the smooth-running system.

'In this case, however, we have a major advantage.'

He was now leafing through Kaz Day's trading logs. The simple question was who she had been trading with, and in what volumes.

'And what might that be?'

'Well, hacking into a security system is an act of electronic violence. It is penetration against the will of the victim, a form of digital rape. And, like most violent crimes, the victim actually knows the assailant. The artful way to hack into a system is to build an algorithm that is a mirror image of the defence mechanisms that bar access – like building a logical virus, a kind of superbacterium that will ultimately walk over the antibodies keeping the invader out. But that takes time, many hours of proposition and rebuttal before the right code is found.'

Samuel began downloading Kaz's trading records. As a

department head, she had notional control over vast swathes of information. But which files to download?

'This way, we get into the system because we know the victim. I have a friend in Paris. Did I ever mention François?'

Kempis nodded.

'Yes, of course I did. I'm tired. Anyway, he's given me the top-level access codes. At least, the highest level he's aware of. The trick is not to go into this system in secret, but to do so unobtrusively. We are safe because we leave everyone in the dark as to who we are and where we are.'

He tapped at the keyboard for a few moments, pausing occasionally to satisfy the prompts required by some computer, presumably located in Paris. Although François had once mentioned a data back-up on some supercomputer in Arizona.

'Now, let's see,' he murmured. The cursor blinked, and Samuel gazed into the middle distance. His fingers hovered over the keys. François had shown him the codes for a few seconds in Paris. It seemed like weeks ago. But it was probably enough. The system required three strings of letters and numbers, each of them twenty-six characters long.

Samuel murmured to himself as he tapped them out: 'S!3OUKEN252TGFY35JMLPE70D9 and . . . enter.'

The sub-digital quality of the connection and the need to unlock three separate security doors made the wait seem interminable. Every second he spent connected to the Ropner Bank system made them vulnerable. The cursor blinked slowly, impassively.

'Entry Level 1. Access authorized,' winked the screen at last.

'Great,' sighed Samuel, and glanced at his watch. It had taken nearly two minutes to log on at the lowest level. That would mean at least four more before he could get to work.

There were none of the architectural tricks he feared on the next two levels. The designers had trusted to the complex security codes for safety. Either you had them, or you didn't. If anyone traced Samuel they would know that he had insider knowledge. That might make François vulnerable when the investigations started, but it was too late to worry about that now.

He now began to download Miller's records. Again he had to guess which files to take. The computer seemed maddeningly slow. Even though he was confident that the access was untraceable, the fact that the bugs had been found must surely have made Ropners extra-vigilant, and every second he was connected meant that there was danger.

Unfortunately, Samuel couldn't download what he most wanted – Khan's trading positions – because, as he had discovered what seemed years ago when he found himself sitting on a surprise fortune as temporary custodian of the proprietary trading book, they were on a separate system and the only person really in charge of that was Khan.

'Well,' said Samuel at last. 'I suppose that will just about do it. It will have to. I'm exhausted.'

'What next?'

'The gory business of analysis. I've got to find the evidence that there was a connection between Kaz and Tungley.'

'And your proof is?'

'Accepted, Peter. My proof would not stand up in court. There is no causal chain. There isn't even a chain of custody for the one piece of concrete evidence that I do have.'

Samuel picked up the archer statue, placed it on the table next to the computer, and stared at it miserably.

Then he sat bolt upright in his chair. There was something else, some other codes on the page of data that François had let him look at. He hadn't even consciously read them, but now, as he pulled the data out of his memory – as he took the pictures down from the attic – he realized that some of the numbers he had scanned were more than just meaningless entry codes. He might, just might, have another way in.

D.FIN 345Y002W
URGENT ATTENTION: NEWS EDITORS, COPY
TASTERS
EX REUTERS NEWS BUREAU, ATLANTA, GA
17.44 EST
FLASH COPY, DRAFT ONE

MARKET RAGE SPREADS TO TAMPA. FOUR
DEAD, FIVE SERIOUSLY INJURED. CASUALTY
COUNT CONTINUES.

By Crawford P King

Angry investor Neville W Bennett rampaged through the
Tampa Bay offices of Merlin Lygo Wealth Management at
16.15 Eastern time today, shooting three Merlin employees
dead and wounding several others before turning the gun
on himself, inflicting fatal head injuries.

The Tampa Bay Police Department confirms four
deaths, including the gunman, and says five others are
'seriously ill' in the Sacred Heart Hospital, Tampa. Up to a
dozen other casualties have been admitted to the hospital.
There are fears that the death toll may rise.

Bennett is understood to have slipped through the
security net at Merlin Lygo – armed guards are now a

standard feature at major financial institutions in the wake of the global market meltdown – and confronted his personal broker. A heated argument apparently ensued, culminating in Bennett, who is understood to have lost almost all of a seven-figure share portfolio in the market crash, shooting his broker in the head with a semi-automatic handgun, before spraying bullets around the Merlin Lygo office.

This is the fourth and most serious 'Market Rage' incident in the United States in the last seven days. Angry investors have gone on the rampage at incidents in securities and brokerage houses in San Francisco, Boston, and Poughkeepsie, NY.

ENDS

26

SAMUEL SCRIBBLED OUT a series of numbers on a scrap of paper. He seemed to be in some kind of trance, like a spiritual medium engaged in automatic writing. But all he was doing was dipping into his subconscious memory, copying out the symbols and images he had seen briefly in Paris.

After a few moments he stopped, looked at the pad on his knee, and began to read.

'This is interesting,' he said, as though the information had been written out by someone else.

'Hmmm,' said Kempis, peering over his shoulder. 'And this jumble of figures has more inherent meaning than the earlier entry codes?'

'I'm not sure, Peter. I think there's a virtual data store, a kind of informational back-up with pictures. There's a chance that the raw data they dump there might be more useful than the audited deal trails I've been looking at. These are the telephone numbers and the access codes. At least, I think they are.'

'You must be the judge of that, dear boy.' Kempis glanced at the window. All was quiet and grey. Oxford could be stupefying in its stillness. The don turned back.

'It sits on the internet, and it'll definitely take time for me to work out what it all means,' Samuel reflected. It certainly was a gamble, a serious gamble. He breathed in deeply. 'OK, let's do it,' he said at last.

He began to eat as he made the wireless connection and got into the Ropner system. He chose a new site aimed at fanatics of football statistics in Frankfurt for the tone box, which faultlessly worked its magic. Let them look for him on ADSL and GSM. He had virtually the same quality and speed this way, but less visibility. If top-quality digital was a Ferrari, this was like driving a souped-up Volkswagen Beetle on the infamous information highway – at night.

Samuel drank tea, consumed some of the admittedly excellent pork pie, and sifted through acres of paper. After a couple of hours he was close to despair. There were a few explicitly identifiable trades executed on behalf of clients, but these were small, and clearly not the large, position-building kind of deals that Samuel needed. There was no motive here for the eradication of two investment bankers.

The dealing records for Miller, Kaz, Diaz and the rest of the team all seemed clean and straightforward. From what Samuel knew of the ticker symbols, some of Diaz's trades looked a little poorly judged, but otherwise there was nothing he could see to raise suspicion. Samuel stared at the suspense accounts for what seemed like days. There were relatively small amounts of money passing through them – far removed from the famous 888888 account that had sunk Barings. But, of course, Khan's trades were not included.

A couple of chats with François and various individuals at cyber cafés had given Samuel an insight into why virtual data storage might be more meaningful than an elaborate toy. The whole point of creating an artificial environment was to harness a logic that allowed people to react in a way that helped them make sense of the data.

François said that chess players remembered the pieces on the board much more effectively if they were arranged in a way that made sense: a position that might have been lifted from an actual game was much easier to remember than randomly arranged pieces.

Easier, he thought, unless you had an eidetic memory, and could recall the shape of the patterns without the need to make sense of them. Still, it was definitely worth a try. The whole point of this type of virtual system was to store data more efficiently – in a way that meant users would understand it better. The digital world was already teaching human beings how to adapt themselves to use it better.

Forward positions on Asian currencies – ringgit and baht against the euro. There was also someone's Asian currency deals against the euro. But whose?

He opened another drawer, which yielded the capital markets' standard trading procedures, house 'good conduct' rules, and, embarrassingly, the mission statement. The mission, surely, was to make as much money as possible.

'How is it?' shouted Kempis from another world.

'Fine,' grinned Samuel. 'Just fine.'

'YOU ARE ONE OF US, *like it or not.*'

'*I am a patriot, but I don't like it, Mr Burrows.*'

'*Look at the bigger picture. And please don't use my name on the phone.*'

'*Sorry, but that was the name you gave me. So, the bigger picture? That we're the guys in the white hats, right? The end justifies the means?*'

'*Sir, you're being of service to your country.*'

'*By stealing my colleagues' trading secrets?*'

'*They run a dangerous, covert operation.*'

'*Does that not seem familiar to you, sir?*'

'*Do you want them to profit from chaos, to ruin economies for their own profit?*'

'*Well ... I guess not.*'

'*No. I know you don't. You're on our side. It's a shitty business. Tell me, do you know how much our country's asset base declines when the dollar falls a cent against the euro?*'

'*You're asking me to value the entire net worth of America?*'

'*How much just disappears when the dollar is manipulated and drops a cent? Well, I'll tell you: over a thousand billion dollars. You gonna let them get away with that because they want to line their own pockets?*'

'I guess not.'

'Damn right. All we want from you is information. We may never use it. But if they mess with us again, you can sleep easy. You've helped your country.'

'If you say so.'

'I do.'

A few seconds later Burrows put down the phone with a frown. His contact, previously so reliable and sober, now seemed dangerously unstable. He would have to report back to Langley. And also to an influential friend in the media who'd been taking a steady, back-seat interest in this operative's case.

27

A LARGE FLUORESCENT orange rectangle floated in front of Samuel. He was familiar with the divisions within the rectangle; they denoted trades in currency cross-rates over various weeks. He had seen something similar on the office reporting screens. But this was different. Instead of old data on yen and dollar contracts, he was seeing current trading positions in eastern European currencies. The bank was testing the system in the most realistic way possible, using real data.

Since the advent of the euro, the eastern European currencies had become extremely attractive to those with adventurous tastes. The economies were wobbly, to say the least. And being outside the euro made the currencies vulnerable to attack from speculators. So countries like Romania, the Czech Republic, Hungary, Bulgaria and Poland jacked up interest rates to attract capital. Perversely, the euro's arrival had not squeezed out trade in eastern European currencies and bonds, but made it more popular. High, 'sexy' returns in bonds and time deposits attracted those who wanted the income and felt they could make a killing on the currency when the time was right.

Samuel looked at the position on the virtual orange card. Something was ... something was familiar. Then he realized: the number in the right-hand corner of the card. He had seen it before. But what was it? He ransacked his subconscious memory once more. There was a maniac in the attic of his mind, looking at picture after picture, and tossing them all away.

And then he remembered the meaning of the number sequence. He punched some more figures onto the screen and soon he was looking at an impressive array of data on trades forward in the dollar against major eastern European currencies. He had little time to read any of the stuff in any meaningful sense of the word, but he made sure he took as much of it in as he could. He noticed that several of the fluorescent data rectangles bore the name 'Pentangle' as counterparty. Pentangle? He flushed hot Pentangle was the name of one of the counterparties that Khan used. It was the name of the firm that Duval had been selling the options to that day that he had been on the wrong side of Khan's trade.

Now he was looking at a file that contained one day of Ropner's trade in the pound against the euro. Samuel recognized the date – it was Black Thursday, the day when Khan was alleged to have made more than a billion pounds betting on the UK currency to fall against the euro. With a surge of excitement he realized that these trades reflected Khan's positions. His hunch had been right. The bank's virtual data store had information that the regular systems did not.

He had found the crock of gold.

Samuel looked at the short accounting names and the numbers, seeking out the various accounts in Ropner Bank's stable that he knew that Khan was responsible for. And Kaz's desk looked to be involved, if he remembered the internal bank code for her department. And the counterparties? He knew almost before he scanned down the file that floated before his eyes, that he would find one name amongst the biggest players.

And there it was, sure enough – the Frankfurt office. Finally – a possible link between Kaz and Dee Tungley.

He must save the data. But as he began to do so, his world turned to inky darkness. Someone, somewhere, had pulled the plug on the system.

'I must go back!'

'Where have you been?' asked Kempis.

'Finding answers in the virtual world.'

Samuel frantically tried to re-enter the system, but whoever had pulled the plug had done so effectively. The Ropner Bank undernet now refused to accept the access codes that had worked moments before. Samuel cursed softly. He had been busted, but he was pretty certain that they would not be able to find his physical whereabouts. They could not have tracked him to Oxford.

'By the way, your last transcript proved most interesting,' said Kempis.

'What?'

'Odd, but most interesting.'

'What are you talking about, Peter?'

Samuel darted across to the sofa and picked up the pile of paper. The transcript of the bugging tape was brief. But it was a miracle there was anything at all. This was the wasted microphone, the bug he had completely written off. The one that had been placed in the basement meeting room they called the cellar.

Feverishly, he read the text. At first, he too was completely mystified. Then he sat down in front of the computer. He had to listen to the original conversation and see if that helped to interpret what had been said.

The audio profile of the tape showed days of silence with a sharp peak of activity in the middle. Conclusion: three days of silence, and one conversation. Using a bug that gave out a very low-frequency continuous signal was a risk Samuel had weighed carefully. Technical surveillance countermeasures routinely scanned for voice-activated bugs. As soon as they switched themselves on, the difference was noticeable, and therefore detectable. But the continuous signal of the bugs Samuel had used could be construed as neon strip lighting, part of the ambient noise of an office or a room.

It was easy enough to scan forward to the activity on the file. He found the active part of the audio file and switched up the monitor volume.

A few clunks. The sound of door locks, heavy bolts, effortful entry. Then dialogue. Two voices. Male. Something about them was familiar, but the quality of reproduction was poor. Samuel and Kempis listened once, twice, three times. The first voice was eager and slightly higher. It was selling something to a deeper, more sceptical second.

'This is the future,' began the first voice.

Silence. Samuel imagined the other guy looking around the bank's deep, dark basement. Then the second voice began to laugh.

'What is this? This is madness, madness. Surely a joke?'

'Oh no. Far from it. This is prudence anticipating the bottom line of the most pessimistic projections for the markets not of tomorrow, but the day after tomorrow. This is what I call the meltdown portfolio.'

'The meltdown portfolio?' Another laugh.

The quality of the tape dipped here, but Samuel was almost sure the next words were as he perceived them.

'. . . a radical alternative investment strategy.'

More static, then:

'. . . what we are facing is simple. It is no more and no less than a crisis of confidence. People the world over are suddenly running from paper assets. They don't trust bankers and brokers and the clever people who work in the financial markets any more. They don't trust the promises of governments. And when they don't trust us, the whole system will come tumbling down. Look what's happening at Eastern Pacific. A major bank goes down, another US corporation admits it's been telling lies about its profits, the US authorities wobble, and suddenly the whole banking system threatens to teeter over the edge as creditors call for their money. What happened in the Depression after 1929 could be with us all over again – but worse, much worse. Run after run after run on the banks – a whole decade when no one dared invest in paper assets or anything that required placing confidence in a bank or bankers.'

'So we're all going to invest in ... what have you got here ... baked beans?' Another incredulous laugh.

'Commodities – soy beans, flour, wine. People will want things, not promises. At least at first. The value of all this will rocket. Of course, we use contracts as well. Futures and options are where the real money is. But if the system cracks, paper obligations won't be honoured. This will be the equivalent of a vault full of gold bullion – a safety net, a thing that ...'

More static, followed minutes later by an excited interjection from the seller:

'... why not? Why ever not?'

A muffled, indistinguishable response, and then the seller in mid-flow.

'... in postwar Germany the initial currency, at the very end of the war when the Germans were on their knees, was the cigarette. A unit of barter.'

It was weird stuff. Inconclusive and weird. A meltdown portfolio? Was Ropner Bank hoarding things in its cellar in the way that medieval peasants did in times of famine? Surely things couldn't be that bad? And whose were those voices?

There was more indistinct noise, and a few bangs and rattles, presumably as they left the basement. The voices exchanged more unrecognizable words until the higher one broke into a laugh: '. . . this space was originally designed as a nuclear shelter. Kind of a neat touch, don't you think?'

Samuel and Kempis sat in silence for a while. Kempis removed his spectacles and pinched the bridge of his nose.

'I remember the end of the second war, of course. Spent some time in Berlin. It's true that a cigarette could purchase virtually anything for a while. As good as, if not better than, the dollar.'

'You were in Berlin, Peter? You never mentioned that.'

'Fighting the evils of communism, my boy.'

'I thought we were fighting the evils of fascism.'

'True, but the weak-minded didn't see that its polar opposite, communism, was just as dangerous.'

Samuel sat down and looked at his mentor. There was so much to take in – the trade records, the weird conversation, and a political past for Kempis that Samuel had never even suspected.

'Tell me, Samuel. I detected a hint of the apocalypse in all that guff about confidence and meltdown and commodities. The apocalypse isn't upon us, is it?'

Samuel shook his head. 'No, Peter. But it might well be that someone would want to make it seem that way.' He was not certain whom the second voice belonged to. But he recognized the first voice, the one that talked so confidently, that had all the bases covered. That was the voice of Khan. Samuel sighed and turned to Kempis. 'It's difficult to imagine things being more apocalyptic than they already are.'

'Mm, I wouldn't be too sure about that, Samuel,' said Kempis, peering through the window as the room filled with a loud throbbing noise. 'Our talk earlier about blissful quietude and pursuers of your liberty may have been premature. I can see a police helicopter hovering above this very college.'

28

'QUICKLY,' HISSED KEMPIS. 'Come with me.'

The noise of the helicopter was even louder now. Its flashing lights could have been no more than forty yards away. It had lowered itself into the main quadrangle of All Souls so that its crew could look into the windows of the studies. It began to move in a slow circle, like some giant, methodically inquisitive wasp.

'Come on, Samuel. Quickly!'

Kempis had opened both of the doors onto the staircase. Samuel was staring out of the window. There was a man in a suit next to a pilot dressed in shades and black SWAT-team gear. Could it be Khan? No, surely not. No. But there was a certain similarity . . .

Kempis shook him by the shoulder and broke the spell. He jumped up, grabbed his bag and took with him the tone box and a memory stick. He found himself trotting after the rapidly disappearing back of the elderly don. Samuel was surprised at the speed at which Kempis could move. Must have been all that cycling to and from north Oxford.

They reached the cloistered gloom of the main quadrangle, but before they began to emerge into full daylight, Kempis had ducked to one side. He was fumbling with the lock of an ancient oak door. The helicopter was even lower now, and the breeze from its blades was a mini-typhoon blasting apart the venerable silence of the quad.

Then suddenly they were in another world again. All was dark and still as Kempis pushed the door shut behind them and locked it.

'Follow me,' he muttered, and guided Samuel to a mouldy length of rope attached to the wall as a primitive handrail. 'Hold on to this.'

They descended a narrow staircase for what seemed like minutes. After the first few steps Samuel expected that his eyes would have acclimatized to the dark. And they must have. But he still could not see his hand in front of his face. They were deep, deep in the earth; there was no light whatsoever. His only guide was the proximity of Kempis, the regular tread of his own footfall; the thick, comforting sound of air forcing its way through his bronchial tract.

At last the staircase came to an end. Samuel stood still, then latched on to Kempis's firm grip as the old man reached for his hand.

'Slowly, now, slowly!'

They shuffled forward together like a couple of blind men crossing the street. After a moment or two, Kempis grunted in satisfaction.

'Here we are.'

Samuel could feel the old man reach up for something. Seconds later what seemed a dazzling laser arc of light illuminated an ancient wall before them. Kempis had a pen torch in his hand. Its sharp light was like a white-hot needle in a vat of pitch.

'Where are we, exactly?'

'Not now,' replied Kempis brusquely. 'Follow me.'

Samuel followed the bright, dancing dot that Kempis shone on the ground before them. He felt vulnerable, childish, following the usherette to a seat in an ancient cinema.

After a while they moved out into a larger space. The air pressure told Samuel this was much bigger than the tunnel they had been walking along.

'What is this, a cave?' whispered Samuel.

'A cave of sorts,' responded Kempis, his deep, booming voice reverberating around the hollow space. 'In the French sense. A cellar, a vast cellar of good things. Sorry about the fiddle in getting down here. It's just that I haven't been here for years, not since my Millbank days, and silence does aid the concentration, you know. Especially at my age.'

Samuel reflected. Millbank? Surely that was the old MI6 building, before it moved to the hideous tower block on the south side of Vauxhall Bridge in London, the one that the IRA had taken a pot-shot at. Had Kempis been part-timing a job in security? But what would the intelligence services want with a Roman Law scholar? Then again, stranger things had happened. What could the security services have wanted with the pompous, camp, art historian Anthony Blunt?

Kempis's tiny dot of light sought out something on the wall. He flicked a switch, and a couple of fat pyramids of light belched out a dusty yellow. Samuel could see they were in a large chamber, roughly the size of a college dining hall.

'That apocalypse conversation struck a chord just now, I must say,' said Kempis.

It was like a dream den, as laid out by the editors of *Boys' Own* in the 1950s. Bakelite radios, stereograms the size of sofas, hunting trophies, ancient car magazines, and racks and racks of wine and tinned food – commodities to guard against the apocalypse.

'What's this? Aladdin's cave?'

'Old age and disuse. You'd think I'd be used to that by now,' said Kempis. 'Haven't been down here for years.'

Samuel followed Kempis, and cast his eyes quickly over the jumble of ancient luxury goods. Some of the wine looked sensational – Cheval Blanc '45, Haut-Brion '29, Château Talbot, Château d'Yquem of diverse vintages.

They were leaving the chamber and entering another dark tunnel when Samuel guessed what he had seen.

'This is an old nuclear shelter isn't it? For all the dons involved in the security services? A bit too close to London to be really safe, but you could all have had a pretty good time drinking yourselves to death before the radiation got to you. It's an old nuclear bunker, isn't it?'

'A long time ago, my boy.'

Kempis was still walking, and Samuel had to hurry after him for fear of losing the old man.

'Long ago, Samuel, and apparently long forgotten.'

They were ascending another staircase, and Kempis was breathing heavily.

'There are only two other dons here who to my knowledge could possibly know about all this. One of them, I think, has forgotten his own name. As for the Mandarins, I've heard nothing for years. And this place hasn't changed in all that time. There's probably a file mouldering away quietly in an MI6 office, but the odds are that they have completely forgotten about it.'

Samuel whistled quietly to himself in the dark. Peter Kempis, a spook – who would have thought it?

The ascent took a good while. Both men were tired, and the adrenalin of flight was beginning to wear off. At last the darkness began to filter out to grey. They reached the top of the stair and Kempis withdrew his key. After a few minutes' effort from Kempis, then Samuel, the rusty hinges of the door creaked and groaned and the door opened inwards to let in light and air.

'Now, tell me,' breathed Samuel. 'Where are we?'

'Sniff the air,' rasped Kempis. 'You tell me.'

Samuel took a great lungful of air; it was almost sickly sweet. Of course, The Turf Tavern, just at the back of Hertford College, a hundred yards from All Souls. The Turf prided itself on serving an undrinkable mulled wine that smelled like nothing so much as Maple and Walnut tobacco. Samuel slowly pushed aside a few empty beer crates and looked cautiously out of the door. They were in a tiny courtyard the size of a telephone box. Just another piece of innocent, obscure Oxford and its medieval quaintness.

'So what do we do, Peter? Go and have a pint?'

The thrum of helicopter blades told them this was inadvisable.

'I just brought you here so there are no surprises when you come out again. I suggest we go back down and do some thinking. Then I must go and see what the police or whoever it is want with us. Or, more precisely, you.'

A few moments later they were seated at a dusty Hepplewhite table. Kempis had opened a bottle of 1914 Armagnac. Its mellow taste was comforting.

'Peter, what do you make of it all?'

Kempis sipped and ruminated.

'What was the identity of the parties in the cellar, those discussing the baked beans? Am I right in surmising that one of them was this Merlin figure – the trader chappy?'

'Khan?'

'Precisely, Khan. And he was the purveyor of doom, the man with the ultimate contingency plan, yes?'

Samuel nodded.

'Hmmm. It seems to me that your former employer is playing a game rather similar to the little pantomime that we all went through in the late 1950s and early 1960s.'

'Khan and games do go together, that's for sure.'

'And do you think his games are valid?'

'Valid? That they have worth in any real sense? Well, they certainly make money. Khan is a brilliant player of the market, a brilliant bluffer and creator of images. So in that sense his games and stratagems are *validated*.'

'Which a fine mind such as yours understands full well is very different from the idea of these games being valid. He could buy a ball of fluff for a million pounds, but if he can persuade someone in the market to buy it for a million and one pounds, his initial, invalid decision is validated.'

'Ah, maybe now I see perhaps where the Master's thinking comes in, Peter.'

'Precisely,' said Kempis. 'The great attraction of your thesis on the Master of Biblos was the fact that it mirrored the man's work. It was the Master, the man who came after all the glossists, who had to sift through the thousands of margin notes to the texts of the jurists, who brought a unifying clarity to the law. He focused on the essential, and let the games take care of themselves.'

'And this is what I must do. Make the real world come to the game-playing world, and see which wins.'

Kempis nodded.

'Your search is for truth, a higher truth. Seeking the killers of your American friends may be one way to find it.

But perhaps that door is already closed. You have a mountain of inconclusive evidence, drawn from unlikely sources. Will the trading records you have produce some magical line of accounting audit to the person who dispatched your colleagues?'

'If I'm right, then it can only be one man. Or at least one man gave the order.'

'Khan?'

Samuel nodded.

'Hmm. It is possible you will have the time to discover the right trail, but the odds are against you.'

'The only real link I've established so far is this.' Samuel reached into his bag and took out the Bourdelle miniature 'Kaz stole this and I found it in Khan's flat. So what should I do, Peter? What would the Master do?'

'I believe he would do what he habitually did. He would look at the issues of principle, the big picture as it is styled nowadays, and formulate a model of truth that was consistent with the facts with which he was presented.'

Kempis took a slow sip of brandy, then continued softly. 'The truth may be that for the ultimate perpetrator of these deaths, the lives of Miss Day and Mr Tungley are entirely incidental. They – and you – may be no more than pawns in a more important game. It's a risky strategy, but it is the best I can suggest. To get to the truth, you must find a way to import reality into his world of game-playing.'

'And then, in theory, I will win. We hope the truth will win.'

'Well, Samuel, think of this bunker. There was a lot of posturing in the nuclear age. But it was a game. The Cold War was a safe war. Bunkers like this were part of the process. The self-delusional mindset that lacks a basis in reality needs convincing props to justify itself. There never was a nuclear war, and there was never going to be while the Cold War continued. Now, with genuine fanaticism about, and Russian soldiers unable to feed their families, the possibility of a little freelance terrorism involving nuclear weapons bought for a few dollars is all too real. But that's another tale.'

'OK, Peter. Let's use a chemistry metaphor, and imagine we have a murky potion in front of us. If we say that adding truth to the mixture is a way of guaranteeing that the solution clears, then fine. But I still have the small problem of finding a way of doing just that.'

'The tactical elements, my boy, I leave to you. You have more knowledge of this man Khan than anyone else. I judge, from what you have said, that he is fond of you. Perhaps he needed you as a cog in some Mephistophelean device at the beginning. But the rescue from the police, the kind gifts . . . I believe he is genuinely fond of you. You do have an appealing quality, Samuel.'

'Mm. The police certainly want me.'

'Enough. I must go back to my rooms and deal with what pass for the forces of law and order. Before I do, let me offer you this: the reality is that you are not being hunted. You are the hunter, my boy. Ill-equipped, perhaps, but the hunter. And they are coming after you precisely because you are dangerous to them. Your next step must be to go to them, to face them down in their lair.'

'What? Go back to Paris?'

'Go to the heart of the matter. Show these forces pursuing you that you know the truth, and that you have seen and understood their game, that you are the hunter. Where you do it makes no difference. Here!' Kempis placed a set of ancient keys and a small modern key ring, with a couple of Yales attached, on the tabletop. 'The Yales belong to the flat of one of my research students in Mansfield Road, just around the corner. I'm sure he wouldn't mind if you borrowed his laptop out of term. And you can keep these. I imagine this place would be an excellent location from which to explode the bunker mentality and the game-playing of your adversary.'

Samuel ran his hands repeatedly over his shaved head.

'Khan, my adversary,' he murmured.

'If you seek the truth, he is your adversary. I am convinced of it.'

'And I will expose his falsehoods . . . How?'

'Well, as I said, the details are up to you, my boy. But one very effective way to start things off would be to make him lose money. A great deal of money.'

'So I'm going to take on and beat one of the world's best traders by playing him at his own game?'

'Not just you, my boy. The Master of Biblos. And the truth. I know you can do it. Be strong.'

Samuel picked up the miniature archer figure and admired its taut intensity, the coiled purpose of Hercules's back.

'You must be the hunter now,' said Kempis. And with that, he was gone.

THE MOBILE RANG.

'Yes?'

'Hi it's me.' A familiar Good Ol' Boy voice.

'What is it? Now's a bad time.'

'Sorry. This can't wait. I've got a favour to ask.'

'Company business?'

'Not the Company you're thinking of. It's a favour for an influential friend.'

He listened carefully, said little, and agreed to the proposition easily and quickly. It was about time, after all.

29

SAMUEL WALKED WARILY down the road to the research student's flat. It was a three-minute trip, but he knew that an assailant might emerge from any shadowy enclave or an assassin could be waiting around the next corner.

The helicopter at least had gone and there was no sign of a heavyweight police presence. Whether this was a good omen or something to be worried about, he could not be sure. Samuel brandished the Yales, and let himself in.

The flat was a classic of student transience. Posters, boom box, iPod and dock, course books, light philosophy and popular fiction. A faintly unpleasant smell emanated from the tiny sink-top fridge, as though something of high protein value had gone irredeemably rancid many months ago. Samuel had no intention of investigating. In the corner was a laptop, hooked up to speakers and a couple of quite interesting but rather mysterious-looking bits of kit.

He knew it was dangerous, but he couldn't resist. In a few seconds, the laptop had come to life. Introductory fanfares issued from the speakers. Within a couple of minutes he had navigated his way to where he wanted to be. He logged into one of the fake IDs he'd created at the Jersey internet café, and sat through the obligatory succession of adverts. And then, as he had somehow always known it would, the mail icon flashed. He clicked, and there it was:

'Remember what it is that you are supposed to do. You're on the right track. Keep going.'

Who had him tagged? His heart raced. Was it a member of the security forces trying to play him along, stalling for time as the helicopters flew in? He crashed the system, folded the laptop into a bag and hurried out onto Mansfield Road.

Samuel was almost trotting as he turned the corner and rounded right, back towards the Turf and the King's Arms. A thumping shock: a police roadblock. It stood between Samuel and the All Souls bolt-hole. Damn, damn, damn.

He slowed his pace and lowered his gaze slightly. There were plenty of people in the street, and the crowd was thickening. The police at the roadblock were scrutinizing and stopping occasional students and passers-by. Except, of course, that no one was just passing by without very careful examination.

Samuel could see that the police were stopping individual men. They were looking for a lone male. They would have his description, and they would arrest him. A radical haircut was one thing, but he had done nothing else to disguise himself – he wasn't wearing contact lenses to change his eye colour; he was still the same height and build, still looked the same age, if a little tired. A dozen or so policemen were standing on their cars, scanning the crowd. If he executed an about-turn they would certainly notice.

He was finished, gone, trapped at last. The only questions worth considering now were where they would take him, what he would be charged with and under which jurisdiction. The crowd was edging him forward; he would be in their power in a few moments.

'Hello.'

A voice from behind, and a familiar hand linked into the crook of his elbow.

'Just keep moving forward,' coaxed the voice. 'Although a friendly kiss would be nice.'

The scent, the touch, the voice. He turned and smudged his lips against her cheek.

'Darling.'

'Yes, darling?'

Lauren draped her arm over his shoulder and laid her head against him. Then she whispered in his ear.

'We are in love. Remember that. Act stupid. You are stupid with love, understand?'

Samuel rested his head back against hers and began to kiss her, passionately. Some of the crowd were beginning to mutter in the way that students do about civil rights and police states and the failure of market capitalism. The gentle ebb and flow of discontented people soon took Samuel and Lauren past the gaze of the police. Their interest in each other made them invisible to the eyes raking the crowd – a pair of lovers, not the right criteria. A single student with an armful of theology books and a prodigiously bushy beard was stopped as they breezed by. As the couple turned down Bath Place, they heard his forthright views on the right of the individual to walk the streets without police interference fading into the distance.

They stopped a few steps into the alleyway.

'Well,' said Samuel, unable to suppress a grin. 'Wherever did you come from?'

'Are you surprised?'

She looked intently into his eyes. They were still locked in a lovers' embrace. Eventually, Lauren sighed softly.

'Your family friend, Dr Kempis. I knew you were going to him, so I called. He said to come. That you needed me.'

'You called him?'

'Yes. I wanted to come. I knew as soon as I got back to Paris. There is no present, no future, just a past back there. So here I am. There is nothing more to say.'

'Nothing and everything.'

Samuel held her close. She had saved him. She had come from the relative sanctuary and safety of Paris. Come to help him. But was she being watched? Was she part of some trick? An agent of Khan's after all?

Lauren saw the questions in his eyes, and shook her head. She held his face and forced him to look deep into her own gaze.

'Look at me, Samuel. Look at me. What can I say? I ... I am here. Believe it. Believe in me. Or go back to all the doubt and insecurity. That is what created your universe of pain. But I am not Gail. I am Lauren and I am here because you are one of the few people I love.'

'What are you saying?'

'I love you, you imbecile.' Samuel nodded. Then he kissed her. They had pretended to be lovers to protect his freedom. Now it was becoming reality. He closed his eyes, gave himself to the moment, and felt safe for a fleeting instant. And then, after they had embraced each other tenderly for a little while, he took her by the hand. Soon, they disappeared down into the bowels of the earth, beneath All Souls.

LIVING UNDERGROUND, they quickly lost track of day or night. True, they had watches, but the constant darkness and their ability to regulate the amount of artificial light they imported into a 'day' meant that time was counted out in other measures.

Samuel was working at the laptop, sifting through the data he had gleaned from the virtual databank. It was half a day, he thought, since the last time he and Lauren had made love – forceful, grinding sex on the floor by the scores of wine racks. If she was angry or tortured by the death of Kaz, or the thought of any involvement he'd had with her, it didn't show. The rich, dark dirt of their last coupling was still packed under his fingernails. Lauren had kicked and screamed so that he almost believed she was rejecting him, but when he tried to withdraw, she had only grown more frantic. She had almost brought down the 250-bottle wine rack, which would surely have killed them both. What a way to go that would have been – crushed to death beneath some of the world's finest wine in pursuit of passion.

Samuel tapped away and watched Lauren out of the corner of his eye. He still didn't know what to make of her. Their lovemaking had given them a physical bond, but he felt that there was so much that remained undiscovered, so much of herself that she wasn't giving – or maybe couldn't give.

She was reading some of the printouts. He couldn't get back into the virtual database, which seemed to have been totally shut down. They had to go with the printouts from the regular database. Perhaps Lauren would make a connection he had missed. Soon it would be time for her to go up and check the lie of the land, see Kempis, and get some more food. They had plenty to eat, but the feeling of entrapment was turning into one of entombment, and they both needed to feel that exit was at least theoretically possible.

But Kempis pre-empted them. They both started as they

heard the door of the chamber open, and there he was. Bright-eyed, torch in hand. The old man's face was still flushed and somehow boyish with the challenge of combat.

'Hail! Well met, you two. It's only me,' he called.

Samuel sat back down in his chair. Lauren walked over and kissed Kempis on the cheek. They came from completely different worlds, but they were united by their desire to save Samuel and establish his innocence. And they were both lawyers, of course, although their attitudes to the law were derived from diametrically opposed political positions.

The three of them moved to the far side of the cellar, which had at first seemed like a roomy two-bedroomed flat. But already Samuel could feel the weight of the world outside pushing the walls closer and closer together. They sat on fold-up camp chairs at the Hepplewhite table.

'So?'

Samuel poured out a large measure of Haut-Brion '29 and handed it to Kempis.

'And so they came, and so they went,' smiled the don. He winced slightly at the textured, complex pleasure of the Bordeaux, which he was gulping rather hastily.

'Which is to say?'

'Which is to say that after a little bit of straight-batting, they had to go. Special Branch detectives. High-handed, and utterly moronic. Nothing changes.'

'You mean they've gone?'

'No doubt they're still watching me on some level. But they appear to have gone, yes. How they came knocking at the door is the mystifying thing. I wondered whether there might not have been some kind of radio implant hidden inside you for them to pinpoint you so accurately, but I believe now it was more mundane than that. I suppose that anyone who bothered to find out anything about you, my boy, would know that you would come to me if you were in some kind of trouble.'

'Someone was definitely onto me when I hacked into Ropner's data store, but I'm pretty sure they couldn't have located me physically.'

'Of course, they know me of old, or at least several members of the Branch's supervisory board and liaison committee do. But I have committed no crime. There are certainly no grounds for jailing a harmless old buffer like me. Sheltering a family friend, hospitality extended by a doddering long-fang like me — these are not the causes of incarceration. Not in this country at least. And they only have a suspicion – no proof.'

Kempis avoided Lauren's look, as though he wanted to add some unfavourable comparison with the situation across the Channel. He explained for her benefit that the authority of the police did not technically extend to the university, which had its own legislature and its own police force, known as bulldogs. Kempis had invited the police officers in on sufferance, and they had taken his laptop away under his watchful eye. They had clearly been perplexed as to how Samuel – who they presumably knew had been with Kempis in his rooms – had disappeared. But there was no evidence, no power of search. Their only option had been to maintain a polite, if furious, silence.

Kempis laughed at the end of his tale and poured a second glass of wine for himself and a partial refill for Lauren.

'And so, Samuel, have you found a way forward? You have had a day and a half now to make your plans. Have you decided on anything? We are safe for the moment, but ancient wheels in Whitehall will be turning and dusty filing cabinets are doubtless being brought to the light of day as we speak. They may suddenly remember the existence of this place, so you need to get a move on.'

'No. We have no plan, but we will find one,' said Lauren. She looked about her, defying the darkness superbly.

Samuel reached out and took a glass, which he half-filled with wine.

'Actually, I believe I do have an idea. There is a whole game to be played here, and I think I know the playing field. It reminds me somewhat of a piece of advice I once had from Miller. Do you remember that German American fellow I told you about, Peter?'

Kempis nodded, but looked troubled. 'He sounded an odd sort.'

'Strange, undoubtedly. But he once said something about making the first move that seems to make sense now. He who makes the first move reveals himself and loses the battle.'

'So what are we going to do?' asked Lauren.

'It is *The Art of War*, is it not?' asked Kempis. 'If I am right Samuel does not even now know the precise detail of what he will do.'

'Exactly, Peter.' Samuel sipped at the wine. 'To discover what happened in the past I may have to make my man reveal himself in the future, but I'm not quite certain when or how it's all going to happen. When I do move, it will be with perfect precision.'

Kempis looked at Samuel for a moment, then raised a glass: 'Let's hope so, my boy. Let's hope so.'

SAMUEL AWOKE in what his watch told him were the early hours of the next day. Lauren lay next to him, her outline dimly visible in the gloomy light thrown out by a lamp in a distant part of the cavern. He sighed inaudibly. In the slow climb to wakefulness he had confronted the fear of abandonment again. But there she was, breathing softly. He stretched over and stroked her hair for a moment, then climbed stiffly from his camp bed and made his way to the latrine in the far corner.

His mind was full of partial solutions to problems half understood, small creatures that flitted through his consciousness and mocked his attempts to pin them down. Once awake, he knew that these demons would not let him sleep again for hours.

Wearily he sat at the makeshift operations centre they had set up behind a wine rack full of Cheval Blanc and Grand-Puy-Lacoste. The laptop whirred into life, and Samuel called up a newswire. Lauren's mobile, using the cord of the old Bakelite telephone as an aerial, beeped once and remained silent. Bullet points of news from the Far East, Russia and central Europe poured slickly, line by line, onto his screen. Europe was waking up, and soon – it was 5.45 a.m. – Britain would be dragging itself out of bed.

Samuel gazed at the lines of information blearily. Nothing particularly caught his attention. But then he saw an unremarkable little headline that had him reaching for the mouse straight away. It was a Reuters story.

> 6.38 POLISH BONDS SHARPLY LOWER IN EARLY
> TRADE – major activity – government defends credit
> rating.

The related article was equally unremarkable.

> WARSAW, September 30 (Reuters) – Poland's offer of
> 2.6 billion zlotys of short-dated bonds at the first of five
> primary auctions this morning saw prices sharply lower
> in heavy trade.

In this primary tender, investors were offering well below par, with bid orders of 85 against stock nominal par of 100 being offered in the market. Dealers attributed market nervousness over the offer to fears of possible devaluation of the Polish zloty, which has been an oasis of calm during recent market turbulence.

'The values we're seeing today say that the market expects the zloty to fall completely out of bed. We're looking at a devaluation of 20% if these bonds are priced correctly,' said one trader.

The Polish finance ministry pointed out that it reserved the right to change the offer according to market conditions and said it would 'defend the credit rating of [its] sovereign debt at all costs.'

For more information about Polish debt double-click on <PLIFMN>

Warsaw newsroom, tel + 48 22751 6700

ENDS [Qs8097501]

Samuel looked around. The bunker was as quiet as ever, the silence punctuated only by the slow rhythm of Lauren's breathing. He checked the screen, reread the story.

'This is it,' he muttered. 'This is it.'

The next hour was spent loading the laptop with the simple instructions he needed. Just as he was finishing Lauren came over. She put her hand briefly on top of his, stooped and kissed him gently on the mouth. A plate of bread and jam was pushed his way, and she peered at the screen.

'Is this it? Is this the move?'

'I believe so.' Samuel reached for the bread and began to munch.

The programs loaded, he flipped back to the news wires. The wire agencies' Warsaw newsrooms had been working overtime. The Polish government debt market was moving down ever faster, and a flurry of short bulletins was being filed as the agencies built the story.

In addition to the debt, the currency markets were now building their own positions in the zloty, which was off more than 15 per cent. They weren't just selling Polish government bonds, they were selling the zloty against just about anything else, using futures and options contracts. Samuel watched the monitor. The whole market was betting against the Polish currency, effectively crushing it.

A statement from the foreign investment agency PAZ insisted that investors had nothing to fear and that their commitment to Polish business would be profitable in the long term 'once the market bubble has burst'. But tens of millions of dollars' worth of capital was oozing out of the country at the speed of each electronic pulse in the fibre-optic cables of the dealing rooms. Investors saw that they had already lost 15 per cent of their outlay and feared that worse was to come. Better to sell now and buy back later, when things were really cheap, after Poland's economy had bled to death.

Then the story Samuel had been waiting for finally materialized.

'Oh yes,' he breathed, copied the story into a word-processing program, logged off the news wire, and hit the execute function on the trading programs he had loaded up.

'This had better work,' he muttered under his breath.

'What if it doesn't?' asked Lauren, now standing over his shoulder.

'It has to. It's this or something very horrible, probably involving prison.'

'When will it work?'

'Oh, very soon. Just depends on the market, and how quickly prices fall. I think they'll fall fairly sharply. Look.'

He called up the last news story. Lauren read it once, twice, then shook her head.

'I'm not sure I understand. What is this?'

'It's what it looks like, an appeal by Khan for order in the markets. He was asking for a currency board and an end to financial instability last week, and here it is – a further appeal for good order, decency, common sense.'

'Precisely. But surely this runs against your theory?'

'That Khan is running a vast speculative position selling the Polish zloty? That he is trying to break the currency and bankrupt an entire country purely for personal gain? Absolutely not.'

Lauren pushed her breakfast dish aside, sipped at her coffee and lit a cigarette.

'OK. Maybe I see after all. By appealing for order, the master of chaos makes the markets think he is worried. So, of course, it's every man for himself, all running in different directions. Maximum mayhem is created.'

'Precisely. When a prominent trader starts wanting to be on a currency board and appealing for an end to the volatility out of which he's made millions over the years, it means one of two things. Possibility number one is that he's old and past it and can't handle the pace any more.'

'And number two? No, don't tell me, I love the capitalist logic of it all, the ruthlessness. Scenario number two is that he himself has made a massive bet that the market will run one way. By pleading for it to go the other he's virtually certain to get what he wants.'

Samuel laughed.

'That's it. Buying and selling is a vast game of poker, based on confidence and bluff. Those who know Khan will suspect that he's got a huge bet against the zloty. You're a lawyer-turned-trader. Congratulations.'

'But tell me, how do you make use of this theory?'

She was sitting on his lap now, her breasts pushing into his face. As he hardened beneath her, she squirmed and wriggled against him.

'Well, it's only a theory – a good one, but a theory. If I'm right, there'll be a systematic selling of the zloty and Polish bond futures that will tilt the market radically downwards. Then, having sold the zloty at the higher price, the traders will go back into the market when the currency is worth virtually nothing and buy it back. It's called covering a short position.'

She had begun to unbutton his shirt. Her hand was working over his chest.

'But even if you're right, how do you stop Khan making his billions?'

'Oh, er . . . by cheating. Watch this.'

Samuel slipped from beneath Lauren and slid a disk into the laptop, which flickered an acknowledgement.

'This is a gift from the gods. The programs I've loaded up are the converse of the automatic sell programs that you get in many automated trading systems. You can buy very good ones over the counter now for a few hundred dollars. These are programmed to buy massively once the target price hits certain lows.'

Lauren had removed her own blouse and presented a plummy pink nipple an inch from Samuel's mouth. He licked it slowly. Lauren shut her eyes and tilted her head back.

'Keep doing that,' she commanded, 'but tell me more.'

'Well, as the market falls we keep buying and buying and

buying,' he said between moments of passion. Lauren had removed his shirt, and her hands were working busily on the belt of his trousers.

'But that just means we become poor as the speculators get rich, no?'

'No, not at all,' said Samuel with some difficulty. Lauren had taken him in hand and the cool caress of her fingers was irresistible.

'You see, we really are cheating. You can't play Khan at his own game and win. Unless you bend the rules, that is.'

'And how do we do that?'

She had pulled him inside her now. She straddled him on the floor, as Samuel tried to keep the monitor in sight.

'By being Khan himself. I have all the access codes for the counterparties he uses. I had a quick sight of them on the virtual databank at the Ropner Bank undernet. What's then needed – providing I remembered the numerical codes correctly – is a word transmitted to a voice-recognition security program. Once the program recognizes the digital make-up of the authorized voice it will execute the trades.'

'*Mmm. C'est bien ça. C'est bien.*' She was riding him now, harder and harder. 'And how do we become the voice of Khan?'

'We use the voice he gave us. I just loaded a data stick of emails that came to me in his own digital voice. As far as the computer is concerned, it's the voice it's programmed to recognize. Oh God!'

'And is it happening now? Are we making Khan destroy his own profit, eat his own capitalist speculation?'

They were near the point of climax now.

Samuel could see the mid-price of Polish government bonds showing red, then blue as his buy order kicked in, followed by a sea of sell orders. Buy, sell, buy, sell, buy, sell. The ruby pixels on the laptop danced a bright fugue of market frenzy. The computer trade had fooled its automatic counterparty, and Khan's major account was now trading against itself. Millions were pulsing in and out, in and out, all around the world.

'Oh, yes,' gasped Samuel.

The bond futures contracts had kicked in now. The whole screen shot blue, then red, then blue, then red again, like police lights.

'Oh yes, it's working.' And then he closed his eyes, lost in ecstasy.

HE WATCHED *the figures turn red and felt a hot flush of anger. It was happening again, he was sure. Another major currency play, another piece of mischievous magic happening somewhere out there in the world of mystery – offshore, numbered trusts, dealings in the ether. He snapped his screen off and stalked out of the office.*

It was earlier than they might have wanted their operative to show his hand, but he no longer cared. It was time to act.

30

KEMPIS WAS SERVING UP a breakfast of Brannigan's finest venison sausages when the phone rang.

Samuel lifted his head from the newspapers. The *Wall Street Journal* had almost got the story right, and had given it a bigger play than its competitors. They were bang on the nose about the externally observable facts, as were many of the competition. The headlines lay strewn over the table – POLES ON BRINK OF DEFAULT, WARSAW ROCKED BY CREDIT DELINQUENCY FEARS, POLAND MAY BE FORCED OUT OF OECD.

But heavy volumes in the currency and bond markets and the plunge of a minor currency were hardly the stuff of front-page splashes after the dramas of the summer. The US government had called out its reservists, fearing civil unrest. The southern states, in particular, were on the edge of revolt in response to higher gasoline prices, government measures to curb consumption, and the increasing scarcity of basic provisions. The White House had made a statement saying that hoarding and survivalist practices were destroying the fabric of society. The number of gun-related murders had quadrupled in Alabama and Missouri. There had even been a rash of killings in New Hampshire.

But this morning, despite all the US news it could have printed, the *Journal* had come closest to getting the big international story right. It hadn't followed the now standard tactic of calling Ovid La Brooy, the suddenly and spectacularly popular Guru of Gloom from Ropner Bank, for a quote. Instead, there was an intelligent, independent analysis of the day's events. The *Journal* suspected that big fish had been moving in the deep, even if the surface of the water showed no more than a little roiling.

The fact was that Samuel's strategy of buying massively on Khan's account must have more than counterbalanced the Ropner Bank sell orders. The Polish government bond market had finished the session heavily down as the market scented the move, and the zloty had been pummelled. Yet no one had worked out that the man at the heart of the oil coup that had sparked the whole crisis had been trying to extract another billion or more from the chaos he had created. Samuel however knew that Khan had lost heavily – not just because his bunker trades had hurt Khan's positions, but because of Khan's dealing costs. Every time there was a sell, there was a counterbalancing buy order and commission to pay. Khan's losses had to be massive.

The phone was still ringing, an ancient sound from a black and white movie. Lauren had come from her bed to the table, and Kempis now looked over at Samuel. Who could it be? Who on earth had the number?

'Something tells me this will be for you, my boy. But I'll get it if you wish.'

'No, no. I suppose I've been expecting this.'

Samuel rose and walked across to the phone, set on its little stand. He picked up the handset rather gingerly and spoke in his most neutral tone.

'Hullo?'

'Ah, as I thought, a loyal subject of the British Empire.'

'Defence of the realm and all that, Khan.' Samuel couldn't help grinning slightly. He rubbed his hand over the top of his head, where a golden stubble was beginning to grow.

'You do realize, old thing, that you can't possibly win this game? Yesterday was a clever stunt, but it was no more than a stunt. The counterparty account codes have been changed. The security systems have been completely overhauled. But, ah, *chapeau, félicitations*, as the French say. You have cost me a billion dollars through fraudulent means.'

'How did you get this phone number?'

'Contacts, diligence, a little mental acuity. As you know, that combination goes a long way. Which means that while I can't be absolutely certain of your whereabouts now, I can make an intelligent guess. You can't be far from the habitat of your friend Dr Kempis. By tomorrow there'll be no need for guessing.'

Lauren and Kempis were staring at Samuel, desperately trying to imagine the unheard half of the conversation. Samuel ignored them, and waited impassively for Khan's next words.

'Hmm. Aren't you the quiet one?' said Khan at last. 'This may amuse you: the telephone identity of the trader who bet against my own position yesterday belongs to the British Ministry of Defence. Beyond that there is – for the moment – a brick wall. Embarrassing to be outmanoeuvred in the markets by the military.'

'Maybe some things really are destined to remain secret in this world.'

'Not if I inquire after them, Samuel. You will be found very soon.'

'Perhaps. But I shan't be using any Ropner kit.' Khan said nothing – a tacit admission?

Samuel looked over at his bag. With or without a bug Khan was right. They would be found very soon. People tend to come looking for you when you start bending the markets for hundreds of millions of dollars. Determined people do the looking.

'So, Samuel, here's my offer. And believe me, it is a friendly one. Despite – or perhaps because of – the fabulous expense occasioned by being your acquaintance, I do believe it would be better if we got together and had a chat. Better by far that I bring you back into the sunlight than that you fall into the clutches of some brutish policeman. They really don't know how to behave with any decorum, you know.'

Samuel knew. He wondered what the British equivalents of Blondeau and Bouchinet might do to him.

'So what are you suggesting, Khan?'

Samuel listened for a couple of minutes, nodding occasionally. Then he read back a list of places and times. Eventually, he put the phone down and turned to Lauren and Kempis, who were bursting with curiosity.

'I have a luncheon invitation.'

'From Khan?' Lauren looked incredulous.

'Yes. I'm tempted to accept.'

'But you can't! It's far too dangerous.'

'I don't really see that I have much choice, do I, Peter? He knows I'm here with you.'

Kempis scratched his chin.

'Don't despair, Samuel. There are those who spend their lives creating the illusion of knowledge. Inviting you to lunch suggests he may not know as much as you fear.'

'But surely you're not going?' asked Lauren, still incredulous.

Samuel looked at the ground pensively.

'I think I must.'

'Well, I'm coming with you,' said Lauren.

'Why? Why endanger yourself?'

'So you admit it's dangerous. It's probably just as dangerous for me to stay here, in that case. I'm coming with you.'

Samuel shook his head.

'Peter, will you reason with her?'

Kempis put his hand on Samuel's shoulder: 'I would, Samuel. But I have a sneaking suspicion that Lauren may be right. And to verify that, I intend to accompany the two of you. There may not be safety in numbers, but there is some comfort. There is no doubt that Khan is dangerous.'

Samuel saw the conviction in Kempis's eyes. He needed that certainty with him. Samuel looked around the cellar. It did feel like a prison now, and he was tired of running away.

'OK,' he said, and smiled. 'Get your toothbrushes. The hunter will face down the enemy in his own den.' He gathered a few things together and put them in his bag, the final item being the archer statuette. He held it in his hand for a moment and smiled.

THE DAY SEEMED glaringly bright after the long stay underground, but the feel of the sun and wind was revivifying. Samuel was standing with Kempis and Lauren on the unclaimed marshland on the north-west edge of Oxford, where the Cherwell is at its most indigent and indecisive. Samuel looked at his watch. Ninety seconds to go, and still he could hear and see nothing.

He noticed the tiny black dot on the horizon just before the thick sound of its rotor blades began to swell and dominate the birdsong and the riverbank gurgle. The thock-thock-thock of the chopper's blades soon put all the wildlife to flight. This was a large beast, no police or military markings, but privately owned. Samuel could see the mirror-shaded pilot manoeuvre the craft down to within a few inches of the ground.

The noise of the blades and the wind rush they created were deafening, intimidating. Samuel hesitated. The pilot saw his indecision and grimaced, a shrug of the shoulders as if to say 'Why waste everyone's time?' The pilot gestured again, and Samuel picked up his bag and ran to the chopper.

'Sit down. Don't make a noise, or you will die.'

He felt the cold of the gun touching his neck, and did as he was bid. There were three in the body of the craft. All of them were horribly familiar: the thin man from the cell in Nanterre, Bouchinet – and Blondeau, who was pressing the gun into the side of his neck. A gag was slipped over his mouth, and his hands were pulled behind his back and tied quickly and expertly. He was pushed down into a bucket seat. Lauren stepped up next and was taken and trussed too. Kempis sensed the danger and yet he came meekly, offering no resistance.

Within what seemed no more than a few seconds, the three of them had exchanged freedom on a fine day for imprisonment and a fate that would be entirely decided by Khan. Samuel was furious with himself. He'd had few options, true. But to walk into this? He had never really expected outright violence from Khan. Then again he had been consistently outguessed by him. Samuel should have known better.

'So nice to be together again,' shouted Blondeau above the noise of the engine. His face split into a cruel smile. He was sitting behind Samuel, gun in hand, with Bouchinet next to him. The thin man had retired to the furthest corner of the craft behind them.

The chopper was heading off eastwards, Samuel guessed. He made signs and tried to speak. Blondeau looked towards Bouchinet. She leaned across and removed their gags.

'Thank God,' said Kempis. 'I thought I was going to suffocate.'

'So, Monsieur Spendlove, it seems we will have our little talk at last,' shouted Blondeau in English. 'Or should that be – we will have our last little talk? Forgive me, my English is not good. I don't have the benefit of your education.'

Samuel tried to make out landmarks and guess the direction they were heading in, but all he could see was clouds and sky.

'What do you want with them?' said Samuel in French, gesturing at Kempis and Lauren. So far they seemed surprisingly calm. He owed it to them to show no fear.

Blondeau smiled. Raising his voice above the noise of the chopper required him to expel a lot of air and, even in the thin, chilly climate of the cabin, the staleness of his breath was unmistakable. 'You know the answer already. If we had left them behind, they might have alerted the British police.'

'If we are implicated with the activities of Mr Spendlove, why would we have done that?' asked Kempis. Blondeau made a grandiose gesture, arm aloft, gun pointing upwards as if to reassert his authority over them. He looked down at the old man.

'You may have,' he said, and undid Kempis's wrist bindings. Samuel looked at Lauren. She said nothing, but the set of her mouth betrayed a grimness that Samuel had seen before. It reminded him of the hell hound on the trail of Kaz's murderer. And of course she still was on that trail, except this time they possibly really were all bound for hell.

They all sat in silence for a few minutes, and Samuel fingered his wrist which, although bound for only a short time, was aching. Kempis caught his eye and then gave a knowing wink. Samuel shook his head, but should have known that once Kempis had decided to do something, there was no stopping him. The don suddenly lurched forward and tried to grab Bouchinet's gun. Bouchinet struck Kempis on the head and then Blondeau grabbed both his hands, binding them again.

'I will shoot if you try anything like that again!' he cried, his gun trained on Kempis.

'What the hell's going on there?' called the pilot. Everyone ignored him.

'We accepted an invitation to lunch,' said Kempis at last. 'This is no way to treat guests. Your discourtesy may prove fatal for us all.'

'Kill the silly old fool,' hissed Blondeau.

Samuel glanced at Lauren. She seemed as surprised as he at the ice in Kempis's veins. He really had seen service, then.

'Just shoot him,' cried Blondeau angrily.

'Shut up,' barked the thin man. 'Shut up.'

'Do you want me to radio for help?' shouted the pilot anxiously.

'No, no,' said the thin man at last. 'Just get there.'

'I wonder where we're going,' breathed Lauren to Samuel.

'I don't know, but it can't be very far. These things can't have that huge a range,' murmured Samuel, not taking his eyes off the other three for a second.

Three quarters of an hour later they came in to land.

Samuel peered out of the window. As he feared, a police cavalcade was pulling up to the helicopter. Blondeau looked out of the window and smiled across at Samuel. His number was up now.

They were at a big military airfield in France, he thought, from the notices on the hangars. Moving across the tarmac was the cavalcade. Police motorbikes were escorting a fat, black Citröen Safari. It was the kind of beautiful, ancient beast that once ferried de Gaulle around. A passenger door opened, but no one emerged.

Eventually the rotor blades of the chopper came to a halt. The cavalcade was silent and stationary, but, Samuel noticed, not in SWAT team gear. There were no Kevlar jackets, no marksmen that he could see. Silence fell. The stand-off was complete.

Then, at last, a figure emerged from the car and began walking easily, confidently towards the helicopter. A handle was engaged from the outside and the door swung back. Blondeau grudgingly removed the bindings from Kempis's hands.

'Welcome,' said Khan. 'I thought you might bring body-guards of a sort, Samuel, but I am flattered, truly flattered.'

Khan gestured with a small hand, immaculately manicured as ever.

'Dr Kempis, Mademoiselle de la Geneste. Delighted. Will you join me?'

Samuel felt no surprise. Cat and mouse tactics were Khan's signature, the gesture of his soul.

'Get rid of these oafs, will you, Khan?'

'Not really my prerogative, I'm afraid, Samuel. They're not in my control. They can be over-enthusiastic about their duties sometimes. But they will accede to my wishes, I trust.'

A pointed look in the direction of the thin man. A nod of acquiescence.

'Very good. Do come with me.'

Samuel looked at the other two. Khan had made his point. He had power. Samuel rose to go and Kempis and Lauren followed.

Within moments they found themselves in the old-fashioned luxury of the Citroën with a couple of large men in the front, but no obvious sign of coercion.

Perrier was passed out from the car's capacious drinks cabinet, and, to Samuel's bemusement, Khan and Kempis began to behave like intimates. They defaulted into a protocol of polite, counterfeit mutual interest – High Table talk. A discursive conversation sprang to life on semantics, philology and the possible grammatical structure of Linear B Script.

Samuel gazed out at the rolling countryside. He squeezed Lauren's hand and got a quick grip back. He sensed her tension – was it fear or anger? Probably both. Kempis talked all the while as though he had bumped into an old friend. It was hard to believe that he had just been hit over the head with a gun.

It was only as they rushed westwards from Bastille, then turned north instead of pushing on to Concorde, that Samuel saw they were not going to Ropners as he'd expected. They threaded their way through the Marais, with its boutique restaurants, gay bars, café-theatres and sweatshop costumiers. Of course. Now he understood the police escort.

They turned off the rue des Archives, slipstreamed through the security check, and drew to a halt in a familiar courtyard. The door was opened for them, and Khan stepped out, followed by Kempis and Lauren. Samuel remained in the soft leather seat for a moment staring at the back of one of the big men in front. A mental picture, an unpleasant picture, was slowly coming into focus.

When he emerged, Khan was just finishing a cordial embrace with their host. He then introduced Kempis and Lauren and finished by turning to Samuel, with what might even have been a hint of pride.

'. . . and, Patrice, you have already met Samuel Spendlove.'

Gourdon led the long crocodile of Khan, Kempis, Lauren, Samuel and assorted minor officials and bodyguards through a succession of anterooms. As they trudged down a corridor Samuel caught a glimpse of the thin man standing in the courtyard, smoking a cigarette, sharing silence and diffidence with Blondeau and Bouchinet.

Through the fifth or sixth set of double doors lay the room in which they had dined so exquisitely on Samuel's last visit. Now, however, all was changed. The art had transmogrified into a succession of drinking and libation vessels, each mounted on tall, slender plinths. A casual glance revealed one to be Etruscan, from the fifth century BC. Of the gorgeous paintings that had bedecked the walls nothing was now more recent than the Renaissance – a Fra Angelico, a Caravaggio, others he could not identify.

But the most startling contrast from his earlier visit was the white rectangular image projected onto the bare wall.

'So. Please.' Gourdon gestured, and they took seats at a large oval-shaped table.

'First of all, Monsieur Spendlove, thank you for coming.'

'Did I have a choice, Monsieur le Ministre?'

Gourdon's smile flickered for a moment and then he resumed. 'Moreover, allow me to congratulate you on your ingenuity. It has been fascinating. Guessing your next move was not easy. And, I must confess, it was uncomfortable when we got it wrong.'

Here Gourdon looked at Khan in a pointed way, but he did not react.

'So, welcome, everyone, to the project we call Olympus. We have long been seeking a solution to a difficult problem. At one stage, I believed that you might be an impediment to that solution. Now, perhaps, you may become part of it.'

Kempis looked at Lauren and Samuel. They exchanged shrugs.

'Forgive me, I am being unnecessarily obscure,' said Gourdon. 'Allow me to shed some light.'

The ambient lights dimmed; the white rectangle on the wall burst into life.

'It's an office,' exclaimed Lauren. 'Just an office.'

'Yes, Mademoiselle. And so is this,' purred Gourdon. Another office scene replaced the first. More men and women sitting at terminals.

'And this, and this, and this.'

Samuel knew what was coming next.

'Of course. Ropners.'

'Yes indeed. The demigods of the financial world. All here singly, or ...' Gourdon flicked a switch, and the screen divided itself into a dozen compartments '... together.'

'These demigods, as you style them, all visible through the pool of Olympus,' muttered Kempis.

'This is outrageous,' cried Lauren, springing out of her chair. 'You control everything like some Orwellian state. You run the capitalist system for your own benefit.'

'My dear lady, please do sit down,' interjected Khan. 'I'm afraid you have exactly the wrong end of the logical stick.

Patrice does not have the ideological baggage of those who call themselves communist – unlike you, I believe. But he has a strong, socialist, humanist bent. These screens are in place not because Patrice's government controls capitalism, but precisely because it does not.'

'So this is a spy-master command and control centre?' Samuel interjected.

'A surveillance centre, certainly,' volunteered Gourdon. 'You must remember, these people are on our soil. We have the right to know what they are doing. Whether they regard themselves as Masters of the Universe or not, they are in France.'

'Samuel, don't you understand these things?' Khan asked quizzically. 'Surely you, with your classical training, can see the ugliness of market economics for what it is. This violent, turbulent scrapping about, dignified by the name of the Market. It's nonsense, chaos with no one in charge.'

'But you're the king of chaos, Khan. You've made a fortune from it.'

'Perhaps. But I prefer the beauty of classical structure and form.'

'Is that why you sent a hitman after me?'

'A hitman? Samuel, please. Would I do something so obvious?' Samuel regarded him doubtfully. He was so plausible, so civilized, so charming. Khan looked at Gourdon, then walked over to Samuel and placed a hand on his shoulder.

'Samuel, I want you to come and join us. We can make the world a better place. Not the world of tomorrow, but the day after tomorrow. Our weapon will be what I call the meltdown portfolio.'

'The meltdown portfolio?' In his head, Samuel heard echoes of the taped cellar conversation.

'Yes. Don't you see? The whole empire of sand that's called capitalism is built on confidence, nothing more. When people lose that confidence they won't trust bankers and brokers and the clever types who work in the financial markets any more. They won't trust the promises of governments. And when that happens, the whole system comes tumbling down. If we're prepared for it, we can win the new game, and build a beautiful, structured system.'

'With you at the top.'

'With us at the top, administering it fairly.'

Samuel stood up and walked slowly to the window, then turned to Khan.

'The beauty of classical structure? Isn't it more accurate to say that you believe in winning, by fair means or foul?' He pulled the archer miniature out of his bag, and placed it in the centre of the table. 'How do you explain this? The woman you took it from was Kaz Day – a former colleague, a dead former colleague. What did she discover, Khan?'

Gourdon looked at it: 'A preliminary study of Bourdelle's Hercules, no?'

Khan reached out a hand and examined the figure. 'Yes, this is the piece that Samuel pilfered from my flat. An unusual thank you note, considering I saved him from the tenderness of the security forces.'

'But you got it from Kaz, didn't you?' pressed Samuel. 'Did one of your thugs bring it back as a trophy after the murder? Snow White's heart?'

'My thugs? Dear boy, I am a collector. Money and taste are the only servants I need, and they did not have to work hard to procure this little artefact. There must be a score of these . . . these baubles.' Khan smiled, apparently quite pleasantly.

Lauren reached out.

'This is the one Kaz and I had. I'm sure it is.'

'Really, Mademoiselle? The word of a self-confessed amateur art thief is to be relied on? Patrice, may we move on?'

Gourdon turned to Samuel.

'Please, sit down. I hope we can find a solution to our problems like reasonable people.'

'My problem, Monsieur le Ministre, is that my life is in danger, I have been falsely accused of murder, drugged, held captive, beaten and had a gun put to my throat by one of your men – whether we pretend he's a civil servant or not. I'm sorry I accidentally killed one of them.'

'Killed one of them?' Gourdon looked at Samuel in puzzlement.

Samuel looked to Kempis for support and inspiration even as these ugly revelations issued from his mouth, like crows falling on carrion.

A moment's silence. Then Kempis cleared his throat: 'As the Master of Biblos would have said, "I believe I have the essence of it." And a few facts, too, if Samuel's testimony is to be believed. Your theoretical model, Khan, and perhaps yours too, Monsieur le Ministre, is based on the need to control. No wonder you wanted Samuel to be styled the rogue trader: you could destabilize the markets, make your billions in the carefully orchestrated chaos, and blame him.'

Khan was glaring at Kempis – an unusual loss of control. The academic paced across the room, admired the beauty of a Macedonian drinking vessel, and turned back. 'But the practical difficulty was that Samuel was better at running away than you imagined. I believe that between you, you created far more chaos than your plan had bargained for, no? It has been expensive for you, Khan, though I imagine money is still not important. Especially to you, Monsieur le Ministre.'

Gourdon poured a glass of water. 'What you say has much truth, Dr Kempis. Money is everything and nothing. Mainly nothing.' He stood up, and walked over to a window looking out on the courtyard. 'Samuel, I do offer my sincere apologies for the indignities you have suffered, but now I also invite you to join us. We are civilized people, as you must see; we are the forces of order. We are the Platonic concept of the mind, ναυσ, imposing order on chaos. We use chaos as our slave, and we can create fear and disorder with it, but ultimately we can rebuild a world on classical lines – pure lines of ordered thought. We can build a concept of a market that recognizes human beings and respects societal values. The ruthless neutrality of money chasing after itself will be no more.'

Samuel felt his temper rising hot within him, but looked at Kempis and thought of the cool, clear lines of the Master, the model of the man he was now measuring. Funnily enough, there was an echo of that in the sharp cleanliness of the Bourdelle sculpture. 'And I am another bit of chaos to be brought to order, just unruly enough, with just enough information to make you uncomfortable? I can't prove that you had Kaz Day killed, or Dee Tungley come to that, but I can embarrass you and Khan by revealing what I know of the truth.'

'I assure you, I know nothing of the deaths of these people. Nothing whatever,' said the minister hastily.

'Well, I can't join you in this . . . this exercise in megalomania. And I'm almost certain that you or Khan had them killed. I just can't prove it yet,' retorted Samuel.

At that moment, the door behind him opened. He did a 180-degree turn. Standing before him was the last person he had expected to see.

'No proof?' said the man. 'I may be able to help you there.'

HE SWITCHED *his computer screen off and headed straight home.
The Métro ride was much more tolerable after rush hour, the only
time he ever caught the train. Not that that mattered any more*

*Once indoors he located the memory stick he had taped beneath
the kitchen table, and uploaded the information from it onto the
virtual site. If anything went wrong, at least he'd leave a mess
behind him.*

*Then he phoned personnel and told them he was sick. Which
was true, but not as they understood it: he was sick of the whole
damn business. The next step was to hunt out his old Langley pass
and the ancient service revolver.*

All he had to do then was wait for the call to come.

*Sure enough, the next day brought the conversation he'd been
expecting – an apparently civil arrangement between friends organ-
izing a lunch. So he tucked the gun into its holster, slipped on his
jacket, and headed out into the street. He noticed that a number of
shops and restaurants had signs saying things like: 'Real assets only
– gold, jewellery, cigarettes. No notes.' The system was breaking
down. It was probably already too late. He quickened his pace.*

*The guards had required little convincing. His American accent,
his work ID, the Langley pass and the fact that he knew exactly
who was expected were more than sufficient. They waved him*

through in a minute. The guard on the door of the room required a little more persuasion. He was a skinny, awkward kind of guy with thick lenses to his glasses and a neat line in 1950s FBI-style suits. Well, needs must. A tap over the back of the head with the heel of the gun did the trick and sent him out cold.

He stood outside the door, listening carefully and bristling at the sheer pomposity, the wilfulness of those within. They just could not be allowed to play God like that. Then the moment came. He turned the handle of the door, and pushed it open.

Khan was there, as was Gourdon, plus the aggressive, dark-haired woman, and an old guy he'd never seen before. Right in front of him was Spendlove, who was staring, open-mouthed.

'No proof?' he said. 'I may be able to help you there.'

31

Samuel looked round, then back at the man in the doorframe.

'Miller! What are you doing here?'

'Good question, Spendlove. Maybe you could say I was doing the right thing, for once.'

'Well, Anton, that certainly would make a pleasant change,' said Khan icily.

'How did you get in here?' asked Gourdon angrily.

'The same way as everyone else, sir. Influence,' said Miller. He was very still. Samuel thought he was even thinner than he remembered.

Miller considered Gourdon. 'Monsieur le Ministre, you may have respect for dignity and the life and liberty of the individual. But someone here is horribly cavalier about human life and human suffering. Tell me, do you know anything about Khan's real plans? About his secret plan to bring even you within his power?'

Khan shot him a look, but Miller kept his gaze trained on Gourdon.

'I see not. Perhaps Khan hasn't told you the master strategy, the governing dynamic? To reduce the world to chaos. To reduce the existing system to one where confidence is so low that barter is a fact of everyday life, where the only tradable commodities are foodstuffs, cigarettes and the most basic services. Prostitution would do tremendously well under the brave new world of classical values as adapted by Khan.'

Gourdon looked at Khan.

'What is he talking about?'

Khan said nothing, but his face was pale and his jaw muscles were working furiously.

'Khan wants to reduce the world to medieval values, but without the spirituality,' continued Miller. 'If his Polish play had succeeded, he would have bankrupted a whole country. The former Eastern bloc countries have only just stopped accepting tax payment in food, for God's sake, and Khan wanted to rape a sovereign currency.'

'Is this true?' asked Gourdon.

'It's, ah, an observation,' said Khan.

'Oh it's more than that,' said Miller. 'Here.'

He tossed a data stick across the table.

'I listened to your spiel about classical structure and all that rubbish, Khan. You tried the same trick on me. "Come join me, climb to the top of the mountain and let all this be your kingdom." It's crap. It's like the demented ramblings of Hitler in his bunker. All you care about is power for you, nothing more. You have no respect for life, nor the dignity of man, none whatsoever.'

'I have as much respect for the dignity of man as you, Miller, you desiccated cretin,' said Khan, who had become more animated than Samuel had ever seen him.

'Mmm. I wonder. I have plenty of evidence that indicates otherwise.'

Everyone was watching as Miller began to walk slowly

round the table, staring at Khan all the while – the snake mesmerizing its prey before it strikes.

'Well, you don't have to take my word for it. Why would you? But when you take the data from that stick, Samuel, I think you'll discover an audit trail that shows Khan has been fixing attack after attack on any and every currency he chooses. His principal accomplices in these covert trades were, I think you guessed, Katherine Day and Dee Tungley.'

'Preposterous,' spat Khan. Then he muttered less certainly, 'And impossible to prove.'

'Admit it, Khan. You just loved unleashing the power you had for its own sake. You needed henchmen, games players who liked the thrill as you did. What went wrong, though? Why did you have them killed? Did they threaten to spill the beans? Did they want a bigger share of the spoils? Or were they appalled by your will to destroy the very system that brought you these riches?'

Gourdon was looking at Khan intently. Lauren sat, eyes cast down, apparently deep in thought. Kempis had ceded the floor to Miller, and stood still, waiting for the next move.

'Do you have conclusive proof?' asked Samuel.

'As you know, Samuel, Khan was careful to ensure that he had his own data systems, and that very few had access to his trading records,' said Miller. 'The weakness of large organizations is that they pander to the giant egos of the largest revenue generators. By letting Khan do what he wanted pretty well unmonitored and at the same time allowing him access to the vast resources of the bank's own capital, Ropner gave him the tools to destroy the world financial system. I think you worked that out.'

'It was you telling me to keep going! It was you who sent me the emails, wasn't it?' blurted Samuel.

Miller had moved on.

'. . . and some of those market raids were maybe a little too daring. The publishing company, Gallimard, involved relatively small amounts of money, but it cost you your friendship with William Barton. I think you would agree that he is a dangerous enemy.'

Samuel blinked. Miller knew about Gallimard, about Barton? How could that be?

'I have – how shall I put it? – a wealth of enemies, Miller,' smiled Khan. 'Admittedly, few are wealthier than Barton. Such a poor loser. It was a pleasure to make sure that one of Patrice's companies gained control. It's a cultural crown jewel of France, after all, isn't it, Patrice?'

Gourdon looked at Khan and shook his head: 'Market chaos, Khan? Barter? Prostitution?'

'You wanted me to intervene, Patrice,' said Khan, tension audible in his voice. 'It was a minor breach of securities law, executed under your nose, whether or not you admit that you gave me your explicit consent.'

Khan rose to his feet and walked to a mullioned window. Samuel watched his former boss gazing down at the courtyard and sensed the gathering of internal resource. This was the cornered tiger marshalling all of his energy for a last, desperate attack.

'Where to begin?' Khan turned to face them now. His poise in the face of his antagonists was once more chrome-plated, unblemished. 'I am, I think, disappointed to some degree in all of you. Ah, with the exception of Madamoiselle de la Geneste, whom I hardly know, and who owes me no favours.' He gave a slight bow in Lauren's direction.

'Patrice, I am surprised that you can give credence to these bald hypotheses. Perhaps you will feel differently when I have finished.'

Gourdon nodded. He would reserve judgement for the moment.

'Miller, you are a marvellous creature. You live in a world of fantasy, driven by whatever demons animate what's left of your personality. This anal fact-gathering, this obsession with spying on me, your colleagues and God knows who and what else, is utterly pathetic. Lots of speculation which never seems to reach a conclusion. You are an odd fellow, best suited to living in your own twilight world and the porn sites that the dealers say you visit. That's the most charitable construction I can put on things.'

Khan walked over to the table, poured a glass of water, and resumed his place by the window. The room was totally quiet. They were all waiting for him to continue. He took a slow, considered sip of water. His hands steadied and then he continued.

'Now, Dr Kempis. Your elegant theorizing based on a few facts. Hmm. Tell me, Samuel, were you aware that Peter and I are old friends – well, acquaintances?'

Samuel gazed blankly at Khan.

The trader reached into his jacket and produced his wallet.

'I see you are at a loss, Samuel. A rare moment indeed. But it was not just me. Dr Kempis was a particularly close friend of your father. Here.' He tossed a couple of faded photos on the table. 'What do you think?'

Samuel picked them up. One was a detail of a stock college photograph. He recognized the background as Brasenose College Deer Park in the first photograph. In the foreground he noted a number of young, slightly fuzzy faces. One of them was unarguably a youthful Khan, sitting a couple of rows behind a beaming don – Peter Kempis.

'Khan, I thought you went to Cambridge, then Princeton?'

'I started a Bachelor of Civil Law course at Oxford. It did not go well. I left early.'

He shot a glance at Kempis. There was bitterness in Khan's dark eyes.

Samuel turned to Kempis in astonishment. It was the don's turn to look into his lap.

'Peter, you knew Khan? Why didn't you say?'

'Look at the second picture, Samuel,' said Khan.

The second photograph was of two men huddled together over drinks. They had the look of conspirators, but as Samuel examined the picture he realized there was something more to it, a clear intimacy implied in their posture. These men cradling shots of vodka were close, probably lovers. The older man's arm over the pretty boy's shoulder implied a dominance, an assertion of possession.

'So . . .' Samuel's heart pounded in his chest. He showed the picture to Kempis. 'Peter, say it isn't so.'

Kempis glanced at it briefly, then away. He shook his head. 'For once, Samuel, things are as they appear.'

The shock was like a sledgehammer beating against his ribcage. Samuel looked down at the photo again: his father, a love slave to Kempis. The happy couple were draped round a bottle of Stolichnaya, overlooked by a giant poster of some hero of the Soviet class struggle.

Khan let him digest the implications, then deftly gathered the pictures.

'Well, Samuel, what do they tell you? I know you resented my using you for my supposed convenience. But what about our mutual friend, Dr Peter Kempis? You have been the grateful recipient of his bonhomie and succour. Is it possible that he was simply using you, as he used your father? As he tried to use me?'

'Peter?' Samuel felt his pulse throb in his temples. 'Tell me this isn't so.'

'Your father was a fine young man, but he got sidetracked, Samuel. He was seduced by drink and communism.'

'And by you, Dr Kempis, I think,' interjected Khan sharply. 'For all your high-minded talk you never could resist the kisses of a pretty boy. Nor behave decently if your desires were unrequited. I have nothing against homosexuality, though seducing eighteen-year-old boys was against the law at the time. But you abused your power. A boy who didn't comply with your wishes could forget about alpha grades, no matter how clever he was. If he didn't get sent down, that is.'

Khan took a step towards Samuel. 'You were lucky to meet your father's "mentor" in his twilight years. Was he not, Dr Kempis?'

Kempis did not return Khan's stare.

'So you see, Samuel, I was helping you all along. You might call it manipulation, but I could not see you suffer at the good Dr Kempis's hands in the way that your father did. I called for you, and the timing was perfect: you came.'

Samuel looked down. He felt his brain would burst. His father and Kempis; Khan had known everything all along; the implication of Kaz and Tungley in a deadly game. He thought again about his father. Suddenly his sadness and his rapid decline seemed more explicable. He looked across at the don.

'I meant you no harm, Samuel,' said Kempis vehemently. 'Your father and I . . . It was a long time ago . . . I meant you no harm. Less than this monster, who's put you in fear of your life.'

Khan waited for the outburst to finish. 'Away from the harmful influences of Oxford, it was all going swimmingly.'

He spoke softly to Samuel now, as though no one else was present. 'It can go swimmingly again, Samuel. You understand why things are wrong, and you can help me put them right. But you should understand this: it's not about power and control. It's about replacing chaos with order. We can bring order to this universe.'

Khan extended a hand. 'Come, join me. These baubles, these trinkets, they can all be yours, yours to command as you please.'

Samuel was staring at the table, aware that all eyes were upon him. 'I discovered something I wasn't supposed to, didn't I?' he said at last. 'Or I was about to, wasn't I, Khan? I would have made a difference – if you'd let Kaz live.' Samuel looked at Lauren, who was staring straight ahead.

'I do wish you would let this obsession with that vulgar woman go, Samuel. It's your downfall. Vulgarity,' said Khan impatiently.

Khan and Kempis looked at each other. Whatever ancient bitterness divided them, they were briefly united: Samuel's concern with the practical, the real world, was his undoing. They were agreed on that.

'So you admit it!' shouted Samuel. 'You don't care for anything other than your own vanity and power. Kaz and Tungley wanted something, or were maybe even going to speak to the world about your game. Whatever it was, she wasn't going to be allowed to tell me about it, was she?'

Khan saw that he had lost Samuel, and looked at Gourdon. 'Your obsession with this practicality is dangerous and damaging, Samuel. You have spoiled a grand design today. But let us indulge you further, and hypothesize for a moment. If Kaz had discovered something of our plan, how would I have kept it secret? And if she had told you, it would have compromised you beyond redemption.'

'Don't play God with me, Khan. Throughout all of this, you have only thought about yourself. Miller is right. You wanted everything – power beyond the dreams of avarice and egomania. Even if it meant disrupting the lives of millions.'

'Samuel, Samuel. You diminish yourself. You concern your-self with the details of a mere trader's demise, when the larger picture is there to be observed. I am afraid I shall have to leave you now.'

'I think not, Khan. We have some important matters to discuss,' called Gourdon.

'I beg to disagree, Patrice.'

Khan pressed at his wristwatch and the next moment two muffled shots were fired outside. Then the door burst open. A large black man in a dark suit pointed a silenced gun muzzle about the room, covering against any opposition. No one moved.

'I was really hoping to avoid such an eventuality,' said Khan. 'But it seems that circumstances militate against a civilized resolution. Pity. Now, I shall have to consider what to do with you, Samuel. Albert here has been dying to see you again,' he gestured at the assassin, who was holding up a mutilated hand in front of a bandaged head. Albert was looking in Samuel's direction and smiling.

Miller could feel the gun in his waistband.

'Khan, what have you been reduced to? This is pitiful,' Gourdon called out from the far side of the room.

Everyone was staring at the barrel of the gun as Khan's

henchman walked into the centre of the room. Khan smiled, his eyes darting from face to face. He licked his lips, like a predator ready to pounce.

'This is unfortunate, yes. But I must go. I cannot be bound by the pathetic constraints the rest of you live by. Your shoddy little bourgeois morality plays, your mean existences, your tunnel vision, your meaningless lives . . .'

The gunman had a smirk on his face and was walking towards Samuel now, gun trained at his head.

'You are unlucky. I don't die that easily,' he said. 'How about you? Shall we see whether you bounce too?'

'No!'

Lauren had been staring into space for several minutes, impassive to what had been going on around her. But now she wheeled round as the gunman was passing and crashed the archer statuette into his groin. He doubled up in agony. The gun fizzed twice more – one shot zoomed harmlessly into the high cornicing of the grand room and the other produced a high-pitched scream.

'My God! I'm shot,' wailed Khan, holding up a shattered hand.

'All right, enough. Everyone keep calm. Give me that gun!' Miller produced his revolver.

A security guard rushed into the room, screaming at everyone to keep down, a shiny firearm pointing at the grounded gunman. Miller showed his Langley identity card as another half-dozen heavies poured into the room.

'I'm shot, I'm shot,' shouted Khan in a frenzy of pain.

'Yes, Khan,' said Samuel, slowly getting up and walking over to Gourdon. 'You are.'

32

SAMUEL AND LAUREN had declined an invitation to dine with Gourdon that night. Samuel had quietly assured the politician that he did not wish to discuss the backfired assault on the global markets any more. He merely wanted his life back. The statesman had nodded, and arranged for food to be brought to them in the guest wing of his residence, where they had been invited to stay for a few days. Gourdon was clearly embarrassed about the way that Samuel had been treated, and of course by his covert involvement in keeping the Gallimard publishing house in French hands. He was now determined to put a smooth political gloss on things, and made it clear that Samuel should lie low whilst he did the fixing.

There was a knock at the door of their bedroom and a liveried servant brought Lauren and Samuel a tray of exquisite cold cuts and a bottle of Meursault. Lauren sat on the bed whilst Samuel rearranged magazines and books on a low table to make space for the tray. The servant retreated and Samuel went over to the bed and, putting his arms around Lauren, tried to persuade her to eat. She had been very quiet as the true story of Khan's deceit had unfolded. Now she was indignant.

'I still want justice for Kaz,' she said.

'Well, Gourdon is promising that charges will be brought if that brute of Khan's confesses.'

'Oh, the charming Albert? I hope I can do better than that,' said Gourdon, smiling at them from the doorway. 'Excuse me,' he said, seeing their surprise. 'But the door was open.'

Samuel waved a hand and Gourdon sat on the chaise longue opposite them.

'I have spoken with Khan. He claims that his associate, the man who attacked you, Samuel, was acting on his own initiative.'

'In attacking Samuel, or murdering Kaz?' asked Lauren.

'Both. But the evidence against Albert and his boss is far from conclusive.'

'Impossible! You must pursue this all the way!' she said, leaping to her feet.

'Be certain of it, Mademoiselle de la Geneste. Khan will stand trial for Katherine Day's murder and conspiracy to murder three security guards, including Blondeau and Bouchinet. Killing members of the security services is tantamount to treason and carries a very heavy sentence.'

Samuel grimaced and said nothing. It was difficult to mourn that pair.

'And he will also stand trial for fraud and grand larceny. I doubt if he will ever be released from prison. What I am saying to you is that he is likely to be locked up for the rest of his life.'

'But what about you, Monsieur le Ministre?' Lauren asked. 'Won't that compromise you irretrievably?'

'Well, it will be embarrassing. But there was no formal relationship between myself and Khan, and few witnesses to testify as to its existence...'

He looked at them, a question unspoken on his lips.

'So if we don't make the market destabilization conspiracy public, it will make the passage of prosecution easier?' asked Lauren.

Gourdon nodded. Lauren sighed and shook her head, leaving Samuel to take up the argument.

'So Khan admits that he allowed Kaz to be disposed of. A small person who dared to get in his way.'

'On the contrary, he denies any involvement with Katherine Day's death.'

'I think it is possible that she discovered the extent of his manipulation of the markets,' Samuel replied. 'Maybe he lured her in with the small play, the ramping and manipulation of the share price in Gallimard. But if she then realized his real plan was to wreck the whole system, no wonder she began to keep trading records. I think Kaz had worked out that Khan wanted to replace the markets with ... well, with himself as the sole arbiter of power, the dispenser of goods. Once Khan discovered he had been found out, she had to go. Arrogance and too much power stripped him of his humanity.'

'A plausible theory, but it will take some time to work out who was responsible for Mademoiselle Day's death and what their motive was.'

Samuel sipped at his wine. 'And what about Tungley?'

'Well,' said Gourdon, 'as you know, that all happened in Frankfurt. We can't be quite certain what precisely occurred there either, but the best guess must be a problem with drink, gambling or drugs. Khan and his thug certainly deny all knowledge and I think that I believe them. It's quite possible that Tungley had an addiction problem – just look at the profiles of the traders in the dealing rooms we have been surveying in the Olympus project. They live on the edge, with caffeine, alcohol, sex and drugs to help them along. Tungley must have fallen foul of a high-rolling bookmaker or drug dealer. He was probably unable to repay a debt and paid for it with his life instead.'

'But wouldn't that mean that the criminal would have to write off the debt?' asked Samuel rather naively.

'There are so many traders who imbibe and snort and roll dice that the occasional extinction of a bad debtor is written off as an operating cost. It must concentrate the minds of those in arrears quite wonderfully.'

Samuel laced his fingers behind his head and looked up at the ceiling.

'And the markets?' interjected Lauren. 'Samuel is a rogue trader, all ready for crucifixion.'

'My friends at the finance ministry in Bercy tell me there's plenty of bounce around.'

'Bounce?' repeated Lauren, dubiously.

'Bounce, Mademoiselle de la Geneste. A great deal of it, apparently. I share your distaste,' he smiled quietly. 'A very Anglo-Saxon concept.'

'So . . .' Gourdon turned at length to Samuel. 'Do we have a deal?'

'I think,' Samuel said at length, 'that I'm done with deals. Look at my deals – with Kempis, who wanted to exploit me as he did my father; with Khan, a monomaniac who thinks nothing of the lives of "little" people. I'm sick of deals, Monsieur le Ministre.'

'I understand. But can I rely on your discretion?'

A beat passed. Samuel sighed. 'You can rely on my discretion.'

Gourdon lost the whimsical smile, and nodded sympathetically.

'It has been a very difficult time for you, Samuel. You both look tired. Let me leave you to your dinner and then we can discuss this further in the morning. I am planning to make a statement tomorrow, which will completely exonerate you. I will show you the press release before it is sent out.'

Gourdon's political career was at risk and he was employing all his powers of charm to persuade Samuel and Lauren to cooperate. Nevertheless, Samuel sensed the man was trying to right some wrongs. In any event, he was bored of quizzing the minister about the finer details of what had happened. He thanked Gourdon for his hospitality, and bade him goodnight.

As Gourdon left the room, Lauren threw herself onto the bed and started crying softly. Samuel went to her and gently embraced her, stroking her hair and kissing her on the forehead. And then they lay together, clasped in each other's arms, wondering if the events of the last few weeks were really true. At least they now knew – or thought they knew – who had been responsible for Kaz's death, but it was such a waste of a vibrant life. Kaz had been talented and beautiful. Yes, there had been problems in her life, but there had been everything to live for. As Samuel tried to comfort Lauren, the memory of Kaz's corpse, its skin waxy and discoloured from being in the water, came back to haunt him. Khan had lost all sense of what was right and wrong. His megalomania had driven him to madness. There could be no other explanation for his actions.

Lauren had stopped crying now and had fallen into a shallow sleep. Samuel leant across and switched off the lights, listening to the slow rhythm of her breathing. The curtains remained open and dim light came in from the courtyard. He could hear the cascade of the fountain in the centre of it, a sound that seemed to promote joy and hope. What would the future hold for him and for Lauren? His eyes closed and he too fell into a shallow slumber.

It was the middle of the night and Samuel and Lauren were still lying fully clothed on top of the bed covers. Lauren awoke first and gave Samuel a tender kiss on the cheek.

'Are you feeling a little happier, my darling?' he said, stretching and yawning before putting his arms around her and hugging her tightly.

'I do feel better. Until I think of Kaz. She was a good friend to me and she did not deserve to die. But one good thing has come of all of this. You and I have found each other.' She kissed him again. He kissed her back, full on the lips, urgently. Then her tongue was in his mouth and she was gently biting his lower lip. He shivered and began to unbutton her blouse.

'I never thought that I could love a man the way I love you, Samuel.'

'Did you think that you preferred women?'

'Few men understand the sexual needs of a woman as you do.'

'That didn't stop my marriage from falling apart.'

'Enough of that!' commanded Lauren. She began to unzip his trousers.

'We must both put the past behind us now, darling. No more talk of Kaz or Gail. We are both in mourning in different ways, but we must let go.'

Her hand was moving softly, deftly, and Samuel let out a quiet groan.

Lauren moved down the bed and enveloped him in her mouth, propelling him into another world – one of ecstatic pleasure, where nothing else mattered except for the sensations of the moment. He ran his fingers through her dark, thick hair. Lauren pushed her way back up the bed towards him. Her tongue was in his mouth again and he could taste himself.

The blouse was gone. Now the bra. Her soft, ripe breasts filled his hands. In a moment, his tongue was teasing her right nipple. He could sense her excitement and stopped for a moment, gazing into her eyes.

And then he was inside her, thrusting deep, listening to her groans of joy. He pushed down and then rose up, lost in the intensity of the moment, wanting it to last for ever.

They were kissing again, tongues entwined. And then they exhaled two simultaneous cries of satisfaction. He lay on top of her, feeling the contractions of her around him. They were both panting. Kaz had bequeathed Lauren to him. He had given himself to her. Their lives had changed for ever.

GOURDON, SAMUEL and Lauren sat at one end of a huge mahogany dining table. Gourdon's personal letters were brought to him on a silver platter along with a paper knife. He pushed them to one side. The rituals continued whether he wanted them to or not, but he had more pressing business to deal with this morning.

'Did you both sleep well?' he asked brightly.

'After the traumas of the last few weeks, sleep has not been coming easily to us, Monsieur le Ministre, but thank you for asking nonetheless.'

'As I told you, Samuel, it is my intention to put out a statement today declaring your innocence and making it clear that you were the victim of the forces of evil. We cannot say that Khan is guilty, of course, until he has been tried, but we will make it clear that he is being held on a number of serious charges, including conspiracy to murder. You will be portrayed as the hero who brought the financial markets back from the brink of collapse.'

'Are you sure that the world's media will take that line? I was the ultimate rogue trader – murderer, rapist, you name it.'

'Well, my people have had words with influential figures in that world . . .'

'Don't tell me you've been talking to the Barton empire?'

'The truth of it is, he has a certain claim on that company he covets.'

'So you've agreed to let him have it? The puppet owners, or whatever they are, relinquish control?'

'Do you care, Samuel?' asked Lauren. 'He was right, according to the crooked rules of his crooked game.'

'I think the answer to your question is that I don't care. Not at all. Not about the whole ridiculous business. I choose to believe that truth, ultimately, will always come out.' Samuel looked at Gourdon defiantly.

'Talking of which, Lauren and I have been discussing your unfortunate position for the last couple of hours, Monsieur le Ministre.' Samuel paused and Gourdon looked at him expectantly, his face drawn.

'And?' Gourdon could wait no longer.

'I don't care what deals you do with media moguls. That's just a stupid game. But we want Khan to have a proper trial, and the full weight of French law to be thrown at him. There must be no deals with him. Zero tolerance. If you can guarantee that, then we'll keep quiet about what we know of your relationship with Khan. I think you've done the right things in the aftermath of this catastrophe. And there's the issue of common decency: Lauren and I are grateful to you for giving us refuge.'

Gourdon tried to respond, but Samuel told him that there was nothing more to say. He took the archer miniature from his pocket and placed it in front of Gourdon.

'A reminder of what we have all had to endure. The property of the French state I believe.' Samuel rose from the table and turned to Lauren.

'Are you coming, my darling?'

'Where to?'

'I don't know. I'm not making any promises or plans. I'm going hunting. Want to come?'

'What are you hunting for?' asked Lauren, reaching for her bag.

'Well,' said Samuel, 'now there's a good question.'

WILLIAM BARTON watched the cello curve of his wife's naked back slide into the bathroom. Japanese girls. They really had something indefinable, ultimately unobtainable. Irresistible for the man who had everything. Not that Barton would ever truly have Reiko. Perhaps that was why Mrs William Barton Mark IV would last.

He could hear the soft tinkling of water as she teased away the odours and the juices of their lovemaking from her taut, youthful flesh.

Maybe language was the partner of truth. Or maybe the unknown and the unknowable were the only truths. It mattered little.

He picked up a vermilion and cream paperback version of *Exile and Kingdom*, the Camus masterpiece, and read:

> From the dawn of time, upon the dry, barren soil of
> this immeasurable land, a small band of men had trod
> relentlessly, owning nothing, serving no one; the
> wretched but free lords of a strange kingdom.

A Gallimard publication. The book was light in his hand, almost curiously so. How could the emblem of something he wanted so much be so insubstantial – just a few pieces of paper bound together?

The surround-sound speakers suddenly stopped the Mozart piano and violin sonata and issued an urgent warble. An incoming call. Barton looked at the number flashing on the high-definition screen on the opposite wall. Switzerland. Lausanne. Why was his friend Alberto calling on a Sunday? He let the call go through to answerphone, and instantly recognized the voice. Not Alberto, Khan.

'Hello, William. What can I say? Perhaps "well done" – though that's a little banal in the circumstances. I think we need to talk, don't you? You have the number.'

Barton sat up. So Khan had made it to Switzerland after all, and was taking refuge with a mutual friend. God knows how much money he had made in deals with Alberto. Probably a lot more than Barton himself. That meant Khan was still a player, still someone to be reckoned with. He was damaged and diminished, but not destroyed.

Barton weighed the Camus in his hand again. A wretched but free lord relentlessly treading the earth. Was that a neat summary of his own life? Or perhaps it better described Khan. Except for the 'free' bit of course. Khan wouldn't be travelling much outside the safe haven of Switzerland and he'd be seeing plenty of the inside of courtrooms. Barton almost felt sorry for him. Almost.

Reiko came in from the bathroom and smiled coyly at him. He smiled back. She would last. Barton wouldn't. He coughed and felt a deep, ominous rattle in his chest. He would be gone sooner or later. A decade? A year? Tomorrow?

Who cared? Gallimard would soon be his. He lay back and sighed into the expensive scented fabric of his pillow, the man who owned nothing, but possessed everything.